Dear Sandy

I hope you enjoy this little "tale" of neurosurgery —

Brent Anderson M.D.

6/93

Knife under fire

Brian Andrews, M.D.

CADUCEUS PRESS
San Francisco

ISBN 1-885129-02-9

Book Jacket Design by Craig Frazier

Manufactured in the United States of America
First Edition
987654321

Knife under Fire

Brian Andrews, M.D.

"The erect and the fallen are but the same man standing in twilight between the night of his pygmy self and the day of his god self."
Kahlil Gibran
The Prophet

Dedicated to all
those before me
who have woken at sunrise
on the morning of a tough case
to gaze at the ceiling
in the darkness
and plumb the depths
of their confidence,
judgment, and surgical skill—
and trusted their luck,
once again.

And to the memory
of Thoralf Sundt, Jr.,
a master neurosurgeon.

Dr. Jack Phillips closed the kitchen door softly and walked out to the driveway. Opening the door of his car, he noticed that the morning breeze was already edged with warmth. He glanced at his watch, and then overhead. The sky above Mount Tamalpais was just becoming light, the darkness of the night receding into a pleasant late summer indigo. He stopped to study the silhouette of the mountain behind his home for a moment, before tossing his briefcase and athletic bag onto the passenger seat of the light metallic blue Mercedes 280 SL. He climbed in and started the car, backed out of the driveway and quickly drove down the hill.

The Mercedes gave off a pleasant growl as he accelerated. Jack had found the car several years before, stored for over a decade in a widow's garage; the combination of relative light weight, the simple but powerful six-cylinder engine, and Germanic quality provided a degree of performance and comfort that wasn't available today. Under Jack's watchful eye, the sports car had been lovingly restored from the ground up by a shop in Berkeley that specialized in such vintage automobiles. The smooth tan Connally leather, imported from England, gave off a pleasant aroma that mixed with the faint cool smell of the natural red-wood forest around him.

As he reached the bottom of the hill, and the small business section of Mill Valley, the physician guided the Mercedes towards the freeway, feathering the accelerator and heel-to-toe braking as he shifted the car with precise and automatic motions. He wanted to beat the city-bound morning traffic, and the invariable bottleneck of cars that occurred at the toll-gate on the Golden Gate Bridge. He accelerated sharply and merged aggressively over into the fast-lane heading south, becoming one in an endless thread of early risers commuting to the city. Jack snapped open his briefcase and pulled out a microcassette recorder, and the top one of a thick stack of manila folders. Each folder was labeled with the name of a patient, and after matching his speed with the traffic, he took his eyes from the road for a moment to glance at his handwritten notes on the top sheet inside the folder. This folder was for a postoperative patient that Jack had seen in his clinic the day before: a thin, pleasant-appearing young woman with a malignant brain tumor. He had operated on her six months before, partially removing the growth. The neurosurgeon recalled her features in his mind purposefully, because this helped him to remember the details of her current examination. Her hair was still thin where the radiation treatments had been applied, covered now with a brightly colored scarf. The weakness on her left side, reflecting the location and damaging effect of the tumor, was still improving, and was now quite subtle, although still obvious on careful testing, Jack reflected, as he began to dictate a letter to her referring physician, *she would most probably be dead within three years, maybe five.* But of course he didn't put this into his letter.

As he did every morning, he also glanced at the clock on the dash of the Mercedes and timed the drive to the hospital. It usually took him no longer than twenty-five minutes to get from his home to his personal parking space at St. Joseph's hospital. He wanted to be in the intensive care unit at six-thirty sharp, for morning rounds with his resident, so that he could be in the O.R. by no later than seven-thirty.

It was a ritual with Phillips to be there, in the operating room, to see the patient, and place a reassuring hand on their shoulder. And to let the patient see him, their physician, before the anesthesiologist's infusion of Pentothal led to an abrupt lapse into unconsciousness. For the patient today it was especially important. She had a difficult problem, an aneurysm hidden in the deepest recesses of her brain. Only 10 days earlier the weakened artery had ruptured, causing a sudden, explosive headache. Thankfully, she had survived the initial hemorrhage without damage or neurological impairment. But now the sac threatened to rupture again, its thin wall held together by a tenuous bloodclot which was already beginning to dissolve and weaken from the body's natural healing process.

The night before, as Jack had sat with her and her husband discussing surgery, she had remained silent, struggling with the fact that just days before she had been a healthy woman, never really sick a moment in her life, and now she faced a life-threatening problem. And possibly a life-threatening solution. It had only taken a brief time to explain what he had to do. So simple really, to place a small titanium metal clip across the neck of the weakened vascular sac, to permanently close it off, and keep it from rupturing again. But despite his gentle and confident voice, he had been clear and nearly blunt in detailing the risks of the procedure; if the aneurysm ruptured while he was operating, before he could control the bleeding, she could easily be left with the permanent paralysis of a stroke, or locked in the unconsciousness of a coma, or quite possibly she could die. Unfortunately, the alternatives were even worse if the aneurysm were left alone.

As Dr. Phillips had left her room, the woman was still shaking quietly, too afraid to cry, as her husband stood numbly beside her bed. The neurosurgeon looked at the clock on the dash again as he guided the Mercedes through the gently banked turns leading down to the Golden Gate Bridge, and the awakening city beyond.

*   *   *

The irregular, rounded aneurysm had a brittle yellow plaque of atherosclerosis covering part of its neck. Through the wall of the weakened sac Jack Phillips could see the blood pulse inside the aneurysm, swirling in a vortex with each heartbeat. He gripped the mouth trigger with his teeth, releasing the magnetic locks on the Zeiss operating microscope. There was an audible, hollow metallic click as the microscope head released and floated freely on its counter-balancing mechanism. He shifted his head slightly to the left, moving the microscope with the mouthpiece he gripped through his mask with his jaw, and focused the lens on three small arteries that came off the neck of the aneurysm and entered the white matter of the brainstem. Jack Phillips was of medium height, with rather plain brown hair cut short under his surgical cap. He had grey eyes, a somewhat lantern jaw, and a lean, compact but muscular build. When under the microscope, he moved with precise, efficient motions.

"Those perforating arteries are really stuck down to the aneurysm wall. I'm going to have to free them up before we can clip this thing." Phillips' voice was soft, matter-of-fact, his comments directed towards a tall, thin man standing to his right, staring intently through the assistants' viewing ports on the microscope. Dr. Aaron Richards, now in his fourth of six years as a resident training in neurosurgery, said nothing, concentrating on the highly magnified view of the aneurysm, its parent artery and the three perforating arteries In reality the perforating vessels were only four or five hundred microns in diameter. Under the bright tungsten lights and high degree of magnification, these vessels were clearly visible as pulsing red columns of blood, with translucent walls on either side. They were tightly adherent to the side of the aneurysm sac. Richards knew that those seemingly insignificant little arteries supplied critical bloodflow to the thalamus and upper brainstem. Damage to even one of them, and the woman they were operating on might never wake up again, her reticular activating system, the brain centers for awareness, destroyed. If she lived, she could well be left in an irreversible coma.

Those little vessels, reflected the resident as he watched Dr. Phillips dissect the perforating arteries with delicate microinstruments, were why this woman had come all the way from Idaho to San Francisco. Many neurosurgeons wouldn't operate on an aneurysm in this location of the brain. These arterial sacs were rare, and deadly. You couldn't operate on this kind of case once a year and get away with it. Besides, as a referring doctor had once wryly said to him: "If you did try to operate, someone lying in the hospital in coma for a month before they die is just bad advertising..."

"What's the blood pressure?" Phillips didn't take his eyes from the microscope as he listened for the anesthesiologist's answer, but continued to work using a dissector to gently lift the smallest of the three perforating arteries from the aneurysm neck. With each high-pitched beep of the electrocardiograph, crystal clear cerebrospinal fluid, CSF, seeped into the operating field, caused by the momentary, pulsating enlargement of the brain simultaneous with the heart's contraction. Aaron Richards brought the tip of his micro-suction into the field to drain the fluid away. He could feel sweat drip down between his shoulder blades under his cotton gown but tried to ignore the discomfort.

"Ninety over fifty," called a woman's voice in a clipped Scottish brogue. Dr. Sylvia Martens had trained in Edinburgh in what was then still the infantile subspecialty of neuroanesthesia. Dr. Phillips had met her at a conference in London and soon recruited her to come to San Francisco. That was nine years ago. At first she had been restricted to only the safe, simple cases performed by the residents. Now she worked only with Phillips.

"Well, the two smaller ones have come away well enough. Let's see about that larger perforator." This artery arose behind the aneurysm sac, and its origin on the large, midline basilar artery was hidden between the aneurysm and the upper brainstem.

As he worked, Phillips pondered, as he always did when he reached this point in the case, that this was where some neurosurgeons lost their nerve. They might try to visualize the origin of the perforating artery once, but even that was more than many could do without developing a nauseating sense of impending disaster. And then they might blindly slide the clip on the aneurysm neck, sincerely hoping to God that the perforator wouldn't be damaged. The outcome was nearly predictable.

"I'm going to need a little help here, Sylvi. Drop the systolic blood pressure down to 70, would you?" Phillips backed away from the microscope as the anesthesiologist began to infuse medications into the intravenous line which would relax all of the blood vessels of the body, and lower the blood pressure. He looked up at Aaron Richards. Now, with a few moments to wait, he was more expansive, using his hands to diagram for the resident what was to come.

"I need to see behind the aneurysm, to isolate the origin of that perforating artery. This situation is typical. The aneurysm dome is tilted back, pointing into the brainstem. I'm going to rock the dome forward, once the lowered blood pressure has allowed the aneurysm sac to soften up. We'll dissect the perforator off, and then clip the neck."

Phillips enjoyed teaching. He was one of only a handful of neurosurgeons in the country who would walk a resident through a case this complicated. It was partially for this reason that the San Francisco Neurological Institute had become one of the most sought-after neurosurgical training programs in the United States. As a result, the residents were usually from the upper 5% of their classes, from the top medical schools in the country.

"The systolic pressure is 70." Sylvia Martens watched the continuous blood pressure tracing on the monitor, measured from a catheter within the radial artery in the wrist.

Phillips moved to the instrument table before looking again into the microscope eyepieces. He surveyed a tray of 40 or 50 aneurysm clips of various shapes, angles and sizes and nodded towards one group of titanium clips set slightly aside with their special bayonet-handled clip appliers beside them.

"Betty, I want that straight 12 millimeter Nakamoto mounted and ready to go. Give me a number 2 Penfield dissector in my left hand and a number 7 Rhoton in my right." The patient was positioned lying on her left side, her head directly facing the surgeon's left. Phillips returned to his position at the top of her head, and peered into the microscope. Working from above the patient's head was routine in neurosurgery, and Phillips had long ago lost the confusion of trying to understand anatomy and remain oriented within an inverted skull. The narrow opening in the temporal bone, above the right ear, was directly below the lens of the microscope. Two self-retaining retractor arms, attached at their base to the back edge of the bony opening, curved up and forward into the field, the flat blades at their tips holding the base of the brain up, to expose a one-inch gap. The aneurysm was located at the geographic center of the woman's brain. Phillips held out his hands for the two dissecting instruments.

"OK, Aaron, I'll want you to aspirate the CSF for me."
Phillips looked away from the microscope as he took the two instruments. First, under direct vision, he guided the tips of the dissectors down to the narrow craniotomy opening. Only then did he look into the magnified view to guide them further into the depths of the exposure. As he moved the tips more deeply he increased the power of the electronic zoom lens on the scope using a control pedal at his left foot. Slowly he eased the flat blade of the number 2 Penfield dissector in his left hand between the aneurysm dome and the brainstem. The glistening white fiber tracts of the brainstem deformed slightly under the pressure as he slowly, steadily forced the dissector into the plane, expanding the space and lifting the aneurysm out of its nest within the brain substance. Synchronous with the audible beep of the electrocardiogram, the aneurysm filled with blood, swirling inside the nearly transparent dome around the tip of the Penfield dissector. Jack could feel the pulsation forcing the blade of the dissector back into the brain tissue.

"Give me a systolic of sixty." This kind of low blood pressure couldn't be used for long without the added risk of causing a stroke, but he had to have the vessels as relaxed as possible to gain the exposure he needed.

"One minute." Sylvia Martens increased the rate of the intravenous line that fed the vasodilator sodium nitroprusside into the left arm. She watched the digital readout from the arterial pressure monitor, as these numbers slowly fell from the effects of the drug. "OK, the systolic is sixty."

"Watch the time, and let me know every ninety seconds, will you?" Jack Phillips' left hand had not moved, and now he continued to advance the tip of the dissector, prying the aneurysm from its bed. The largest of the three perforating arteries could now be seen running back from the basilar artery trunk into the brainstem, but its origin was still obscured by the aneurysm dome. Aaron Richards positioned his long thin suction tip into a corner of the operating field, and taking extreme care to stay away from the two dissecting instruments in Dr. Phillips' hands, he quickly sucked away the clear CSF that was welling up into the field before withdrawing his instrument back out of the field.

Phillips now had the entire aneurysm dome tilted forward out of its bed within the front of the brainstem. He used the narrow, sharp-edged microdissector in his right hand to follow the critical large perforating artery to its origin on the basilar artery, just below the site where the aneurysm ballooned out of a collar of brittle yellow atherosclerosis. The perforator was adherent to the aneurysm dome here, but with gentle strokes of the microdissector, the artery fell away from the aneurysm, now fully exposing the neck of the sac.

"There's a lot of atheroma at the neck. I hope it won't be too stiff for the clip to close completely."

As Jack Phillips spoke, the pressure of the pulsating, swirling blood, which had once already caused the aneurysm to burst, and had relentlessly pounded the weakened sac for over a week, did so again, rupturing the tenuous film of fibrin and blood coagulum that had held the aneurysm intact. Perhaps weakened by the manipulation, the translucent dome suddenly exploded. Abruptly the highly magnified field of vision through which both surgeons worked turned completely red, as the narrow intracranial space filled with hemorrhage.

Phillips' head recoiled momentarily from his eyepieces. As he'd experienced each time he had witnessed an intraoperative aneurysm rupture, he felt a slight shock at the abruptness of the change under the microscope. An electrical sensation ran down the back of his scalp, but he ignored this as he brought his right hand carefully out of the field and quickly looked back into the eyepieces.

"It's ruptured," he announced. His voice was calm but louder, direct, and clearly audible to everyone in the room. "Watch the blood loss and check the time. Sylvia, keep up with me...you had better get some blood into the room. Aaron, keep sucking. Betty, give me a large bore sucker in my right hand at full power. Get that clip ready." He paused for a slight moment, taking a deep, calming breath. "Everybody quiet." The latter point was quite unnecessary, as each member of the surgical team concentrated on their duties.

Two Japanese neurosurgeons, who were visiting San Francisco specifically to watch Dr. Phillips operate, had been softly speaking to each other in their native tongue as they watched on a television monitor in one corner of the room the view seen under the microscope. They both fell silent, and one sucked in his breath as the TV screen suddenly filled with blood. *How would the American handle this disaster?* As they watched intently, the pool of blood gradually shrank as Phillips brought the large-bore sucker down into the narrow opening. The vacuum pumps, set on full power, drained the field to expose a large rent in the side of the aneurysm, which squirted a column of blood with each systolic pulse of the heart. Phillips brought the sucker tip down to directly cover this opening, diverting nearly all of the flow into the suction tubing, which was now a solid column of blood out to the collection canister at the wall. With the bleeding diverted, Phillips could once again see the neck of the aneurysm, still held forward by the number-2 Penfield in his left hand. It was still clear of the perforating vessels.

"Aaron, come out with your sucker." Aaron Richards thankfully backed his narrow Frazier tip out of the operating field. Under the magnified view the resident couldn't help but notice a visible tremor in the tip of his instrument. At the rush of blood following the rupture, Richards had suddenly felt a wave of horror and nausea. He now prayed that his hand and the instrument in it wouldn't touch anything important. As the tip of the sucker came out of the cranial vault, he pulled his eyes away from the microscope for a moment to visually guide the sucker away from the field.

"Betty, give me that Nakamoto in my left hand." Phillips slowly pulled the Penfield dissector out of the field, not taking his eyes away from the microscope, but instantly memorizing the anatomy of the aneurysm should things become obscured by blood again. He brought his hand forward, where the scrub nurse quickly took the dissector and immediately replaced it with the Nakamoto clip applier. The straight titanium alloy spring-clip was secured with the blades open, in the jaws of the applier, and as the clip applier touched the neurosurgeon's fingers, the nurse pushed it towards him slightly. By reflex, Phillips gripped the instrument, and then brought it down towards the craniotomy opening.

"Guide my hand, Aaron."

The operative exposure between the retracted temporal lobe of the brain and the floor of the skull was too narrow to return the instrument into the the field without direct visual guidance. As Jack Phillips concentrated on diverting the flow of blood from the ruptured aneurysm into his sucker, Aaron Richards backed away from the microscope and brought his hand up, lightly grasping Phillips' wrist. Watching the tip of the clip applier with direct vision, the resident guided the Nakamoto clip into the microscopic field. Phillips used the control at his left foot to back the zoom lens out, giving him a wider visual image and greater depth of field. Upon seeing the aneurysm clip under the microscope, he could now guide it himself down to the neck of the aneurysm. He simultaneously increased the power on the lens to again give him a detailed view of the aneurysm. The collapsed sac was now held by the flow of blood into the suction tip, and Phillips could see the neck of the sac and confirm that the three perforating vessels were still clear. Slowly he advanced the blades of the clip over each side of the aneurysm, nudging the largest of the perforating arteries away with the blunted tip of one blade.

When the blades were just beyond the far side of the aneurysm neck, he gently squeezed the hand-piece of the applier, releasing the locking mechanism that held the clip. He then slowly relaxed his left hand, opening the applier, which allowed the clip blades to progressively close. As the blades came together and occluded the lumen of the aneurysm, the torrent of blood pulsing into the sucker in his right hand progressively diminished, and then stopped. The clip was now fully closed, the force of the blades crushing the brittle yellow atheroma within the aneurysm neck.

After releasing the closed clip, Phillips slowly pulled both instruments out of the field and backed the zoom out on the microscope. He inspected the clipped aneurysm for residual leakage, and found none.

"Blood loss?" Phillips eyes didn't move, as he continued to stare at the Nakamoto clip which pulsed against the brainstem with each systole. His voice was slightly husky, which irritated him, as he coughed slightly to clear his throat.

"560 cc's," responded the neuroanesthesiologist in her Scottish brogue.

"Bring her blood pressure up as fast as you can, Sylvia. We need to perfuse her brainstem." Phillips looked over his mask at Aaron Richards. The resident could see no real emotion in Jack Phillips' face, but noticed perhaps for the first time the lines of strain that framed his professor's grey eyes. Richards himself still felt stunned and emotionally drained by the abruptness of the near disaster.

"Time from rupture?"

"Three minutes, fifteen seconds," replied Dr. Martens.

"Aaron, close her up. Good job, everybody." He paused for a moment and looked at the younger doctor again. "Aaron, don't worry about that tremor too much. That's just nerves. It will go away with time." Phillips pulled off his gown and gloves and left the room.

*   *   *

After the aneurysm, Jack looked in on the case that his Chief Resident was performing under the supervision of Fred Steele, the Assistant Chief of the Neurological Institute. They were in the operating suite next door, and Phillips walked in and stood at the head of the table, looking over the drape that stood between the operating field and the anesthesiologist. They were doing a lumbar laminectomy, Jack observed. He was pleased to note that the Chief Resident continued to work, removing the bone overlaying the spinal canal, and seemingly ignored him as he stood there, remaining focused on the case. Fred Steele, however, looked up and nodded his head.

"How did it go?"

"Ruptured as I was getting the last perforator off." Only as Jack recounted the problem did he notice the tense ache between his shoulder blades and the sweat bonding his scrubs to his chest.

"Tough break...Will she be OK?" As the Director of the Neurosurgical Intensive Care Unit, it was necessary that Fred know the clinical condition of each patient admitted there, as the woman with the aneurysm certainly would be for several days.

"I think so. The period of ischemia was less than three and a half minutes. But she could have a stroke if we're unlucky." Jack shook his head as he turned to leave. "I guess I'll be more gentle the next time..." Fred nodded his head in mock agreement, both of them knowing that perfection of technique sometimes had little to do with surgical success or neurological outcome.

Phillips climbed the stairs up to his office, feeling the fatigue in his legs from the tense concentration of the past hour and a half. The office was one floor above the four neurosurgical operating suites, and directly down the hall from the six-bed neurosurgical ICU. Jack had played a major role in designing the layout of the Institute, which directly adjoined the 560-bed Saint Joseph's Hospital. His corner office was large and bright, and he entered through an adjoining reception area and waiting room where his secretary, Louise Brannan, kept his potentially hectic life in order.

As he walked into his office he glanced out the window. On clear days Alcatraz could be seen in the distance, and beyond that Angel Island. Today, a thick grey rolling fog, typical for late summer in San Francisco, filled the bay. Jack bent and turned on a television monitor which faced his desk from the opposite corner of the room. The color picture was focused on the plate of bone that Aaron Richards was now wiring back into place, covering the brain, in the woman with the aneurysm. Jack briefly adjusted the color setting and then sat down to a stack of mail and telephone messages. As he leafed through these, Mrs. Brannan came in with a cup of fresh strong drip coffee. Jack shunned coffee in the morning because it gave him a perceptible tremor under the microscope, but after his cases were through for the day he drank it, enjoying the taste and using the mildly euphoric stimulant to energize him for the tasks of the afternoon.

While he worked, he intermittently glanced up at the television to watch the resident's progress in closing the craniotomy. When they first arrived to work at the Institute, the young doctors considered the impassive eye of the overhead television camera a sort of eavesdropping 'big brother', but eventually they simply learned to ignore it. On Jack's desk was a channel selector which allowed him to switch to each of the four operating suites. Jack noticed that among his messages was a second one from KQPK, Channel 3. An aggressive assistant producer there had been trying to reach him for several days, to do a segment on his work. Complete, no doubt, with the gory details from the operating room, he reflected. He knew that the publicity would probably be good for St. Joseph's and the Neurological Institute, but he hated the thought of an interview, and the potential invasion of the OR by a television crew.

On the television monitor, the resident was now closing the scalp, using interrupted sutures of blue monofilament nylon. Jack punched the intercom button. "Louise, please send for Mrs. Willmeyer's family, would you?" By routine, Jack spoke with the patient's family members after he had completed the critical part of the operative procedure, but he usually waited until the residents were nearing completion of the case, so that should any late complications arise during the closure, he wouldn't be caught unaware. Phillips himself rarely performed either the opening or the closure of the surgical procedures. After carefully going over the planned craniotomy for the senior resident, diagraming the exact exposure needed on the shaved and iodine painted scalp of the anesthetized patient, he then left the opening for the resident to perform on his own. Only after the brain was exposed did he come back into the operating room, to place the brain retractors and proceed with the critical elements of the surgery. After the important part of the procedure was finished, he then again left as the residents closed the case. This freed Phillips from the somewhat mundane and time-consuming aspect of the surgery to pursue more important tasks. But as far as family members were concerned, once Dr. Phillips left the operating room, surgery was over.

Jack shut off the television monitor just as Mrs. Brannan knocked on the door. His secretary showed in a heavily-set man of about fifty, with calloused hands, wearing a checkered western-style shirt, blue jeans and well-worn cowboy boots. He was accompanied by a thin younger woman in her thirties who also wore blue jeans. Jack motioned for them to sit at a large cream-colored couch opposite his desk, below a Leroy Neiman serigraph of the 1984 America's Cup sailing match. He sat down on a leather and chrome chair facing the family, and leaned forward with his elbows on his knees.

"Mr. Willmeyer, your wife is fine." Jack still wore his pale green operating room scrubs, under a starched and pressed white coat with sharp creases down each sleeve. He believed strongly in the power of appearance, and consciously he meant for the coat to indicate neatness, accuracy. Perfection. Consciously also, he remained at eye level with the patient's husband, never standing above, his manner never condescending in any way.

His voice was even, nearly soft, his words holding deep, important meaning to the people in front of him. Dr. Phillips avoided technical terms or medical jargon. "We were able to secure the aneurysm safely. I don't believe that it will bleed any more." He paused for a moment. "I think your wife is cured."

The bulky farmer from Idaho slumped a little with relief, glancing over at his daughter. He had slept in the same bed with her mother every night for 29 years, since the day they had been married, until the aneurysm had first ruptured the week before. The thought of losing her was simply overwhelming.

"We aren't out of the woods yet. She might still run into difficulties while she is recovering, but we'll do our best to get her through all this and back home."

Phillips did not need to tell them about how close the woman had really come to dying, or to sustaining permanent damage when the aneurysm had ruptured. He sat with them for a few more moments and answered their questions.

"When can we see her?" The daughter had a look of relief on her face. She had four kids and an unemployed husband to take care of. God only knew that she didn't want to care for her father, too, if her mother weren't there.

"After she comes up from the recovery room, in the Neurosurgical Intensive Care Unit on this floor. Probably another hour or so from now. Mrs. Brannan will show you where the Neuro ICU is." With this, Jack got up and showed the family to the door.

"Doc, thank you." The farmer grasped Jack's hand and pumped it before he walked out. "They said you were the best." In the firm grip of the other man Jack could feel the thick callouses that came from years of keeping a hard sod farm alive in the plains of Idaho. After the family had left, Jack sat for a moment, reviewing the case in his mind. *He was damned lucky with the hemorrhage that it had clipped as easily as that!* Then he turned the television monitor on again and went back to his desk. He worked for another hour on dictating letters and operative reports, and editing the final draft of a manuscript for the Journal of Neurosurgery.

At a quarter to five Jack hit the intercom button.

"Louise, page Mark Chin down here, would you?" Each of his six residents spent their third year of training doing research on the nervous system, working with one of the staff members at the Institute, usually Fred Steele, who did the bulk of the research because he had a slower clinical practice. But Dr. Phillips himself tried to stay involved in the work as best he could.

The residents looked forward eagerly to their year of research, not only because they might learn some interesting laboratory techniques or make a contribution to neuroscience or the clinical advancement of neurosurgery, but because it offered them some reprieve from the constant 100-hour-per-week schedule they endured when they were on the surgical rotations at the Institute. Dr. Mark Chin was currently doing his research year, and though Jack no longer had the time to spend in the laboratory himself, some part of each day was devoted to the lab resident, going over the progress of his work.

Mark Chin arrived, knocked on the closed door softly and then stood just outside Jack's office. He knew not to just walk in without knocking. Like all of the residents, soon after arriving at the Institute fresh from his Internship in General Surgery, he had been called down to see Dr. Phillips, and when he arrived he had promptly strolled right into the Chief's office. He remembered painfully the brief but sharp look from the Chairman.

"Shouldn't walk into anyone's office without knocking, Mark. I might be talking with a family, or scratching myself, or something."
Dr. Phillips had said it matter of factly, but with clear meaning in his voice, and after that moment had been as courteous as always. Chin had decided that it was simply one way that Dr. Phillips quickly put a new resident in his place. But after the first time, everyone knocked before walking into his office, even Dr. Steele, the Assistant Chief of the Institute. Phillips called the young resident in and they went over Mark's most recent laboratory work on the use of robotics in neurosurgery; the resident had taken an advanced degree in mechanical engineering before medical school. They also went over a review of patients with tumors of the third ventricle which the resident was preparing for presentation at the upcoming national meetings and later on, formal publication in one of the neurosurgical journals. They worked in part from the Cogent Systems computer work station that was on Jack's desk. This tied into all of the other terminals in the Institute, and a hard disk system which contained the entire database for all patients ever treated at the Neurological Institute.

Cogent had originated in a garage in San Leandro four years earlier, a company that had been started by an old undergraduate classmate of Jack's at Stanford. At his wife's encouragement, Jack had speculated in the company in the beginning. Since then Cogent had moved over to Menlo Park, in the heart of the Silicon Valley, and onto the Pacific Stock Exchange.

After Mark Chin had left, Jack looked at his watch. It was nearly six. He looked out the window, and saw that the fog still blanketed the bay. He picked up the telephone and pushed a four digit number.

"Recovery room," a woman's voice answered.

"Hi, Bernice," This is Dr. Phillips. How is Mrs. Willmeyer doing?"

"She's fine, Dr. Phillips. She's awake and following commands and has stable vital signs. Dr. Richards is here; do you want to speak with him?" the nurse asked.

"Yes." He waited for a moment. "Hi, Aaron. Any problems?" Jack listened as Richards briefly detailed the woman's neurological status.

"Fine. Keep her intravascular volume up overnight. Monitor her blood pressure and pulmonary-artery pressures closely. I want you to check her neurological exam a couple of times during the night, too..." The residents knew that this did not mean to take a brief look at the patient before going to bed for the night. It meant getting up out of bed at least twice to closely re-examine the patient. It was not unheard of for Dr. Phillips to call at three a.m. and ask for an update. And it had better be accurate, because rumor was that with a new resident he would also call the supervising nurse in the ICU to ask for her own update on the patient.

Jack Phillips paused for a moment. "That was a good job you did today, Aaron. Handling an intra-operative aneurysm rupture takes a real team effort." Jack didn't compliment the residents very often; he was not one to glad-hand or saccharine-sweeten the training program. However he did try to acknowledge when a resident did a particularly good job, if only to reinforce the behavior as part of the resident's training. He remembered only too well his own training in neurosurgery under Dr. Winston Sharp at the Montreal Neurological Institute. Years of tolerating the man's constant criticism and deprecating manner had only taught Jack that such sheer abuse was counterproductive. This was one of the many lessons, both positive and negative, that he had learned from carefully observing his own professors, and used in shaping his personal style and manner.

"I've got a squash match at six o'clock. I'll be on the beeper till about eight, and then home." Jack played at a private club near the hospital three times a week. Tonight's match he knew would be particularly challenging. His close friend, Raleigh Stevens, was the same age, fourty-six, and had a similar level of skill. But more importantly, Raleigh was a criminal defense trial lawyer. Their competitiveness arose from a professional source.

*   *   *

Jack guided the Mercedes from Doyle Drive past the Army Presidio onto the freeway towards the Golden Gate Bridge. He still had a slight sheen of perspiration on his forehead despite the shower after the match. He smiled to himself. As usual it was a tough one, but today Raleigh couldn't handle his passing shots. He wiped his forehead with a towel which stuck out from his well-worn leather athletic bag. The

Mercedes' exhaust resonated as Jack shifted down from third to second and he drove through the toll plaza at twenty miles an hour onto the bridge, heading north.

As was typical for mid-September, it was still light out, but the entire span of the bridge was shrouded in thick, moving fog. He could see the massive orange suspension cables climb upward until they disappear into the gray mist as they ascended. As Jack picked up speed, the fog coalesced into droplets on the windshield, and he turned the wipers on to the intermittent setting. He shifted into fourth and reached seventy miles per hour. As he came off the bridge and approached the sweeping curves of northbound Highway 101, the fog broke, except for protruding tongues, tinged with pink from the setting sun, creeping in between the hills of the Marin headlands to the west. He drove through the Redwood Tunnel with it's multi-colored rainbow painted over the entrance, and then into the softening light of dusk past the town of Sausalito. As the freeway began to descend from the coastal headlands, he could feel the air temperature warming through the vent. He opened his window, and enjoyed the wind as he drove.

He turned off at the Mill Valley exit and within a few minutes passed through the small downtown area with its bus depot, bookstore and shops and three Italian restaurants. He turned up into the hills that shouldered the base of Mount Tamalpais. The road wound up under the cover of the redwoods, and Jack could feel the air become cooler and moist in the shadows under the large trees. A quarter of a mile up the hill he turned into the short private road leading to his driveway. The tires of the Mercedes made an irregular rough sound on the cobblestones that covered the road.

As Jack entered the side door into the kitchen, he saw Barbara preparing a salad on the large butcher block next to the sink. After having their older daughter Christine, she had limited her management consulting work to half time, and after their son Darian had been born she worked just two days a week, at an office close by in Tiburon. She liked being at home when the kids returned from school, and preparing a meal that for the most part the whole family attended. She and Jack had met when he was a medical student at Stanford, but they had waited to get married until he had nearly completed his training in Montreal. She had long ago become accustomed to his twelve and fourteen hour days.

"Hi, sweetie," Jack kissed his wife on the cheek and then threw his beaten leather bag and briefcase on a kitchen chair. "Where are the kids?" He opened the door to the refrigerator and pulled out a tonic water. Today had been one of Barbara's work days, and she was wearing an apron over her dress. A dress that flattered her figure, Jack noticed. Barbara still had a slim, athletic build, with rather broad shoulders for a woman, a testament to years of competitive swimming in school, and narrow hips and waist, which she toned with regular

14

aerobics. Her blue eyes and small, pretty face were framed with deep red hair.

"They're both in their rooms doing homework. Dinner is nearly ready." Barbara fed several carrots into the Cuisinart. Jack stood back a little watching her, flexing his fingers unconsciously. He had an aversion to anything with whirling blades.

He walked through the dining room and down two carpeted steps into the living room, with its high, peaked beam ceiling. The house had been designed by an innovative young Marin architect, to take full advantage of its location on the mountain overlooking Mill Valley, with the bay and the city of San Francisco in the distance to the south. Jack sipped his drink and looked out through the large picture windows which came together in a gentle V-shape facing south. The sun was going down, and to the west above the mountain the sky was now a faded pink, but darkened to deepening shades of blue towards the east, over the hills of Oakland and Berkeley. He could see the layer of fog that still blanketed the bay, obscuring Angel Island and Alcatraz. Above the fog, the tops of the larger buildings in the city reflected the last light from the setting sun.

"Hey, dad!" Jack's eight-year-old son ran out of his room wearing bright multi-colored shorts which went down to his knees, and a baggy t-shirt, emblazoned with the name of a rock group that Jack had never heard of. On his feet, which seemed too big for the rest of him anyway, were high-top tennis shoes that looked as though they were inflated somehow with air, unlaced at the top and flopping open. Jack grinned at the ungainly image.

"See my new haircut?" Darian's light brown hair was now cropped down to a fuzzy crew cut, apparently all the rage among the eight-year-old set.

"Seems to me that I had one just like that a few years ago," Jack replied with a laugh.

"Yeah, it's great!" Darian ran up to his father and started to punch him playfully in the stomach. Jack put his tonic water down on a glass-and-marble coffee table and used his arms to feint and block his son's blows. Then he grabbed Darian around the shoulders.

"Holding! Holding!" the boy laughed, trying to squirm free.

Barbara came into the living room. "Darian, get cleaned up and help me set the table."

Jack walked down the hallway that led to the bedrooms. The door to his daughter's room was closed. He knocked, and then walked in. The room was painted a light mauve. Christine was sitting over a textbook, and looked up as he entered.

"Hi, dad." Christine was fifteen, and had just begun her sophomore year in high school. And she had suddenly developed from a little girl to a very attractive young woman, somewhat to Jack's amazement. He came over to her desk and put his arms around her. He looked down at the book that she was reading.

"So what are they teaching you these days?" he asked. He tried to keep up with what the kids were learning in school, but usually failed to do a very good job at it.

"Anthropology," she said, briefly making a face as she closed the book. "I've also got Math, and French, and a bunch of others." Christine kissed him on the cheek and then got up. She was tall and athletic, like her mother, Jack thought. "I'll go help mom get dinner on the table," she said.

Jack walked back to the kitchen with her and retrieved his briefcase and bag. Then he went down to the end of the hall to the master bedroom. He dropped the athletic bag on the bed, and walked into the adjoining study. The study was at the end of the house, where it was the most quiet, beneath a stand of tall redwoods, which Jack could see through a clear skylight above him. The walls of the study were lined in grass cloth. Two of the walls were nearly covered with his diplomas and degrees, and pictures taken during his medical training and the year of army service spent after his internship. The third wall was taken up with a large rosewood bookcase which contained most of the important historical literature in neurosurgery. The original writings of Harvey Cushing, Walter Dandy, Sir Geoffrey Jefferson and Wilder Penfield, as well as a number of other rare first editions by lesser known authors. Jack had started his book collecting during medical school, and over the years had made it a point to browse antique book stores, to add to his collection, whenever he was in a another city, while at medical conferences or on vacations. These days he also used a broker in Boston, who kept him informed when important books became available. Jack's collection wasn't large, but over the years he had accumulated the nucleus of classical teachings upon which the practice and science of neurosurgery were founded.

He opened up his briefcase on his desk, a slab of polished granite supported by two blocks of black marble. The desk faced a window on the south side of the room, which, like the living room, looked down the mountain, towards the city. Jack lifted out the manuscript for the book that he was writing on vascular malformations of the brain. He had spent the past year organizing and writing the first eleven chapters, and now faced a December deadline for completing the first draft. He also pulled out a floppy disk that held the working manuscript. He did all of his data base management, statistics and word processing by computer. The PC on his desk was identical to the one in the office, and he could connect to the system at the Institute using a modem.

"Dinner's ready," Barbara called from the kitchen. He left his things organized for work later in the evening, and went out to the dining room. Darian and Christine were helping to bring the dishes out. Darian's hair stuck straight up in its new found freedom. With the close cut on the sides, the haircut made his ears seem to stick out. Jack looked at him and smiled as the family sat down to eat.

2

The freighter Devil's Wind, out of Hong Kong, moved through the darkness from the west. The first mate stood on the bridge and looked at his watch. Two-thirty a.m. He cupped a mug of hot tea in his hands to warm them as he again scanned the dense fog which enveloped the ship. In the distance he could just see a dim glow from the lights of the city beyond. The freighter was running through moderate seas at a steady eight knots. She was low in the water, heavy with a cargo of Taiwanese steel bound for the boom of commercial construction in California. The first mate checked the ship's position again in the orange sweep of the radar. Her heading would take them directly under the gently arching center of the Golden Gate Bridge six nautical miles away, at the entrance to the San Francisco Bay. He began to watch for the signal light, as he picked up the ship's telephone and dialed two digits. He waited for a brief moment and then spoke in sharp guttural tones.

On the aft deck, three crewmen quickly prepared their cargo, clipping small waterproof radio transponders to each of two smooth black rectangular fiberglass cases. A tiny check light on each transponder glowed green, as a crewman activated the nickel cadmium current sources. The cases were ballasted with specially designed semi- permeable bladders, built into the casing walls. Once in the water, they would remain afloat for only one hour; if not retrieved by then, the bladders would fill and the cases would sink, their contents crushed by the weight of the sea, and kept out of the wrong hands. Two of the men loaded the cases onto a metal pallet, as the third crewman went to the starboard crane, and climbed into the narrow cabin. He activated the crane's articulated arm, swinging it up over the two other men, and lowered the cable, which was quickly attached to the pallet. He then dialed the bridge, spoke briefly and began to wait in the darkness.

The first mate again lifted the telephone to speak, this time politely, informing the captain that the preparations were complete. In a moment the senior officer, who had not been asleep, was on the bridge. He went to the radio and, placing headphones over his ears, began to turn the frequency setting as he watched the digital UHF readout. He listened for a moment to the audible beep from the transponders on the fiberglass cases, each at their expected frequencies. The range of the small radio sources was very short, limited to within half a mile from the ship.

The captain heard a quick cry from the first mate, removed the headphones and went forward to peer through the thick glass of the ship's storm windows. The other man pointed slightly to starboard. Only then could he see the small signal light, faint in the fog. He looked at his watch. Two-forty-two a.m. After their continuous run of twelve days from the Port of Hong Kong, the rendezvous was scheduled for a thirty- minute time window, between two-thirty and three o'clock. The captain smiled privately in the darkness. He nodded as the first mate returned to the telephone and spoke once more.

On the aft deck, the crewman in the crane levered the controls for the crane to gently raise the pallet off the deck. Carefully he swung the articulated arm over the starboard side of the freighter. Another crewman held a nylon check-line in his hand and watched from the railing as the pallet was slowly lowered to within ten feet of the water. With the movement of the ship, the pallet swung slightly aft, as the freighter continued on her course, neither slowing nor changing direction. Finally, the crewmen themselves saw the white signal light, small and still on the water, now close alongside as the freighter moved past. They heard the sudden rise in pitch of powerful twin V-8 engines as the small boat accelerated to match the speed of the ship, the driver positioning the boat below the hanging pallet with its precious cargo. The man with the check line watched, waiting patiently as the boat fought with the countering forces of the ocean's swell and the freighter's wake until finally the signal light changed from white to red. Gently, he pulled the line, tipping the pallet over onto its side, and watched as the smooth black cases dropped and disappeared into the ocean beside the boat. The crane operator drew the pallet back on board, as the others continued to stand at the railing, talking quietly to each other in Cantonese, looking now behind them into the silent darkness.

Twenty minutes later the boat ran south, cutting across the five-foot onshore swell. The powerboat was low in the water, too low to be detected reliably by coastal radar, and she ran without lights except for the instrument panel and the compass, which glowed a dim red in the darkness. San Li looked at the large phosphorescent hands on his watch. Three-fifteen a.m. He pushed the throttle forward and the drone of the engines rose as the deep V-hull began to plane, pounding through the crests of moving water. They continued south for another twenty minutes, until San Li could see the lighthouse at Seal Beach, and further in the distance the faint glowing lights of Half Moon Bay. He turned and continued east, moving with the swell, until the breaking waves of Montara Beach were dimly visible half a mile away. San Li spoke rapidly, and shut down the engines. Two younger men, wearing tight-fitting black wetsuits and powerful kevlar diving fins, quickly climbed over the side of the boat and dropped into the water. They clung to the hull as two others, similarly outfitted, lifted one of the black, rectangular cases over the side and into their arms. The two still on board then pulled the other case onto the side of the boat. Nim Choy slid silently into the water, ignoring the shock of the cold, as the second man lowered the case down into the blackness. Nim Choy felt for the molded handles on each side of the mass, and then he held it until his partner Sing Dock was in the water and gripping the other end. The case hung neutrally in the water, neither floating nor sinking.

The other two men were already far ahead, swimming steadily towards the shore, their own case held between them. Nim Choy began to follow, gripping his handle tightly, and pushing with broad strokes of the fins towards the breakers. San Li watched silently until the four swimmers were well clear of the boat, and then started the engines and accelerated out to sea through the chop. Excellent timing tonight, he thought, looking again at his watch. The intercept with the freighter had gone perfectly. Repeated practice of recent months had assured consistency, to the point that retrieval of the containers from the ocean after the night drop from the moving freighter was no longer a problem, despite the blackness and the fog, and guaranteed by the electronic transponders on each container. The Coast Guard had not yet learned to suspect moving ships, San Li reflected with a smile, as he continued west. He would spend the remainder of the night on board, and return to Pacifica midday from his "fishing". He had already loaded the hold of the boat with salmon, to prove the worth of the trip.

The breaking surf tried to tear the container away from Nim Choy. He tightened his grip despite the numbness in his hands from the cold, and held on as he and his partner were thrown onto the shore. They dug in with their feet and fought the pull of the riptide. With the next wave, they were able to climb further onto the shore, and finally get their fins off. They carried their container onto the beach, each holding one end, taking care not to drag the case or leave trailing marks in the sand. Nim Choy's shoulders burned from the strain of the swim and carrying the eighty- pound load. There was no light except from a pale quarter moon which gave Montara Beach a dull faint glow. The fog had cleared slightly, leaving a heavy mist that blanketed the coastline.

They reached a deep cleavage in the earthen wall which buttressed the beach. Here they found the other two men, already stripping off their wetsuits to change into black sweaters and pants, which they had left there earlier in the night. All of the wetsuits were bundled into a large plastic bag. After the men had changed, they began to carry the containers up a narrow path that led from the beach to the two-lane highway, running along a bluff a quarter of a mile away from the shoreline. As they neared the road, one of the four set off at a run towards the highway, and then a half mile south, to the black van which they had left four hours before, hidden beside the road in a wooded area. The other three continued to carry the containers towards the road, and into a small area protected by bushes. Traffic was rare at night on this isolated section of coastal highway. Nim Choy peered north and south in the distance, but saw only blackness. Except for the crash of waves on the beach, there was no sound, until the three men heard the van's engine start. They watched as the vehicle came towards them with its headlights on momentarily. The driver pulled off the road and stopped abruptly, the van's lights vanishing in the darkness. Quickly Nim Choy pulled open the sliding side door, and the men lifted the two containers, then the plastic bag with the wetsuits. The men climbed in and slid the door shut with little noise, as the van started and they began to drive through the darkness north, towards the still sleeping city.

The sky was just beginning to brighten with the first pale rays of sunrise as the van made its way along Sutter Street over Nob Hill, and turned left onto Grant Avenue. In the faint morning light the yellow letters of the "Wan Tow Fish Market" could just be seen on the driver's door below the window. At this time of the morning there were many such delivery vans passing through the early light, supplying the markets and shops throughout Chinatown for the coming day. The fog had disappeared and the sun could now just be seen, rising over the hills of Berkeley to the east across the San Francisco Bay. The van pulled into a narrow alley between the Yan Wah Cafe and the Kam Tom Market. The market sold vegetables and dry goods to local residents; the windows of the shop were lined with Chinese newsprint showing the weekly specials. Immediately, a second van, dirty white in color, pulled into the alley behind the first and stopped, effectively blocking any view from the street. The first van drove to the end of the alley and came to an abrupt halt. The dark brick walls of tenement apartments closed the alley off on three sides. Although every apartment had a narrow window which opened out above the alley, on this morning each was blind to what was occurring below.

Nim Choy slid open the side door of the van. In the adjacent building, he opened a pair of double wooden doors, their paint peeling badly. The driver of the white van came up to help, and the five young men then quickly unloaded the two fiberglass containers onto a low dolly. They pulled the containers into the building and closed and locked the double doors from the inside. Nim Choy pulled a string to turn on a bare overhead lightbulb, as the men rolled the dolly through a narrow hallway towards the back of the building. They reached what appeared to be a shelf-lined wall which held a collection of used paint cans and jars with faded labels. One of the men lifted out one jar to reveal a latch, which he pulled down. A section of the shelving and a narrow false wall swung open, revealing a hidden elevator shaft. Inside the shaft a wooden platform waited, just wide enough to hold the dolly and two men. After loading the containers, Nim Choy turned on another bare electric lightbulb overhead, as the men outside closed the wall behind him. He then untied a rope coiled on the side of the elevator shaft and slowly began to play it out to a pulley overhead. In small jerky motions, the manual elevator began to move downward. Nim Choy continued to let out the rope until he could see a glow of lights coming from below. Then he could hear the voices, speaking in rapid Cantonese. Finally, the platform dropped to the level of a door in the side of the shaft, which opened into a small room. Three well-dressed Chinese men were standing in the room, and watched as he pulled the dolly out into the center of the wooden floor.

The room was one of hundreds like it, in the network of tunnels and catacombs that ran underneath the streets and buildings of Chinatown. Built by cooley laborers under the eyes and threats of the boo how doy, the hatchetmen for the ruling tongs in the early 19th century, the rooms were first used as opium dens, and gambling rooms, and hideaways. Later they were storerooms, and then for decades they had been left abandoned in darkness. A man of about fifty, tall for an Asian, dressed in a well-tailored suit of English wool, glanced at a gold Piaget watch on his wrist. It was six-ten a.m.

"You have made excellent time." Although the man smiled, showing even, perfect white teeth, his eyes through narrow lids remained flat, emotionless, inscrutable. His two companions remained silent, standing with heads slightly but discernably bowed, in respect to the man beside them. They, too, were Chinese, of course, for those of other races were never allowed to enter the tunnels. Nim Choy used a flat-handled metallic key to unlock the latches on each of the four sides of the first container. A slight sucking sound could be heard as the waterproof seal was broken. He lifted the lid away and placed it on the floor to the side. The interior of the container was lined with brick-sized packages wrapped in thin yellowed paper. In the corner of each of the packages was a red seal, the seal of Gojin. Nim Choy opened the second container, revealing a similar cargo, and then the thin young man stood back. The two visitors looked on curiously, as Samuel G. Twan, banker, international businessman, and the head of Gojin Tong, picked up one of the paper-wrapped bricks of pure Burmese heroin and studied it under the bare light. He turned to his guests and regarded them before he spoke.

"At least, my friends, we can once again make good use of these passages and tunnels, a tribute to the sweat of our forefathers' labor." He gazed at the other two men, and smiled once more.

3

"I just couldn't believe it! He clipped the damn thing with his left hand!" Aaron Richards stood in the on-call room of the Neurological Institute, recounting vividly the case of the basilar artery aneurysm, Mrs. Willmeyer, who now a day later was awake, alert and comfortable, in the intensive care unit only for observation.

"I mean blood was pouring out of there, and he just put the sucker on it as if nothing had happened." Richards was talking to one of the junior residents, Murray Walker, the son of a Baptist minister from Tennessee, and a graduate from the Vanderbilt University School of Medicine.

"How's she doin?" Walker's drawl was pronounced all the time, but especially when he was relaxing in the call room, free from being overheard by patients or senior staff members.

"She's perfect. Like all of them. I tell you, Murray, he can sure teach you how to stay cool when things look like they're going to hell." Richards remembered painfully the tension and helplessness he had felt while the aneurysm was bleeding, seemingly out of control.

"That's why we're here, man." Murray got up, stretched, and drank the last of his Coke, throwing the can into the waste basket. "I've still got to see my patients before I head out. All of the new admissions are done." It was just after 10 p.m. The Neurological Institute admitted about thirty patients a week for diagnostic studies or surgery. They performed about nine-hundred major neurosurgical procedures a year, largely because of Dr. Phillips' reputation. But that large number took its toll on the residents, whose job it was to admit the patients to the hospital, and take care of them before and after surgery. In return for the routine ninety to one hundred hours per week each put in, the residents received low pay, mediocre food, a clothing allowance for fresh hospital whites, two weeks a year off, and unequaled training in neurosurgery.

"Well, I'm on-call tonight." said Richards. "I think I'll relax for a couple of minutes before checking the post-op's." Aaron Richards made a point of calling home each night that he was on call, to talk to his wife and their two year-old son.

Walker looked up at the tall resident. "You better be careful, man. My kid is starting to call the telephone 'Daddy'." Aaron Richards laughed and nodded as the other went through the door and walked onto the polished linoleum in the hallway.

*   *   *

In his study, Jack Phillips was sitting at his desk wearing tortoise-shell glasses for reading, a habit he had only grudgingly accepted the year before. After he had spent the earlier part of the evening with the kids, he routinely worked on his manuscript between about ten and eleven or eleven-thirty, to meet the coming deadlines for the book. Open on the desk were several reference articles, and he looked from these to the computer in front of him, concentrating on the discussion section for the chapter on AVM's within the deep midline structures of the brain. The terminal screen glowed with white lettering on a bright blue background, a color combination that he found to be optically comfortable. The writing went slowly, each sentence pondered over and massaged until it had crystallized upon the computer screen to the neurosurgeon's satisfaction. After another half an hour of effort, Jack called the hospital and spoke with Aaron Richards. They discussed the first case for the next morning, a tumor of the pineal gland.

"He'll be prone, in the Concorde position," Jack said, referring to an operative position in which the patient lay face down, with his neck flexed, looking something like the droop-nosed supersonic jet aircraft after which the surgical position was named. "Be sure that they have the CO_2 laser on the microscope. I'll see you at six-thirty."

Jack hung up the receiver, and sat down to place the evening's work into the computer's memory and retrieve the disk from the PC. He walked out of the study and went through the bedroom into the master bathroom, which was large, the countertops shining in dark-green marble. He took off his glasses and looked in the mirror above the sink. Underneath his eyes were dark circles of fatigue. He rubbed his face, and quickly brushed his teeth. His tan from their vacation up at Cortes Island three weeks before was nearly gone, he noticed.

He walked back into the bedroom where Barbara was already lying in bed. She was wearing a tee-shirt with a low-cut neck, and was read-ing a book. Jack could see his wife's long legs under the covers. He glanced at the title of the book. "Competitive Marketing Techniques."

"Hmmm." Jack murmured as he took off his robe and got into bed. "Looks aggressive."

Barbara regarded him as the robe fell, and put the book down on the side table. "It is," she replied. She snuggled next to him and kissed his cheek with moist lips and then bit him gently on the ear. Jack responded by reaching over and rubbing the well-developed swimmer's muscles between his wife's shoulder blades, gently at first, and then more firmly, feeling their bulk, and texture through the thin cotton of her nightshirt. He reached down and rubbed the side of her smooth thigh. He understood perfectly his wife's needs, but he had a case to do in the morning, and had to get some rest. Finally, he reached up and turned out the Pharmacist's lamp at the bedside, and within moments, he was asleep.

*   *   *

The next morning Jack met Aaron Richards in the Intensive Care Unit, and the two of them rounded on each of the twenty-two patients that Jack had in the hospital. The resident had himself already seen each of the patients, and quickly gave Jack a thumbnail sketch of their progress over the previous day. They finished at seven-twenty, which allowed the resident ten minutes to run to the cafeteria for breakfast before they began in the operating room.

The patient was a young, forty-one year old man from northern California named Timothy Morgan. Three weeks before, he had started awakening in the morning with headaches. A few days later he had begun to have nausea and vomiting, along with double vision. He saw his local doctor, who could find nothing wrong with his physical examination, but just to be sure decided to order an MRI, or magnetic resonance imaging study of the brain. The local physician's shock was evident as he had explained to the patient that the MRI had shown a lemon-size tumor. The tumor was blocking the normal cerebrospinal fluid pathways, resulting in hydrocephalus, water on the brain, which was the cause of the headaches.

As Jack walked into the room tying on his mask, the anesthesiologist was about to put the young man to sleep. Jack walked to the side of the bed and looked down at the patient, whose pre-operative nervousness had been erased by a soothing intravenous sedative.

"Are you warm enough?" Jack asked as he put a hand on the man's shoulder. Operating rooms were always notoriously cold, and Jack really meant the question, although he also used that phrase simply as a way to show his concern. The patient turned towards him in a slightly drugged stupor, nodding his head, his eyes not quite focusing. Despite the sedation, Jack could still see the fear in the man's face. "Good. You'll be asleep in a moment." He paused. "I'll take good care of you. Everything will be alright. Just relax." With that, the eyes closed, as the anesthesiologist pushed a large syringe of barbiturate through the intravenous line and into the man's circulation where the effect of the drug was nearly immediate. *Everything, most assuredly would not be*

25

alright. Jack went back to the MRI scan, now hanging on the view box along one wall of the operating room. The tumor was hard to miss, its irregular, invasive borders distorting and compressing the elegant simplicity of the upper brainstem, and the Aquaduct of Sylvius, ballooning the ventricles that drained through the narrow aquaduct. It was probably a malignant tumor, he thought to himself, as he looked at the study once again, and imperceptibly shook his head.

The anesthesiologist finished taping the sleeping patient's eyes shut. They then carefully turned him prone onto the operating table, and Aaron Richards applied a three-pin head-holder which pierced the scalp and skull to hold the head in position, facing down towards the floor. The back of the man's head had been shaved, and now the circulating nurse began a ten-minute scrub of the operative site along the scalp and upper neck.

The tall senior resident and a first-year junior resident went to the sink just outside the operating room to scrub their hands, while Jack used the time to write a note in the patient's medical chart. As Richards came back into the room, Jack carefully described the details of the opening he wanted through the back of the skull. The resident listened intently, and after the nurse had helped him into his gown and gloves, he quickly painted the operative site with iodine solution and began to drape the area.

"I'll be back in fifty minutes," Phillips said, glancing at the clock as he turned and walked towards the operating room door.

Richards knew that he had just that long, fifty minutes, to get it right. He bent over the shaved and orange-painted scalp and held out his right hand towards the scrub nurse.

"Anesthesia, we're starting. Knife, please."

In his office Phillips began to see the first of a series of patients that he would consult on between cases. Mrs. Brannan showed them into his office, where they were each given fifteen to thirty minutes. Since they were mostly referrals, their private doctors had already provided Jack with some details of their neurological condition. Usually they brought with them a CAT scan, angiogram or MRI study done earlier at their local hospital. Jack's history and neurological examination was rapid, and limited to particular questions, and specific parts of the neurological examination, testing of a particular reflex or specific muscle groups, as the problem indicated. This was followed by a rapid review of the studies on an X-ray view box that stood next to his desk. The neurosurgeon would often use the studies to point out to the patient what the problem was, and then discuss with them his recommendations for treatment. Quickly he began to go through his morning appointments.

At eight-thirty Phillips left the office and walked back downstairs to surgery. From the door of the operating room he could see Aaron Richards still concentrating on the surgical field and he could hear the shrill whine of the high-speed air drill as the resident continued to shave away bone from the back of the skull.

As he walked in, Phillips noted with satisfaction that the resident did not look up, distracted by his presence, but continued to work on perfecting the exposure. Jack continually drove into each resident the need for complete attention to the procedure, and the status of the patient, but to ignore everything else that might be happening around him. Including earthquakes. Being in San Francisco, Jack had operated through two minor quakes without missing a beat.

"How's it going?" Jack looked over his shoulder and peered into the incision.

"Tough bone." Richards had exposed the glistening white dura mater covering the cerebellum, the coordination center of the brain.

"I'll scrub. Start to open the dura." Jack went out and began to scrub his hands. When he came back into the room, the junior resident who had been assisting Aaron Richards silently pulled off his gown and gloves and stepped out of the operating room. He would come back later, to help close the incision after Dr. Phillips was through. As the chairman moved closer to the table, the senior resident stood back to let Phillips take the position in which he had been standing. Quickly Jack finished opening the dura mater with fine scissors, and then began to suture the edges of the dura to the muscle surrounding the opening. As he passed each stitch through the thin dura and then the muscle, he would lift the needle for a brief second to allow the resident time to grab the stitch and tie the knot down. Aaron Richards shrugged off his mostly sleepless night to concentrate on following the neurosurgeon, tying sutures as quickly as Phillips could place them. After the cerebellum was exposed, Jack electrically coagulated and cut several distended blue veins that drained the structure from above. The two pale pink lobes of the cerebellum dropped downward, hanging by their more anterior neural connections to the brainstem. This opened up a potential space between the cerebellum and a roof of dura mater, the tentorium, above. Under this roof, peaked in the midline, there was now a trapezoidal tunnel directly above the suspended lobes of the cerebellum. Deep in the center of that opening was the pineal gland, and the patient's brain tumor.

"Microscope." Jack pulled down the head of the microscope, and gripped the mouthpiece between his teeth, his head movements guiding the lens towards the narrow exposure. Under increasing zoom magnification, Jack came upon additional veins draining the cerebellum, which he collapsed and coagulated with a bayonet-shaped bipolar cautery in his left hand and cut with long-handled titanium microscissors in his right. He rested his forearms on the sloping surface of the patient's back, to remain free of any tremor in his fingers caused by fatigue. As the exposure deepened, he neared the attachment of the cerebellum to the brainstem. A veil of translucent grey arachnoid covered the region of the pineal gland. Intuitively, Jack slowed his movements and gently incised the veil with his microscissors. As he cut the membrane, an irregular, rounded yellow tumor mass came into view; fine blood vessels covered the surface of the tumor, each of which turned brown and shriveled as he coagulated the veins with his bipolar forceps. Above the tumor, he could begin to see the massive blue Vein of Galen, which drained blood from the central cerebral hemispheres and upper brainstem. Aaron Richards was impressed by the size of the vein under the microscope. *Stay away from that baby,* the resident thought to himself.

As he carefully exposed the pathology, once again Jack experienced the deep pleasure that performing neurosurgery held for him. The subtle, precise exposure of a difficult location by simply opening the natural folds and cleavage planes of the brain. And to do it with as little manipulation as possible, avoiding damage to the critical structures that were the very essence of the patient's mind. To do this, and go where nature didn't intend, leaving little remaining trace of his presence, gave him a keen sense of joy, control and power.

"Eleven blade." Phillips took the long-handled scalpel in his right hand and cut a window into the exposed surface of the tumor. It had a soft, necrotic consistency.

"Pituitary forceps. Let's send a frozen section on this." Jack used the fine, cupped forceps to grasp and bite a small piece of the tumor. He gave this to the scrub nurse and it was immediately sent off to the pathology lab for freezing, staining and examination by the neuropathologist. Once the specimen was sent, he continued to work, removing more of the tumor.

Within ten minutes an older man came into the operating room. Even in his surgical scrubs, Dr. Norman Kelsbach looked rumpled, strands of grey hair escaping wildly from under his surgical cap. He wore thick black horn-rimmed glasses, through which his eyes appeared magnified and watery.

Jack looked up from the microscope. "Hi, Norman."

"Jack, this looks like a highly malignant tumor. It has many bizarre cells, and necrosis. Could be a glioblastoma, but I can't be a hundred percent sure about the tissue type until I look at the permanent sections. Can you give me some more tissue?" The older man's voice sounded hopeful.

Jack nodded. Dr. Kelsbach could be reliably counted upon to never feel one hundred percent sure about any diagnosis by the frozen section alone, and as reliably to always want more tissure for further study. But it wasn't surprising that most of the time he was right, after further staining and later scrutiny of the tissue under the light microscope in his laboratory confirmed the diagnosis. Jack worked on and delivered more tissue which was carefully wrapped and handed off to the circulating nurse who labeled it and gave it to the neuropathologist. The older man peered from a safe distance at the operating field, and happily nodded his head as he was given the additional specimens, before starting for the operating room door.

"Thanks, Norman." Jack spoke without looking up. He was already back at work under the operating microscope, gutting and removing the center part of the tumor.

"We'll remove as much as we can safely. This is obviously a malignant tumor. He'll need irradiation and probably chemotherapy later." The neurosurgeon spoke in a low, matter-of-fact voice to his resident. Jack knew that the best result now could only come from not hurting the patient with an overly aggressive tumor removal. Damage in this region could disturb the patient's wakefulness, balance or vision.

As he removed the softer parts of the tumor, he came upon a more firm area, attached to deeper structures. It was larger than he optimally would like to leave for later irradiation, but the gritty nature of the tumor nodule made removal difficult without pulling on deeper, more important structures. He took several samples from the area as additional specimens for the pathologist.

"Let's try the CO_2 laser." The expertise in the Silicon Valley just sixty miles south of San Francisco provided a variety of compact but powerful laser systems for medical use. Lasers provided the ultimate in "no touch" surgical technique, allowing tissue to be evaporated from an exposed surface.

The circulating nurse went around the room and put clear safety glasses on each of the scrub personnel, to prevent eye injury from a stray reflected beam of light. Then she turned the on-off key for the 50-Watt Narion CO_2 laser, and punched in a 6-digit access code on the small keyboard on the control panel. She proceeded through the start-up sequence, and finally a green light began to glow on the panel. An articulated arm connected the laser beam by co-axial mirror to the operating microscope, where a small manual joy stick controlled beam direction.

"You're at four watts, Dr. Phillips." The circulator checked everyone again for safety goggles.

Jack looked through the microscope, and using the joystick in his right hand, directed the red pinpoint dot of the ruby aiming laser onto the tumor mass. He defocused the beam somewhat, dispersing the red light over a larger area. This would widen the track of the CO_2 laser and slow its evaporation of tumor tissue. He put his foot into the covered control pedal and stepped on the power.

There was a sharp hum as the tissue under the ruby aiming beam suddenly glowed yellow and then disappeared layer by layer. Blue smoke curled up, away from the thermal reaction in the evaporating tissue. Jack sucked the smoke away with the sucker in his left hand as he moved the beam from side to side to direct it onto fresh tissue. At the edges of the laser track a thin margin of black char developed. Tumor pieces broke off as they were separated from the body of the tumor, and these Jack sucked up and pulled out of the incision, where they were quickly pulled off the sucker tip by the resident who used a moistened gauze pad.

"Suck the smoke, Aaron; its starting to look like Los Angeles down here." With this the resident brought his free right hand up to pass a second sucker tip into the narrow exposure. The smoke then funneled directly into the two suctions, allowing a perfect view of the evaporation track. The resident concentrated on watching Dr. Phillips' hand, which might come out for the instrument to be cleaned, while at the same time guiding his own suction within the surgical field.

"See the Vein of Galen above us? We'll leave that alone." The large blue vein became more distinct as additional tumor was removed. After working for thirty-five minutes, there remained only a shell of charred tumor against the brainstem and pineal gland.

"We had better quit before we hurt him." Jack had over the years developed a sixth sense that told him when to stop, most of the time soon enough, to avoid escalating the risk of an unwanted neurological deficit. Jack used the bipolar cautery to control a few small bleeding sites, and then used the foot pedal control to back the microscopic zoom lens out of the depths of the exposure. He moved away and silently began to pull off his gloves and gown, and then he wrote a brief post-operative note in the chart. The junior resident, who had returned and scrubbed once again, began to assist Aaron Richards with closing the incision.

"I'll go and speak to his wife. Aaron, let me know how he is when he wakes up." Jack paused for a moment. "Call me if he doesn't wake up," he added, before walking out of the operating room.

Slowly, he climbed the stairs to the office. When he arrived, Mrs. Brannan looked up from her desk. He nodded and walked into his corner suite. Jack sat down somewhat heavily at his desk, and rather than turn on the OR television monitor, he rummaged through his mail without thinking as he waited for a little while before speaking to the wife of the young man still on the operating table. He remembered that they had two children, younger than his own. Jack suppressed the abstract sense of comparison that sometimes came so easily when he dealt with patients near his own age. He had long since learned to control his emotions about any particular patient, after having advised and guided hundreds of wives, parents and children through the diseases of their loved ones. But he realized that personally he had the most difficulty dealing with those patients unfortunate enough to have malignant brain tumors. Such tumors were so mindless and irrational. You couldn't prevent them, and in reality you couldn't really cure them. Eventually, it became like trying to hold back an inexorable, slow, exhausting tidal wave of disease, and medicine became the futile struggle of delaying the inevitable.

Phillips hit the button on the intercom. "Louise, call Timothy Morgan's wife in, please." Quite soon there was a knock on the door, and Louise Brannan showed in an attractive tall blond woman in her late thirties. Jack got up and walked to the door and took her hand.

"Please, sit down." Jack directed her to the couch under the Leroy Neiman, and sat next to her. "Your husband's operation went beautifully, and so far he's come through it just fine." He paused for a moment. "But I couldn't remove all of the tumor safely." He looked directly into the woman's eyes. Her mascara was running slightly from below her eyes.

"Was it malignant?" The young woman gripped Jack's hand more tightly.

"We won't know until we can make a more accurate diagnosis under the microscope. But I'm sure that your husband will need further treatment, including radiation therapy."

Jack looked at the floor with this technically correct yet somewhat deceptive answer, as Regina Morgan started to cry softly. Despite his deception, she already knew the truth. Jack supressed an urge to put his arm around her and tell her that everything would turn out fine, that the father of her children would live, and that the two of them would grow old together. But he could only hold her hand and let her cry, for he knew that this very likely wasn't to be. After Mrs. Morgan was gone, Jack sat at his desk and for a long while looked out the window at the fog on the bay.

A short time later there was a soft tap on the door. Jack recognized the pattern and turned back into the room. "Come in, Louise."

The secretary entered, with a yellow notepad in her hand. "There are a couple of appointments that I want to go over with you before I firm up the schedule. First is Mr. Weinberg. He wants to sit down and talk with you again about what happened to his wife. He has some more questions..."

Jack Phillips expressed a slight grimace, although he had to forcibly quench a rapidly flaring sense of anger. He had already spent over an hour with this man, after the sudden and unexpected death of his wife. Mrs. Weinberg had entered the hospital a few months before with a slowly worsening compression of the spinal cord in th neck, due to nothing worse than arthritis of the cervical spine. But the problem was rendering her progressively more paralyzed, and, at a spry seventy-three years of age, it was appropriate to correct the compression. Surgery had gone well, and for the first two days she had looked fine. Jack still remembered the phone call from the resident on-call at three a.m. to inform him that the night nurse, making her routine rounds, had discovered Mrs. Weinberg dead in her bed. An autopsy had shown a massive pulmonary embolism, with clotted blood obstructing the blood flow to both lungs. The fatal clot must have been forming in the deep veins of the woman's legs and pelvis during her days of relative inactivity after surgery, to then break away, suddenly strangling the lungs. There was nothing more to say to Mr. Weinberg.

"No." The frustration was clear in Jack's voice. "You tell Mr. Weinberg that I don't feel that further discussion is going to be helpful. We have already gone over every detail of what happened on several occasions." The obvious question that was still in Mr. Weinberg's mind was why the problem wasn't prevented. Indeed, Jack had already explained to the husband that they had used their usual protocol to prevent embolism after his wife's surgery. She had been kept in intermittent compression hose, which had continuously helped to wring out the legs and keep blood flowing, and she had received low-dose heparin, to thin the blood and prevent a clot from forming. Yet an embolism had still occured. Mr. Weinberg simply couldn't understand that sometimes, despite all of the wonders of modern medicine, *things just happen*.

"He mentioned getting a lawyer." Mrs. Brannan's voice was purposefully soft and even, as she knew that the words alone would be provoking enough.

With that, Jack's level of frustration reached new heights, and the control seeped out of his voice. "So tell him to get one!" Jack immediately reflected that it was obvious that there had been no malpractice here. The patient's death had occured in spite of doing everything correctly. And eventually, should Mr. Weinberg find a lawyer willing to bring a malpractice suit against him, not all that likely, given Jack's reputation, and should all of the details of the woman's death yet again be combed over and scrutinized, the neurosurgeon knew that a suit would eventually be either dropped or lost by the plaintiff. Yet this would happen only after an extremely long, expensive, and time-consuming process which would keep him from other, more important duties. And Jack knew that the Neurological Institute was an attractive deep pocket. Mr. Weinberg would probably be able to find some lawyer who would accept the case just for the nuisance value, to harass them, and try to get them to pay off on a worthless lawsuit just to get it out of their hair. He shook his head as he reflected: *The American legal system is a disaster!* Part of the problem, of course, was that patients and their families expected that nothing would, or should, possibly go wrong. So that an unexpected death must have been the result of an error or mistake.

Jack sighed. "Why don't we see Mr. Weinberg one more time." Maybe that will do it." But Jack had his doubts as he tried to free his mind from this frustrating case and turn to tackle the other problems of the day.

4

Samuel Twan got into the driver's seat of his maroon Jaguar XJ-S and put the key into the ignition. The interior of the automobile carried the unmistakable odor of calfskin, and the banker glanced appreciatively at the smooth mahogany finish which formed the surface of the dashboard. He turned the key in the ignition and there was an immediate smooth growl as the large V-12 engine came to life. He pulled out of his personal parking space under the First Bank of Num Hoy and turned onto Vallejo Street. An elderly Chinese woman, broken and bent with years of manual labor, hurried to get across the street and out of the way of the sleek automobile. Samuel Twan came to a full stop to let her past. He had great respect for the elderly. His own parents, immigrants from the fourth district of Canton in mainland China, were still alive, and living in what was for them unbelievable luxury, in a large apartment in one of the rental complexes that he owned.

Twan glanced at the gold Piaget on his wrist. Twelve-fifteen. He had a luncheon meeting with several other businessmen at Chez Martine, on Union Street. It was just a ten minute drive. Sam Twan liked to drive himself, although his lieutenants within Gojin Tong had requested several times that he no longer do so. They urged him to use a driver and a bodyguard. With increasing power, they argued, his life was at increasing risk for an assassination attempt by a rival gang, especially in the recent months, with their successful control of the heroin market on the West Coast. Up to now Sam Twan had laughed at the advice. He had come up through the ranks of Chinatown youth gangs. He could take care of himself. The fog remained thick as he accelerated up Vallejo Street and turned right on Pacific and then left on Union Street. He passed the highrise apartments of Nob Hill and descended west towards Van Ness Avenue.

The Jaguar looked completely at home on Union Street, a wide, comfortable boulevard of small exclusive shops and restaurants. Tourists strolled along the sidewalk, window shopping. A light rain had begun to fall as Twan arrived at the Union Street Garage and pulled into the entryway. He opened the trunk latch from the remote control on the dashboard and got out of the car. From the trunk he pulled out an expensive tan overcoat, to protect his suit from the drizzle.

As he stood facing the inside of the garage and started to pull the heavy coat on, Sam Twan didn't notice, nor would he have cared had he seen, the slight figure of a young man moving across the street towards him. The boy wore a loose-fitting black jacket above dark pants of a coarse material, and black slippers. His face, wet from the rain, carried little expression as he walked into the garage entrance. Twan moved away from the Jaguar and reached to get his arm through the coat sleeve. As he noticed the young man staring at him, a look of impatience began to spread across his face, which transformed into a look of disbelief as the boy turned to face him squarely and pulled a blunt-nosed 9 mm pistol out of the folds of his jacket. Sam Twan tried to turn away as the *boo how doy* aimed the weapon at his head and fired. The copper jacket of the bullet pierced Twan's heavy overcoat and drove through his upraised left elbow, piercing the bone. Then the bullet, now deformed and tumbling, passed through the coat-sleeve and ruptured first the globe and then the thin bony orbit of his left eye, severing the optic nerve, and finally, its kinetic energy spent, came to rest near the base of his brain.

As the banker fell heavily to the ground, the garage attendant, about to give Twan his parking receipt, stood silently, staring at the body in horrified disbelief. Blood flowed freely over the left side of the man's face from the mutilated eye. The gunman rotated on both feet, and again in a relaxed open stance aimed for the heart and squeezed the trigger, firing again, into the left side of Twan's chest cavity. Not even glancing at the garage attendant, the assailant calmly tucked the gun back under his loose coat and walked towards the street. The attendant finally found his voice, but in some primitive reflex of self-preservation could utter only low, gasping moans. A battered car pulled up to the curb, and the door was pushed open from the inside. Unhurriedly, the young gunman climbed in and the car began to move away as curious people gathered on the sidewalk, staring at the body on the ground. The garage attendant gazed absently as the assassin's car accelerated down the street. The vehicle was dark green; a Ford he thought. He tried to focus on the license plates, but already it was too far away to see the numbers. The car turned right at the corner and was gone

*   *   *

The radio and telemetry operator was sitting in the small cubby-hole off the emergency room at Saint Joseph's Hospital, drinking a diet coke and reading the sports section of the afternoon paper when the Code 3 call came in. He looked up at the radio loudspeaker as it abruptly burst into a series of scratchy transmissions. God damn it, he thought, this was the second time his reading had been interrupted within the last half hour.

"St. Joseph's. This is Paramedic Unit Eight. We have an adult male, multiple gunshot wounds to head and chest. Vital signs are unstable, repeat, unstable. We're on Code 3 transport, over." The radio operator dropped his newspaper to the floor and tossed his remaining soda into the trash can. He punched the call return button on the mike.

"What's your ETA, over?"

"Four minutes. This man has active blood loss and his vital signs are deteriorating. We have one large IV line in and we're running lactated ringers solution wide open. Any instructions, over?"

"Hold on, Paramedic Eight."

The radio operator picked up the desk phone, punched in a three-digit number and put the phone back down. Within 30 seconds a large black man wearing a wrinkled white laboratory jacket over operating room scrubs came to the radio room. A number of biological fluids of varying ages covered the sleeves of his coat. The red beeper that had just come to life on his waistband designated him as the senior surgical resident on the Trauma Service, on call for the Emergency Room.

"We've got a single male, gunshot wounds to the head and chest, who will be hitting the door in four minutes, doc. He's bleeding and has unstable vital signs. They want instructions."

The trauma surgeon picked up the mike and keyed the call button. "What's the current blood pressure, and do you have an airway, over."

"BP's seventy over thirty. We've got an oral airway and a 16 gauge IV in place. He's ventilating OK, but there is active bleeding from the left eye, over."

"OK. Close the lid and compress the orbit. Run lactated ringers solution wide open, start another IV if you can find a vein and get him in here ASAP!" The doctor picked up the telephone and dialed zero. "This is Dr. Jarmain in the ER. Page neurosurgery and trauma surgery to Trauma Room 2, stat!"

Murray Walker was standing in the cafeteria waiting in line with his lunch on a plastic tray when his beeper went off with a shrill whine, sending a distinct and immediate sense of disgust through the resident. "Come to Trauma Two stat! Come to Trauma Two stat!" The message was static clogged but unmistakable, and abruptly the resident's mood changed to anxious anticipation. He looked down at his tray of food. He was hungry, but he would have to forget it for now. He gazed past the take-out line, and saw an empty table. The resident got out of line and walked up to the cashier. She was an older woman whom he knew well from endless days and nights of living at the hospital.

"Bernice, I got a stat page. OK if I leave it here and come back?"

"Alright, darlin'." Bernice nodded. She tried to be good to "her boys" in the hospital. Murray put the tray down and quickly went out of the cafeteria and began to run down the nearby stairway towards the ER.

The ambulance moved up Fillmore Street with full lights and wailing siren. The driver kept his left foot over the brake pedal but slowed only slightly at each intersection, as traffic pulled to the side or stopped to allow the heavy truck through.

In the back of the ambulance, the other paramedic used heavy scissors to cut open the patient's suit coat, vest and shirt. She found the entry wound in the left chest, sucking and bubbling air as the patient attempted to breathe. She quickly reached to a side shelf and ripped open an occlusive sterile dressing and slapped it over the wound. She then stripped lengths of three-inch wide tape from a role suspended from a clamp on her belt and taped the dressing in place. Much of the tape wouldn't stick because of the flowing blood that covered the lower part of the chest, and so she just held the dressing with her hand. She had already placed a wad of sterile four-by-four inch gauze pads over the left eye, but these had soaked through and blood was dripping off the gurney and onto the floor. The patient breathed through a clear plastic mask carrying oxygen from a green tank that was strapped to the side of the cabin. His chest heaved, and he coughed heavily, and then abruptly he stopped breathing altogether. The paramedic grabbed the partially inflated rubber bag connected to the mask, and began to ventilate the man's lungs by hand. She grabbed his right wrist and felt for the radial pulse. It was barely palpable.

"He's apneic, but he's got a pulse. What's your ETA?" She barked the information to the driver and looked forward into the cabin, bracing herself against the gurney as the ambulance sped around a right hand turn.

"Ninety seconds. Hold on." At the next intersection, the driver hit the brakes hard to avoid colliding with a blue sedan whose owner, in indecision over the screaming siren bearing down on him, had come to a complete stop in the middle of the crossing. The irritating two-note wail abruptly came to a halt, as the ambulance finally turned onto Pacific Avenue. The large concrete mass of Saint Joseph's Medical Center extended the length of the block. The ambulance pulled into a wide covered driveway, made a quick U-turn, and then backed up to the doorway of the emergency entrance. Two hospital attendants, hands sheathed in rubber gloves, and wearing long plastic aprons to ward off blood and other fluids, stood waiting. As soon as the ambulance stopped, they pulled the double rear doors open. The floor of the ambulance was covered in blood. The attendants quickly entered the cabin and lifted the gurney up, while the paramedic continued to ventilate the patient and tried to compress the left orbit. Together they pulled the patient out of the ambulance, and unlocked the gurney carriage, allowing the frame and wheels to unfold by gravity and drop to the ground. The frame automatically locked in the upright position as the two attendants hurried the patient through the double doors and into the emergency room.

Murray Walker heard a second urgent page on his beeper as he was running down the last flight of stairs three at a time, and arrived in the ER ten seconds before the patient. As he got into Trauma Room 2 he saw the Attending Physician for the ER and the Chief Resident on Trauma. They both wore surgical gloves, and three nurses were quickly unwrapping sterile trays to prepare for opening the chest and placing intravenous lines. Two interns were putting on gloves and nervously glancing at each other, as suddenly the doorway was filled by the paramedics and attendants as they rushed the patient inside, leaving a trail of blood on the brightly polished floor.

The Chief Resident on Trauma brushed off his fatigue as he began to systematically examine the patient. He had already spent six weeks of what would be a three-month rotation, day and night in the hospital. After a moment he looked up at the neurosurgical resident. "Murray, we've got a gunshot wound to the brain and chest. He's apneic and has an unstable pressure. We've got an OR ready. I'm going to have to take him to the operating room pretty quickly for this chest injury from the looks of it."

Murray quickly went to the phone and called the office. One of the secretaries answered.

"Dr. Steele there?" Murray looked at the clock. Twelve-thirty. So much for lunch, he thought.

"He's in the OR. Dr. Phillips just got up here."

"Let me talk to him." Murray's drawl actually became more pronounced when he got into a stressed situation. By his voice and the commotion in the background noise over the telephone, the secretary could tell something was up. Murray waited while he watched the large round overhead surgical lights being directed onto the patient's bare white chest. The anesthesiologist extended the patient's neck and peered down the man's throat to place an endotracheal tube into his airway to ventilate him. He ignored the blood that still flowed from the right orbit as he began to fill the air-starved lungs with oxygen.

"Dr. Phillips."

Murray Walker quickly outlined the situation in the ER. It was likely that the patient would have to go directly to the operating room for his chest injury, he explained. Usually Dr. Steele covered the trauma cases, and any other patients that came in through the emergency room. But the Assistant Chief was tied up in a major spinal decompression, and wouldn't be out for several hours.

Jack could hear the rush of commotion over the telephone as one of the paramedics loudly issued a quick statement of injuries and vital signs.

"All right, Murray, call me when you start to go to the OR." In his office, Jack hung up the telephone and felt a slight surge of excitement in the center of his abdomen. After Viet Nam, he thought that he would never want to see another trauma case. But after a few years, he had discovered that he still liked the excitement and intensity.

In Trauma Two, what was left of Sam Twan's expensive woolen suit was now completely cut away, and the two interns wiped down both ankles with an iodine solution and promptly began to make incisions in the skin to isolate and catheterize the greater saphenous vein in each leg. Another resident quickly prepped the right groin and began to feel for the femoral pulse.

"No femoral pulse, chief." The resident made a guess as to where the femoral vein would be and passed a large bore needle into the groin. He withdrew on the syringe and came back with dark red blood. Quickly he drew off a large sample to be sent for laboratory analysis and to the blood bank for crossmatching. The Chief Resident felt for the patient's pulse in the neck. There was none. The nurse had placed electrocardiographic leads on Twan's chest. The green line flowed across the face of the EKG monitor, monotonously, ominously flat.

"Ok, we'll have to do a thoracotomy here." With hurried but calm movements the Chief Resident pulled on sterile gloves and picked up a small paint brush from a tray, quickly painting the left side of the chest with iodine. He then took a scalpel and made a long incision from below the nipple to under the arm. The skin edges parted to expose the yellow fat in the subcutaneous tissue, and deeper the red striated layers of muscle. There was little bleeding as he pushed the smooth surface of the pink and black mottled lung back and out of the way. The Chief Resident placed a rib spreader in the wound and began to rotate the handle on the device to expand the opening and expose the chest cavity. A large amount of blood poured out of the chest and over the gurney onto the floor. He reached for the heart, which lay still and felt empty and flaccid in his hand.

"The heart's empty. Give him volume. Let's get some type specific blood down here." The Chief Resident began to massage the heart, pumping what little blood there was in the chambers into the circulation. "Give him two units of bicarb. Let's get a blood gas, and keep that volume coming!" he barked as he kept up cardiac massage. Two interns and a nurse squeezed manual reservoirs which pumped crystalloid salt solution into Sam Twan's empty blood vessels.

Murray Walker pulled on a pair of sterile latex gloves and moved in between the anesthesiologist and the ER Attending, who was trying to start yet another intravenous line in Sam Twan's arm. He lifted the gauze pad from the left orbit. The eye was destroyed, and with the vitrous fluid from the eye gone, the globe lay collapsed within the bony socket. The bleeding had stopped. Murray looked over to one of the nurses who didn't look too busy.

"You'd better let Ophthalmology know we're going to need their help here." The resident then lifted the right lid and shined a penlight into the eye. The pupil was large and irregular in shape and didn't respond to the light. He touched the outer part of the eye with a cotton swab. The eyelid didn't flicker in irritation with the normal corneal reflex. He held the head and sharply turned it to the right. The eye remained unmoving within the orbit, turning along with the head. So the oculocephalic reflex is out too, he thought. Murray then grasped the endotracheal tube that the anesthesiologist had secured in place with adhesive tape and pushed it back and forth to stimulate a gag and cough reflex. Only then did he find that the patient made a weak attempt to cough through the tube. Murray looked at the Chief Resident who was still massaging the heart.

"What's the story from your end?" he asked.

"We're getting some volume into him with the type-specific blood. I've found a lacerated pulmonary artery and got it clamped. The bullet to the chest missed the heart, but just barely. I'm going to cardiovert him now." The Chief Resident picked up two thin long-handled defibrillator paddles and placed the sterilized metallic contact disks at the tips directly on each side of the heart.

"Give me 50 watt-seconds. Everyone stand back." All of the personnel around the gurney took a step away as he pressed the red button on the end of the right hand paddle. Sam Twan's body arched suddenly from the electrical charge and then lay still. The Chief Resident put his hand back into the chest cavity and felt the heart, as he looked up expectantly at the cardiac monitor.

"OK, we've got a rhythm." He peered up at the green line that traced across the screen. It was a grossly abnormal, wide complex rhythm, slow and sluggish as it labored across the screen.

"Give him atropine, one milligram IV. We've got to get upstairs. Is the OR ready?" The Chief Resident loosened the rib spreader and pulled it out, and then quickly covered the thoracotomy opening with a sterile towel. With the increasing pressure in the circulation, blood again began to well up from the left eye. Murray Walker went back to the telephone and dialed Dr. Phillips' office.

"What's the situation?" Sitting at his desk, Jack looked at his wrist-watch. It had been eight minutes since the first call.

"He has a left orbital entry wound which appears to have entered the skull. There's been a lot of bleeding from the orbit. It only stopped when he had a cardiac arrest. They did a thoracotomy and got his heart started again. He has a laceration of his pulmonary artery which they've got clamped. Trauma wants to go directly to the OR. Neurologically, all he's got are a gag and cough, but he was just being resuscitated when I examined him, so his blood pressure was too low to really call it." Murray finished and leaned up against the wall next to the telephone. He watched them wheel the patient towards the elevator. At this rate, he probably wouldn't get dinner either, he thought to himself with notable irritation.

Jack pondered his options. There weren't any. "We obviously can't study him any further. I'd like to know whether the bullet injured his major intracranial arteries. We'll have to make do with plain X-rays. Once they get him upstairs, get a set of skull films to localize the site of the bullet. I guess we'll have to assume that he injured the carotid artery, and explore him to control the bleeding source, if it's not just coming directly from the eye." The neurosurgeon visualized in his mind the possible path of the bullet, and the blood vessels and neural tracts and nuclei that it may have damaged. "Did Ophthalmology see him yet?"

"I've called for them and they're on the way."

"I'll come down to the OR now." Phillips got up from his desk and put on his long white laboratory coat. He turned to Mrs. Brannan as he went out the door. "I've got to go to the OR." As he went down the hall, one of his patients who was walking turned to say hello. Jack smiled and stopped for a moment. Mrs. Kuboski was recovering from a brain tumor operation, and with the complete removal of the growth, relieving the pressure on the base of the frontal lobes, had changed from an apathetic and sullen, depressed woman into a feisty chatterbox. She now patrolled the hallways as her "therapy", and every time she saw Dr. Phillips, she stopped him to let him know how well she was feeling. It was definitely time to send her home, he decided, as he finally escaped to the stairwell. He hurried down the stairs towards the operating rooms.

In the OR the trauma surgeons had re-opened the chest incision and were exploring the left lung for the lacerated branch of the pulmonary artery. Feeling along the back wall of the chest cavity with his hand, the Chief Resident on Trauma stopped as he came onto the rough edge of a fractured rib, and next to it an irregular firmness within the muscle.

"I think I've got a bullet here." He looked up at Dr. Gregory Johnson. The sixty-three year old Chief of General Surgery had scrubbed in once they had brought the patient into the operating room. The resident could see the craggy, wrinkled lines that framed the older man's eyes above his surgical mask. The only time that Dr. Johnson didn't have a cigar in his mouth was when he was scrubbed and masked.

"You had better get it out of there and send it to the police for ballistics. Try not to mark it up too badly as you work it out." Dr. Johnson used the large flat blade of a retractor to compress the lung forward and expose the back of the chest wall. The Chief Resident worked through the muscle and soon had the bullet visualized, but still buried in tissue. He used the electrical cautery to cut some of the muscle away. The blue smoke generated by the cutting current curled up and out of the incision. The chief resident ignored its acrid odor trying to peer through the haze. Dr. Johnson stuck a suction tip down into the thorax and suctioned the smoke away.

The Chief of Surgery spoke to the circulating nurse as he worked. "When this bullet comes out, you need to begin a written documentation of whomever has it. And don't let it out of this OR until the police are here to pick it up themselves." The resident used a pair of smooth forceps and gently rocked the bullet loose. Finally, it came free from the tissue and he pulled it out of the chest cavity. He looked at it closely. The dull grey metal was flattened into an irregular oval, and was split open along one edge. It felt suprisingly heavy in the forceps.

"Call the police and let them know that we have this thing out." He handed the bullet to the scrub nurse who placed it into a glass cup on the table with the surgical instruments.

Murray Walker quickly changed into scrubs and was tying on his paper mask as he walked into the operating room. He glanced at the trauma surgeons working in the chest and then pulled on examining gloves and went to the head of the bed. The bleeding from the left orbit continued at a slow ooze.

"How's his pressure?" Murray looked up at the blood pressure monitor and then at the anesthesiologist.

"It's still low. We're giving him pressors and some blood. I can't give him much anesthetic because as soon as I do, his pressure bottoms out. But his cardiac rhythm is OK."

Murray looked for the circulating nurse. "We need to call X-ray for AP and lateral skull films stat. Y'all had better get ready for a craniotomy." He wanted to get these things moving before Dr. Phillips came in. Just then a slender middle-aged man entered the room and walked to the head of the table.

Murray nodded. "Thanks for coming, Dr. Moss." He then quickly outlined the problem to the ophthalmologist, who nodded his head with each new piece of information. The ophthalmologist then tried to examine the orbit using a suction to clear some of the flowing blood away. After a moment, the older man stood back and shook his head just as Jack walked in, tying his scrub mask on. He nodded to the other man.

"Hi, Bob, what do you think?" Jack moved to the head of the table and gazed at the ravaged eye with the steady stream of blood still welling up, dripping to the floor. He glanced at the man's other features momentarily, and although the patient's visage was obscured by the tape holding the endotracheal tube in place, somehow the man seemed vaguely familiar, although Jack couldn't place where he had seen him before.

"Well, the globe is destroyed. It will need to be enucleated at some point. I can't tell about the bleeding. It could be from the remnant of the ophthalmic artery or from the globe itself, but the bleeding looks like it's coming from the orbital apex." He paused as he considered the situation. "It's probably from inside the head." The three of them stood back as an X-ray technologist rolled in a large portable X-ray unit and positioned the cathode tube above the patient. She slid a film cassette underneath the head and prepared to shoot the film.

"Well, let's get a look at these films and then make a decision," Jack said as he walked up to the table and looked over the shoulder of the Trauma Chief. "Hi, Greg. What's up?"

"Hello, Jack. Well, we've controlled the bleeding from a lacerated branch of the pulmonary artery. I want to do a wedge resection of that segment of the lung. His heart is in better shape now that he's gotten some volume. We dug a bullet out of the chest wall. Looked like a thirty-eight to me. After we do the lung resection, we're going to tidy up and go home."

All of the surgeons except Dr. Johnson, as well as the anesthesiologist and the scrub and circuating nurses, stepped out of the room as the tech shot the X-rays. The old trauma surgeon shook his head. "I'm getting too old to worry about a little radiation," he grunted, and continued to work in the chest as the X-ray machine emitted a high-pitched beep as it exposed the film cassette.

The doctors walked back into the room and the anesthesiologist busied himself with transfusing additional cross-matched blood from the blood bank into the patient's dwindling circulation. He turned to Jack. "I'm going to have real trouble keeping up with that blood loss from the eye if you can't control it. It's not slowing down at all."

Jack nodded, pondering the information as the X-ray tech walked back into the room carrying the two radiographs, and handed them to Murray Walker. The resident slid the two blackened sheets of exposed film up onto a viewing box on one wall of the operating room and clicked on the lights. Jack and the ophthalmologist walked over and the three of them stood looking at the large irregular gash of bright whiteness against the muted, softer grey tones of the skull and surface tissues. They could see that the bullet was well inside the cranial vault, in the midline, above and behind the eyes. There were numerous smaller bright fragments scattered nearby.

"That's one hell of a place to get shot. It looks like it's right about inside the third ventricle. I sure don't want to go chasing after that," Jack muttered, nearly to himself, as he stared at the films. "If the damage along the bullet tract didn't kill him, more injury to that area certainly would. It has probably injured the left carotid artery on its way through." He went back to the head of the bed and looked at the man's face once again, vaguely troubled by the familiarity of the patient's features. *Where have I seen this guy before?*

He shook his head and stared at the floor, pondering his options. "I hate like hell to operate on him, but we can't leave him with a persistent bleeding site. He'll just exsanguinate and die for sure. And we have got to assume that it's coming from an intracranial source. I guess that we could just pack off the orbit and tamponade the bleeding. That would probably stop it, but he would just bleed around the brain, or into it, and I don't think that he would survive." Jack looked again at the films on the viewbox. How many times had he held similar X-rays up to the bare light bulbs of the operating rooms in Viet Nam, trying to localize the fragments and hurriedly plan an approach. They hadn't had CT scanners or other fancy technology back then, but somehow they had managed to get the job done.

"Murray, let's get the head prepped and scrub. We'll also need to prep the left neck in case we have to clamp the carotid artery to control the bleeding. We can repair the defects in the dural lining as best we can when we're finishing."

The ophthalmologist turned to leave. "Jack, call me when you're through, so I can remove what's left of that globe and debride the orbit. Do either of you know about him or whether his family has been contacted?" Jack looked at Murray, who shrugged, and turned to the trauma surgeons.

"Did y'all hear about a family on this guy?"

The Trauma Chief Resident nodded his head. "They were making some calls from the ER as we were coming upstairs. Apparently this guy is one of the trustees of the hospital. Rich, too...he had seven hundred dollars in cash in his pocket."

Jack glanced at the resident. " A trustee of Saint Joseph's?"

The resident nodded again. "His name is Twan, I think."

Of course! Jack looked again at the face on the operating table. He had met this man at several of the monthly executive meetings. Indeed, at a recent meeting where Jack had presented, along with the Chairman of the Department of Radiation Therapy, a tentative plan for building a sophisticated stereotaxic irradiation unit for the Neurological Institute, Twan had asked several questions about the bottom-line financial solvency of such a unit, informally called a "Gamma Knife". The system was quite expensive to put into place, and with the current climate of dropping reimbursement provided for such hospital-based treatments, it might never generate a profit, or even pay for itself. However, stereotaxic irradiation was clearly a technology that was needed for treatment of some difficult brain problems, and Jack was convinced that it was necessary for the Institute to develop the technology. To his frustration, by the end of the meeting they had come to a relative impasse, and Jack clearly recalled that this man Twan had remained critical about the cost-effectiveness of the proposed facility. The issue was on hold for now, until a Board of Directors meeting coming up at the end of the month. Jack gazed again at the face covered by tape and bandages and flowing blood from the destroyed orbit. "I wonder why in the world he got shot," he muttered to himself, putting other thoughts to be back of his mind.

As he spoke, Fred Steele walked into the operating room. The Vice Chairman was shorter than Jack, and had a stocky build. Although he was only a year younger than the Chairman of the Institute, he already had a head of prematurely grey hair. "I heard that a trauma came in. We were finishing up the laminectomy case. I had Aaron Richards go in to help finish closing."

Jack Phillips nodded towards the wall. "Take a look at those skull films, Fred."

The other surgeon went to examine the X-rays still up on the view box. "Holy Christ! How'd that happen?"

"Apparently he was shot out of the blue by some guy down on Union Street. He's one of the hospital trustees. His name is Twan. Have you ever met him?"

The Assistant Chief's voice rose an octave. "Hell yes! He's a big deal businessman and banker down in Chinatown." Fred looked back towards the body on the operating table. "I met him with my wife at a fund-raiser for the hospital a few months ago." Fred's wife was a third generation Chinese-American. She had been a registered nurse at Saint Joseph's before they were married. Now she remained socially active within the Chinese community in San Francisco.

"He's donated all kinds of money to charities in the city; a real philanthropist." Steele gazed up at the skull X-ray on the viewbox. The brightness of the bullet was stark against the bony outline of the skull. "Isn't he the guy who wants to torpedo the Gamma Knife?"

Jack nodded as Dr. Steele walked back to examine the patient's face and ruined eye. "He's got a youngish wife, as I recall, but I don't think any kids. How the hell did this happen to him?" The Assistant Chief put a glove onto one hand and opened the patient's good eye. The pupil remained enlarged and totally unreactive to light. He glanced up at the arterial blood pressure monitor. The pressure, with the added blood already given, was low but now adequate to perfuse the brain. Steele pushed his horn-rimmed glasses up on his nose, and turned to his older associate. "Jack, this guy looks like a goner. His good pupil is fixed and dilated despite an adequate blood pressure. With the location of that bullet, I don't think that he ever had a chance. You want me to take care of this? I can put in an intracranial pressure device and pack off the orbit. He won't last long, that's for sure."

Jack thought for a moment. Fred usually did take care of the trauma cases. He was technically good at it, and the cases gave him an excellent chance to teach the residents. Plus the work kept him busy, since his practice of the more interesting elective cases had remained somewhat

44

slow over the years. Yet, despite that, Jack did like to take care of an occasional trauma case. And he disagreed with Fred that the patient was absolutely destined to die from this injury. Probably so, sure. But, particularly when it was one of the trustees of the hospital, he felt that everything that could be done probably should be done. And it would probably look better for the Neurological Institute if the Chief did the operation, he decided.

"Thanks, Fred, but I'll take care of this one. I think that we had better do everything that we can here, regardless of the outcome. And anyway, I could use the practice," he joked lightly. Jack knew that Fred Steele chafed to the degree that Jack performed the majority of cases at the Institute, particularly the ones that were the more difficult and challenging. Those were the types of cases referred to Jack, and he wasn't about to give them away to anyone, including his younger associate. His referring doctors expected Jack to take care of the patients sent to the Neurological Institute, not Fred Steele. Both men loved to operate, to perform as much surgery as possible; Fred Steele's strong desire to do surgery was exceeded only by the desire that burned within Jack Phillips. In addition, although just below the filmy surface of consciousness, as a neurosurgeon Jack had a driving, relentless need for the challenges that difficult cases presented to him. The patient before him, although almost assuredly stricken with a fatal injury, offered just such a challenge.

Fred stood still for a moment, gazing at Phillips silently. Given that Jack was already focusing his mind on the complexities of the surgery at hand, he failed to notice the edge of tension that built around the other man's eyes above his surgical mask. Dr. Steele turned again to look for another long moment at the X-rays and the stark, white bullet in its dismal location within the head, and then, unnoticed, shook his head silently and walked out of the room.

Hurriedly, Murray shaved the patient's head with clippers and then used a hand razor to get a close cut from the ears forward. He wiped the scalp down with soapy water to rinse away the hair, and then dried it with a towel. Blood continued to ooze from the eye and run in a stream down onto the headrest and from there to the floor. The resident slipped a little in the puddle of fluid that had formed underneath the operating table. He used the sticky side of a a length of wide tape to pull away any remaining hair from the scalp. He looked at the circulating nurse.

"Can you do a quick scrub of the head?" She nodded as Murray hurried out of the OR to join Dr. Phillips, who was already washing his hands at one of the large stainless steel sinks. Murray picked up a packaged scrub brush, opened it and began to lather his hands and arms to the elbows.

"What do you think his chances are?" he asked Dr. Phillips. Murray had assisted on only one other gunshot wound to the brain. Unlike their prevalence in other cities, such wounds weren't all that common in San Francisco, although with the increase in inner-city gang violence caused by the extremely competitive market of crack cocaine, that was changing. Still, here people were more likely to fall off bar stools or get run over jaywalking.

"I treated a lot of patients with gunshot injuries in Viet Nam. They were generally a lot worse, from high caliber rifles or shrapnel. Usually a lot dirtier, too." Jack could remember the young men brought in with penetrating injuries and fragmented skulls, and the endless days and nights spent trying to put them back together in the humid, suffocating air of Southeast Asia. *The tons of human wreckage and hundreds of devastated lives that he had witnessed!* After a while he had begun to ignore the human side of it, and each patient became just an anatomic jigsaw puzzle to be put back together, problems of physiology to solve. Jack reflected as he lathered his hands at the scrub sink: You had to stop feeling for each one of them, because back then there were just too damn many.

"I don't think that his chances are very good at all, given how poor his neurological exam is, and the location of the bullet and all. But we'll control whatever bleeding that we find and debride the brain. Then we'll try to get a reasonable repair of the dura if we can."

Jack rinsed his hands and walked into the operating room, dripping water from each elbow. Murray continued to scrub for the required five minutes, pondering his Chairman's words, and then followed Dr. Phillips in. The trauma surgeons were just finishing their closure of the chest incision, rapidly placing a final layer of metallic staples in the skin, as the the two of them gowned and gloved for the procedure.

After shaving, and a brief scrub with surgical soap by the nurse, the scalp had been painted an orange hue with iodine solution, and now shone under the operating room lights. Phillips took a number ten blade and gently marked the incision that he planned to make, starting from just in front of the left ear and curving up and then forward towards the hairline. A thin trickle of blood began to run down from the skin mark as the neurosurgeon and his resident quickly surrounded the incision with towels and completed draping. They also draped out the neck to expose the common carotid artery if they needed to. Quickly they connected suction tubing and the electrical cautery, and were ready to begin.

Murray had automatically moved to the right side of the head to get ready to assist the Chief. Phillips stood back and motioned to the resident to move to the left side of the table.

"Open this up. Quickly," Jack said, as he himself went to the right side and stood, waiting.

For a moment the young resident hesitated, as he felt his pulse begin to race. He had assisted Dr. Phillips many times before, but had never done a major case himself. The scrub nurse was holding out the scalpel with a fresh number-ten blade attached to its tip. Murray could see the blade shining under the hot lights of the operating room. He gazed down at the orange scalp with its thin line of dripping red blood, and felt sweat break out on his forehead. He swallowed. Dr. Phillips had placed a sponge on the edge of the skin mark and held a sucker in his hand, ready to assist him.

"Go ahead, get started." Phillips' voice was soft, nearly casual, as he waited for the resident to begin. Murray took the knife in his right hand, and looked towards anesthesia.

"We're starting." With slightly self-conscious, hesitant movements at first, Murray opened the scalp and temporalis muscle and, reflecting these forward, placed three burr holes into the skull. He connected the holes using a pneumatic side-cutting saw. As he gently lifted the bone flap out of the head, they could see that the dura mater covering the brain was tensely bulging and had a blue discoloration.

"Looks like a subdural hematoma, Dr. Phillips. "Murray felt an exhilarated sense of elation that the Chief was letting him perform the surgery. His eyes fixed upon the operating field; every sight, every sound, every sensation was acute and focused; he missed nothing. His responses and movement became sharp, perfectly controlled, nearly automatic as he worked, with Phillips silently giving him the exposure, the assistance that he required. Indeed, Murray didn't realize that the actions of his professor were in essence unfolding the procedure before him, directing him as to where to go, and what movements to make next. Murray's back was now covered with a fine sheen of sweat, and he could feel the operating gown cling to his skin. But he didn't care. This was one of the great experiences of his lifetime.

"Open the dura, Murray."

The resident used a sharp hook to pick up the tough outer membrane and cut into it with a narrow scalpel blade. Immediately, a stream of dark, semi-clotted blood squirted through the incision, and Dr. Phillips quickly suctioned it away. Murray continued his incision around most of the circumference of the bone opening. After folding the dura to one side, a thick layer of residual blood remained, compressing the brain.

"Suction out the clot," Phillips said. "Carefully." His voice was still relaxed, conversational, urging the resident onward with the case.

Murray still couldn't believe that he was being allowed to perform so much of the case. He worked to coordinate his hands with the quick and precise movements of the Chief, as he watched Phillips use a broad-tipped forceps to lift up the dark blood clot away from the brain, so that the resident could safely use his suction to remove it.

After all of the visible blood was gone, they could begin to see the brain start to pulsate. Jack also noticed that there was a steady ooze of brighter blood from the underside of the brain, coming between the frontal and temporal lobes.

"That bleeding is most likely coming from a tear in the internal carotid artery." Jack watched the blood well up, and continued to suction at it absently. He began to feel a slight uneasiness inside of him. He hated to be out of control, ever. This was a situation where that could very easily happen. He wondered whether he should open the neck to expose the common carotid artery in case he needed to clamp it off temporarily to control the bleeding. As he stood there sucking the blood and going over the possibilities in his mind, his confidence returned and he decided that whatever he might find, he could most likely deal with it from inside the head.

"I had better take over from here. Good job, Murray."

The resident stood back to let the Chief move to the left side of the head of the table. He was exultant, and now he tried to impress Dr. Phillips by doing everything possible to continue to make the surgery go smoothly, by being the perfect assistant.

The neurosurgeon clamped the metallic base for the self-retaining brain retractors to the skull at one edge of the bone opening. He brought one of the articulated arms around to the top of the head and moved the second arm down over the patient's ear, and then began to use the flat blades at the end of each retractor to spread the frontal and temporal lobes of the brain. As he moved more deeply under the frontal lobes, they began to see increasing damage as they got closer to where the bullet entered. Phillips was having to suck away increasing amounts of blood from the field. It was bright red blood. *Probably from the carotid artery, but not too bad so far.*

"Let's bring in the microscope." The scrub nurse quickly draped the microscope with a sterile plastic cover, and then the circulating nurse pushed the base of the instrument towards the table. Jack grasped the handles and directed the microscope field into the exposure. Once he got into focus, he continued to retract the brain with the articulating arms of the self-retaining retractor. The bleeding increased.

"Murray, give me some suction in here." The resident placed his sucker into the exposure as Jack retracted the frontal lobe even further. Under magnification they could see the optic foramen that opened into the eye below and further forward. Around it the normal surface of the brain was unrecognizable, the grey and white matter destroyed and mottled with hemorrhage. The dural membrane overlying the orbit was torn, and fragments of fractured bone were embedded in the brain substance. Deeper in the field of view, there were strands of brighter white tissue that glistened under the bright light, before coming together as a thicker stump.

"Looks like that is what's left of the optic nerve. What a mess." Jack used his suction tip to show the resident the severed nerve. "It's pretty clear that the optic chiasm and hypothalamus are destroyed. I don't think that this guy has any chance of recovery from this injury. And if he did, he'd at the very least be blind, and have terrible problems with water balance, hot-cold regulation, and other metabolic problems from damage to the hypothalamus."

Murray Walker studied the field through the teaching head of the microscope. He couldn't recognize much of anything that looked like the normal anatomy he had memorized from his textbooks.

"Jesus", he murmured. He had never seen that much damage to the brain before. He worked to keep clear the steady stream of blood with his suction tip.

Jack wanted to get just a little more retraction further back to expose the internal carotid artery. Gently he compressed the wide retractor blade with his hand. He could feel the brain slightly relax and begin to fall away from the force of his retractor pressure. *Just a little further....*

Suddenly there was a rush of blood from behind the retractor blade. The view through the microscope became completely red. Jack could feel his heart start to pound. *God damn it!* The carotid must be completely torn, he decided. The blood began to pulsate and pool with each heartbeat, and the narrow exposure rapidly filled up with blood despite the suction.

"Murray, compress the carotid artery in the neck. Now!" The resident looked away from the scope and grappled for the exposed area on the patient's neck, searching with his fingers for the pulsation of the artery that supplied the brain. When he finally felt it, he used four fingers and pressed hard, squeezing the artery in the neck down onto the front of the spinal column. As he did this, he reflexly lifted his left hand and sucker out of the operating field. Within seconds the narrow exposure was overflowing with blood, which spilled out onto the drapes and from there onto the floor.

"You're going to have to suction, too. I can't see a thing." Jack raised his voice with irritation. "Anesthesia, we've got a lot of blood loss. Let us know how much it is and keep up with it." Jack could see that compression of the carotid in the neck was making no difference on the rate of blood loss.

"Give me a larger sucker tip! All suctions to full power."

"Murray, you've got to suction for me!" His voice was emphatic. "And compress both carotids!"

Murray turned his right hand and used his thumb to press on the other side of the neck to occlude the opposite carotid artery. His forearm was starting to ache from the effort, as he craned to see through the microscope and with his left hand keep his sucker tip inside the head.

Even with both of them suctioning, Jack still couldn't see through the pool of red. The anesthesiologist looked over the drapes. "His pressure is dropping, Dr. Phillips. Now ninety over fifty."

"Keep up with the blood loss!" the neurosurgeon barked. He worked with a small cotton patty trying to identify the exact site of bleeding. The blood was still pulsing from the depths of the exposure at a tremendous rate, despite the compression in the neck. There was a loud rushing noise as the two suctions drained the vital fluid away from the field. Jack listened as the anesthesiologist called to the circulating nurse for more packed red blood cells from the blood bank. And make it STAT, he added. Jack became aware of the high pitched beep of the EKG monitor, indicating each heartbeat. He noticed this because the rhythm had changed. It was now fast, and irregular.

"We've got ventricular tachycardia," the anesthesiologist called out, notifying everyone, but no one in particular, in a high, tense voice. He grabbed for his medication tray and began to draw up lidocaine and epinephrine. Murray Walker's right arm and hand burned as he bore down on the neck with his fingers. He tried to ignore the discomfort and looked up at the blood pressure monitor. It read forty over twenty. That low a pressure allowed essentially no perfusion of blood to the brain, he thought to himself. The beep of the EKG monitor was still irregular.

As the blood pressure dropped with the hemorrhage and cardiac arrhythmia, Jack could finally see one torn end of the artery. Quickly, he used his sucker tip to remove a thick rim of the surrounding brain, until more of the artery was exposed. It still pumped blood, but it was a much weaker stream.

"OK, give me a straight 8 millimeter Nakamoto clip!" He held out his right hand. The scrub nurse groped around looking for the clip applier. She hadn't been prepared for needing the aneurysm clips.

"Ventricular fibrillation!" The anesthesiologist nearly yelled the words. "Someone had better start CPR on the chest."

"Come on!" Jack's voice was louder, impatient. The nurse finally found the applier and loaded the clip into it. She then placed the applier into his fingertips. He tried to be smooth but saw with excessive irritation that there was a visible tremor in his right hand as he guided the clip to the stump of the artery and closed it. By now there was much less bleeding, as the exhausted and empty circulation provided little blood to the brain. He placed another patty onto the skull base where there was still an ooze and looked away from the microscope.

"What's going on?" he looked up at the EKG monitor. The pencil-thin line on the monitor was flat except for tiny irregular flickers off the baseline. The blood pressure was zero. One of the nurses was up on a stool over the drapes and leaning forward, using her shoulders to compress the front of the chest with an intermittent, steady rhythm. As she pumped, the sterile dressing over the chest placed by the trauma surgeons was becoming soaked with blood from the underlying incision. The blood began to soak the palms of her hands.

"He's in V. fib. and not responding to the drugs. We're still trying to catch up with the blood loss." The anesthesiologist was squirting the paddles of the defibrillator machine with conductive gel.

"Put it on 400 watt-seconds." The anesthesiologist moved in next to the nurse performing CPR. He nodded and the nurse quickly stood back and away from the table. Phillips watched as he applied the paddles to the chest wall and leaned in over the table, keeping his body well away from the patient to avoid being shocked himself. As he punched the red button on one of the handles, the patient arched off the table in a tetanic muscular spasm, and then flopped back down and was still. All of them, doctors, nurses and the X-ray tech standing in the corner of the room, looked at the monitor. The green line continued to trace flat across the dull screen. The anesthesiologist held the paddles to the chest again. He punched the button and there was a spark and a burning smell as one of the paddles momentarily lost contact with the skin. Again the body jerked and was still, but the green line steadily traced its unwavering course. His eyebrows raised slightly over his mask, the anesthesiologist looked up at Dr. Phillips. "Looks pretty grim," he muttered.

Phillips shook his head. "Let's call it quits," he said quietly. "He wouldn't have survived the brain injury anyway. Everybody agree?" The anesthesiologist nodded. Jack looked at the others on the team They were still staring up at the green line, which continued to arc in flat desolation across the face of the monitor.

Murray Walker was shocked. It had happened so quickly. Everything was going well and then all of a sudden the guy hemorrhaged, arrested, and now he was dead on the table. Murray looked at the body. There was still a trickle of blood oozing from the craniotomy opening. Only moments before the entire team was focused on keeping the patient, a human being, alive. Now they seemed to consciously ignore the body on the operating table. The circulating nurse was wasting no time in trying to clean up the mess on the floor. The anesthesiologist reached up and switched off the EKG monitor. The green line blinked out and was gone forever.

Jack turned away from the operating table and looked at Fred Steele, who must have come back sometime earlier, and was watching silently from the side of the room. Jack shook his head as he pulled off his operating gown.

The younger man looked at him and nodded in understanding. "Too bad, Jack. But this guy was a goner anyway. Christ, look at the location of the bullet. That cardiac arrest did him a favor..."

"Well, his carotid was transected. I couldn't get control of the bleeding quickly enough." Jack wearily pulled off his scrub mask. The excitement and anxiety of the case was starting to wear off, leaving a distinct sense of frustration. He sat down heavily on one of the metal stools on the side of the room, and after searching for a pen in his pocket, he finally borrowed one from the circulating nurse and began to write a note in the chart. He felt embarrassed that the bleeding had gotten away, and somewhat irritated that he had operated on the patient at all. Now it was going to be an operative death in the record books. When he finished writing his note, he got up and rubbed his face with both hands. Fred was waiting for him. Together they turned and walked out the door.

*　　　　　*　　　　　*

Samuel Twan hadn't arrived at the restaurant by one o'clock. Joseph Lo got up, and excused himself from the other two men at the table. He walked towards the pay telephones, trying to control his anger. Lo was a prompt man, to whom time was very definitely money. He looked again at his wristwatch and then dialed the direct number to Sam Twan's office in the First Bank of Num Hoy. He stared at the door to the men's restroom impatiently and counted four rings before a woman's voice answered.

He spoke in rapid Cantonese. "This is Mr. Lo. Mr. Twan has not arrived for our luncheon meeting. Did he not remember?"

Samuel Twan's personal secretary was a slim, middle-aged woman of supreme efficiency. She prided herself on keeping Mr. Twan's busy schedule perfectly coordinated. She sounded surprised.

"Of course he did, Mr. Lo. He left at least forty minutes ago. I can't imagine why he is not there."

"Well, I will wait no longer. Tell him to contact me as soon as possible." Lo briskly hung up the receiver and walked back to a table secluded in a rear corner of the restaurant. The lighting was dark and intimate. Two other men, both Caucasian, sat smoking silently.

"Apparently, Mr. Twan left his office nearly an hour ago. He should have been here by now. He had suggested that we meet to hear his proposals. I can wait no longer. I apologize to you for Mr. Twan. This is not at all like him." Lo spoke in smooth, accent-free English. He was the third generation of his family in San Francisco, and had received his undergraduate education at Yale before receiving his MBA at the Harvard Business School. He got up, nodded and walked towards the door.

Twan is a fool, he thought as he left the restaurant. In those two, there was a business deal of great importance to be made. They offered a golden opportunity to launder drug money from the Far East through legitimate corporations in the United States. But wasn't it unusual...He couldn't remember a time when Sam Twan was even five minutes late for a meeting. Lo walked up Buchanan and turned right onto Union Street. The rain had stopped, but it was still wet and cold. He glanced upward, displeased that he had not brought his umbrella with him that morning. A dull metallic sun could just be seen through the overcast above.

Lo continued to walk, gazing at the sidewalk in front of him, deep in thought. He looked up as he heard a car drive by at high speed. It was a dark sedan, and had a red light blinking in the corner of the rear window. He followed the car with his eyes and then suddenly he stopped. Fifty yards ahead he could see broad yellow police barrier tape cordoning off the sidewalk. It was at the entrance to the garage where his own car was parked. The street was full of marked and unmarked cars, pulled up in front of the garage, blocking the entrance.

Joseph Lo went to the curb and looked each way before he slowly walked to the other side of the street. He continued down the block until he was directly across from the garage entrance. People were milling around him on the sidewalk, looking across the street towards the open entryway. The slightly built Chinese man remained quite still, hidden in the crowd, and caught a glimpse of the rear end of a dark burgundy metallic sedan. He suddenly felt his blood run cold as he recognized the Jaguar. He turned and went inside a men's clothing store behind him, which faced the garage. The door was open and a young male clerk was standing just inside with his arms folded, watching the scene on the street. The young man was wearing a bright yellow teeshirt with contrasting suspenders under a broad-shouldered sports jacket. His short spiky black hair was tipped in bleach blond. Lo looked at him with mild but silent contempt.

"What happened?" He kept his voice casual.

"A guy was shot, right in the head." The salesman laughed nervously, and didn't notice the slight narrowing of Joseph Lo's eyes.

"Really? How terrible." Lo nodded to the young man and then walked out of the store. He walked calmly, slowly, for an additional two blocks. Then, at an intersection, he hailed a cab and climbed in.

"California and Grant." It started to rain again, a grey, flat drizzle. Joseph Lo gazed out at the street but didn't notice the trails of water streaming down the windows. As the cab sped away, he began to consider his options.

*   *   *

The intercom buzzed, and Jack Phillips hit the receiver button on his desk. "Yes?".

"Mrs. Twan is here to see you." Mrs. Brannan sounded subdued and professional.

"I'll come out." He quickly got up and pulled a freshly laundered and pressed white coat from the closet behind his desk. He was no longer in surgical scrubs, having dressed before leaving the surgical suites. He checked the knot on his tie as he walked to the door and opened it.

Standing in front of Mrs. Brannan's desk was a strikingly beautiful asian woman of about thirty years old, Phillips judged. She wore an obviously expensive fur coat over a dress of dark material. When she looked at him, he saw that her almond-shaped eyes were dark, nearly completely black. She had been crying; there was a slight smudge where the tears had smeared her mascara. A small, somber Chinese man stood behind her. He wore black, and held a hat in his knotted, elderly hands.

"Hello, Mrs. Twan? I'm Dr. Phillips." He held out his hand, and she took it for a brief, delicate moment.

"Please, come into my office." Jack stood back to let them enter and then closed the door softly behind them. After they had sat down, the woman looked toward the elderly man.

"This is Mr. Chow, our lawyer and an old family friend."
Jack nodded and shook the older man's hand with a firm grip. Once they were seated, Jack sat down on the leather-and-chrome chair facing the couch.

"What has happened to my husband?" Her voice was quiet, and she looked down at the floor.

Jack chose his words carefully, and then spoke in a gentle but firm voice. "Your husband came into our Emergency Room having been shot in the chest, and in the head. By the time he arrived, his heart had stopped, but we were able to get it started again. He had massive bleeding inside his chest, and bleeding from a torn blood vessel in his brain. We had to take him directly to the operating room to try to control the bleeding. While we were trying to do this, his heart stopped again. Despite our repeated efforts to resuscitate him, his heart would not respond ." Jack saw the woman look up sharply at him, her eyes wider. Jack was taken aback. Hadn't she heard already? Didn't she know?

"Oh no, this cannot be!"

"Mrs. Twan, your husband is dead." He paused. "I'm sorry," His voice was soft. "I thought that you had been told."

She turned and buried her face in the shoulder of the elderly man sitting beside her, and began to cry again. The older man slowly put his arms around the woman, his face grim, his eyes closed.

Phillips looked at them. These people's lives were forever changed by what he had just said. Yet, wasn't it odd, he reflected, that he felt no real emotion himself, except a very distant, abstract kind of sadness. The emotions he felt were more of self-reproach. He had made a surgical decision, a momentary judgement, and it had led to the patient's death. He looked down. His hands were gently clasped on his knees. They were lean and strong hands, with slender, tapering fingers. His wife had once said that they were beautiful hands. When they made love she sometimes stroked the back of them, lightly feeling the texture of the coiled veins and smooth tendons through the surface. Now, they felt utterly useless.

Mrs. Twan slowly controlled her crying and then got up, followed by Mr. Chow. Jack also got up. He opened the door and they stepped out. Jack walked behind them to the door to the office. He watched as they walked down the hall, and he then turned and went back into his office. Mrs. Brannan looked at him as he walked past. He shook his head a little. After he entered his office, he took off his white coat. Slowly he hung it up and closed the door to the closet.

Outside the sky was dark, and there was a black rain falling. He sat down at his desk and rubbed his eyes. The case today reminded him of another patient, from another time, long ago, when he had made a similar decision. With the same result, he remembered. Christ, it had been years since he had thought of that. He hated the sense of helplessness that he felt...a vague gnawing dissatisfaction in the pit of his stomach.

Fatigue gripped him, as he stared at the manuscripts and work on his desk. He could feel his usually intense motivation to complete the day's work, to strive forward with his clinical practice, his research, the things that he cared so deeply about, dim and fade away.

Suddenly Jack felt a need to be with his family. So many times in the past he had found solace from the sadness that he faced, in the simple pleasures of his home: his wife and the children that he loved. Children that were young and healthy and free of the pain that was such a part of this career that he had chosen. While he was not able or willing to feel deep emotion for the tragedies that sometimes occurred in his practice, just the opposite was true with his wife and children. There, and there alone, he could allow his emotions to come to the surface. To free himself from the burdens of his practice, he needed his family. He looked at his watch, which showed five-thirty p.m., and dialed the telephone.

"Hey, dad!" His son's voice was high-pitched, enthusiastic and full of energy. Jack smiled to himself.

"Hello, Darian. What are you up to?"

"I'm trying to get my homework finished. There's a show on TV I want to watch tonight."

"What are you studying?" Jack found comfort in just listening to his son's voice, in letting the stresses and concerns of his practice fall away for a few moments. He leaned back with his eyes closed and smiled.

"Oh, algebra." His son's voice dropped a little. "I don't like it much." Jack knew that his son had some trouble with math. "What are you doing, dad?" Darian's voice rebounded, a little more hopeful.

"I'm coming home!" replied his father.

5

The room was dark and narrow, with a low ceiling. The walls could just be seen in the light of the candles that lined either side of the large statue of Kwan Tai, the God of War. The smell of incense from the burning joss sticks filled Nim Choy's nostrils, as he kneeled facing the icon. The red and gold painted face of Kwan Tai flickered in the candlelight. Below, a thin boy with short black hair kneeled and looked down at the floor in silence. He was fifteen, and tonight he was choosing his destiny as a member of Gojin Tong. Nim Choy looked around. The room was filled with other senior members of the guild. San Li was there, the older man looking straight ahead impassively. Nim Choy looked at the others in the low light for signs of sorrow, like that he had felt in the weeks since the death of Samuel Twan. He could detect little expression in the faces. Only the hardness that was a requirement for survival in this world.

An elder of Gojin Tong, Robert Chun Ling, who had taken over as acting head of the guild after the death of Samuel Twan, stood to the side of the statue of Kwan Tai and recited the words of the initiation rite. He wore traditional robes, as had been worn by the elders of Gojin Tong since its inception in the mid-1800s, here in San Francisco. Originally formed by immigrants from the Fourth District of the Canton Province, the tong was part of the Luck Dai Gong Sue, or the Six Companies, from the six districts in the Canton region. The tongs were initially organized to provide mutual protection for their members from the oppression of the large family guilds that first ruled with an iron fist within Chinatown: the Wongs, Lees, Chins, and Four Brothers. As they became more powerful, the tongs themselves began to take over the gambling, prostitution, and opium trade, brisk because of the ready wealth created by the California Gold Rush. Throughout the years, Gojin Tong had remained powerful and influential, and now controlled heroin and cocaine importation, as well as gambling, and prostitution. And the original objective of the tongs, protection, also remained an important function: Gojin Tong had the largest extortion ring in San Francisco.

The ceremony was taking place in one of the basement rooms of Robert Chun Ling's expensive home, which overlooked the entrance to San Francisco Bay, on the outer edge of the city. The new young recruit continued to look at the floor silently. He was not afraid. He was the youngest son of first generation immigrants. Both his mother and father scraped out a living through constant work, his father as a waiter in a restaurant and his mother sewing in a garment shop. They were fools, he had decided. He already made ten times as much money as they did, selling heroin and cocaine in the elementary and junior high schools, and extorting protection money for Gojin Tong from shop owners in Chinatown. He recalled with grim pride the elderly owner of a fish market who had dared to resist him because of his young age, and smiled inwardly as he remembered the punishment that he had exacted.

Robert Chun Ling suddenly stopped his incantation and turned. With both hands, he picked up a black lacquered bowl containing a mixture of cock's blood and wine. He turned and carefully handed the bowl down to the boy. To the new initiate who drank the mixture, it would give courage. The courage to prove himself, and eventually become a feared *boo how doy* for the triad. The boy took the bowl in both hands and lifted it to his lips. He drank the tepid fluid slowly, until there was no more, and handed the bowl back. Then he stood, and the elder finished the ceremony by gripping his narrow shoulders in both hands and telling him to go and be strong, but above all, true to the ways of Gojin Tong. The boy turned and walked away from Kwan Tai, his head straight and proud. He went to the back of the narrow room and kneeled down, now a full member.

Robert Chun Ling now stood in front of the group and addressed them. "Members of Gojin. It is with unrelenting sadness that I think of our past leader, Samuel Twan, who was gunned down without mercy only a few weeks ago. Killed at a time when Gojin is the most powerful of tongs. Killed at a time when we have nearly total control of the heroin trade from all of Asia, and at a time when our other interests are at a peak. It was through the efforts of Samuel Twan that we have become what we are. But it is also because of this strength, this power, that others strike out in fear."

The elder waited for a moment, and spoke in a quieter voice. "Through the efforts of several of our members, and by walking the streets and listening to the wind, it has become apparent who is to blame for our leader's death." The group was totally silent. Kneeling in his place, Nim Choy suddenly stiffened and stared at the elder. Who had done this to Samuel Twan, the one who had given him his own beginning in Gojin? Nim Choy suppressed an urge to get up and shake the older man to extract the name.

The elder continued. "But it is not for me to tell you who killed our leader. For tonight, we have a new leader who will speak. I, and the other most senior members of Gojin, have chosen from among our own, one who will continue to direct us to our destiny, as Samuel Twan would have done were he with us." Robert Chun Ling turned to his right and held out his arm. From the shadows a small, thin man entered, and walked to stand directly in front of the statue of Kwan Tai. The candles glowed, and formed a halo around the silhouette. Nim Choy strained to see the face of the man in the darkness. The man's voice was thin and reedy, but distinct and sure in its message.

"Gojin Tong. We will remain all powerful. But first we must demand that those responsible for Sam Twan's death be punished in the same way. We now know that it was the Wan Fung Tong that planned and carried out the assassination of our leader." Murmurs and whispered conversations erupted.

Joseph Lo stopped and stared out over the group. Wan Fung Tong was a triad that had originated in Taiwan. They were as yet small, no more than a collection of petty criminals. But they were steadily becoming more powerful. Lo could see the reaction in some of the faces in the candlelight. He saw in them looks of hatred, and looks that spoke of revenge. Good.

"But there is more." The faces turned back to him, and once again there was silence. "We have also found that Samuel Twan was not simply killed by the bullets from the guns of these treacherous hoodlums. We are told that from these wounds he might have survived. The Wan Fung Tong somehow gained influence over the Western doctors that held the power and skills to save our leader's life." Lo's voice became bitter and heavy with emotion. "In doing so, they guaranteed that he would die."

Nim Choy remained still, his gaze transfixed on Joseph Lo.
The older man continued, his voice rising and becoming more emphatic. "We must retaliate against Wan Fung quickly, and forcefully, to make them pay for the death of Samuel Twan. We must also weaken them, for they surely have additional plans to further attack us and infiltrate our markets. Plans to take from us what is ours!"

"What about the Western doctors?" asked Robert Chun Ling, "Do we know who was influenced?"

"This also is quite clear. Our sources within the hospital itself tell us that he died at the hands of one doctor, the Chief of Neurosurgery at this hospital. His operation was apparently ill-advised and flawed; he allowed much of it to be performed by an assistant with little or no experience. I am told that there was excessive bleeding which caused Samuel Twan's heart to stop. Bleeding that this doctor would usually have been able to control." He paused. "My consultants tell me that he is particularly skilled." Lo stopped for a moment, his voice becoming quieter, but clear in the silent room. "Yet, instead, he fufilled the murderous ambitions of the Wan Fung Tong."

Nim Choy felt the dark room close in on him. The potent smell of the incense was suddenly sickening. Samuel Twan had been his guiding light. The man had nurtured him from the time that he had been a child in the streets of Chinatown, without goals or purpose, after his own father had died. Nim Choy was shocked and disgusted that a physician, one committed to the preservation of lives, could be bought in such a way.

Lo went on. " As well, it was distinctly unusual for this Chief of Neurosurgery to care for patients with this type of injury, yet he did so."

"But we are not completely sure?" asked Robert Chun Ling.

"No, not completely. However, I feel that we must respond to this murder, to this threat to Gojin Tong, on all fronts." The frail man banged his fist down on a table next to him. "He must be punished with the rest of them."

Nim Choy felt a rush of hatred flow through him as he stared at Kwan Tai, the red-faced God of War, and vowed personal revenge for the death of his friend.

*   *   *

Murray Walker got up from one of the front seats in the small auditorium and walked to the podium. His short white coat was dirty and stained, and he wore a wrinkled blue scrub suit that stunk from the sweat of the previous night on call. The resident was exhausted. He had been up for most of the night, caring for the patients that had been operated on the day before. But before he could go home and get some sleep, he had to get through the weekly Saturday morning conference.

He carried a cup of coffee in his left hand and as he got to the podium he looked at the sheet of paper in his other hand. It contained the morbidities and mortalities, or "M and M's" for the previous month. The junior resident on the clinical service was responsible for getting these organized and presented. Murray looked up at the group. Dr. Phillips, as usual, sat in the front row, his long white coat glistening with razor sharp creases. He wore an expensive but conservative tie and a starched collar, and was freshly shaved. Under Dr. Phillips' impassive gaze, Murray ruefully thought of his own stubble. Dr. Steele sat a few rows further back, leaning back in his seat, sipping from a cup of coffee. The rest of the staff and residents tried to offer the appearance of being fully awake.

"The first case that I would like to discuss is Mr. Twan, a 52 year-old Asian male who was admitted to the emergency room in full cardiac arrest after having been shot through the left chest and the left orbit.

60

He had an ER thoracotomy and was resuscitated and taken directly to the operating room. During this time he had pretty well continuous bleeding from the left orbit, and ophthalmology felt that it was most likely coming from the brain. We performed AP and lateral skull X-rays, which I have here." Murray turned and placed the films up on the viewbox. Several residents in the audience sat forward on their chairs to get a better view.

"As you can see, there is a large bullet fragment in the region of the hypothalamus and third ventricle." Murray paused. He felt as though he had cobwebs in his head, as he tried to put his thoughts in order despite his fatigue.

"We performed a left-sided craniotomy to debride the brain and control the bleeding. The optic nerve and chiasm were destroyed, as was just about all of the base of both frontal lobes. As we were trying to identify the carotid artery, there was suddenly massive bleeding. Anesthesia couldn't keep up with the blood loss and he went into ventricular flutter and then V. fib. He couldn't be resuscitated, and died." Murray finished, feeling drained. He looked at the floor, still remembering the abruptness of the patient's death, and feeling again the emotional letdown, from euphoria to hollow futility, that he had experienced on that day.

"Murray, what did the autopsy report show?" Dr. Phillips asked, his voice even, and mildly curious.

"The autopsy showed massive destruction of the base of the brain as we had determined at the time of surgery. The bullet was lodged within the third ventricle, and had destroyed both optic nerves, the optic chiasm, and the hypothalamus. The left carotid artery was completely disrupted." The resident looked at Dr. Phillips and thought that he seemed pretty relaxed about the whole thing.

Jack got up and turned to the group. "Well, I've thought about this case for some time. Neurologically, he was pretty well devastated at the time that he came in from the initial injury, and this was further complicated by the cardiac arrest. A lot of people wouldn't have operated on him at all. Indeed, Fred Steele came into the room at the time, and suggested a conservative approach, just packing off the orbit and placing an intracranial pressure monitor. In retrospect, that was clearly the right thing to do. I don't think that there was any way that he would have survived though. His intracranial pressure would just have climbed up from the bleeding and eventually killed him. My thought at the time was to try and control the bleeding at the source, which turned out to be the left internal carotid artery, followed by a standard debridement and closure."

He stopped and shook his head as his mind reviewed the details. "It was a mess. About the only thing from a surgical point of view that we might have done differently was to have had the carotid exposed in the neck so that we could have cross-clamped to gain proximal control when the thing ruptured. But even with Murray occluding both carotid arteries manually, there still was tremendous bleeding."

"I agree, Jack." Fred Steele took off his glasses and cleaned them, gazing myopically around the room at the residents and other members of the faculty. It wasn't lost on him that Jack had acknowledged his own input into the case. It was typical of Jack to do so. But it still irritated the Assistant Chief that he had operated on the man at all...it had simply been a waste of resources, and a kind of surgical grandstanding that Fred Steele personally found distasteful. It hadn't been the first time that Jack had ignored his advice and performed some technically difficult or dangerous procedure in a patient under less than optimal circumstances...although he usually he got away with it. It was definitely an ego trip that Jack Phillips relished. And in this case it belied a lack of understanding on Jack's part about gunshot wounds to the brain. Fred Steele continued his discussion: "As is always the case, a bullet wound that crosses the midline structures of the brain, in a patient who comes in with absent upper brainstem reflexes, is fatal from the word go...this guy's chance of dying from this injury was 100% at the time of admission. But it is true that it was hard to ignore his continued bleeding from the eye. And it's nice to know that there are some things that even you can't handle."

Several of the more senior residents laughed, and Phillips himself smiled, as he sat down. Murray got on with the rest of M and M's. He wanted to get these things over with, so that he could get out of the hospital, and home to bed.

Later in the day, from his office, Jack called home. "Hi, Barbara. Listen, how about if we go out and get a bite of dinner tonight? The kids will be OK, won't they?"

"Hmmm. That sounds nice. Christine is going with some friends of her's to the movies." I think that Darian can probably stay over at the Williams house after he does his homework and watch TV or something. I'll call Linda and check. Will you make some reservations?"

Jack looked out the window. Indian summer had arrived, and it was spectacularly clear outside. The clouds and fog that normally hung over the bay the entire summer were finally gone. Through his window, Jack could see Alcatraz clearly. The stark grey and white walls of the old prison were bright in the blue water of the bay. "Yeah, I've got just the spot."

*   *   *

Far below, the lights of Marin, and further eastward, those of Berkeley and Oakland, glittered in the distance. The sky was perfectly clear, a dome of deepening indigo as the evening approached. Inside the darkened interior of the restaurant the mood quiet and relaxed. A single candle glowed in the center of their white linen-covered table. The restaurant was one of their favorites, perched on the shoulder of Mount Tamalpais along the winding two-lane road to the summit. The windows next to their table were opened outward, and the scent of the mountain forest surrounded them. There was just the hint of a breeze, the air surprisingly warm. From the chill of the evening in Mill Valley below, Jack had noticed the temperature climb as they had driven up the mountain with the top down. Beyond the subdued sounds of the restaurant, Jack could sense the stillness of the oncoming night. They had ordered a Napa Valley sauvignon blanc, which was excellent, and they sat and sipped the wine.

"How was your day?" Barbara looked at Jack and smiled. She was wearing a low-cut white satin dress. She had little need for a bra, and Jack could see the soft outline of her breasts under the thin material. He felt a vague, deep stirring.

"I'm finally getting a real handle on the book. That deadline for the final draft is coming up." As usual, he had spent the Saturday at the hospital. After the morning Grand Rounds conference, he had worked at his desk on the computer for most of the day. At first Barbara had complained about the time that he spent away from the family. But over the years she began to realize that he wouldn't, or couldn't, change. Somehow the inhumanely long hours of internship and residency training had accustomed him to a deeply ingrained work ethic, which had continued as he had moved up the academic ladder and finally to the Chairmanship of the Neurological Institute. In striving to develop a busy practice, and achieving a national reputation for the hospital, and himself, Jack had continued to work as much as he ever did. Barbara's complaints, no matter how bitter, seemed to have no effect upon her husbands ability to see that he was missing or ignoring the most important years of their childrens growth and development. She had basically raised the two of them by herself. The kids thankfully, had learned to enjoy the brief hours that Jack was home, but silently his wife resented all of the time that her husband spent away from the rest of them. She considered him excessively driven. But in reality, in his pursuit of medical excellence, Jack was a tortured man.

"What did you do?" he asked.

"I took Darian to soccer practice. They are having their first game in a week. I hope that you can make it."

"I've got it on the calendar. I'll be there," he promised. Jack did try to spend time with his kids, especially Darian. The two of them loved to hike through the headlands of Marin and out to the coastline of Point Reyes. Most Sundays, after the one morning of luxury sleeping late and reading the paper in bed, he spent the rest of the day with them.

The waiter came and took their order. Both had decided on a Ceasar salad and fresh grilled Coho salmon. Barbara sipped her wine. "I read something in the paper today about that man that you operated on. Twan, was his name I think."

"Oh, really? We talked about him at the conference this morning."

Jack was only mildly interested in knowing more about the man. He had tried to forget about the case.

"The article said that he had connections to organized crime in San Francisco," She paused. "and that it was a gang-related assassination."

Jack was surprised. "A gang? You must be kidding. The man was a trustee of the hospital!" He pondered the information for a moment. "Well, whoever shot him did a good job. He took one bullet in the head and another in the left side of the chest, near his heart."

He paused. "I had gotten the impression from Fred that he was a model businessman. Did fund-raising, that sort of thing."

"Fred knew him?"

"He said that he had met him at one of his wife's parties. Those Chinese gangs are mostly kids, aren't they?" he asked.

"It didn't go into much detail." She looked up as the salad was served, the waiter grinding pepper with a large wooden peppermill onto each of their plates. They began to eat. Jack continued to enjoy the panoramic view, noticing the stars as they began to appear in the still night sky.

"There really wasn't very much that we could do. His head injury was going to be fatal, sooner or later. It would have been much worse if he had survived. He never would have recovered. At best, he would have been left blind and vegetative." Jack chewed his food as he reflected. "Did I tell you about his wife?"

Barbara shook her head.

"She was young, maybe early thirties. I had to tell her that he had died." Jack once again remembered the discomfort that he had felt as he had talked with her. "She took it pretty well, considering." He remembered how dark her eyes had been, and her tears. Then he pushed it from his mind.

"I'm glad that I don't have to deal with many of those. Fred usually handles the trauma that comes in."

"Why is that?" Barbara asked.

"Well, he's good at it for one thing. And his practice is still a little slow, I guess. He doesn't mind the work. He wanted to do this one...Christ, I should have let him."

"Is he still running?" She remembered that Fred was devoted to jogging and other forms of physically stressing himself.

"Oh yeah, he still runs from the hospital across the Golden Gate Bridge every day after work. He's nuts. Eventually his knees are going to need to be replaced."

The main course was presented with a quiet flourish, and the waiter brought them fresh glasses for a half bottle of good Chardonnay from the Sonoma Valley. They relaxed and quietly finished their dinner. Jack gazed out the window and let his mind forget about the tensions of work. A full moon had risen and given the surrounding mountainside a pale glow. Afterwards they held hands as they walked out to the car. The Mercedes growled to life and Jack began to follow the narrow two-lane road down the mountain, passing no houses or street lamps for several miles. Jack drove at a leisurely pace, with the side window down, listening absently to the pleasant exhaust note of the sports car.

After a short period, he thought that he heard a different sound, more rasping, and high-pitched. Vaguely the noise became louder with each turn of the winding road, coming up behind him. Jack looked in his mirror but couldn't see anything except the red glow of his own tail lights, and the trailing road behind, pale in the moonlight. They rounded a long turn that led onto a short straightaway. Here there were a few houses, and a single streetlamp lit the roadway. Barbara had turned on the stereo, so that Jack could no longer hear the sound clearly. But he was curious, and watched in his mirror after they had passed under the lamp. There! A brief flash under the light. About two hundred yards back a car was behind them, without lights.

Christ Almightly! thought Jack. What kind of fool would be driving without lights! He's going to run himself off the road! He continued at his comfortable pace. The steering of the old sports car was quick and accurate and light. As he came around a long gentle bend, he suddenly noticed the rasping sound abruptly increase in pitch. It rapidly became louder and louder, until it seemed to be on top of them. Suddenly, there was a glare of lights right behind them. He's going to hit us! Jack clenched the steering wheel and veered to the shoulder of the road. To the right was a steep drop-off. Barbara screamed, and by reflex Jack hit the brakes, knowing in an instant that this was a mistake. Immediately the tires began to skid in the loose gravel on the side of the road. He wrenched the steering wheel back to the left, but the car continued forward, the front tires plowing, without any grip, sliding toward the edge of the cliff. Jack felt, more than saw the other car flash past within inches of his door. It was dark in color, a low sportscar, with the convertible top up. The Mercedes shuddered as it scraped up onto a narrow ledge of rock. Beyond there was only a blackness. The car ran up, onto a large boulder, which jammed under the front suspension. With that the Mercedes came to a halt, the right front wheel suspended over the edge.

Jack was shocked. He found himself staring into the darkness, his hands braced up against the steering wheel, expecting to feel the car tumble down the mountainside. He could still hear the rasping noise of the other car as it disappeared into the distance down the mountain. He felt a sharp pain in his right knee. Barbara had gripped the armrest on the door, but with her left hand had grabbed his knee, her nails digging into the flesh. Slowly, he began to unclench his hands from the wheel, the usually calm, sure hands trembling in the darkness. The radio was still softly playing classical music. He reached over and shut it off. Then he noticed that the engine of the Mercedes was still running. Somehow he had pushed in the clutch with his left foot and the car hadn't stalled. He moved his hand again and slowly turned the ignition key off.

"Are you OK?" He reached down and loosened Barbara's grip on his knee. She continued to clutch his pantleg.

"My God! What happened?" Her voice was high and panicky.

"That sonofobitch ran us off the road!" Jack slowly got out of the car. In the full moon he could see the roadway clearly. There were no lights except the headlights of the Mercedes which glared out into the pitch blackness of the night. He walked around the front of the car and looked underneath. The right side of the car was jammed up on the boulder which had prevented them from going off the edge. Jack walked back to his door. Barbara was still sitting motionless in her seat.

"Barbara, get out on this side. We'll walk back up to those houses and call the police." He reached in and shut off the lights, and then gently gripped her arm. He helped her climb over the center console and then out onto the road. With the full moon, they had no difficulty walking back up on the edge of the pavement. No cars passed by them, and the only noise was the sound of their shoes crunching on the gravel.

"Why would someone do that?" Barbara had calmed down and walked holding Jack's arm tightly.

"I just don't know. It was probably some crazy kids. Driving without lights! And then that stunt! Jesus, we could have been killed."

About a half mile back was the streetlamp that they had passed. A driveway turned in off the road, and they followed it to a small cottage. Lights were on inside. Jack followed a walkway to the front door and knocked. He heard steps inside. The door opened part way and Jack could see an older man with a large belly standing in a flannel housecoat.

"What do you want?" the man demanded.

"I'm sorry to bother you. We were run off the road about half a mile down. The car can't be moved. Can I use your phone to call the police, and a tow truck?"

"Run off the road?" The man saw Barbara standing behind Jack and opened the door fully. He backed up to let them in. "The phone's in the kitchen." He led them into the small unkept kitchen. There were dishes in the sink. The stale smells of cooking filled the room. Jack dialed 911, and once they answered, he described what had happened. Then he hung up.

"They said to go back to the car. They're sending the Highway Patrol and a tow truck," Jack said.

"You want a ride back?" The old man asked.

"That'd be great, if you could." They waited as the man changed into his clothes. Jack gave Barbara his sports coat to wear over her thin dress, as the night was getting colder. The three of them squeezed into the cab of the man's pickup truck and drove down to the car. As they arrived, they saw lights flashing around the stranded car. Highway Patrol and local police officers were standing in front, inspecting it with large flashlights. Jack and Barbara got out and walked over to the group of officers.

"This is my car. I was run off the road by a dark sports car."

They looked at him. "How did that happen?" one of the officers asked as he looked Jack up and down and glanced at Barbara. Jack could see that they weren't convinced about his story. They probably thought that he was drunk at the wheel or something. His temper flared.

"Look. We were driving down the road, and this car driving without its lights on nearly ran into the back of us. I swerved, and he missed us by about an inch. We're just lucky that we didn't go off the edge! And that's what happened. The guy was crazy! You should be out looking for him!" He finished, and looked from one officer to the others.

One of the Highway Patrol officers directed the two of them to his cruiser. "Let's get a report. We'll need a description of that car. I'll radio for a tow truck, and then we will get you home." It took another hour and a half. They sat in the patrol car, listening to the intermittent crackle of the radio. A tow truck finally came, and pulled the Mercedes off the boulder. Jack winced as the front suspension grated and dragged across the boulder. The right front wheel stuck out at a sick, abnormal angle. Finally, they lifted the front end and hauled the car away. Jack watched the red tail lights fade away down the mountain road. He still couldn't quite believe what had happened, but he felt lucky that it hadn't been worse.

The patrolman gave them a lift home. He told them that the Highway Patrol would look into it, but it was pretty unlikely that they would locate the car that had caused the wreck.

It was two-thirty in the morning when they finally arrived at their doorway. The kitchen light was on, and they found the kids asleep. After undressing, Jack went into the bathroom. He looked into the mirror. His face was haggard, and he felt exhausted. Thank God tomorrow was Sunday! He rubbed his hand through his hair, and then brushed his teeth. When he came back into the bedroom, Barbara was already asleep. He crawled into bed after her. But in the darkness, again and again, he saw the headlights as they came up behind him, and felt the sickening shudder of the car as it slid out towards the cliff. At last, he fell into a troubled sleep.

6

The small diner was hidden down a flight of stairs at the basement level, on a narrow alley off Grant Avenue. Not many tourists to Chinatown came into the restaurant. From the street, only the hand-written signs of yellow paper could be seen in the low window, posting the specials of the day for the local residents.

The proprietor, Ping So, cooked behind a short formica-covered counter. The smell of fried vegetables and chicken filled the air. There were three people at the counter, including Chun Wong, who owned a dry cleaning and laundry business on the floor above, as well as the building that they were sitting in, with its three additional floors of tiny apartments above the laundry. His wife and her two sisters were still working upstairs, but he had come down for his lunch, as he did every day.

Two Chinese youths sat at one of the small booths. The taller of the two wore jeans and a red leather jacket. He had a bandana around his neck, and his hair was greased into a high pompadour. His chrome sunglasses reflected the light from the fluorescent lamps in the ceiling. The second was shorter, and wore a simple white teeshirt under a loose-fitting black jacket. His hair was cropped short on the sides and in a flat razorcut on top. The young men spoke little as they waited for their meal. The one in red, facing the street from the booth, kept his eye on the door of the diner, and on those who entered the restaurant. Since the Twan killing, they had been extremely cautious, and had been in-structed by their elders to halt their usual duties of collecting protec-tion money from the shop owners over on the west side of the city, in the Sunset and Richmond districts. The Wan Fung Tong had also slowed down its drug distribution, and was running only the most hid-den of its gambling rooms, with the most stable, exclusive clientele. The elders of the tong kept their personal bodyguards with them at all times. They expected a retaliation, and were ready for it.

The shorter of the two young men watched idly as an old lady got up from her seat at the counter and began to make her way out of the diner. Her face was wrinkled and wizened by years of hard physical labor, and her thin white hair was covered with a bright red scarf. She stood hunched forward, and walked with slow, arthritic steps using a cane. The boy's eyes, devoid of emotion, followed her as she went to the register and paid for her meal out of a small change purse. As the old lady opened the door and finally began to make her way up the stairs, the boy turned back around and shrugged.

A half a block away, three men sat in the rear compartment of a white van. There were no windows, and it was beginning to get hot in the darkened compartment. San Li glanced down at the MAC 10 that he held in his hands and made sure that the safety was off. The presence of the older man calmed the two younger men with him. They had both swiftly volunteered for the duty, and now they followed San Li's example. One of them had already experienced the intense edge of danger in a gun battle, and now recalled the heady power of wielding his weapon for a just cause. The other had not yet, but was committed to proving himself within Gojin Tong. They had been informed that members of the Wan Fung Tong would be in the restaurant at lunch time.

San Li remembered the discussion as they had been briefed for the hit. "There will be two bodyguards. You must kill both of them. The two were directly involved with the murder of our leader. They will be with Chun Wong, an elder of Wan Fung triad."

That man is a fool, thought San Li. He eats in the same place each day. He must think that he is impervious because he owns the building.

"Tell him that you are unhappy tenants and want your rent reduced," one of the gang members had joked before they had left the safe house.

Nim Choy watched impatiently from the driver's seat of the van. He had parked in a loading zone. He looked at his watch, and started the engine, but kept his eyes fixed on the exit from the small alley. He was worried, because the traffic on the street was at its heaviest around midday lunch hour.

The van would be seen. There was no avoiding it. That morning they had placed fresh license plates, stolen from a car in the financial district soon after the morning commute. The owner probably wouldn't even have reported it before he would be confronted by the police looking for the van. By then the plates would be at the bottom of the bay.

Suddenly, Nim Choy saw what he was looking for. The bright red scarf could just be seen above the flow of pedestrians on the sidewalk, as the woman exited the restaurant, and then it quickly mixed in with the noontime crowd. The scarf confirmed that the three were there, in the restaurant, as expected. He shoved the van into gear and, glancing into his mirror, pulled out and accelerated down the street.

Inside the restaurant, Ping So was serving their meal. The shorter youth glanced at his companion, who was beginning to eat, and then he looked at his own plate of rice and fish. He was hungry. You cannot be suspicious of everyone, he told himself, thinking of the old woman. He started to eat, and as he did so his eyes wandered around the room, and fell on the worn formica countertop, next to Chun Wong, where the elderly woman had been sitting. He stared impassively for a long moment, unsure of his vague concern before he realized what he was looking at. What was bothering him. It was strange enough that the old peasant woman was eating in a restaurant at all. But there! He looked at her plate, as Ping So was lifting it away to put in the sink. The plate was still full of food. She had barely taken a bite! He emitted a short guttural sound, and began to get up from the table. His partner looked at him in puzzlement as the shorter youth tried to reach into his loose jacket for his machine pistol. Suddenly, the windows and the door of the diner exploded in a shower of glass.

After the windows were gone, and San Li had encountered no opposition, he waved to the two younger gunmen, who moved down the steps and crouched to spray the diner further. A large mirror behind the counter shattered and fell to the floor. The three gunmen stopped only when their clips were empty. San Li could see four bodies, lying like broken dolls among the shards of glass. The air was smoky and thick with the sharp smell of cordite. The three ran back to the waiting van and climbed inside, ignoring the frightened pedestrians running away from the gunfire. As San Li slammed the side doors shut, Nim Choy pulled out into the traffic, which had continued to move around them on the street. The whole thing had lasted less than a minute. At the end of the block he turned right, and then at another intersection turned left, and disappeared into the traffic and congestion of the city.

*   *   *

Joe McAllister scanned the report quickly the first time, and then read it again more slowly. A look of disgust began to cross his face as he leafed through the pages. First the Twan murder, and now this. A hit by three Asians in broad daylight in one of the busiest sections of the city! Walked right up and put five hundred rounds into a restaurant at lunchtime. Four dead. The fucking gangs were doing anything that they goddamn well pleased1 They were lucky that no tourists had been killed, for Christ's sake, he thought angrily. Then you would have seen some action from the mayor's office. The aging detective took a swallow of coffee out of his styrofoam cup. Made that morning, the coffee had long since gone cold and stale. He looked around the office, spotted a trash can up against one of the drab metallic desks, and tossed the cup in, still half-full. The brown liquid slopped up out of the can and onto the floor, but he didn't notice as he kept reading the report through to the end.

As the homocide detective assigned to the Twan murder, McAllister was tired and frustrated. The investigation was going nowhere. The locals were so goddamned tightlipped! It was as if Chinatown were zippered shut. Even the young Chinese plainclothes officer that he had assigned to check up on leads in the area could get no one to talk. All they had come up with were the witnesses to the shooting itself. It had been clean, fast, and hadn't left a single shred of evidence. The gun, the car, the plates, had all been recently stolen. The car was later found a hundred and fifty miles away in an abandoned junkyard.

McAllister walked down the hall and knocked on the captain's door. He went in, not bothering to wait for a response. Captain James, Jesse they called him behind his back, was sitting in the cracked leather chair at his desk, the receiver of the telephone wedged between his shoulder and his ear. The detective stood and waited. As the captain finished talking, he looked up.

"Hi, Joe. I see you've already gotten a look at that report." The captain's eyes were a little bloodshot, only in part from overwork, McAllister suspected. He nodded.

"What a goddamn mess. Who do you have assigned to it, Captain?"

"Epstein went to the scene and did the initial report. But I want you to take it over."

McAllister had been browsing through the papers again and looked sharply at the captain, who returned his gaze.

"You know that the Twan case has gone nowhere so far," said McAllister.

"Yeah, but you've got a few leads. Maybe the two are related." The captain stretched, and then got up and went over to a coffee pot sitting on a filing cabinet. He poured himself a cup of the black liquid. He looked at the detective, raising his eyebrows. "Coffee?"

McAllister shook his head. "I'll talk with Epstein to see if there is anything that isn't in the report that might be useful. We have been getting nowhere beating the streets on the Twan case. Can I use Jim Leong full time on this?" The legwork was mounting up. He needed another pair of feet, preferably Asian.

"Sorry, but I can't do it. With the hiring freeze this year, we're thin enough as it is. He's already got two other assignments. You're on your own unless you can talk him into some serious overtime." McAllister nodded his head. He had already known the answer, but was just testing to see if the old man was getting soft.

McAllister walked out of the office and went back to his desk. The grey surface was littered with old reports, used styrofoam cups and scraps of paper. He glanced at his watch. Four-thirty. If he got over to the Medical Examiner's office soon, they would probably still be doing the autopsies on the restaurant shooting victims. The detective pulled on his worn tweed sportscoat and left the office. The walls in the Central Police Station were a drab shade of institutional green. There were wooden benches along one wall. The air in the building had a tired, stale smell. The hallway was as familiar as his house. McAllister had been working the homocide detail for the past fourteen years. He moved heavily down the stairs and into the parking garage, and walked to his brown Ford sedan. After a couple of tries the car started, and he drove up and out of the parking garage.

It was pleasant outside, clear and warm. Early fall weather, he noticed. McAllister drove to the Medical Examiner's office. It was only five blocks away from the Central Station, but he'd rather drive than walk the distance. Besides, with the police plates on the Ford, he could double- park wherever he wanted.

He looked into the rear view mirror for a lane change, and glanced at himself. His grey hair was getting too long, he noted. His skin was sallow between the mounting wrinkles, an unhealthy yellow from too much time indoors. I'm getting just too goddamn old for this, he muttered to himself. Retirement was a year away. It wouldn't be soon enough. He lit a cigarette, and began to look for a likely place to leave the car. He waited as someone backed out of a parking space, and pulled the Ford in. He turned off the key, but the engine kept turning over in a gasping manner for a few moments, until it finally coughed to a stop.

McAllister walked up two steps and through double glass doors into a drab gray stone building office. There were a few people milling around in the waiting area. A woman was dabbing her eyes. Probably here to identify their family members, he thought. He glanced at them. No Chinese, he reflected.

The detective waved at the receptionist behind the counter, and waited as she pushed a button to let him through a heavy locked wooden side door. The stone building was quiet and cold. He could feel the chill through his jacket and thin shirt. As he walked down the staircase to the morgue, he began to sense the familiar odor of the place, a mixture of disinfectant and, something, he wasn't sure. It was faintly unpleasant. At least today they weren't burned, or pulled out of the bay. He reached the bottom of the stairs and walked through another door.

On the stainless steel dissection tables there were five bodies, all naked. A large white identification tag hung from the right great toe on each. McAllister walked along the tables. One of the bodies had medical catheters protruding from an arm, and an endotracheal tube jutting out of the mouth. An older Caucasian male, it had already been autopsied. The long y-shaped incision extending from each shoulder to join at the bottom of the breastbone before continuing down to the pubis had been closed with heavy nylon suture. Sent over from some hospital, he thought. The other four were more interesting.

The detective walked over to a man wearing a shiny black rubber apron and heavy surgical gloves, busy closely examining a heart, which was still attached to the lungs, and abdominal organs, all of which had been removed en bloc from one of the corpses. McAllister looked at the body with interest. It was an Asian male, thin, and no more than twenty years old. He could see six or seven entry wounds in the chest and abdominal wall. They were small blackened punctures in the mottled white skin. The trunk incision was splayed open, revealing now only the empty chest and abdominal cavities from which the organs had been removed. Dark blood pooled in the back of the chest cavity, layering on each side of the spinal column.

The forensic pathologist, Dr. Sebastian Greco, was a short, swarthy man. He used a scalpel to deftly open the chambers of the heart, and then washed down the organ with water flowing from a plastic hose before prodding it again with his finger. The blood washed across the metallic table to side gutters and from there into a sink at one end.

McAllister looked on curiously. "Whatcha got, Doc?" The shorter man looked up.

"Well, Mr. McAllister. How are you?" The pathologist grinned. His heavy afternoon shadow could have used another shave.

"This man died of a gunshot wound through the left ventricle of the heart, not to mention several others through his chest and abdomen. Look at these." The pathologist pointed to a collection of bullets grouped near the head of the cadaver.

"All from this one?" the detective asked.

The pathologist nodded. "They were just inside the chest wall and in the abdomen. Pretty low velocity, I'd say. Surprising. I would have expected more penetration."

McAllister nodded. "Silencers, Doc They used silencers on the weapons, which slowed the slugs down."

The pathologist nodded thoughtfully and returned to his examination. "All of them died of multiple gunshot wounds using similar weapons. I've got plenty of samples for your ballistics lab."

McAllister walked around the table to look at the faces on the two younger bodies. Neither was damaged much, although the taller one had several cuts from glass fragments, each of them bloodless and gaping. He looked at the toe tags and checked the names. Same as on the report he had read through earlier.

"Doc. I'm going to have the photographer come by in the morning and take facial pictures to show to witnesses. I'll send someone from ballistics down tonight for the slugs." The shorter man nodded, as he continued to work, dissecting the viscera down, and recording his findings into a microphone hanging from the ceiling.

McAllister left the Medical Examiner's Office, and drove back to the Central Station. It was already starting to get dark earlier in the evening now, he noticed. When he got back to the office, he went to his desk and unlocked one of the drawers. He pulled out the Twan file, sat down, and flipped through the pages. By now he pretty well had it memorized. He read again the description of Twan's assailant. One of the bodies in the Medical Examiner's Office sounded like a pretty good fit.

He then browsed through the report on the restaurant murders again. Tomorrow he would interview the known witnesses to the shooting, including the wife of Chun Wong, the victim who owned the building and ran the laundry on the second floor. When she had heard the shooting, she had apparently run to the window and seen three gunmen load into a white van. They had been wearing ski masks. Ski masks. Silencers. Five hundred rounds through the plate glass in less than a minute. This little get-together had one purpose, he said to himself. But could you believe it? No one had gotten the license number on the van! Not that it mattered that much; they wouldn't have been so stupid as to use the real plates. Well, at least there was an APB out on the vehicle.

McAllister looked at his watch. Six-thirty. He stretched, and then scratched the scalp under his thinning hair. He was hungry. He'd go over and take a quick look at the murder scene and then get something to eat before going home.

He went back to the car. It was colder now in the darkness. The heater in the car was just starting to exude warm air when he arrived at the restaurant site. The alley had been cordoned off with yellow plastic police barrier tape, although the shops on either side of the alley were still open, trying to entice the tourists, who walked past along the sidewalk and looked curiously at the wreckage.

The detective ducked under the plastic barrier and walked into the narrow alley and down the stairs. There wasn't much light, and so he went back to the car and got a flashlight before going into the diner.

Glass was strewn over the floor. McAllister's shoes grated on the fragments as he walked. The mirrors and glass display cases behind the counter were shattered. Brightly colored lanterns lay on the counter top, torn and fallen from the ceiling. Bullet holes had perforated the upholstered booths and the back wall of the room. There wasn't much blood. The lab detail had already gone over the scene that afternoon. They would come back tomorrow to go over it again. Christ, what a goddamn mess this place was! McAllister left the room and walked back up the stairs. A shootout in broad daylight! They were out to show somebody something, he decided. He left the narrow alley quite certain that the shooting was related to the Twan murder.

The detective stopped at the Golden Gate Cafe on the way home. Since his wife had passed away two years before, he rarely cooked at the house anymore. The Golden Gate was inexpensive and the food good. He knew the waitresses; they always treated him pretty well. He gave the girl his order and lit a cigarette as he waited for the meal. It came after a few minutes, pot roast and potatoes, and he ate in silence, pondering the two cases, looking for the similarities and the differences. He smoked another cigarette as he drank his coffee. Well, it opened up a few leads, and that was definitely better than what he'd had before. Finally he left the restaurant and drove home in the darkness through a misty fog.

He pulled up to his small home, one of a long row of similar older tract houses in the Sunset district. A small patch of uneven brown grass in the front yard was unmowed. There was a built-in garage which he no longer used; years ago his wife had used the garage for her gardening tools. She had kept a small but immaculate garden. He and his wife had lived in the house for twenty years before she had passed away. They had never had children. After she was gone, McAllister had lost interest in the place. He turned on a few lights and got the heater going. His bed was unmade, as he had left it that morning. He hung his sports jacket up and kicked his shoes off, and then turned the television on and lay down on the bed, still dressed. He glanced at one of the shoes and noticed without interest that the sole was almost completely worn through. He gazed vacantly at the television, as his mind cast randomly upon images of the restaurant murder-scene, and the bodies of the young men lying lifeless in the morgue, until sometime later he fell asleep.

7

The thin cervical laminae covering the posterior aspect of the spinal canal came away easily. Jack Phillips watched as Aaron Richards used a narrow rongeur, slipping the small foot plate of the instrument under the bottom edge of the lamina to bite away the bone in even, controlled pieces. He worked up either side of the spinal canal, lifting the center section, which would be replaced later. The patient laying face down on the operating table was just nine years old, and at that age the plate of bone over the spinal canal was still quite soft. Phillips didn't say anything, but concentrated on providing the resident with the assistance he needed to complete the laminectomy.

One month before, the boy had begun to stumble as he had tried to run at school. After that, his arms and then his legs had become progressively weaker, and he had started to lose sensation. A week ago a magnetic resonance imaging study had shown an abnormal fullness of the spinal cord within the neck. With intravenous contrast, the swelling had proven to be a sausage-shaped tumor within the cord. The boy's parents had pushed his wheelchair into the preoperative area, where his dad had then lifted him, tenderly, and placed him on a gurney, and then waited, holding his hand until the anesthesiologist had taken the child to the operating room. The boy didn't say a word as they wheeled him away, too quickly to notice his mother's tears.

The laminae of the fifth, and then the fourth and the third cervical vertebrae were lifted, still connected together by their attaching ligaments, and then the entire segment was removed, exposing the glistening white dura mater. As Aaron Richards continued to work with the rongeur, Phillips used the bipolar forceps to grasp the thin-walled, full blue veins that coursed across the dura and electrically coagulate them, the veins abruptly shrinking into irregular, collapsed bands of fibrous tissue.

"The dura looks full, don't you think, Dr. Phillips?" The neurosurgeon nodded in agreement, as he continued to coagulate the small bleeders with the bipolar. In a child, controlling the blood loss was critical, since children had less blood to begin with. The resident worked quickly but carefully, to complete the laminectomy.

"OK, Aaron, that looks pretty good. Now dry it up so that we can open the dura." Phillips waited to let the resident finish tidying up the edges of the exposure. Aaron Richards inspected the entire five-inch incision, which ran down the back of the neck from the base of the skull, to control any tiny bleeding points. Then they switched positions to let the resident assist and the neurosurgeon do the work.

"Dural hook, and eleven blade." Phillips lifted the dura away from the spinal cord and gently used the tip of the blade to make a small incision in the mid part of the thin, leathery covering. He used fine scissors to continue the incision the length of the exposure. Immediately there was a small flood of crystal-clear cerebrospinal fluid which streamed, and then pulsated out of the dural sac. The spinal cord lay white and glistening within. Near the center of the exposure, the cord was markedly swollen with a central yellow area of discoloration.

"Tack the dura back and then we can go ahead." The resident used a fine needle holder and small curved needles to pass thin silk suture through the dural edges and then through the soft tissues more superficially. As Jack tied down the sutures, the dura tented away on each side to more completely expose the cord. With each beep of the electrocardiogram, more cerebrospinal fluid welled up and flowed out of the opening. The spinal cord, which had been floating in the CSF, began to sink down toward the floor of the canal.

"Microscope in, please." Phillips reached for the operating microcope and adjusted the eyepieces, before focusing down on the exposed cord. There was a faint electric whine as he used the foot control to adjust the fine focus. Aaron Richards adjusted the assistant's eyepieces and oriented himself visually within the operative field.

"So, we see this area where the cord is obviously swollen, and discolored." Phillips spent a moment to carefully inspect the abnormality. The fine dorsal sensory rootlets coming off the posterior aspect of the cord were pearlescent under the bright tungsten light of the microscope. Further out to each side they bundled together with the motor rootlets from the anterior surface of the cord to form the bundled nerve roots which then exited the spinal canal to innervate the neck muscles and upper extremities. Under the magnified vision, the abnormal area of the spinal cord appeared to be exploding from within. As the nerve fiber tracts passed down to supply the trunk and legs, they were thinned and stretched around the yellowish abnormality.

"We'll dissect this area to get a biopsy, and then see how easily it dissects from the surrounding elements of the cord." Phillips continued to work as he spoke.

"Call pathology and tell them that we'll be wanting a frozen section in a minute. Eleven blade.

He held up his right hand and then closed it when he felt the handle of the scalpel touch his fingers. Under the microscope, he used just the tip of the narrow blade to nick the veil of translucent pia mater which covered the neural tissue. There was no bleeding, but they could see small areas of previous hemorrhage within the neoplastic tissue.

"Fine biopsy forceps." The cupped jaws of the instrument closed down on the pathological tissue and pulled away a specimen.

"Here's tissue for a frozen section."

Phillips handed off the specimen, and then began to work inside the tiny space that he had created, taking additional bites with the biopsy forceps.

"There seems to be a dissection plane here with the normal cord substance." Phillips continued to work, separating the yellow tumor from the normal grey and white matter of the child's spinal cord.

"Let's send a message to the family. Let them know that their son is doing just fine." The message passed from the circulating nurse to the front desk and then by telephone up to the nurse on the pediatrics floor where the boy's anxious parents waited.

The frozen section diagnosis came back over the intercom.

"Astrocytoma." Aaron Richards watched Dr. Phillips' grey eyes as the doctors listened to the information. Phillips continued to stare in the direction of the loudspeaker, considering his options. The resident knew that in many parts of the country the procedure would now be terminated, and plans would be made for giving the boy's spinal cord irradiation. Classical teaching was that these tumors were infiltrative into normal healthy tissues; that they couldn't be removed. Only recently in a few centers were some surgeons attempting a possibly curative complete removal.

"Well, let's keep working in this plane. If we can follow it maybe we can remove the bulk of the tumor." Phillips returned to the microscope and continued to slowly follow the plane between the normal and abnormal tissue. He wedged fine cotton pads into the space and then worked along the length of the abnormality until he reached where the surface of the spinal cord finally looked more normal. He meticulously avoided pulling or stretching the normal fiber tracts, glistening with their individual coverings of lipid myelin. On one side the cord substance was reduced to a mere sheet of neural tissue over the neoplastic growth.

Jack felt a keen sense of exhilaration as he worked to remove the tumor. The function of this child's spinal cord, whether the boy would wake up able to move his extremities or wake up irreversibly paralyzed by the surgery, depended largely upon the neurosurgeon's skill and judgement. Judgement of course was much more important than pure skill or dexterity. It was a fact that most normal adults had the motor skills and hand-eye coordination necessary to perform neurosurgery if the neccessary techniques were used. But to work too hurriedly, or stretch the fiber tracts too much, or to lose the dissection plane but risk continuing on: it would have been his judgement that had failed then. Jack worked with absolute confidence in himself. Finally, after an hour and a half of careful work under the microscope, most of the perimeter of the tumor was dissected free.

"Laser on, please." They waited as the circulating nurse went through the start-up sequence for the CO_2 laser. The glowing green light indicated that it was ready. The nurse checked everyone in the room for protective goggles.

"Aaron, suction the smoke." Phillips manipulated the joystick, focused the light of the red ruby laser directing beam. Then he began to evaporate the tumor with the CO_2 beam. The tumor glowed yellow and a thin layer of carbonization formed at the edges of the beam path. The resident suctioned the thin blue smoke produced by the laser, as Phillips slowly debulked the tumor. Finally, only a thin shell remained.

"We'll remove what's left over manually with the bipolar cautery." The remaining rind of tumor came out piecemeal. In one area, tumor and normal cord substance became one, the dissection plane becoming obliterated. Jack opted to leave some tissue that was possibly residual tumor rather than risk damaging the spinal cord.

Finally, he inspected the resection cavity carefully, under increased magnification, for microscopic areas of bleeding, controlling each with tiny bursts of the bipolar. "Well, I think that this is the best that we can offer him."

In several places, the residual spinal cord was thinned to a mere sheet of tissue, hollowed out by the surgical resection. Aaron Richards wondered how any impulse transmission could take place through such an insignificant ribbon of remaining spinal cord. *Jesus*, he thought, shuddering to himself, *this kid could easily wind up a permanent quadriplegic.* Just the possibility of causing such a disability in a nine-year-old was devastating.

Phillips glanced up at the clock. Three-fifteen. They had been at work continuously for close to five hours. "Aaron, I have to catch a flight at five o'clock. Let's get this dura sutured and then I want to have one of the junior residents help you finish closing. OK?"

The senior resident nodded. They began to reconstruct the dural covering using fine silk suture. As the resident passed the curved needle through each side of the incision, Phillips grasped the thread and tied it with quick, precise movements. Soon it was sewn completely watertight. The older surgeon backed away from the operating table and pulled off his gown and gloves. Only then, as he wrote an operative note in the chart, did he feel the tightness and fatigue in his neck and shoulders, the build-up of many hours of intense physical effort. Finally, Phillips turned to leave.

"I'll call you after I get into New York tonight. Are you on call?" It would be midnight by the time he telephoned back to the hospital. The resident nodded affirmatively.

"Good. I'll see him in recovery before I leave. If there's a problem later, Dr. Steele will be available." Then Jack left the room, and went up to the pediatric floor in the main hospital to see the boy's parents.

Later in his office, Jack leafed through the work that he planned to take with him on the flight: a couple of manuscripts and one of the chapters for the AVM book. He placed these in his briefcase. Mrs. Brannan brought in a cup of coffee, and he returned phone calls and dealt with office work for another thirty minutes. Finally, he picked up the telephone again and dialed Barbara's office number. Today was one of her work days.

"Hi, Hon. How are you doing? I'm getting ready to head to the airport."

"I'm fine. Pretty busy. Did you pick up your car?"

After three weeks in the shop to replace the right front suspension pieces, Jack had picked up the Mercedes from his mechanic in Berkeley that morning, after dropping off the rental car.

"Yeah. It seems to run OK. I'm glad that the insurance covered the bill, though." Jack had pretty well put the whole incident up on the mountain out of his mind. The Highway Patrol hadn't gotten anywhere with finding the car that had run them off, and finally concluded that it was just a prank. Some prank, he reflected.

"I'll call you from New York tomorrow evening. My flight gets back in the early afternoon the next day." He hung up and then dialed the extension for Fred Steele's office.

"Hi, Fred. I'm going to the airport for that New York meeting. I'll be back Thursday. I just finished a kid with a cervical cord astrocytoma. I told Aaron to get in touch with you if there's a problem, and I told the kid's parents that you would be available."

"Sounds OK to me. How did the surgery go?" Fred sounded cheerful enough. He must have done a good case himself, Jack thought. He was always in a cheerful mood after doing an interesting surgery. As with Jack, operative neurosurgery was a drug that he couldn't get too much of.

"We found a real nice plane of dissection. I think that we got the entire tumor out. I told his parents that he'll probably be weaker for a while. Anyway, thanks, I'll see you in a few days." Jack replaced the receiver and picked up his briefcase. He had packed a suitcase that morning and left it in the trunk of the car. He nodded to Mrs. Brannan and walked down the stairs to the parking garage.

As he left the garage, he saw that the city was blanketed by a low overcast. It was cold, nearly drizzling. So much for Indian summer, he thought to himself. The Mercedes started right up though, and seemed to run as well as ever, as he listened with a critical ear. Shifting crisply into second and then third, he particulary appreciated the sports car after having driven the sluggish American sedan the rental agency had provided him, with soft suspension and no power. As he drove, he first used the cellular telephone in his car to dictate his operative note on the boy with the cord tumor, and then he dictated letters to his referring physicians into his small cassette recorder, for later transcription by his typing service. It took twenty-five minutes to get to the airport and park. He arrived as planned, exactly ten minutes before the scheduled departure time.

The flight to New York was crowded, but Jack flew first class so that he could spread out and guarantee that he would get some work done. He ignored the cocktails and movie, and by the time the plane was at full altitude over the Sierras, he was concentrating on one of his manuscripts. After he tired of editing the paper, he picked up a medical journal and began reading. He worked this way until they were over Utah, and dinner was served. After an excellent meal, without wine, he once again went back to his manuscripts and journals for the remainder of the flight. As they finally landed at La Guardia, he snapped the briefcase shut, satisfied with his progress. The weather here was colder than in San Francisco. Jack quickly found a cab for the trip into the city. It was a clear night, and he relaxed and enjoyed the skyline as his taxi crossed over the Triboro Bridge into Manhattan.

*   *   *

Christine Phillips was walking to meet her ride home. The Carolyn Smythson High School that she attended was small and private, and located in a quiet, exclusive suburb of Marin County couched in a valley below Mount Tamalpais. She had worked out in the gym after class, lifting weights, doing aerobics and stretching for an hour. The weights were good for her dancing, and helped to tone and define her lithe build. She usually met her ride at a church about half a mile from the school.

The street that she walked was lined on either side by tall shade trees, their leaves just turning and beginning to fall. With the heavy overcast, there was little light in the grey afternoon, but a pleasant wet smell hung in the air. She walked quickly, in part just to stay warm. She carried her books in a brightly colored nylon backpack. The school stressed academic excellence, and although the work was difficult, the majority of the students were later able to have their choice of colleges. Christine didn't mind studying. She and her brother were invested with an intellectual curiosity that both their mother and father had encouraged and made enjoyable. She didn't really know what she wanted to major in at college yet, but she figured that there was still plenty of time to think about that.

The street had only a few houses, and most of these were set back behind expansive lawns and hedges. There was little traffic at this time of day. The damp air coalesced into a fine light rain, as the teenager kept up a steady pace. A few of the other kids drove by in cars, and one rode by on a bicycle, the tires sending up a spray of water from the roadway. Christine enjoyed the rain and the fresh smell of the trees. She thought about her dance class later that afternoon.

As Christine left school, she hadn't noticed the black van parked up the street. As she walked now, she wasn't aware of it until the van had slowed down next to her. She was walking on the right-hand side of the road, and she looked up, puzzled, as it moved slightly past but then slowed to the same speed that she was walking. She thought that perhaps it was one of the other students, wanting to offer her a lift in the rain. As the cab of the van passed, she couldn't really see anyone, and had merely caught a glimpse of the driver. He seemed to be young, and, she wasn't sure, maybe oriental.

Suddenly the double side doors next to her burst open. Two men jumped out and grabbed her by the arms and began to pull her toward the open doors. They were both short, and wiry, and wore ski masks that covered their faces. One of the masks had a bright orange and white checkered pattern. As she realized what they were trying to do, she struggled and began to let out a panicked scream, but one of the men had already clamped his hand over her mouth. Together the two dragged her into the back of the van. Christine could see only a bare metal floor and the inner walls which had some kind of wooden slats bolted to them. Her left leg banged up against the open door of the van as they pulled her inside. Already they were accelerating down the street. The double doors slammed shut, and all she could see was darkness.

As the doors closed, she fought the two men, kicking and biting, trying to lash out with her restrained arms. But finally they forced her down to the metal floor, and blindfolded her, tying her hands behind her back. The metal surface jarred her over the irregularities in the road. The hand over her mouth slowly came away.

"Where are you taking me?" Her voice was high and tremulous, as her mind twitched from shock and surprise, to the physical pain of her awkward position, to pure fear. There was no verbal response to her question. She could see nothing through the blindfold. She tried to scream again, but was cut short once more as the hand was quickly clamped over her face. A gag was forced into her mouth, the rough cloth smelling strongly of gasoline. The van picked up speed, and Christine could hear the sounds of other cars. They were on a freeway. She felt frightened, and angry, and her arms were already beginning to ache from being tied up. What could they want with her? But she decided that her best chances to keep from getting hurt would be if she didn't fight. She could hear the men, voices near her, speaking in an Asian language. But she couldn't tell what language it was. Japanese? Chinese? After one of the comments, the other two men laughed. The intense smell of gasoline in the van sickened her. But she kept quiet, and listened for sounds that might tell her where they were, or where they were going.

A little while later, she couldn't tell how long it was, the van slowed, and then stopped for a moment, before accelerating again. She heard a muffled voice saying, "Thank you". What could that be? Christine thought for a moment, and it came to her. *They must have gone through a toll booth!* It could be the Richmond Bay Bridge, or the Golden Gate. Those would be in different directions. She tried to think, and as she concentrated on thinking, her fear lessened a little. When she had first been pulled into the van, she was sure that she was going to be raped, but as long as she didn't move or struggle, the two men seemed to be leaving her alone.

She couldn't imagine why they had taken her. Could it be that they had kidnapped her for money? She knew that her parents were comfortable, but they weren't millionaires. She tried to remember other cases of kidnappings that she had read or heard about, but she couldn't get the thoughts straight in her mind. The gasoline smell on the floor was overpowering and made her nauseated. Her arms hurt badly now from her position.

The van lurched as it began a series of sharp right and left turns. From the traffic noises, it sounded like they were in a city, but she couldn't tell whether it was San Francisco or Oakland. After more bouncing turns, a series of stops, and lurching up and over a steep hill, the van slowed and made one final turn before coming to a stop. She heard a metallic scraping sound. The van pulled forward, and now behind her she heard the scraping again, and then a door loudly slam shut.

The men grabbed her by her clothes and picked her up and onto her feet. As she stood, her head struck hard against the roof of the van. She heard the side doors of the vehicle open, and then she was forced out.

There were more voices outside the truck. They led her across a smooth floor, concrete, she thought, and then along a walkway that felt wooden under her feet. They pushed her down a series of creaking stairs. One of the men clutching her arm seemed to be talking to her in a loud, continuous stream of language she couldn't understand. The air seemed to get colder as they descended. She felt better now that she was moving, and her arms ached less. She decided that the voices were probably Chinese. She remembered the singsong voices of the waiters in the Chinese restaurants that she had gone to a few times with her parents. They would usually go with Dr. Steele and his wife. She re-

84

membered Dr. Steele's wife ordering for them, speaking to the waiters in a rapid tongue, with gestures at the menu. Usually she would get exotic dishes for them, whole fish steamed in spices, quail eggs. For some reason, blindfolded here, she could somehow faintly detect the same odors that she remembered from those restaurants.

The hands pushed her onto a flooring that bounced slightly with her weight. Some kind of platform; it felt wooden beneath her feet. Suddenly the platform dropped a few inches. The sensation of movement startled and terrified Christine. Then the platform began to descend in a series of jerky movements. She could hear squeaking sounds above her that matched the movement of the platform. Finally, they came to a halt, and she was turned and roughly pushed forward. She stumbled and nearly fell on a ledge. It felt like dirt or gravel under her now. The air was very cold, and damp, permeated with a stale, earthen smell. They led her along a walkway for twenty or thirty paces, and then stopped. She was pushed down into a rough hard-backed chair, and she could feel her brutal hosts, securing her hands behind her, tying them to the chair. Her captors pulled the gag away from her mouth, and finally she was left alone.

*   *   *

The bleeding wouldn't stop. He had tried all of the things that he knew of to do, but the pulsatile flow continued. It must be a huge tear in the vessel. The entire field under the microscope was red, and the suctions couldn't keep up. Anesthesia was yelling at him, telling him the patient's blood pressure was falling. They were pouring fluids into the intravenous lines. The blood continued to gush out from a place that he couldn't see. He tried to pack it off, to buy time, just a little time, but it wouldn't work. The blood still came. He would lose the patient if he didn't do something quickly! Not again, he couldn't let it happen again! But what could he do? What else is there? And then the telephone. Of all things at a time like this! Would someone shut up that goddamned telephone!

Suddenly, he jerked awake in the large bed, but could see only the darkness. An unreal sense of fear gripped him. Disoriented, he was clutching one of the pillows. He slowly released it from his hands, and realized that next to him the telephone was ringing. He turned and groped for it on the nightstand next to the bed, and finally found the receiver. The clock next to the telephone showed three-ten a.m.

"Hello?" his voice was hoarse, his mind still clouded and vague.

"Jack?" It was Barbara. She didn't sound right. "Jack, something is terribly wrong! Christine has been kidnapped!"

He jerked up in bed, now completely awake. "What?"

"Listen to me. She's been kidnapped. She was walking from school. One of her classmates saw it." Barbara was crying.

"When? Who did this?" Jack felt a horrible bewilderment. What could they possibly want with his daughter?

Barbara needed a few moments to calm down. "Around four o'clock. The boy from her class said that two men jumped out of a van and pulled her inside. They were wearing ski masks. He called the police, but they couldn't reach me until a while ago. I was in late meetings at work."

"What have the police done? Have they found the van? What have they done?" *My God,* he thought, stunned, unable to believe what he was hearing. *Not Christine!*

"No, they said that they are looking for it. The boy didn't get the number on the license plates. It was too far away, and everything happened too quickly. All he could tell was that it was a black van, with no side windows, like a delivery van."

"Are they doing anything else?" he asked.

"A detective is coming here to talk with me and get some information."

"Where are you? Where's Darian?"

"We're both here at the house."

Jack sat on the edge of the large bed. *Christine!* All Jack could think of was his daughter, trapped, by whom? Would they hurt her? Would they...

"I've got to come back." he said. "I'll go back to the airport now and get the next flight back to San Francisco."

"Please hurry, Jack! Hurry!" Barbara was crying again.

"Barbara. Let me talk to Darian." Jack waited as he heard his wife call for their son to come to the telephone. Why on earth was this happening to them? First the car, and now...this.

"Hello, Dad?" Darian's voice sounded small, and far away. Jack became aware of the static in the long distance connection.

"Darian. This is Dad. Are you alright, son?"

"Yeah. What's happened to Chris?"

"I don't know, but I'm coming right home now. Darian, take care of mom until I get there. And stay in the house. Don't go outside by yourself to do anything! Do you hear me? "

"OK, dad." The boy sounded frightened.

"Let me talk to mom again."

"Barbara. I'll go to the airport right now and get a flight. Something must be going back early in the morning. When I get there I'll come straight to the house. OK?" He had the light on now and was already grabbing his things and throwing them into his suitcase and briefcase.

"Hurry, Jack!" The telephone clicked off. He quickly pulled on his clothes and picked up the telephone. The hotel operator sounded half asleep.

"I need you to get me a cab to the airport right away. This is an emergency. Got it?" She was more awake as he roughly banged down the receiver.

He finished packing his clothes and ran into the bathroom for his shaving kit. He didn't bother to shave or wash his face, but quickly looked around the hotel room for anything that he might have left. The meeting would have to go on without him being there.

Jack hurried down to the lobby, but there was no one at the cashier's or registration desk. He decided that they could deal with the hotel bill after he had gotten home, as he quickly walked out the front door and under the covered entry way. Outside it was intensely cold. With each breath a cloud of moisture dissipated in front of him. No taxi was visible in the driveway or waiting out along the street. *Come on! Where was it?* All he could do was stand there. Through his dress shoes, he felt his toes start to go numb and stamped his feet to keep warm. He looked repeatedly at his watch. Finally, after eight interminable, frustrating minutes, a decrepit yellow cab pulled up the driveway. Jack opened the back door on the passenger side, threw his luggage onto the seat, and climbed in after it.

"Get me to La Guardia as fast as you can! It's an emergency." The driver had been drinking hot coffee from a thermos cup. From the tone of Jack's voice, the driver turned for a moment to look at him. Then the man cracked open his door and tossed the rest of the steaming liquid in his cup out onto the concrete, before hitting the button on the meter and jamming the gear shift into drive.

The old Chevy rattled and shook as they accelerated up the street. Jack watched the intersections go by. Until then, he hadn't even thought about whether there might be a flight, or on what airlines. He would deal with that when he got to the airport, he decided. His initial horror at the kidnapping had turned into a deep foreboding, like a knot in the pit of his stomach. He would do anything to get Christine back. Any amount of money, anything that they wanted. He didn't even really care why they had done what they did, but he wanted it over with, and his daughter safe.

The cab driver was hitting eighty-five miles an hour on the parkway to La Guardia, the cab a few times nearly out of control, it seemed, as it bounced over dips in the road on worn shock absorbers. When they finally arrived at the airport, Jack glanced at his watch again. Five-twenty a.m. The fare was eighteen dollars. He handed the cab driver a twenty and a five and climbed out, dragging his luggage out with him. It was still cold and there was a freezing wind coming from the west. Jack quickly went inside the terminal and began to walk from airline to airline, scanning the departures on the television monitors over the ticket counters. There was nothing to San Francisco before eight o'clock. He felt an intolerable sense of frustration. *Dear God, there had to be some-*

thing available! Ultimately he passed AmerAir. He'd never heard of it, but the monitor showed a flight at six-ten a.m. There was no one at the ticket counter yet, but he decided to wait. He felt worn and exhausted, having gotten only an hour's sleep when Barbara had called. He spotted some vending machines, and bought a thin paper cup of coffee. That was what they called it, anyway. He drank the tepid liquid as he walked back to the ticket counter. At five-thirty a young man arrived and began to organize things behind the counter. A couple of other people were walking up with luggage. Jack was the first in line. "I need to go to San Francisco this morning."

"No problem, we've got plenty of room." The young man began to punch buttons on his computer terminal.

"What time does it arrive?" Jack asked.

"Let's see. San Francisco. Stop-over in Denver. Final arrival at one-ten p.m."

Jesus, a stop-over, can you believe it? But it was the best that he was going to find.

"OK. One person." He pulled out a credit card to pay for the flight. After he received the ticket, he swallowed the rest of his coffee and walked to the gate. Only a small number of passengers were waiting to board the aircraft. It was just becoming light, the morning sky turning shades of pink and blue through the large picture windows in the terminal. But Jack hardly noticed. He stared at the floor as Barbara's word rang over and over again in his ears. He re-analyzed what she had said, to picture what had actually happened. *If they have hurt Christine...* A growing sense of rage towards the assailants gnawed at him. Although it was clearly, objectively irrational, he truly felt that if he could get his hands on those that did this, he would kill them. In his fatigue it seemed that this whole thing was unreal, a very bad dream. But as he stood impatiently, waiting for the plane to load, he knew that it was indeed happening, and all too real.

Jack didn't sleep at all on the airplane, and barely ate when they served breakfast and lunch. He spent the entire time alternately outraged at the kidnappers, agonizing at the slowness of the flight across the country, and guilt-ridden for having been away from home when they had taken Christine. He sat in a window seat in the Boeing 727, and stared out at the clouds below, and the intense blue of the sky above. Memories of his daughter as she was soon after birth, and in her first years as she grew and developed, her first steps, her first boyfriend, interspersed with random images of Christine as a bright young woman. With everything to live for. The trip also reminded him of another flight, another time when again he had felt helpless. There had been cloud cover then, too, but he hadn't seen it, sitting on the hard steel benches in the cargo bay of an Air Force C-131. That flight had landed at the airbase at Kam Loc. The heat and humidity had surrounded and suffocated him as he walked down the rear loading ramp and into the dusty heat of Viet Nam.

As he gazed out the window, he recalled the days after that flight to Viet Nam when he had never left sick bay or surgery. The wounded had just kept coming in. He remembered the clumps of elephant grass under them as they arrived on the litters. Grass that had been pulled up by the roots as the wounded were hurriedly evacuated from the field and loaded into the Hueys. He remembered their injuries too well. The ruined young men, eighteen, nineteen, twenty years old. Not much older than Christine was now. Some were already dead when they arrived. Sometimes the Hueys would fly over, bodies loaded into a huge dark swinging hammock below. Death became commonplace there. The thought of Christine dead was intolerable, and he pushed it from his mind, as he waited for the flight to end.

At San Francisco International Airport, Jack finally got to his car and started it up. As the Mercedes came to life, he pushed the gearshift lever into reverse and backed out of his parking space. He drove to the exit of the garage and paid the cashier, feeling slow and clumsy as he dug for his wallet. As he drove he felt numb with fatigue, and knew that he could easily make a driving error or fall asleep at the wheel. He reached for the receiver of the cellular phone, and dialed his home number. Through the hollow static he heard the telephone ring several times.

"Hello". It was a man's voice. Jack was momentarily terrified that somehow the kidnappers had gotten to his home, and now had Barbara and Darian, too.

"This is Jack Phillips. Who the hell are you?"

"I'm Detective Neal Cochran, with the San Francisco Police Department." The voice remained even, and sounded young, thought Jack. "We're here with your wife and son. Where are you, Dr. Phillips?"

"I've just left the airport. I'm in the car now. I'll be there in about forty minutes." His fear turned into relief. At least someone was with the family. "Can I speak with my wife?"

He waited for a moment until Barbara picked up the telephone. "Jack?" She sounded less upset than during the previous night.

"Barbara, are you alright?"

"Yes. These detectives have been here since last night, in case there were any telephone calls. Where are you?"

Jack held the receiver of the telephone between his head and shoulder and shifted down for a slow curve onto the overpass that would get him up to Highway 280, near the coast. That would be a quicker way to get across the city and up into Marin. "I'm in the car. Just left the airport. I'll be there in about forty minutes, I guess. Has there been any word?"

"No, nothing yet. Please hurry home." She hung up. Jack placed the receiver in its cradle and continued to drive, pushing the sports car up to eighty-five miles an hour on the open freeway. After he reached the city he waited impatiently for the traffic lights on 19th Avenue as he continued northward. Finally he drove through the Presidio and onto the Golden Gate Bridge. As he crossed the bridge, he didn't look as he usually did to catch a glimpse of the skyline of San Francisco. He drove quickly, hitting seventy miles per hour, and sped up even further as he drove up and over the headlands and into Marin. His watch read three-forty p.m. as he finally arrived home.

There were two cars that Jack didn't recognize parked in the driveway. On the street there were several police cars and a van from a local television station, with a white dish antenna on the roof. As Jack began to park, several people got out of the van and began to approach his car. He parked on the curb and got out. Instantly one of the reporters with the television crew held up a microphone and began to ask questions.

"Who are you, sir, if I may ask?" Jack looked at the woman but remained silent. The woman followed him as he began to walk toward the house. Two uniformed officers came up to him.

"I'm Dr. Jack Phillips. This is my home," he said to the policemen. With that, the reporter pushed her microphone into Jack's face.

"Do you have anything to say about your daughter's kidnapping?"

He could feel the camera trained on him by one of her crewmen. A surge of anger swept over him as his mind screamed "Get out of my way!" The last thing he wanted to do is give a statement. *My God,* he thought, *I hardly know anything myself!* He took a deep breath and tried to calm himself as he mumbled, "No, not at this time." He gave a pleading look to the two policemen and one of them moved in front of the reporter, halting her pursuit as he continued to walk up the driveway.

As Jack went into the house through the kitchen door, Darian ran up and grabbed him around the waist. Jack picked his son up and held him tightly for a moment, and then carried him into the living room. There were two men sitting on the couch.

Barbara got up as Jack walked in and hugged her husband, with Darian still in his arms.

"Has there been any word?" He looked closely at his wife. Her eyes were red and puffy.

"Nothing yet. These men have been here waiting with me in case there is." Both of the men had gotten up as Jack had entered. She turned towards them.

One of the men came forward and held out his hand. "I'm Detective Cochran. We spoke on the telephone."

The man looked as young as he sounded, about thirty, thought Jack, as he shook the man's hand. The detective turned to the other man that stood behind him. "This is Mr. Emory McTaub, from the Federal Bureau of Investigation."

The other man was older, about Jack's age, with a thin build. He had very fair, freckled skin, and red hair that appeared to be quickly receding. His neat dark blue three-piece suit had sharp creases in the pant legs.

McTaub shook the neurosurgeon's hand. "We both know what you are going through, Dr. Phillips. We're here to help you get your daughter back safely." He gestured to the couch. "Would you sit down. We would like to ask you a few questions. It might give us some understanding of why your daughter was kidnapped."

"Has anything turned up yet? The vehicle, other witnesses, anything at all?" Jack lowered Darian to the floor and went over to the couch and sat down.

"No, nothing. We know that it was a late model van, black in color, and that's all. Every police force in the Bay area is looking for it. So far, nothing." McTaub sat down across from Jack. Clearly, he was the one running the show. The younger detective stood back, beside the couch, and looked on. McTaub opened a briefcase and pulled out a yellow pad of legal size paper and a ballpoint pen.

"I need to ask you some questions to determine what these people might be after. Why do you think that Christine was kidnapped? Do you have obvious wealth? Enemies? Debts? Do you support any unusual political groups?"

Jack shook his head. "I thought about that during the entire flight back from New York. We're financially comfortable, even wealthy by some standards, but not rich like you're talking about. And no one is really aware of it." He failed to mention Barbara's parents, who in fact were very well off, living in comfortable retirement in the exclusive enclave of Hillsborough, north of Stanford University. He looked at the floor and shook his head. "I'm known within my profession, and within the local medical community, but not beyond that." Jack remembered the television interview that was scheduled for next month. He'd cancel it, he decided.

"We have no enemies that I know of. There have been a few unhappy patients, but every physician has them, especially in neurosurgery."

Jack recalled some of the patients that he had treated over the years. Patients with illnesses that were difficult to treat. Illnesses that sometimes were impossible to cure. More and more his practice had come to include an increasing number of the difficult problems. Many patients had lived, but sometimes it had seemed that just as many had died, or been left with severe disabilities. It was a fact that there were still many diseases that medicine could not cure, but only slow down for a time perhaps, to allow a few additional months. And there were some diseases that medicine had no treatment for at all. And neurosurgery was by no means foolproof. It was performed by human beings, and it was dangerous. Sometimes people died. He recalled his secretary's comments about Mr. Weinberg, the man whose wife had died inexplicably from a pulmonary embolism. Jack stared out of the living room windows at the city in the distance. His thoughts lingered briefly on some of those deaths that had occurred over the years. If Christine had been taken because of one of those cases... He felt a deep sense of bitterness, and disbelief at even the thought that such a thing could happen.

McTaub and the others were silent, looking at him. Finally, he responded. "I've had a few lawsuits in the past, all of which were dropped or eventually cleared. And I don't know of any that are being threatened."

The balding FBI agent continued. "What about debts, or your political persuasions. Anything even from years ago, that might have led to enemies?"

"We have no real debts at this point. We're basically non-political." Jack had gone to Viet Nam with a personal commitment to performing a duty for his country. Later, during his tour he had become aware of the deep-seated discontent among many of the troops about the nature of the war, the way political decisions prevented any hope of victory. He had felt it, too, especially as he cared for those same men as they lay injured and dying. But he had suppressed any questions he had about why they were there, instead concentrating his efforts, his emotions, on each patient. After the war, Jack had purposely remained non-political. His political position, like his religion, was confined to the science and practice of medicine. Right and wrong for him became only what was right or wrong for his Institute and his patients.

McTaub looked at the neurosurgeon and then glanced over at Darian and Barbara. "Pardon these next questions, but they must be asked. What about personal activities. Could there be any jealous husbands?"

Jack felt himself bristle. He understood the need for the question, but Jesus Christ, right here in front of his wife and kid? He looked at Barbara. She wasn't looking at him but was staring at the FBI agent, with a thin, humorless half-smile on her face. "No, there is definitely no possibility of that," he replied curtly.

The FBI agent sat glancing through the notes that he had written on the yellow legal pad. "Well, I suspect that someone thinks that you're worth more money than you say that you are. Most kidnappings are either the result of a fight over child custody, or for a cash ransom." McTaub looked out of the V-shaped living room windows at the panoramic view. There were lengthening shadows and a golden hue in the distance indicating the coming darkness.

"We will be here until six o'clock; then another team will arrive to stay tonight." The FBI man continued. "We would ask that you remain here, and not leave the house unless it is absolutely necessary. I want to discuss with you the possible scenarios should the kidnappers call. We need to discuss what you will say. "

Barbara then got up. "Do any of you want coffee? Tea? Jack, are you hungry?"

Absently, he shook his head, as he continued to sit, staring at the carpeted floor thinking about his daughter. The others shook their heads as well.

Barbara went into the kitchen and in a few minutes came back out carrying a cup of tea. "What about those reporters outside? They're staring into our kitchen window. Do we have to put up with that until all of this is over?"

"Ignore them. I'll have the local police department put up a barrier to keep them further away from the house." McTaub looked up at the younger detective, who seemed to seize upon the task as something that he could do. He went to the front door, unlocked it, and walked out.

*   *   *

Christine was cold. In the dampness, still tied to the hard wooden chair, she shivered despite her sweater and worked her legs up and down to keep warm. Her captors had kept the blindfold over her eyes, but after many hours, after her hands had became painfully numb, they had come back and loosened the ties binding her arms to the back of the chair. She could tell that there was at least one other person with her here. Wherever this awful place was. The guard kept on getting up to move around her. Maybe to keep himself warm, she thought. Several hours before, other people had come in and talked among themselves in rapid, uninterpretable words. And one of them had spoken to her in accented English. A few words. But they had penetrated into the blind-folded darkness of her world.

"Do not be afraid. When your father does what we ask, you will be released. We won't hurt you."

Still Christine thought about what the man had said. Hearing, but not understanding why. Her arms and shoulders ached terribly, but as she opened and closed her hands and flexed her arms, now at least her sensation was coming back. It seemed that the rope restraining her hands was becoming looser.

She heard a match strike, and smelled an acrid odor. It didn't smell like cigarette smoke, but there was something burning. Was the guard building a fire to keep warm? It was freezing cold. In the silent room, any sound seemed to echo and amplify. Christine could hear the guard doing something, over to her right side, but she couldn't tell what it was. There was a crackle that sounded like silver foil, or plastic being crinkled. Then a sudden loud snap cut through the silence. She had no idea what that was. After a few more minutes, the guard became silent.

Christine sat still and listened closely for a long time. The guard also had stopped moving, and the room was utterly quiet. After many minutes, she held her own breath, and listened to the guard's breathing. It was slow and regular and deep. The man was sleeping! She moved her wrists up and down against each other again and discovered that the ties were now quite loose. Her hands were small enough that she could nearly squeeze one of them through the loop in the rope. She pulled harder, and the rope burned as it dug into her right hand above the knuckles, but she continued to pull and squirm her hand within the loop, and it slipped a little more. She twisted her hand in the opening. The pain sharpened, and she bit her lip to keep from crying out. And suddenly the hand pulled through! She stopped, breathlessly, urgently listening for the guard. But his steady breathing continued unchanged. The pain in her hand slowly faded as she opened and closed it behind her.

Christine reached up and silently pulled off her blindfold. Above her burned a single yellow electric bulb, barren and hanging from a wire. She gazed intently around the room, looking for the guard. He had to be asleep not to have noticed her movement, she thought. She blinked and peered through the dim light. Off to her right side, ten feet away, she saw a slumped figure, lying half-upright against the wall. The guard looked Asian. He was young, perhaps her own age. Next to him there was a length of rubber tubing, and a candle that still flickered in the darkness, next to a spoon lying on the floor. The sleeve on his left arm was rolled up above the elbow and in his lax right hand Christine saw a syringe, and the shiny tip of a needle. He had injected himself with some kind of drug!

Christine used her free hand to uncoil the rope from around her body and the back of the chair. Her other hand became looser and finally she was able to pull the length of rope free from the chair, still tied by a loop to her wrist. She tried to do this as silently as possible, as she continued to watch the guard. But he remained asleep against the wall.

The room appeared to have dirt walls, but the floor was covered with bare wooden planks. The light bulb hanging from the ceiling left the corners of the room in shadows. Slowly Christine got up. The chair creaked on the loose planks and she stopped suddenly, staring at the guard, who remained motionless. Her back and legs were aching and stiff from the hours of sitting, and a shooting pain went down the outside of one leg and into her foot, which felt numb and tingling. She gathered up the rope still tied to her left wrist and coiled it in her hand.

There were two open doorways framed with wood, one on either side of the room. Through each, Christine could see only blackness. She walked towards the door furthest from the drugged guard. At the edge of the room, the flooring gave way to a dirt passageway. It seemed to be some kind of tunnel. She looked around, and then saw, next to the sleeping guard, a black plastic flashlight, balanced on end on the wooden floor. She desperately wanted to get out of the room, but the thought of going into the tunnel without light horrified her.

Slowly she crept on her toes back towards the guard. The ancient planks creaked as she moved. Reaching him, she carefully, patiently, bent to pick up the flashlight. She could see the guard's face in the flickering light of the candle. As she grasped the end of the flashlight, the smooth plastic handle slipped out of her fingers, the light toppling over and clattering loudly in the silent room. Unexpectedly the guard sighed, and turned towards her. She froze, bent over, unmoving, unbreathing. In the dimness, she saw his brow wrinkle and then his eyes blink open. Terrified, she looked wildly around the room. In a low pile of debris next to the guard lay a wooden length of two-by-four. It was coated with dirt, and at one end several nails were hammered through and protruding. She grabbed the piece of wood. The guard's eyes were wide open now, as he looked directly at her standing over him. In his drugged state, he seemed for a moment not to comprehend that she was there. But then, in the dim light, Christine saw his eyes narrow as he quickly began to move up from the floor, clutching the syringe and needle in his right hand. By involuntary reflex, the piece of wood was up, above Christine's head, and as the guard came at her, thrusting at her with the syringe, she struck at him with all of her strength. The end of the board hit the man in the face. He groaned and fell back to the floor. Christine was overwhelmed by anger and fear. Again and again the piece of wood came down, striking the guard in the head and neck. It seemed as if she had lost all control over her actions. A dull hollow sound emanated with each blow to the slumped body. Abruptly, she stood with the two-by-four again up, ready to strike again if necessary. The teenager's eyes were wide, fixed on the motionless form below her. Blood oozed from the lacerations in the man's skin caused by the nails in the end of the board.

Christine's breath came in heaves, her thoughts tumbling around her. She suddenly felt nauseated, and dropped the board to the floor with a clatter. She looked for the plastic flashlight. It lay partly underneath the guard's body. She grasped the end of it and pulled it free. The man remained still. Christine looked at the guard's chest. Silently, with an overwhelming sense of horror at what she had done, she realized that he was no longer breathing. She had to get out of that room! Quickly, she turned and, switching on the light, moved towards the darkened passage at the far end of the room.

The flashlight gave off a weak beam which penetrated only a few feet. She shined it on the ground in front of her and went forward. The floor and the walls of the passageway were formed of hard packed dirt. Christine was enveloped in darkness, except for the small pool of light before her. Despite the coldness, she felt a clammy sweat under her clothes.

After about a hundred feet, abruptly, the passageway ended and branched off to the right and the left. She stopped. Her breathing was still heavy, and her throat and lungs burned. She looked behind her but could see only the darkness. What was this place? Momentarily, she was terrified that she would become lost and trapped in a maze of tunnels. But she couldn't go back, towards that room. Towards that guard. Again she saw in her mind the body lying on the floor, bleeding from the face and chest, unmoving. She struggled to push the image away and forced herself to go on. She turned to the right and continued to follow the passageway. The flashlight was getting weaker; the light now illuminated only the ground just in front of her feet. She went slowly. The passageway narrowed, the dirt walls closing in towards her on either side. She shined the flashlight up and could see the ceiling only a foot above her head. And the tunnel seemed to be sloping downward ! Momentarily she stopped, and thought again about going back the other way. But she couldn't go back. If the others found the guard, they would follow her. She forced herself to keep moving.

After another fifty or sixty feet, the walls of the passage fell open. Christine shined the light around. It was another room. A musty odor filled the cold air. There was a dust-covered table, and broken chairs lying beside it on the floor. And nothing else. At the other end of the room the passageway continued. She went on, the tunnel turning right and left. There were pieces of rotting wood on the ground in some places, which she stepped over. She came to another fork in the passage. She went to the right again, not knowing why.

Christine's flashlight flickered, and then, as she watched in horror and disbelief, the yellow glow dulled, and went out. The darkness engulfed her, and she felt waves of panic overcome her, as if she were underwater and couldn't get to the surface. Furiously, she shook the light, but it remained dead in her hand. She opened her eyelids as widely as possible, searching for any light, any shape or form to her surroundings, but the darkness was complete. She stood frozen, sure that she would die in these tunnels as the cold penetrated her clothes. She began to shake uncontrollably, numb from the cold. *She had to move.*

Consciously she forced herself to take a step. With her right hand, she reached for the wall, and felt the roughness of the dirt. Then slowly, a step at a time, she continued forward, holding her left arm in front of her, and her right against the rough-hewn wall. The passageway was level, and after another forty or fifty feet she came to the end of the wall. Gingerly, she shuffled forward, with both arms outstretched. She came upon another wall, in front of her. But it wasn't dirt; it felt wet, and smooth, like ancient cement or some sort of clay. Without reason, she turned once again to the right, and, using her left hand now, followed the wall, step by slow step.

As she walked, she felt the tunnel begin to ascend slightly. Before, the silence had been absolute, but now? She stopped, and held her breath to listen. She heard the dripping of water, and also, another sound. She couldn't tell what it was. She continued forward, and the tunnel rose further. She strained her eyes for any light. Her shoes made a scraping noise as she shuffled to feel for obstacles on the flooring. Then again, she heard a sound. Something. She stopped, and abruptly turned around to listen behind her.

Voices! They were behind her! They were looking for her! In terror, she turned back and, holding her hand out to the wall, began to run, not caring what she might run into. Her footsteps ground on the floor surface, and her left hand struck a piece of wood, protruding from the side of the tunnel. She felt the sharp pain in her wrist, but ignored it as she continued to run. She couldn't let them find her; they would surely kill her for what she had done to the guard. With a shock of pain, the air was knocked out of her and she found herself on the ground. For a moment she couldn't breathe, and felt a sharp ache in her chest and over her forehead. She lay dazed, the ground cold and wet beneath her. She must have hit the end of the tunnel. A dead end? With frantic persistence she dragged herself up, feeling the wall in front of her, cold and rough and solid under her hands. She turned to her left and once again willed herself to move, feeling the wall with her hand. Her left wrist was hurting badly now.

In front of her, in the distance, she began to see a vague shape of dull brown light. She continued towards it and it became more clear: an outline of the passageway! She dropped her hand from the wall beside her, and ran as fast as she could towards the light. Her legs ached and the pain in her wrist was sharp and severe, but she focused only on the light. *Closer, closer.* Behind her again, she heard the voices, louder than before. They must have followed her footsteps in the dirt. She didn't look back, but finally came to the source of the brightness and stopped. She looked up, and could see some kind of air shaft. The light was more a pattern of dim shadows, filtering down the dusty opening and outlining the walls of the shaft. Narrow wooden slats were spaced up one wall, nailed to a heavy beam. Christine felt for the bottom slat with her foot, and stepped on it. The rotted wood creaked, but held her weight. She grasped the slats further up and began to climb. The voices were much closer now, and as she looked back down the passageway, she could see angular, changing patterns of light in the distance. She ignored them and, gazing upward, clutched at the narrow boards, as the rope, still tied around her left wrist, caught up in her legs and feet. She kicked the rope away and continued to climb. Twelve feet up the shaft opened into a small room. Light streamed in through a small window near the ceiling. She scrambled up out of the shaft, and rolled over onto the floor. She pulled the rope on her wrist up and out of the hole, just as the beam from a powerful light glared up from below, illuminating the ceiling above her with a jerky, roving pattern.

Christine lay motionless, trying not to breathe despite the effort from climbing. She could hear the voices, loud below her, and then the creaking sound of someone beginning to climb the ladder. She looked around and quickly saw a small door on one side of the narrow room. She jumped up and went to it, grasping the knob and turning. But the door remained solidly in place. It was locked from the outside! The noise on the ladder was closer. A shout came from down the shaft behind her. She grabbed the knob with both hands and with all of her strength pulled on the door. With a splintering sound, the bolt on the dead lock pulled through the ancient wood. The door swung open, and she went through. Outside stood a thicket of empty packing boxes and other debris which she pushed out of the way. She was in some kind of narrow alley, with dark brick walls on either side. Christine ran as hard as she could toward the entrance to the alley, where there was light and traffic noise and people walking along the street. She turned onto the sidewalk, and continued to run, weaving between surprised pedestrians, who looked curiously at the girl in dirty clothes dragging a length of rope. Christine looked around her in disbelief. She recognized exactly where she was. She had been there with her parents many times. She was in Chinatown. The neon lights above the street blinked and glowed against the aging buildings. At the end of the block she turned down a hill, and ran past long tables filled with vegetables and dry goods and live squawking chickens in wire cages. Elderly locals, mixed with tourists of all ages, were standing and shopping in the open markets. She glanced over her shoulder and, although she saw no one chasing her, she continued to move as fast as she could through the crowd. Bright orange and gaudy red and purple signs in both Chinese and English, advertising the shops and restaurants, jutted out over the sidewalk. The sky was the deepening blue of approaching dusk.

Christine reached the bottom of the hill where there was heavy traffic on Columbus Avenue. She turned left, towards North Beach, and slowed down to a fast walk, looking nervously again over her shoulder. She coiled up the rope on her wrist and stuffed it under her sweater. She looked around for a police car, but saw only the slow moving traffic. Tourists mixed with commuters leaving the city to go home. Several taxis drove by, but she had no money to pay them. The kidnappers had taken her purse along with her backpack.

She continued to walk, trying to catch her breath. Her wrist was starting to hurt again, and she began to shiver in the cooling evening air. She turned again, walking towards the waterfront, and then stopped dead in her tracks. Approaching her were three Chinese youths, walking abreast along the sidewalk. Two of them had on black leather jackets; one had his hair shaved closely on the sides, with razor cuts inscribing a linear pattern on his scalp. One of the boys leered at her, and the three began to talk to one another in quick phrases. To Christine their voices were one and the same as the echoing voices that chased her in the tunnels.

Panic welling up, Christine turned and ran between two parked cars. Barely glancing at the oncoming traffic, she ran into the street as cars squealed to a stop and one of the drivers began to pound on his horn. She ignored the noise, and continued to run to the other side of the street. The three Asian youths laughed as they watched her with belligerent amusement.

She continued to walk through the boulevards of North Beach. Already the Italian restaurants were filling with people, off from work in the nearby financial district. The smells of garlic and pizza and freshly ground coffee drifted out onto the sidewalk, and Christine realized how hungry she was; she hadn't eaten since her captors had fed her a small portion of rice hours before. She had no idea what time it was now. But the sky was dark, with only a hint of orange and pink to the west, over the rim of city hills. They must have had her overnight and an entire day in the undergound cell, she decided.

At Columbus and Vallejo Avenues, a San Francisco Police Department patrol car was double parked, idling. An officer sat in the driver's seat, while his partner finished writing out a parking ticket. Christine saw the patrol car, and ran over to the passenger's side and tapped on the window. The officer sitting in the car looked at her. Her sweater and face were grimy, and her blond hair was knotted and tangled. Probably a runaway, he thought to himself. He leaned over and rolled down the window.

"You've got to help me!" Christine blurted out. "I was taken hostage yesterday by men in a truck." She began to cry with her remaining terror and pain.

Right, he thought. A runaway on drugs, he was sure of it. The officer didn't want to have to deal with the paperwork involved in picking her up. But she kept standing there, and so, reluctantly, he opened the passenger door from the inside and then slid back in the seat. "Sit down and tell me what's really going on."

The officer's eyes flicked over the girl as she got into the car. She was a mess. Her jeans were filthy. "Now, what's your name?" he asked. His partner had walked back and was standing outside the passenger door, inspecting her with quiet disgust.

"Christine Phillips. My father is Doctor James A. Phillips. He works at Saint Joseph's Hospital. I was picked up by men in a truck in Marin County. Yesterday, I think. You have got to believe me! Please, call my home. My mothers name is Barbara. Barbara Phillips." Tears continued to stream down her face.

The driver looked up at his partner, who was still staring at the girl. They had heard about the kidnapping of a teenage girl during the duty report before the shift. And there was an APB out for a black van. *Jesus H. Christ!*

"Was it a van?" He asked, his voice softer now. Christine was shivering uncontrollably. The police officer turned the heater on and the fan to full.

"Yes, a black van. Look at this." Christine pulled her left arm away from her body and the length of dirty twine that was tied to her wrist fell out from under her sweater. There was a deep gash on the underside of her wrist where she had caught it on the wall in the tunnel.

The officer needed no further convincing as he silently picked up the radio.

8

"How could this have happened?" Joseph Lo's voice was low and clipped in fury. "How could the girl have escaped from her guard?" He stood, staring at the young man who dared to consider himself a *boo how doy*, whose responsibility it had been to hide her away until they had made arrangements for the doctor.

The young man hesitated. He knew that he had failed, and would become an outcast from the tong, at the very least.

"Her guard apparently had loosened her restraints and then...fallen asleep." He couldn't bear to mention the syringe and the heroin that they had found next to the man's body. "She must have knocked him unconscious as he slept, and then beaten him to death."

"She killed him?" Lo was astonished that the young girl could have done that. But it saved them from having to do it themselves, he reflected silently. "He didn't deserve to die, but should have had to live on with his shame." *As you will,* Lo considered, gazing at the younger man.

"We chased after her, following her footprints. But she escaped through one of the unused entryways to the passages." He had been the one to climb the ladder and, as he had gotten to the broken door, seen the girl turn out of the alley and on to the sidewalk. He had then decided that she could not be captured on the busy open streets of Chinatown.

"Move everything of any importance out of the underground. She is likely to bring an army of police back into the system." Lo spoke bitterly. For over a hundred years, the tongs had used the hidden rooms and passageways to their benifit. As opium dens, gambling rooms, and as a place to escape from the police or hide the bounty from their criminal activities. In the past, there had been wars just for the right to use the underground network, which extended the length and breadth of Chinatown. Never had the police gotten into the system. Except for a very few, but they had never escaped to tell about it. If the girl remembered the place where she had left the tunnels, that would all change.

"You had better try to conceal the location where she escaped." Lo was beginning to realize just what a disaster this was becoming. With the girl having escaped, not only would Phillips be alerted and out of their grasp, but he would soon be heavily protected. The girl would know that she had been abducted by Chinese and brought into Chinatown, and the doctor could be expected to tie in her kidnapping with the death of Samuel Twan. He would come to understand the threat against him.

"Exactly when was the girl last seen?" he asked.

"At about six-thirty this afternoon," said the lieutenant.

Lo stood, thoughtful for a moment. Perhaps she has not yet reached her father. She may still be wandering the streets. Finally, Lo turned to the others in the room.

"We must move quickly on Doctor Phillips. They won't expect us to act again so soon. And we must also do it where they will least expect it." Lo looked at the group. Several elders of the tong were there, listening to him. They looked skeptical. He would make them understand, he decided.

*   *   *

The telephone rang, and Emory McTaub walked into the kitchen to get the call. The FBI agent had decided to remain at the Phillips home into the evening. When his replacement had arrived earlier, he had sent the man into downtown Mill Valley to get some things for sandwiches. They had all eaten together in the kitchen. Barbara and Jack Phillips had sat quietly, looking frequently up at the clock above the sink. The waiting was by far the hardest part for everyone, including McTaub.

After the meal, Jack and Barbara had gone with their son into his bedroom, to spend some time alone with him, and explain better what was happening. To try to explain why it was happening. Later the boy had fallen asleep with his mother sitting next to him, stroking his hair. Jack had gone into his study. McTaub glanced at his watch as he picked up the receiver. It was seven-twenty in the evening. Jack Phillips came into the kitchen just as the FBI agent spoke.

"Hello?" McTaub's voice was calm and unhurried. He listened for a moment, and then responded. "This is Emory McTaub of the Federal Bureau of Investigation. I'm with the Phillips family." He looked at Jack as he spoke. The physician's face was haggard. He musn't have slept for close to forty-eight hours. After the FBI agent listened for a few moments, he looked at his watch again.

"What time was she picked up?" He looked into Phillips' eyes. They were clear, grey eyes, though now lined with dark rings underneath. But the eyes bored into the agent.

"What is her condition?" McTaub purposely kept his voice calm. He was a man who was trained to wait for all the facts before coming to a conclusion. He continued to listen, but finally allowed a slight smile to cross his face. As he watched, Jack Phillips' shoulders slumped, but the doctor made a fist with his right hand and shook it in triumph. Jack turned to go tell his wife.

The FBI agent continued. "Keep her under extremely careful protection. If the kidnappers are unstable, they may try to go for her again. Get a doctor in to take a look at that wrist injury. I'll come in to see her now, to do some preliminary questioning. We'll do a more formal debriefing later, once she's rested." He thought for a minute. "You'd better get a child psychologist in to evaluate her, too, and see how she is handling all of this." McTaub slowly hung up the telephone and walked back towards the living room. Barbara came running down the hallway. Jack walked more slowly behind her, carrying their son.

"What's going on? Where is Christine?" The woman sounded both anxious and relieved.

"That was the San Francisco Police. It seems that your daughter escaped somehow, and was picked up by a patrol car in the North Beach area of the city."

"My God! Is she all right? Did they hurt her?" Barbara Phillips seemed to be close to tears. Her husband put his arms around her, and held her shoulders tightly.

"Apparently she has some cuts and scrapes, but other than that, she seems to be unharmed. The Police are having her examined by a physician, and I asked them to have a clinical psychologist see her." McTaub couldn't believe their luck. So much more often the victims were never found, or if they were discovered, it was too late. He had trouble believing that the girl could have escaped at all, never mind so quickly. The kidnappers must have been absolute amateurs.

"Why a psychologist?" Barbara Phillips' question broke into McTaub's thoughts.

"Even with adult kidnapping victims, the shock of this kind of ordeal is immense, even when there isn't any physical injury. The emotional damage that a child or teenager goes through is often much more intense."

"When can we go to see her? Is she going to be coming back here?" It was Jack this time. The relief was obvious in his voice.

"She is at the downtown station. I've told them to keep her under close guard until I get there. I think that it is safest if all of you stay here at the house until I can debrief her and bring her back here." McTaub didn't want this to get any more complicated than it had to be.

Barbara spoke up immediately. "Not on your life! We need to see her as soon as possible, and I think that she will want to see us. Jack..." the woman looked towards her husband.

"I think Barbara's right. I don't want to wait here any longer sitting on my hands. She'd probably feel a lot better if all of us were there." Despite his fatigue, Phillips looked resolute. The FBI agent didn't press the issue.

As the two parents went to get their son dressed, Emory McTaub sat puzzling over the case. The police sergeant had said something about the teenager escaping in Chinatown, from some kind of tunnel system. The girl was also sure that she had been abducted by a group of Asians, probably Chinese. McTaub had no idea what the motive might have been. In his experience, kidnappings rarely were the work of more than two or three individuals. What would a bunch of Chinese want from this family? He would have to discuss it with Dr. Phillips, after he had questioned the girl.

The couple returned with their son, dressed now. With the FBI agent, they prepared to go outside and make some kind of statement to the press, and then go into the city.

"Let me speak to them," said McTaub. "It's probable that the kidnappers are following the news reports. We don't want them to know anything about where Christine is, or even whether she has been found. They might take some kind of action that could be unpredictable."

He led them out through the kitchen and towards his plain light blue colored Chevrolet sedan. From the cobblestone driveway, they could see several reporters standing behind a metal police barrier, watched over by a pair of local police officers sitting in a patrol car. There was also a van from one of the local television channels, with a minicam television crew. McTaub went forward to speak to them. As Jack helped his wife and son into the back of McTaub's car, he saw the bright lights of the minicam team flare up and illuminate part of the street and the driveway, silhouetting the slender FBI agent. Jack climbed in next to Barbara, and put his arm around both her and Darian, waiting. In a few moments, McTaub returned and got in the car.

"Keep your windows closed and don't say anything as we get out of here. I told them that we are moving you to a different location for safety reasons. It's true, even if it's not quite accurate. It will get them off of our backs."

A uniformed police officer dragged the metal barricade out of the way, and McTaub backed the sedan out of the driveway. As they pulled into the street, the spotlights of the television crew were directed on the car, and a reporter clutching a microphone moved in and began to shout questions at them through the window. An officer pushed him back. Darian and Barbara looked out at the glare of the lights and the people, but Jack stared straight ahead, trying to ignore the scene. He wanted desperately to get away from the house and the reporters and to see his daughter. Two patrol cars followed the sedan down the hill and towards the Golden Gate Bridge, and the city.

McTaub spoke as he drove. "They told me that your daughter stated that she had been kidnapped by a group who were Oriental. She thought they were Chinese." He looked at Jack through the rear view mirror. "That ring any bells?"

"Chinese?" Jack was incredulous. Why in God's name would some Chinese be after his daughter? His mind seemed to be working in a fog from his lack of sleep. It just didn't make any sense. "I have no idea," he said finally.

Barbara was silent for a long moment but then spoke quietly, her voice surprisingly calm in the darkness. "Jack, what about that Chinese man who had been shot. That man you operated on. The one who died?"

Jack's eyes opened more widely. "Yes. God what a mess. He had come into the emergency room with a gunshot wound to the head. A fatal injury from the moment they shot him. He was hit in the lung, too. I made the mistake of trying to save the guy's life," he added, surprising himself at the sarcasm in his voice.

McTaub considered the information.

His wife continued. "And I had read in the paper that the man was suspected of being a part of a gang in Chinatown. Some kind of organized crime thing. His shooting was more an assassination." Barbara's voice was soft but urgent. "What if they are behind all of this?"

Sounds unlikely, thought McTaub. But obviously worth checking out. He remained silent as he continued to drive, pondering the case.

The downtown station was a large mass of grey concrete, hidden among the highrises of the financial district. The street was still busy with evening traffic and there were no obvious parking spaces. Emory McTaub double parked the Chevrolet and then the four of them got out and walked up the stone steps to a large wooden door. McTaub opened the door, and they entered a small waiting room painted a dull, institutional green. In front of them, a thick bulletproof plexiglass window partitioned the waiting room from the office inside. McTaub went directly to the window and rang a bell. A young uniformed officer came up, and after McTaub showed the man his identification, the reinforced steel door next to the window was unlocked with a metallic click and they were allowed through and taken towards the back of the building. They climbed a flight of stairs, and were met at the top landing by an aging officer with sergeant's stripes on his sleeve. McTaub shook the man's hand, and the older officer led them to a locked door.

"The psychologist has been in there with her for some time. She has a deep scrape on her arm; the station doctor dressed it and gave her a tetanus booster," said the sergeant. He knocked, and then unlocked the door.

Their daughter sat at a long grey table, bathed starkly by florescent light. Her blond hair was tangled and hung loose down over her shoulders. An angry red scratch ran across one cheek, and her face was still dirty, despite her having washed it once. A smallish woman with greying hair sat beside her, holding her hand. A white bandage was wrapped on Christine's left wrist. As her family walked in, the teenager pushed back her chair and rushed to her father.

"Oh, Daddy!" Both parents held her, and then Darian went to her and put his arms around Christine's waist. Jack gripped his daughter tightly and didn't notice the tears that ran down his face and into her hair.

"You're safe now. You're safe now. We love you so much!" He whispered to her. Barbara remained silent, holding her daughter tightly.

"Why did this happen to me?" the girl sobbed.

"I don't know, Honey, but we'll find whoever did this. We'll find them," Jack replied softly.

"They were Chinese, daddy. I was in Chinatown. I knew it from the times you've taken us there. They put me in an underground room of some kind, and there were tunnels. It was so awful." Christine continued to cry uncontrollably.

"Don't worry, honey. You're safe now." But Jack's words seemed hollow as he heard himself say them. He felt helpless, and guilty. How could he have kept her from going through this. How? His guilt at having been away, on the other side of the country when she needed him, burned into his mind.

Finally, McTaub stepped in, and gently spoke. "Christine. We need to speak with you. We will protect you and keep those people from ever harming you again. But we must speak with you. Can we do that?"

Christine continued to sniffle but slowly calmed herself down. Her mother led her to the grey table once again. The clinical psychologist continued to sit, listening to the girl as she spoke. The sergeant brought in some coca-cola in a glass and sat it down in front of her. Barbara sat next to her and put her arm around her daughter.

McTaub questioned her with a gentle voice. "Tell me about when they picked you up. What did you see?"

"There was a black van. It came up right beside me, when I was coming home from school. It was going slowly, and then suddenly these men jumped out. They grabbed me and pulled me in. I tried to stop them."

"How many of them were there? What did they look like?"

"I think there were two or three that grabbed me. I couldn't tell what they looked like at all. They were wearing ski masks!"

"And then what happened?" McTaub had a small tape recorder out on the table, and was also writing notes on his yellow pad of paper.

"I was blindfolded and gagged, and my hands were tied, and they forced me to stay in the bottom of the van until we stopped. The men talked to each other. I couldn't understand it. They sounded Chinese."

"Did they hurt you in any way?"

"My arms and shoulders hurt from the position they kept me in, but no, they didn't beat me or anything. They kept my arms tied behind me for hours." Jack stood behind his daughter and listened. He tensed as Christine talked about her pain.

"Then what do you remember?"

"They took me down some kind of elevator, run by hand I think, down a long way, and then into a room of some kind, underground. It was cold. They kept me blindfolded the whole time." Christine began to cry again as she remembered the tunnels. "After a long time sitting, they loosened the rope on my wrists so that I could move a little. It was so cold and wet! But I was able to squeeze one of my hands through the rope..."

McTaub looked at her. "Didn't the persons guarding you see that?"

She shook her head. "There was a guard. I thought that he had fallen asleep, but after I got the blindfold off I saw a needle in his arm, and some things next to him. A syringe, a candle, and some other stuff. He was using drugs of some kind. I don't know what it was."

"Didn't he wake up?" McTaub had been writing something in his notes, but looked back up when Christine didn't answer. She just stared straight ahead, unmoving. Her dirty face seemed etched in sadness.

"Christine, did the guard stay asleep?"

But the girl remained silent. Jack put his hand on her shoulder. "Christine, can you answer his question? What's wrong?"

"I hit him, Daddy." She spoke in a small voice, nearly a whisper. "He began to get up and he was going to grab me. So I took a piece of wood and I hit him in the head." Her face slowly lost its emotion and became a cold mask. "I hit him again and again. I couldn't stop. And then I left. I had to get out of that place."

Despite his fatigue, a sense of shock ran through Jack as he listened to his daughter's words. *His little girl. What had she gone through?* Yet he felt a queer sense of satisfaction that she had inflicted some hurt and pain on her captors. He looked at McTaub, who sat quietly, looking at the girl for a long moment.

Then the FBI agent spoke softly. "Christine, what you did was necessary for you to escape. There is no punishment, and you should feel no guilt about it. Do you understand?" He waited until the teenager nodded slightly. "Then where did you go?"

"It was dark. I had a flashlight, and followed a tunnel. It was like a maze. I didn't know where I was going. I went through another underground room. And then the light went out and it was completely dark." She stopped for a moment. "I thought that I was going to die in there. Then I heard voices. They were following me. Following my footsteps." Her voice rose as she once more lived through her nightmare. "I had to keep going, to get away from them. Finally, I found light, and a kind of ladder. I got up into a room, and broke through a door to get out. They had nearly caught up to me. But I ran. I was in Chinatown. There were people and cars on the street and I just kept running away from that place."

"Did anyone follow you?"

"I didn't see anyone. Just three Chinese boys. They laughed at me, and I ran away from them, too." Christine slumped a little, and sipped some of her drink. She seemed exhausted. Jack kept his hands on her shoulders.

"Christine, did any of the ones that kidnapped you ask you questions, or tell you anything? Anything at all? Did they tell you what they wanted?"

The teenager turned her head and looked towards her father. She looked at him for a long time before she spoke.

"It was you, daddy." A sickening electrical chill ran up and down Jack's spine, as he heard his daughter's soft voice. He felt as though he were suffocating. "One of them told me that I would be safe once you did what they wanted."

"What was that? Did they say?" asked McTaub.

Christine shook her head as she got out of her chair and buried her face in the front of her father's jacket. Jack slowly put his arms arounds his daughter and held her tightly, as her words echoed urgently inside of him.

9

McAllister picked up the styrofoam cup, swallowed the last of the coffee and then tossed the cup into the trash can next to his desk. He stared again at the files open before him. On top was a black and white photograph of the body of Stewart Wong, taken at the time of the coroner's autopsy. The long Y-shaped incision in the chest and abdomen had been sewn together haphazardly with coarse black stitches that stood out starkly against the pale skin. It had not been difficult to determine that this had been the man that had killed Samuel Twan. The attendant at the parking garage had identified the body as soon as he had seen the photographs. The college kid had said that he would never forget the image of this young man, with rain running down his face, putting a bullet into Samuel Twan's head and then carefully redirecting the muzzle of his gun towards the fallen man's chest before firing again. He particularly remembered the young man's eyes, he said. He had never seen such dark, emotionless eyes.

Stewart Wong was just twenty years old, but had already been convicted on a couple of counts as a juvenile: dealing drugs at high schools in the city, and battery. He had beaten an old store owner in Chinatown, just as two SFPD officers on foot patrol were strolling by. That was about the only way that he would ever have been caught for that offense. The kid was probably punishing the old man for being late with a payment for "protection". But the elderly shopkeeper would never have gone to the police on his own. If he did that, the next time he wouldn't just get pushed around. All in all, it was a pretty sure bet that Stewart Wong had been moving steadily up the ranks in one of the Chinatown gangs.

McAllister felt his left leg begin to ache from his position sitting on the hard chair. He shifted his weight and then leaned back and put both feet up on the edge of the desk. Well, he didn't plug Twan because of the man's looks. It was obvious that Mr. Samuel Twan must have been up to his ass in badness, too. Probably in another, competing gang, figured the detective. The businessman had been a pillar of the Chinese community for years. President of a bank. On the Board of Trustees of Saint Joseph's Hospital. Lots of generous contributions to all the right places. He had probably paid for his goddamned Jaguar with money from kids buying heroin, or extorted from the old shopkeepers that ran the tourist traps along Grant Avenue. He would have to look into Mr. Twan a little more thoroughly, the detective decided. Check on the man's business connections, his personal life, the usual things.

As McAllister sat there, one of the other detectives, Tom Billard, walked by his desk carrying a cup of coffee. "Hey, Joe! How are you doing on that Twan case? Anything?"

McAllister got up and stretched. He loosened his tie.
"Yeah. It looks like a little disagreement between a couple of the gangs." He began to walk towards the coffee pot.

"Well, they must be getting real antzy, 'cause we got another one."

McAllister stopped, and turned back to look at the other man. "No kidding?"

"Yeah. This guy was found yesterday lying in the corner of an abandoned warehouse down near the waterfront. Young Chinese guy. He had fresh needle marks on his arm. But it wasn't the drugs that killed him. He was beaten to death. Whoever did it really hammered him, too, all over his face and head."

"Know anything much about him yet?" McAllister could smell the possibility of a lead. A pretty long reach, really, but it was so hard to get any information on these people that he didn't want to leave any stone unturned.

"Got an ID from his fingerprints. This kid had been charged a couple of times but never convicted. I went to talk to his parents. They live in a nice little house in the Richmond district. They even spoke some English."

"What did they tell you?"

"Said that he had a problem with drugs. His mom was real upset about it all, obviously. He had already been in trouble as a juvenile. Mostly petty stuff." The man took another sip from his coffee cup. "But she said something funny. I don't know what the hell it meant." He paused.

"What was that?"

"She said something about "Gojin". Kept sayin' it. That "Gojin caused it.

"Caused what?" McAllister's curiosity was aroused. It wasn't often that the Chinese said anything to the police, especially where gangs were involved.

"Caused his death."

"What is Gojin, did she say?"

"No, after that, her husband came out and grabbed her and pulled her inside the house. I couldn't get anything else out of them. Sounds like the name of someone.

McAllister thought for a moment. "Yeah, I guess so. Listen, thanks for telling me about the case. Let me know what else you find out, OK?" He nodded to the other man and then turned and kept walking towards the coffee pot.

*   *   *

The First Bank of Num Hoy was an imposing five-story glass and stainless steel structure on Vallejo Street. The location bordered Chinatown on one side, and the expensive apartment buildings and condominiums of Nob Hill on the other. Joe McAllister flipped his cigarette into the gutter and then pushed through the revolving glass doors and walked inside the building. A gigantic Buddha, finished with gold paint and studded with a mosaic of colored glass, smiled benignly at him from the entryway. One hand of the statue reached down and gently touched a green marble base. The combination of modern architecture, decorated with traditional Oriental art gave the building a sumptuous air. He walked over a thick carpet to one of the desks near the entry, where a very attractive Asian woman sat at a desk.

"May I help you?" She smiled pleasantly.

"Yes, you can." The detective pulled out the leather case that held his badge and showed it to her. The woman's smile never even flickered. McAllister was impressed.

"What can we do for you?" Her voice was soft, and her English precise.

"I would like to see Mr. Twan's former secretary, to ask her a few more questions. They might be important regarding his death."

The woman reached for a telephone. "I'll see if she is still in." She dialed a four-digit extension and waited. After a few moments, she looked up at him. "I'm sorry, but she doesn't seem to be in her office."

McAllister wasn't surprised, but it irritated him that she wasn't there. "Then may I speak to the new President, Mr. Robert Ling?" McAllister knew that he was in the bank. He had called the man's office half an hour earlier.

"He is very busy, with the recent unfortunate loss of Mr. Twan. Let me call his secretary." Once again the woman dialed an extension and then she spoke, this time in Cantonese. She then waited for a few moments, and spoke again. Finally, she put down the receiver.

"If you will be willing to wait while Mr. Ling finishes a business meeting, then he will see you for a few moments. Please go to the fifth floor." She directed him, pointing with a small delicate finger towards one side of the building.

McAllister thanked her and walked to the elevators. The doors were covered in gold leaf similar to the Buddha in the entryway. A few deposits had gone into building this place, he thought. He got off the elevator on the fifth floor. The doors opened into a wide hallway lined dramatically with darkened glass. Large pieces of sculpted jade were displayed on black lacquered pedestals on either side of the hallway. The jade glowed from discreetly hidden high-intensity lighting set into the ceiling above each piece. In his frayed coat and worn shoes, the detective felt completely out of place here.

At the end of the hallway a receptionist's desk was positioned near the plate-glass wall of the building. As McAllister approached, he could see a magnificent panorama of the city, with the financial district displayed in front of him, and further in the distance, Coit Tower, with Alcatraz and Angel Island on the water to his left.

"Please take a seat, sir." Another strikingly beautiful Asian woman spoke from behind the desk. "Mr. Ling will be with you shortly." McAllister sat in a comfortable leather chair and looked at the view. This piece of real estate had to be worth millions, not to mention the building itself, and the art, he reflected.

He stared at Angel Island in the distance. When they were much younger, he and his wife would take the ferry from Tiburon over to the island and spend the day hiking on the trails, and walking on the rugged beaches. He remembered the times that they would lie on one of the grassy hillsides, with the entire city before them, and his wife would gently run her fingers through his hair. Her big bully of a policeman, she would call him. He remembered the long picnic lunches that they would have. Even when the bay was covered in fog, they would sit, listening to the foghorns off the Golden Gate Bridge. Where did the years go?

The voice of the receptionist pulled him from his revery. "Mr. Ling will see you now, sir." As the detective got up, he took one last look at the island. Well, his wife was long dead, and he was here to do a job. He followed the woman's direction through a wide door, which she closed silently after he entered.

The office was somewhat barren, compared to the rest of the building, containing only a desk and two chairs, all of an ornate French Provincial style. Behind the desk sat a small, aging but impeccably tailored man. His hands were folded in front of him. He did not look particularly pleased. McAllister noticed that there was very little paperwork sitting on his desk. Strange for a new guy in the hot seat trying to run a bank.

"What can I do for you, Mr. McAllister?" There was a slight wavering in the man's high-pitched voice.

"Mr. Ling, I'm investigating the murder of Mr. Samuel Twan. I have a few questions that have come up since we performed our initial investigation."

"I have already personally answered questions from your office. Have you any firm leads on the murder of our former president Mr. Twan?"

"Yes, but I need some additional information. Can you tell me about the foreign business connections Mr. Twan may have had?"

"You think that he was killed by foreigners?" Ling leaned forward over his desk and peered at McAllister through thick bifocals which made his eyes appear larger than they actually were.

The guy seems kind of overly interested in what we know, thought the detective. "It's a possibility. I just want to check it out."

"Actually he had very few international connections, except of course to the gold bullion and stock exchanges in Hong Kong. Most of our investors are the second- and third-generation families of Chinese immigrants, who have earned their wealth here in California. They are hard working, and they save their money." The older man's voice seemed weak, quavering. Age spots were beginning to show under the thin hair on his temples and forehead.

"How about his local connections. Did he have any unhappy customers in the bank?"

"In the banking business there are always a few people who may be, shall we say, less than pleased. But we do our best, and our clients do very well." He held out his hands and then dropped them to the table. McAllister noticed that they shook as they fell.

"Any other business connections here in town? Ones that you might not have mentioned the last time that we interviewed you?"

The old man replied quickly, becoming curt. "No. Mr. Twan was a prominent supporter of our community, but that was all. This bank consumed all of his energies, and we miss him very much."

The detective was starting to get slightly irritated. This was going nowhere. He decided to take a chance.

"Mr. Ling, have you heard the name Gojin? I understand that Mr. Twan was related to Gojin in some way. Is that true?"

McAllister watched as the Chinese man paused for a moment before answering. He slowly cleared his throat.

"I have never heard that word before, nor had I ever heard Mr. Twan use the term. What is it? Do you know?"

A moment before, the man had picked a yellow pencil up from the desk. As McAllister watched, now Ling gripped the pencil tightly in both hands, the flesh of his fingers white against the colored wood. The old bastard was starting to sweat a little bit, the detective noticed with mean joy.

"No, I thought that you might be able to help us out on that."

"Well, I'm sorry, but I can't. Will there be any other questions?" The banker abruptly pushed the intercom button on the desk and called in his secretary. He seems to be getting a little desperate to get rid of me, thought the detective.

"Well, you've been most helpful. Thank you for helping us try to sort this thing out." McAllister got up as the young secretary came back into the room. He shook the banker's hand. The man's moist and uncertain grip was further proof that, despite its outward appearance, all was not right with the First Bank of Num Hoy.

McAllister left the office and went back down the elevator. As he passed by the huge Buddha guarding the entryway, the detective smiled at the pleasant young lady at the front information desk. She didn't notice him as she appeared to be listening intently on the telephone receiver.

It was four-thirty when he got back to the office. He began to write down some notes on his conversation with Mr. Ling. There were a lot of things that bothered him about the old man, but they were hard to pin down. He was too nervous, for one thing. Of course a lot of people got nervous when the police started asking them about a murder. But he just wasn't the type of personality that McAllister imagined a new bank president to be. *And no papers or work on his goddamned desk!* The detective stared at the piles of recent, old and ancient reports and papers piled on his own dull grey desktop. And what about this Gojin thing. That really made him sing in soprano! But why?

As he sat and pondered, Tom Billard walked by again, his shirt sleeves rolled up, and another of the endless cups of coffee in his hand. He sat on the edge of McAllister's desk with a smirk on his face. It must be gossip. Billard loved to spread the gossip that filtered through the office. The older detective looked up at him.

"Joe, you won't believe this! You remember that case that I was telling you about this morning? The kid that shot up, but was really beaten to death?" McAllister nodded.

"Well, half an hour ago I got a phone call. It was our local friendly Federal Bureau boys. They said to sit tight and they'd be right over. Two of them just rolled into the office and plucked the entire file! They said that they were onto the case and were going to take it from here, thank you very much!" The officer smirked. "Our tax dollars at work!"

"What do the FBI want with a local murder?"

"They weren't talking. They said to just forget about the case! Maybe they've gotten a screaming urge for Chinese food!"

"Well, that's strange as hell." McAllister made a mental note to look into it. He had a buddy in the San Francisco office of the Bureau. He'd give the guy a call in the morning.

10

Tim Morgan was dying. The malignant tumor above the cerebellum that Jack Phillips had subtotally removed, at first had seemed to respond to the focal external-beam irradiation. But then, quickly, it had begun to grow again, unchecked by the treatment. Magnetic resonance imaging studies showed the growth to be larger each time it was checked. The tumor grew upward, spreading into the third ventricle in the center of the brain.

They had brought him into the Emergency Room one weekend, stuporous and vomiting. An emergency CAT scan had shown massively dilated ventricular spaces within the brain, hydrocephalus caused by the tumor finally blocking the normal flow of cerebrospinal fluid. In the middle of the night the residents had performed a shunting procedure, running a thin plastic tube under the skin, from the ventricles of the brain down into the abdomen, to divert the flow of CSF. But the relief had only been temporary, and the tumor had continued to grow.

They had tried chemotherapy, forcing Tim to sit in the hospital connected to an intravenous line infusing the poisonous drugs. He had spent the days with his three year-old daughter or the baby in his lap. The chemotherapy had made him nauseated, and with the earlier effects of radiation, had made all of his hair fall out. His daughter Shauna had said that it made her daddy's head round like a ball. But despite the chemotherapy and its toxicity, the tumor was unaffected and grew relentlessly.

After the shunting procedure, he had felt fine for a while, and had even returned to work for a few weeks. He needed to feel that he could provide for his family. But then the double vision had started, and his headaches had come back. Later, his movements became clumsy and he began to have difficulty walking. His speech became thick, and he had trouble just moving his tongue. He would fall at home, but each time he would pull himself back up, and keep on walking, sometimes holding on to the walls for support. They had put him on steroid medications, which helped, but only slowed the deterioration slightly. Later, he had lost his initiative and drive, and would sit for hours in a chair while his children played around him on the floor. He began to refuse to go to the hospital. All he would say was that he wanted to stay at home. As long as possible.

This time, when his wife had awakened in the morning, he was unresponsive. She could see that he was breathing, but nothing she could do would wake him up. She had called Dr. Phillips' office. Dr. Phillips wasn't there, but his secretary had said that she would page him and suggested that Mrs. Morgan call an ambulance to bring her husband into the hospital. The ambulance came, and the attendants were instructed to take him directly to the neurosurgical floor at St. Joseph's.

When Regina Morgan had finally delivered the kids to her sitter and then driven to the hospital, she found Dr. Phillips with one of the residents. They were in with Tim, examining him as he lay in the bed. He was still comatose. They had looked into his eyes and tapped on his knees, and discussed the findings together in low voices as she sat in the room at the end of the bed. They had already done another CAT scan of the brain and put an intravenous line into Tim's arm to give him fluids and mannitol, a sugar that reduced swelling, and more intravenous steroids. His breathing had become more labored. Then Dr. Phillips had accompanied her to his office.

They sat down together on the cream-colored couch, under the bright Leroy Neiman painting.

"Mrs. Morgan, we need to talk about Tim's condition. The CAT scan shows that the tumor has continued to enlarge. Despite the radiation, and the chemotherapy, it has grown massively from its original site." Jack took her hand with both of his. "Tim is dying. There is nothing more that we can do for him except keep him comfortable. I promise you that we will do that."

Regina Morgan had known in her heart that this was true even before they had come to the hospital, but still she felt the tears come as she tried to wish the words away. The tears rolled silently down her cheek and into her lap. It couldn't be true. *Why us? What did we do to deserve this?*

Jack remained silent, continuing to hold her hand. He was there for her, and wanted her to know that.

"What am I going to do? What am I going to do? My babies. They will grow up and never know their father." The tears were freely flowing now as she turned and pressed her head into Jack's shoulder.

"No, you will teach them about their father. You will teach them to love him, even though he won't be there with you. It will be hard. But you must do it. Your children depend on you." Jack's words came from his heart. Though it agonized him to think about what her life would be like alone, without the father of her children, he had to guide her. Right now, at this moment, he had to cope for her, whatever his own problems.

116

"What should I do now?" she asked.

"Be with him. Although he's not awake, it may make it easier for him and for you to just spend time with him."

"Tim had wanted to stay at home. He hated to come into the hospital. He wanted as much time as he could at home."

"And you helped him have that. But now we can best keep him comfortable here, with the nurses to help you."

"What should I tell Shauna?"

Jack thought about their three year-old daughter.

"Tell her the truth, the best way that you know how. I would have her come in and see him, even though she may not understand why he can't talk to her. Don't keep her away."

Regina Morgan wiped her eyes with a tissue that Jack Phillips held out for her and sat back in the couch.

"It's so unfair. He never had a chance to do what he wanted to do. He had such great dreams."

"It is unfair. And it wasn't Tim, and it wasn't you. There was no way in the world that either of you could have known about this tumor, or prevented it, or stopped it from growing." Jack paused, overwhelmed by the uselessness of medicine for this man and his family. "It just happened."

The woman got up and slowly walked to the door.

"Thank you, Dr. Phillips, for trying. I know that you did the best that you could for Tim."

Mrs. Brannan held the door open for her. The secretary had been waiting on the other side, listening. Jack nodded, knowing that the best, in this case, had been very little indeed.

After Regina Morgan left, the door to the office remained closed for nearly an hour. Louise Brannan watched the time on the clock next to her telephone. And he hadn't called out on the intercom. It just wasn't like him. Even though they had cut down on his patient load since the scare with his daughter, Dr. Phillips had still remained busy, writing and dealing with the administrative problems of the Institute. After a week or so, he had even started to operate again. After the kidnapping, men from the police department had stayed around the office for the first week that Dr. Phillips had come back, but then had decided to just keep an eye on the Phillips home. But they had said to watch out for any unusual activities or strange people around the office. Mr. Weinberg, whose wife had died unexpectedly, had made another call, threatening legal action against Phillips and the Institute, and had been shocked to find three FBI agents at his door within half an hour, questioning him closely about possible links to Christine's kidnapping. They had come to the conclusion that the old man had no involvement. The secretary looked at the clock once more and decided that she had to check on him. Finally, the secretary went to his office door and gently knocked on it.

"Come in."

As she entered, she saw the neurosurgeon sitting at his desk. He was staring out the window at the bay. Although there was a haze, she could still see the waterfront and Alcatraz in the distance.

"I was wondering if you might like a cup of coffee or something?"

"No thanks, I'm fine." He continued to gaze out the window.

"Are you really alright? You have been in here an awfully long time." The grey-haired secretary closed the door behind her and leaned against it.

"I was just thinking about Tim Morgan and his wife. How quickly things can change. Their goals, and dreams, with them one day, and then all of a sudden..." his voice drifted off.

"You did the best that you could."

"It certainly wasn't very much good in this case."

"I remember a time you told one of the residents: That, too, is why we are here. That when we are defeated, we should use it to try to learn, and become better at what we do know."

He smiled slightly. "You're right, Louise. I did say that." He remembered, curiously, that this had been one of the reasons that neurosurgery had attracted him. Not just working with the nervous system, and the surgery. But that there were many problems that remained unsolved. That patients did die. He had always looked at the deaths as challenges to both his intellectual and physical skills. To do better somehow, the next time.

Louise Brannan decided that it might be good for Dr. Phillips to talk. "How is your daughter?"

"She's amazing. At first they kept her home from school, and she was pretty devastated by it all. But now she's back to her old self, as if nothing had happened."

"Did they find out anything about the people that tried to take her?"

"Not much. After what they described as an 'intensive investigation,' the FBI concluded that it must have been done for money. The rich neurosurgeon would pay whatever ransom the kidnappers demanded." He turned again to stare out at the bay. Another example of how things can change suddenly. Once they had found out that the kidnappers were Chinese, they had considered the Twan case as a possible motive, but dismissed it. Jack, too, refused to believe that the death of the patient had had anything to do with the kidnapping. Emory McTaub had said that they would keep investigating the case but that they might never find out who was responsible. He had recommended that Jack try to forget about it. Not an easy thing to do, he had found.

"Why don't you go on home. There is nothing more that you need to do here. Dr. Steele has taken care of the monthly morbidity and mortality reports and reviewed the budget for next year. Everything else can wait until tomorrow."

The sky was beginning to darken with clouds, becoming a leaden

118

grey. Out on the bay, the searchlight on Alcatraz flashed at regular intervals and then disappeared as it rotated away.

"I don't know what I would do without Fred." Phillips glanced at his watch. Quarter to five. Still pretty early, but what the hell... "I think that I'll take you up on that."

Jack took the elevator down to the garage level. He no longer took the stairs like he used to, on the advice of the FBI. They had given a lot of advice. But not many answers. A week after they had gotten Christine back, a specially armed force of FBI and SFPD had raided the tunnels under Chinatown, going in through the entrance that Christine had identified for them. They had found tunnels and rooms, yes. But nothing else. Not even footprints in the dust.

Jack got out of the elevator and began to walk towards the Mercedes. He always parked it down at one end of the garage, in a corner behind two heavy structural pillars, to keep other people from hitting the side of the car with their doors. As he walked he looked down at the smooth concrete and the yellow painted lines that marked out the parking slots. Christine had a dance rehearsal tonight. Maybe he could get home in time to see it. He looked up and noticed that his car was obscured by a truck parked next to it, some kind of delivery van. He wondered what the traffic on the bridge would be like. As he came around the back of the white van, he shifted his briefcase into his left hand to search for his keys. Then he stopped short.

The door of the Mercedes was open. A pair of legs were sticking out from under the dashboard. *Jesus Christ!*

"What the hell are you doing to my car?" he yelled at the figure.

With surprising agility, a young man squirmed out from under the dashboard and landed on the ground in a crouch. Jack instinctively lifted his briefcase and threw it at him, hitting him over the head and shoulders and knocking him back down. The briefcase landed heavily on the other side of the man. Out of the corner of his eye, Jack noticed that the back doors of the van in the next stall were starting to open. He quickly turned and violently shoved the door shut, and then he ran, sprinting back towards the elevators. The staircase was right there next to it. Behind him he heard a loud report. Christ Almighty! They were shooting at him! He didn't stop to look, but kept running. A compact car was coming down the parking lane towards him. Jack ran to the other side of it and crouched, trying to use the car for cover. He heard sharp cracks as bullets hit the car. The driver slammed on his brakes with a squeal. Suddenly Jack felt a sharp stinging burn in his left hand. He ignored it, as he got to the elevators. Next to them was the stairway entrance. The heavy steel door at the bottom of the stairs was painted a bright green and was closed. He grabbed the nob and turned it and began to pull with both hands. He looked behind him and saw two men closing in at a run. They were about thirty feet away. The door slowly came open, and Jack slipped through, leaving a thick black stain on the door edge where he touched it. He ran up three stairs at a time. As he got to the first landing, he slipped and fell onto his hands. Behind him he heard glass shattering. He pushed himself upright, and as he turned for the next flight, he saw that the two men were shooting at him through the small glass window in the door.

Jack got to the first floor landing. It opened out into the main hallway of Saint Joseph's Hospital. Directly across from the stairway was the security office, he remembered. He grabbed the knob and pulled it. His left hand was beginning to hurt, a numb, burning sensation that he hardly noticed. He ran across the hall in front of startled pedestrians and into the office.

"Get your gun! They're after me!" He yelled at a security guard who was sitting in the office. The guard on duty had just recently started to work at the hospital. He was in his fifties and had grey hair and a sizeable paunch. He looked incredulously at this guy who was bleeding like a stuck pig all over his desk.

"What the hell...! Who are you?"

"Two men!" Jack gasped from fright and exertion. "After me with guns! They're coming up the stairway!" Jack huddled down behind the desk. The guard pulled out his gun, a bright silver 45 that had seen its only use on the practice range. He looked tentatively across the hall at the door to the stairs. It remained closed. People were staring into the office from the hallway. Maybe this guy is some wrist-slitting psycho from the emergency room, thought the guard.

Just then, his supervisor, a big burly guard who had been at Saint Joseph's Hospital for fifteen years, strolled into the office carrying a diet coke. He stopped in his tracks when he saw the gun out and the blood all over the desk. The new guard gazed up at him with wide eyes and then looked again down at Phillips.

"What the fuck is going on here?"

"I don't know, Don. This guy just ran out of the stairwell saying that people were shooting at him. He's bleeding like crazy!"

"What's going on, fella?" The supervisor bent over and grasped the man's shoulder to turn him. Jesus, the guy is shaking like a leaf, he thought. There was blood all over the tile floor below the desk, and on the man's clothes. Finally, he got a look at Jack's face, recognizing him immediately.

"Holy Christ Almighty!" He looked back quickly at the new guy. "Go get some help from the ER. Now!"

*   *   *

120

It was evening, and unseasonably warm for December. Emory McTaub listened to two tourists laughing as they went by on the wicker seat of a rickshaw drawn by an old man on a bicycle. He continued to walk slowly along the sidewalk, stopping to browse, like any of the thousands of tourists a day that still crowded Chinatown in the winter months. He spent a full minute looking through a large plate glass window at a vast assortment of intricate brass ornaments and woodcarvings. As he had done five times in the past half-hour, he slowly turned his head and scanned the faces of the people on the sidewalk for any possible tails, any faces that he recognized from earlier in his stroll. But all he saw were curious sightseers, and an endless number of locals, the young and old that inhabited this ten-block square of San Francisco that was Chinatown. He shifted the canvas satchel that was strapped over one shoulder and kept walking.

McTaub paused as he came to a restaurant with pagoda-style architecture. Garish green and yellow neon glowed in Chinese lettering on the sign overhead. He turned his head to glance casually across the street. He was looking at the entry into the alley that Christine Phillips had directed them to, after her escape. To one side, a brightly illuminated curio shop took up the first floor of a four-story building. Bordering the other side was the entryway to an ancient brick tenement apartment, where a single lightbulb glowed above the doorway. At the back of the alley, McTaub could just see the small wooden shack with the door that the girl had broken out of. The door that led into the tunnel system.

McTaub had been angered and disappointed when he and others in a combined team of FBI and SFPD had searched the passageways through the same entrance ten days before. Although they had been impressed with the size and complexity of the tunnels, there hadn't been a shred of useful evidence despite an intensive search. It had been too clean. He had been more impressed with what wasn't there than with what was; there hadn't even been cobwebs in the corners. They had found some old broken-down furniture in one of the rooms, but it had looked too neat, too clean, not haphazard enough to be real. He was sure that Christine's story was accurate. Who could make up something like that? Obviously someone had done a very careful tidying up before they had gotten there. He had decided that a second look a little more informally might be useful. He had never before been one to break or even bend the rules, but this case had him frustrated. How could these people seemingly just disappear into thin air? He planned on only a little nighttime search for evidence on his own. Nothing too radical. That just wasn't his nature.

McTaub continued up the block and then crossed the street at the corner. The streetlamp illuminated his shadow on the sidewalk as he strolled back towards the alley. He shifted the canvas satchel on his shoulder once again, as the weight of the contents caused the strap to dig in. He stayed close to the buildings as he walked. As he passed the apartment house, he casually turned into the alley and began to walk slowly and silently towards the back. Wooden boxes and crates discarded from the curio shop lined the sides of the narrow passage. Above him on either side, McTaub could see the windows of tenement apartments. He knew that in many of these apartments several generations of a family lived together in a few rooms. McTaub felt naked and exposed. Even though it was dark, anybody looking out might easily see him as he walked below.

As he reached the back of the alley, the agent stopped for a moment to allow his eyes time to adjust to the dark. He looked straight up, between the buildings. Above, in the darkness, the fog was beginning to filter across the city, but he could still make out one or two stars through the grey mist. The sound of two people talking loudly to each other in Chinese echoed into the alleyway, the voices a harsh cacophony, as though they were arguing. After a moment, he went to the door of the shack and kneeled down on one knee to take a look at the door, and stared in surprise. When they had left the tunnels after their search a few weeks before, the rotted wood on the edge of the door had still been shattered from when Christine had broken out. No lock had been left on the door after that. Now McTaub could see that the doorframe had been rebuilt and a heavy new padlock was in place. It looked like a strong, solid, professional job. When they had tried to determine who owned the tiny building, the records had shown that the owner had died years before, and no one had claimed the title since then. McTaub silently swore as he realized that they should have had the alley under surveillance. He would be very interested in whomever it was that had arranged for the door to be fixed and a new padlock installed.

The FBI agent placed his canvas shoulder bag on the ground beside him and opened it. He picked out a small leather packet which he unsnapped and opened. He chose from a selection of lock picks and went to work on the lock. He tried to work silently, conscious of the light and windows around him. After ten minutes, he gave up in frustration. The lock seemed to be unpickable. Sweat was beginning to drip down the inside of his shirt. McTaub placed the picks back in the bag, and, after a moments hesitation, pulled out a long screwdriver. He wedged the end of it between the new doorframe and the side of the door. The doorframe loosened a little as he pried it, but there was a tremendous creak, which echoed in the narrow alleyway. He quickly stopped and crouched, trying to become invisible in the shadow of the wooden shack. The noise had seemed deafening, and he was sure that someone would come to their window to see what it was. But no one came. And the frame was looser. After three solid minutes of silent immobility, he wedged the screwdriver back into the space and pried again. This time there was less noise, and the frame splintered and gave way where the new latch was screwed into it. McTaub looked around him and up towards the entrance to the alley. No one seemed to have noticed the sound. He pried once more, and the latch pulled completely off the doorframe, several of the new screws falling to the ground. He picked them up and put them in his pocket. Maybe the lab could tell what kind of screws they were and where they had been bought. A longshot, he thought, but what the hell... McTaub pulled some thin leather gloves from his bag and put them on. Then he grasped the doorknob, and pulled it. The door opened and the agent quickly entered the small building, dragging his satchel in behind him.

Xiang Pin was seventy. But even at that tired age, her hearing was as sharp as ever. This she attributed to her life of moderation and a healthy dosing of the correct herbs and medicinal salves, which she rubbed into her skin. As she sat in her tiny apartment, three stories above the pavement, she worked a needle and thread with her fingers. Her sewing basket was still half-full with the mending which she did for the laundry down the street.

She stopped working and looked up. What was that? Ever since her husband had died five years before from stomach cancer, she had become very curious about what went on around her apartment, and in her building. That noise had sounded like something breaking. It came from below her window, which was held partly open by a piece of wood that her eldest son had fashioned for her. At her age, the woman liked her room to remain cool. The breeze, moistened with the sounds of the busy Chinatown street at the end of the alley, was pleasant in the nighttime. Xiang Pin put down her sewing and slowly got out of her chair. Her arthritis still caused her pain, despite her salves and the ginseng tea that she drank daily.

The old woman made her way over to the window. Probably those hoodlum teenagers who don't have anything better to do. She peered down into the alley below. Her vision wasn't quite as good as her hearing, but still she could see something. What was it? She went back and turned off the light, next to her chair, and then looked down again. It was a man! What was he doing? As she watched, he took a long piece of metal and pried open the door to the wooden shack. He shouldn't be doing that, she thought! Only recently, after the police had come and gone into the small shack, had her landlord arranged for that door to be fixed. In fact, one of his assistants had personally come up to her apartment and asked her to keep an eye on the building after they had fixed it. Xiang Pin clucked to herself. People have no respect for property these days! Not like when she was a girl, back home in the Canton Province. She watched the man pry the new boards completely off the door frame. Then he entered the shack and closed the door behind him. In a moment, she could see angular, flickering beams of light through the small window next to the broken door.

The old lady moved away from the window and turned back into her room. There was a telephone at the end of the hall on the ground floor of the apartment building. She went to her purse and with arthritic fingers pulled out two dimes. Then she went to her drawer, where she kept her telephone numbers in a small book. Mr. Lo's assistant had given her a number to call if she saw anything unusual. Well, this was definitely unusual! She shook her head in disgust at the thought of more trouble, as she picked up her cane and hurriedly began to make her way towards the stairs.

Once inside the small shack, McTaub, closed the door and lifted a powerful, wide-beam flashlight from his bag. He turned the light on, careful to keep it directed down at the ground, and shined it into the gap in the floor that led down into the tunnels. The opening was black, a gaping, lifeless hole. The agent felt a shiver run through him. This whole tunnel and cave business was eerie. But he quickly put that out of his mind and, once again shouldering the bag, slipped down into the dark silence. He felt for the wooden rungs that were nailed into the side of the opening, and lowered himself down one step at a time. He stuck his flashlight into the front of his jacket, shining it back up onto the wall in front of him, so that he could see the wooden slats. The slats were rotted, and as he pressed down on each one with his toes, he could feel the soft wood give way a little. He guessed that it was about fifteen feet to the bottom. The tunnel had a musty, dank smell, the same as had been evident the last time he had been there. Then, there had been ten armed police with him; they had simply slid a heavy aluminum ladder down into the hole and climbed in, using large and powerful hand-carried lamps for illumination. Now he was alone, and all that he could hear was the sound of his own breathing. He thought about the Smith and Wesson that he had tucked into his bag. That gave him some solace, but not much. This place was still damned strange!

McTaub reached the bottom of the shaft, and dropped down off the makeshift ladder to the dirt floor. It was bitterly cold. He put his flashlight on the dirt floor and zipped his jacket up to the neck. He also pulled some leather gloves out of his bag and put them on. The agent picked up the light and shined it towards the left. The passage went about twenty feet and then turned. He shined the light the other way. The tunnel ran straight ahead, the light outlining a black empty hole. As Christine had run towards the light, the ladder had been to her left. That would mean that she had come from this direction. McTaub started forward, but then stopped, and after a moment's reflection pulled his revolver out of the canvas satchel with his right hand. He released the safety. The weapon felt foreign and unwieldy through the glove. He held the light in his left hand, shined it forward and began to walk.

As he moved, the FBI agent heard only a crunching sound from his shoes on the dirt and gravel floor. His breath evaporated in the light in front of him. During the first exploration of the tunnels, they had gone this way, trying to follow back in the direction that Christine had come. They had discovered several branches off of this passageway, and had followed two of the paths extensively. Both had eventually led into black empty rooms. McTaub knew that they hadn't found the room where Christine had been held hostage. *Where she had killed the guard.*

McTaub shuddered involuntarily, remembering the face on the body that had been found on the waterfront. What kind of fear must it have been, for a young teenage girl to do something so violent. Later, she had remained silent as he had told her that the guard had died of an overdose of heroin. But that had actually not been true, although the toxicology screen had shown both heroin and cocaine in the man's bloodstream. The drugs hadn't killed him; the girl had beaten him to death.

When the police had come into the tunnels the first time, they had not completely explored some of the smaller side passages for lack of time. That had bothered the young FBI man, and in large part led to his decision to return to the tunnels tonight. McTaub remembered that one of the small tunnels had branched off the passageway that he was now in. After moving a hundred feet or so, he found the entrance to the small tunnel that he had recalled. The entrance was partially blocked by ancient boards and the floor covered with heavy debris. He pushed the wood aside and climbed through. Further in, more debris and a low pile of dirt occluded the passage. The agent picked up the wood and threw it out into the main tunnel. Then he brushed the dirt to the sides with his gloves. Finally, he moved forward. This passage was much smaller than the others had been. He shined the light onto the dirt in front of him as he walked, and then stopped to study the floor in his beam of light. The ground looked cut up, and there were shovel marks. As if someone had shoveled the dirt out into the end of the small passage, to close it down even further, he thought. Who knows how old the marks might be, but it was different than they had seen in the other passages.

The tunnel started to slope down slightly and became even narrower. McTaub had to stoop to get through. One wall was wet, and there was a green slime built up on what seemed to be a kind of cement face. He shivered involuntarily in the wet cold. The passage made several turns, and the walls closed in even more. The agent felt a sickening sense of claustrophobia, made worse by the complete darkness around him. He stopped for a moment to calm himself. He felt a deep urge to turn back, as he gripped his gun with his fingers, which were becoming numb with the cold. *It was insane to be here!* McTaub could feel his heart pounding in his chest, and in the silence he could nearly hear the blood pumping into his temples. The vapor from his breath continued to cloud into the light in front of him. He forced himself to slow his respirations, to relax his muscles. He sensed his heart rate begin to slow. Finally, he continued forward.

After another fifty or sixty feet, the tunnel entered a small room. Could this have been where she had been hidden? He searched the room with his light. But the floor here was dirt. She had said that the floor in the room was covered with wooden slats. At the other end of the room, the tunnel continued on.

McTaub's arms were getting tired from carrying both his gun and the flashlight. He clicked the safety back on, and put the weapon back in his satchel. He continued to shine the light around the room, looking for...who knows? Something. Broken furniture was stacked on one wall of the small room. A table, thickly covered with dust, stood empty, for who knows how many years?. But there were footprints on the ground. Signs of life, from how long ago? He went to the other end of the room and continued forward. After sixty or seventy more feet, he came to a new passageway off to the left. He decided to go on straight, and kept going for about ten feet. Then he stopped. He went back to the side passage. He tried to remember what Christine had said. When she had still had the flashlight, she had taken several turns, each to the right, and then gone through a room! The agent stood in the mouth of the new tunnel, trying to reconstruct her path in his mind. His instinct urged him on, battling with his growing fears, of the black unknown in front of him.

The FBI agent went into the new side passage. He walked slowly, carefully, listening for any new sounds. After thirty or forty feet, he stopped, and after a moment of deliberation, he shut off his light. The darkness that engulfed him was total. Even knowing that he had a flashlight in his hand, McTaub felt a deep panic well-up inside of himself. He remembered how he had been so afraid of the dark as a child. Now it was the same, a raw visceral fear that couldn't be controlled by reason. How Christine must have felt, as she was trapped in this darkness alone, not knowing a way out. Quickly the agent clicked the flashlight back on and, after a pause to calm himself, moved forward again. The passage began to widen, and rise slowly upward. McTaub's thin shoulder ached from the weight of his canvas bag. He shifted the bag to the other shoulder, and heard his handcuffs rattle inside. That was a joke, he thought grimly. As if he were going to find someone down here, and arrest and cuff them before he dragged them back out of this place!

Ahead, McTaub saw the tunnel abruptly dilate, into another room. He stopped and his body tensed as he peered forward and shined the flashlight towards the ground. This room was different than the others, the floor covered with wooden slats. The agent moved more slowly, continuing to examine the flooring. Here the grey wood was not covered with dust, but appeared to have been walked upon recently. He stood at the entrance to the room and began to shine the light from side to side, until the beam caught and froze in one place. Outlined in the light was a squat black rectangular case sitting on a low wooden pallet. McTaub moved into the room and inspected the container more closely. It seemed to be made of metal, or perhaps fiberglass. Circling the edge of the case were two metallic bands, obviously where two halves came together.

The agent shined the light around the rest of the room. In one corner, the wood on the floor was blackened and stained. He moved silently, and crouched down to inspect the area more closely. The stain was dried blood, he was sure of it. The blood confirmed for him that this was the room where Christine had been held. Where she had killed the guard.

McTaub silently dropped his bag down on the ground and, shining the light inside, pulled out a small plastic container. He used his screwdriver and gently scraped some of the dried blood off the decaying floor surface. He carefully dropped the small flakes into the container, and then snapped it closed and put the things back into the bag.

The FBI agent stood up and inspected the room in more detail. The chair to which the teenager had been tied was gone. The girl had said that she had picked up a piece of wood, with which she had beaten the guard to death, from a pile of trash. But all of that was gone too. He turned back to the case, guessing as to the contents. McTaub opened his canvas bag again and pulled out the screwdriver. He propped his flashlight up on the bag and shined it at the case. Then he fit the corner of the screwdriver between the two edges of the seam around the container. The metal strips bent where he pried them. He continued to work the seam to one side. The top half of the case appeared to be coming free slightly. He went to the other side and worked the edge the same way. Some kind of lock on the damned thing prevented it from coming open! But it was looser now. Just a little more... McTaub was kneeling down, concentrating on the metallic edge in the light.

"Stand up!" The agent froze, bent over the case. The voice was very loud, coming from behind him. He turned his head slightly but could see nothing in the glare from his own light.

"Stand up, and move away from there!" The voice had a distinct accent. McTaub slowly got up off his knees, and began to turn towards the voice, trembling slightly. He looked down at his canvas bag, and tried to judge whether he might be able to get to his gun. He attempted to swallow, but the saliva had evaporated from his mouth.

"What is in the case?" His voice was dry and rasping. In the darkness he could see only the faint image of a figure, about eight feet away. The other man did not speak for a long moment.

"What is in the case is no business of yours." More silence. "But, in fact, it is heroin. Pure heroin, from Burma."

McTaub stared at the figure, shocked that the other would so readily admit to him the contents of the case. He could feel more than see the gun trained on him from beyond the light. The FBI agent tried to control the rising fear in the center of his stomach. There was only one reason that the man would tell him so readily, even casually, the contents of the container. McTaub realized that he was going to die. Suddenly, he became angry, the fear melting away inside him, and his words came loudly and recklessly.

"Why did you kidnap Christine Phillips?" If he was going to die, he had to know why they had wanted the girl.

There was a long silence. "For her father, obviously." The man's form shifted on edge of the darkness.

"What do you want with him?"

"He must be taught a lesson. A very important man died at his hand." The voice remained calm, matter of fact.

Suddenly, a name and its larger significance crystallized in McTaub's mind. "Samuel Twan." But he still didn't believe it. It made no sense.

"Twan had been shot in the head." The agent's words spilled out as his mind worked in desperation. Maybe he could buy some time and figure a way to distract the man facing him. "Phillips had nothing to do with killing him, for God's sakes! He was trying to save the man's life!"

"Dr. Phillips had every chance to save him. He could have saved him. Had he wanted to." The voice became louder, angrier yet. "But he was a part of the conspiracy. He let Samuel Twan die. And so he must pay for his alliances."

"He did the best that he could for Twan! You must believe it!" McTaub wanted to keep the figure in the shadows talking. Keep the man distracted, focused on the doctor.

"If *you* believe it, then you are a fool."

The FBI agent could almost physically feel the muzzle of the gun boring down on him. Pressing into him. Abstractly, he wondered how much pain there would be when he was shot. *In this God-forsaken place,* he shuddered.

And then McTaub couldn't take it any longer. He felt the panic well up and crest and he tried to control it, but couldn't. He kicked the flashlight away with his foot, and grabbed for his canvas bag. The light spiraled wildly as it slid across the wooden floor and into the dirt wall. He tried to crouch, to hide in the darkness. For a moment, he thought that he might get to his gun. His hands were clutching at the bag, tearing it open. He was abstractly surprised at how much time he had, as he groped for his weapon. But then there was a deafening sound, and a flash that filled the small dirt room under an empty street in Chinatown.

11

The tungsten bulb of the operating microscope threw a two-inch spot of intense white light onto the surgical field. Under magnification, the light glistened off strands of flexor tendon. The Senior Resident in Orthopedics gently held open lacerated layers of skin and subcutaneous fat with delicate, sharp-hooked retractors held in each hand, as the Chief of Reconstructive Surgery peered at the magnified view of the tendon, and the joint underneath. The two of them sat, one on either side of the hand and outstretched arm, to the left side of the sleeping patient.

"I don't know, Bill, the joint doesn't look like it's salvagable," the older surgeon said finally after inspecting the damage. The surface cartilage and bone had been shattered by the bullet. The tendons of the finger, normally firm strong bands of tissue, were split into eight or nine fragmented white strands, the frayed ends completely torn from their insertion distally at the finger tip.

"Could we replace the joint with a prosthesis?" asked the resident, as he reflected with discomfort over how devastating it would be if the specimen under the microscope were his own hand. A surgeon's hands are his life, the resident thought to himself as he repositioned his retractor hooks to better expose the remains of the joint capsule.

The Chief shook his head. "No, with the digital arteries completely gone, the distal part of the finger would have very poor blood supply, and I don't think that the reconstruction would hold up. Even if it did, with both digital nerves out, there would be little or no sensation at the finger tip. I don't think that it would prove to be as useful to him as a well-healed amputation with intact sensation."

It had been even less of a question when they had looked at what was left of the fifth finger. The bullet had amputated the finger nearly completely at the proximal joint near the hand. The remaining end of that finger was much too damaged to re-implant. It still remained hanging, within the operating field. They would complete that amputation once they had made a decision about the fourth finger.

"With this amount of damage, the joint would fuse if we left it in place, wouldn't it?" asked the younger man.

The Chief nodded.

"Will he be able to operate with these amputations?" It was a question the resident had been thinking but dreaded asking.

"You bet. He can, and he will," replied the older surgeon. "There are many excellent surgeons with less than ten fingers. My old Chief of Surgery lost two fingers on one hand in a farming accident when he was a kid. He operated for forty years, and it never slowed him down a bit. He had special gloves made with just three fingers built into them. I knew a general surgeon one time that had a total of only six fingers, and he did just fine! There is an informal club called 'Less Than Ten' made up entirely of surgeons in the United States with finger amputations! The Chief nodded his head again. "He'll need to retrain some, but knowing Jack Phillips, he'll be back, I can guarantee you."

The resident shook his head in disbelief as the older surgeon leaned back on his stool and swung the overhead mounted microscope away from the surgical field.

"We won't need magnification for this. The amputations will go faster if we get rid of the scope." The resident stood up and with the sterilized handle pulled a large overhead light in above the table. Then he sat back down and the two men concentrated on finishing the job.

*   *   *

The grey concrete was smooth and shining, and the bright yellow lines seemed to go on forever. He ran, gasping for air. Where was the door? Where was the goddamned door! He searched for it frantically, and then glanced behind him as he heard another sharp metallic report from the gun. His breath was coming in heaves, his lungs burning from the exertion. He would have to stop soon. He would have to do something! In front of him there were cars parked on either side. He turned and ran between two of them, ducking down low as bullets shattered a window next to his head. The space between the cars was narrowing. Too narrow! He squeezed to get past the cars to the other side. Then he would be safe! But now the other end was blocked! In horror, he turned towards his assailants. They were there now, facing him, standing still on the shiny concrete. They were wearing business suits, he saw. Somehow, that surprised him. He watched as the muzzle of a gun came up slowly, towards his own chest. At his heart. He stared at the man's face, with the smooth Oriental features set in a mask of hatred.

Abruptly, Jack became warm, and the air became hot, and humid. He looked up, distracted by a sound. He knew the sound, as he felt the air pressure beat on his face and in his ears. Approaching Hueys. Medivac choppers, loaded with casualties. They always kept coming. The sky was brighter now, but the sun was hidden with a brown haze of choking dust. He could see the white-painted underbelly of the helicopter as the pilot centered the craft for landing. God, it never ended. But not here! Don't land here! He looked again in front of him. The gunman was transformed. It was the same man, the same face, but now he wore traditional black pajamas, his hair hidden by a broad, leafy covering. But the face was the same. He no longer held a handgun, but instead trained an AK47 assault rifle, shifting the weapon to aim directly at Jack's head. Shot in the head. It would be fatal, he was sure of it. Once the carotid artery ruptures, you just can't get control of it. *Christ, it was hot!* He winced as the orange flash came from the rifle. What will the kids do, Darian and Christine, when I'm gone? They're good kids. It's not fair. It was never fair. *Dear God, why me!* The thought screamed in an echoing void as the bullet crashed into his brain....

"Jack?"

The voice was far away. But still there was the hot, bright, orange-yellow light.

"Jack, are you awake?"

He cringed again, still waiting for the pain of the bullet.

"Your operation is over." He recognized the voice, but couldn't place it. Still the bright light of the sun shined down on him. Slowly, he realized that the light was coming through his eyelids. He opened them. Above him, a bright examining light was shining down from the ceiling, into his eyes. He squinted. His head hurt, and the pillow behind his neck was soaked with perspiration. Barbara's face came into view over him. Her eyes were red. She looked down at him, blocking the light in his eyes and kissed his mouth.

"Where am I?" His voice croaked. His throat was sore; he needed water. He tried to get up off the bed, but Barbara gently pushed him back down.

"You're in the recovery room. Your surgery is all through. Don't you remember going to surgery?"

His memory came back, slowly, in fragments, as the anesthetic continued to wear off. Going to his car, the men chasing him, getting the heavy door in the stairway open. The black stain on the green paint. The burning in his hand. His hand. Jack looked down toward his left hand. It was covered in a white mound of bandages.

"What did they do?" He looked up at his wife.

She didn't say anything but continued to look at him with tears in her eyes.

"They took care of you. You were shot in the hand."

He remembered the blood on the door. And the burning pain. He was silent for a moment.

"Who did the surgery?" he asked finally.

"Dr. Williamson. He'll be here to see you soon."

"I need some water." The hand was beginning to hurt again, as the effects of the anesthetic wore off further. It was mostly the fourth and fifth fingers, and the outer side of the hand. Barbara held up a plastic pitcher of water with a straw, which he took in his lips.

"Just a sip, Doc Phillips, till you're more awake." It was Ida, the black nurse who worked in the recovery room.

"OK, Ida." Jack looked around. He was alone in the recovery room except for one other patient across from him. An old man, clutching his belly. It felt strange to be in here, a room he knew so well, lying flat on his back. He was faintly embarrassed.

"What time is it?" he asked.

Barbara looked at her watch. "Eleven-thirty. In the evening."

"Where are the kids?" As his mind began to focus, Jack lost his concern for himself. They might be after his family again.

"They're at home. Two police officers are with them."

Jack looked at his wife. His hand was hurting badly now.

"This can't go on. The men that shot at me." He took a deep breath. "They were Chinese again. They won't stop. Did the police catch them?"

Barbara's face became a rigid mask as she tried to hide her emotions.

"No," she said, finally. "Apparently they escaped right away, out of the parking lot."

Jack felt an agonizing frustration inside of him.

"They were the same ones that had taken Christine. I know it! They were even using a van, like before! Christ...what do they want with me?!"

Barbara was holding him now, leaning over the bed, her head next to his. Jack felt a warm wetness running down his neck. "I'm sorry, Jack. So sorry that this ever happened to you." Her words were muffled and so soft that he could barely hear them.

Jack reached up with his good hand and put it softly around his wife.

Later, in the darkness of his room, as he lay in bed with his left hand propped up on several pillows, two detectives from the San Francisco Police Department came in to talk to him, to get a description of the assailants. The more senior investigator asked most of the questions.

"Did you recognize their faces? Had you ever seen either of them before?"

Jack shook his head. He was sick and tired of questions, with no answers in return.

The detective went on. "These gangs can get pretty big, but they usually leave this type of thing to their more experienced members, or contract it to somebody else sometimes. Either way, they are professional hit men, basically."

"So this is a gang then, that has been doing this?" Jack looked at the police officer closely.

The older man nodded. He shifted in his chair, resting a scuffed and worn shoe on the bottom edge of the bed frame.

"I'm sure of it. I've been investigating the murder of Samuel Twan. You do remember him, don't you."

Jack stared at him. "Yes, the man that I operated on," he paused, "The one who died...."

"Nearly a month ago, in Chinatown, four men were gunned down inside a small restaurant. A van drove up, and men wearing ski masks got out, and shot the place to pieces in broad daylight at lunchtime. Over five hundred rounds in under a minute. Three of the men that were killed were members of the Wan Fung, a tong gang in Chinatown. One of them was the man who had murdered Samuel Twan."

"So Samuel Twan was a gang member of some kind? He was a respected businessman. My God, the man was one of the trustees of this hospital!"

"He probably wasn't just another member. We know that many of the senior members of these tongs are older, well-established in completely legal businesses of all kinds. He must have been important, probably one of their senior members, or elders. Kind of like a Don in the Mafia."

"But why the hell do they want me?" Jack's voice was accusatory.

The detective remained calm. "For revenge, I would guess."

"Revenge!" The neurosurgeon's anger quickly flared, his voice rising, incredulous. "I was the one that tried to save the guy's life!"

Jack's anger turned to disbelief. It was inconceivable to him that these people wouldn't understand that he had done all that he could for the dead man. Up until this moment he had refused to believe that anyone could want to punish him for trying to help another person. For trying to save a patient's life. It made absolutely no sense.

"Twan died while you were operating on him. Somehow they must hold you at least partly responsible for the man's death."

"Those bullet wounds were fatal! He was dead from the moment he hit the ground!" Jack was upright in bed, his good right hand clutching the sheets next to him, his knuckles white.

The detective was silent, giving him time to quiet down. "Obviously, that's not the way they see it," he said, with observed calm.

Jack looked at the detective. "Can't you find them and talk to them? Tell them the truth?"

"It's not that easy. We're looking for them, but we don't know who they really are, after all of this."

Jack held up his bandaged left hand. "Well, if they didn't kill me, they made goddamned sure that I could never make the same mistake again!"

The detective waited a long time. Ignoring the No Smoking rule in the hospital, he took out a cigarette, lit it, and inhaled deeply, looking out the window at the lights across the bay, in Tiburon and Belvedere, twinkling in the darkness. His silence invited the neurosurgeon to speak what was going though his mind.

Jack shook his head angrily. "You know, for years I have thought that some patients expected too much. You get a bad result, whether or not you committed malpractice, and they want to sue you. They expect to be paid for the misfortune of having a disease that can't be treated, or a procedure that doesn't get the results that they want. They expect medicine to be perfect every time, with a perfect outcome, and when it isn't, it must be your fault, and never their own responsibility."

He stared silently down at the sheets in front of him, bitterness welling up inside of him. "But medicine isn't perfect. Some people remain sick, and some people die, and sometimes there is nothing that you can do about it." He was silent for a moment as he ran his good hand through his tangled hair. "So instead of money, why not take it out even more directly on the doctor. Cut off his fingers, or kill him! I shouldn't be surprised." He spit the words out.

McAllister broke into his anger. "We have an APB out for the van that the two men were using. Anybody that looks suspicious will be stopped and questioned, I can assure you." He used a soft but steady, calming voice. Over the years he had dealt with many angry, distressed people.

The two detectives got up to leave. Jack looked at the older one more closely. Even in the dim light, he could see the lines and creases on the man's face, around his eyes. The man's skin had a sick, grey hue. He looked tired. Not just fatigued, but irreversibly worn down by the years. "What was your name again?" he asked.

"McAllister." He handed Jack a business card. "Joe McAllister. If you think of anything else, just give me a call." He began to walk out, but then stopped and turned.

"By the way. You should know that things could have been worse. We checked out your car. Those guys were wiring nearly half a pound of plastic explosives into your ignition. If you had left work a little later, when you tried to start the car you would have been history." McAllister's voice was matter of fact. "We had the bomb squad remove it."

Jack was shocked into silence. If he had turned on his key.... All he could do was nod at the two investigators as they walked towards the door. Finally, as they were about to leave, he called to the older man.

"McAllister, does the FBI know about all of this? They were working on my daughter's kidnapping. A man named McTaub. It's obvious now that the two are tied together."

The older man stopped and turned again to look at the neurosurgeon sitting in the bed. For a long moment he didn't say anything, but finally he took a deep breath.

"McTaub's missing."

"What?" Jack's voice was urgent. "What did you say?"

"McTaub hasn't been seen since he left the office four days ago. The FBI don't know where he is. They're looking for him."

McAllister himself had been skeptical when the district chief from the San Francisco office of the FBI had called him on the telephone and told him. They had no idea where the man was, and it was completely unlike McTaub to remain out of touch like that.

He continued. "We have a twenty-four hour a day police guard standing duty at your door here at the hospital. No one will go in or out of here unless they are medical staff or you know them." The detective wearily turned away to leave. *What a nightmare*, he reflected, as the door finally closed behind him.

Jack stared at the ceiling. It was painted a pale blue, the same as the hospital rooms in the Neurological Institute. Over the years, Jack had learned to ignore the color as he had walked into the rooms a thousand times to see his own patients. Now it bore down upon him, focusing him on the fact that he was here, imprisoned in his own hospital.

And with everyone gone and no distractions, the pain in his hand was more noticeable. Earlier, before the detectives had arrived, he had refused a shot of morphine offered by the nurse. He glanced at the digital clock on the nightstand beside him. Nearly two o'clock in the morning. An hour before the police had driven Barbara home. Now he missed her.

He looked down at the swath of bandages on his left hand. It was strange. After he had awakened from anesthesia, he had numbly listened to Dr. Williamson, the Chief of Reconstructive Surgery, tell him about the findings at surgery. When the hand surgeon had told him that they had amputated most of his fourth, and all of his fifth finger, in an isolated, clinical sort of way he had understood the words, but not really believed them. Not really felt their truth inside. Even now it was hard to imagine, because he could plainly feel his fourth and fifth fingers, there within the bandages. He tried to move the fingers inside the dressing, and the pain suddenly intensified, as if raw nerve endings were being dragged across the coarse, dry gauze.

As he looked at his hand he began to feel a deep, bitter sense of loss. What would it be like performing the intricate and delicate surgery he did, without his fourth and fifth fingers? Dr. Williamson had been quick to point out that it wouldn't affect him at all; that he could expect to return to full function after he healed up. But Jack couldn't be so sure. He wasn't the same. A part of him was missing. He was less than one hundred percent whole.

Jack had always been astutely conscious of his own physical abilities. His love of medicine was in part the result of his awareness of man as a superbly designed, biological machine. His skills as a neurosurgeon were dependent upon the natural ability of his body to translate the visual input from the operating microscope, silently, swiftly, into precisely controlled responses with his hands. His hands were his life-blood, his tradition, his very being.

And what would potential patients think, when they saw him for the first time. Would they want brain surgery performed by a man without fingers? *Would he?* Once his referring doctors heard about it, what would happen to his practice? He was good, but so were others. Patients might just as easily be referred elsewhere...to neurosurgeons with a full complement of fingers. Finally, what about his confidence, so important to his surgical skill. How would he feel doing his most delicate surgery, *risking patient's lives*, and knowing that there may be a movement or manipulation that he could not perform? He shook his head in anguish, and then pressed the button to summon the nurse, to ask for his pain shot.

The nurse was young, and attractive, one that had cared for some of his patients in the past. Someone that he had given orders to.... He felt embarrassed as now she directed him to turn onto his side so that she could lift up his hospital gown and give the injection into the left cheek of his buttocks.

A little while later, he lifted the bandaged hand up off the pillows and looked at it. Funny, it *really did* feel as if he still had a fifth finger. There was pain where he perceived the finger should be. He knew that it was a trick played by his mind, made worse perhaps by the shot of morphine. His brain still functioned as if he had the finger; the severed digital nerves still transmitting impulses from an imagined place. It was a strange, eerie sensation. He was exhausted, but calmer now from the effects of the strong narcotic. He turned out the light beside the bed and tried to sleep.

As he lay in the dark, once again he saw the images that had haunted him earlier, while he was awakening from anesthesia. In the blackness above him, he couldn't escape the hating look in the man's face, the rifle rising, slowly towards his head. He winced and forcibly tried to jerk his head away as in his mind he saw clearly the muzzle flash. The image wouldn't go away. Over and over, the flash of deadly orange. He became aware that his breathing was fast and shallow. His heart was pounding in his chest, as he lay alone in the dark room. It left him shaken and exhausted as he tried to calm himself. Finally, the sedating effect of the morphine took hold, and he fell into a troubled sleep.

The next morning he lay in bed, trying again to remember the details of the previous day. The man lying in his car, the chase to the stairs, the pain in his hand, and later, the trip to surgery. It was a lot clearer than the night before. He repeatedly looked down at his bandaged hand, still not believing what had happened to him.

Just after eight a.m., Barbara walked into the hospital room, carrying some flowers and a book. She kissed him on the lips, and he could feel the coarseness of his whiskers on her smooth skin. He hadn't yet even thought of shaving.

"How are you feeling this morning, Jack?" Her voice was soft and caring. Her anxiety from the previous night seemed to have disappeared.

"Better, thanks Hon." He glanced down at the book that she held, and recognized the cover: My Medical Career, by Harvey Cushing. He had been trying to read it at home. It was sort of a joke between the two of them. Every evening when he went to bed, he tried to read for pleasure. Inevitably, he fell asleep after a page or two, the book resting on his chest.

She looked down at it. "I thought now that you have a little time..."

"Thanks," he replied. "Is my briefcase still here at the hospital?" He really didn't want to waste time reading, when he could lay his things out on the bed and maybe get some work done. The deadline for the manuscript on arteriovenous malformations was at the end of the month. He suppressed his irritation as Barbara shook her head.

"No. I'm sorry, I took it home with me last night, with your clothes." She sat down next to him, and looked at the bandages on his hand. "How is it?"

"It's all right. Hurts a little, I guess." Jack couldn't look into his wife's eyes as she stared at the dressing. He wondered what she really felt, now that his hand was injured. Now that his career was on the line. Now that he was less than whole.

His entire life had been devoted to perfection, from his medical studies to his surgical skills, and later the development of the Institute. All came from an inner quest, an inner need for perfection. And now that was impossible. Jack gripped the bed sheets with his right hand, and gazed down bitterly. He couldn't bare to look at his wife.

As if she were reading his mind, Barbara spoke in low, even tones. "You know, Dr. Williamson said that you will be able to go back to doing surgery. It may take some re-training of that hand. But it's not impossible." She shrugged her shoulder, looking at him. "Maybe in a way this is telling you to slow down. Pace yourself just a little...you've been on such a steamroller of a career for so long now." She paused. "It's been hard."

The nurse walked in to give him his morphine shot. Barbara glanced at her and then got up off the bed. "I've got a few things to do," she said.

He looked at her. "Thanks for coming. And bringing the flowers," he replied, as she turned to leave. "Oh, do you happen to have my office keys with you?"

She shook her head. "I can bring them back later, with your briefcase."

He nodded. "I'd like that." She bent to kiss him, and cupped his head with her hands for a moment. He could smell her perfume as she held him: it was the one that she had gotten on Rodeo Drive, on a trip to Los Angeles earlier in the year. The name of it was "273", he recalled. Then she was gone.

The nurse smiled at him. "Time for your shot, Dr. Phillips," she said cheerily. Her good mood only added to his irritability, made worse by the increasing pain in his left hand. "How about a sponge bath?" she asked.

He shook his head. "I'll tell you what I want," he replied curtly.

Her eyes opened wider for a moment, and then she quickly administered the injection and escaped from the room. Jack shook his head, disgusted with himself, and gazed absently out the window. He hated being a patient.

Dr. Williamson came in, on morning rounds with his residents. Again the older surgeon was supportive, telling Jack that he would be back operating before he knew it. After that, Mrs. Brannan came into the room, tears in her eyes, obviously distraught over what had happened to him. Jack grasped her arm with his good right hand.

"Louise, listen to me. If you hadn't sent me home early, I wouldn't be here at all. You saved my life, really."

"It's so unfair, after all of the good that you have done for other people."

"But it's happened. We'll get through it," he said hollowly. But the woman was inconsolable. After several more minutes, she calmed down somewhat, and as she left, she promised to bring him his mail and any administrative work that he could look over as he lay in bed.

In the afternoon, Barbara brought in the children. Darian tried to put on a brave face, but Jack could see the fear in his son's eyes as he peered at his dressings. But Jack was more worried about Christine. His daughter was so quiet, withdrawn. She barely looked at him as she sat near the end of his bed, silently. Before they left, Jack held her for a long moment, but still she was stiff and far away.

Much later, there was a soft knock at the door.

"Yes. Come in."

The door opened and a small, delicately coiffed woman entered, softly closing the door behind herself.

"Hello, Susan." Jack put down the medical journal that he had been paging through, and leaned back against his pillows.

"Hello, Jack." She remained near the door initially, but then came forward and sat in a chair next to the bed, smiling, although the sadness was plain to see, as her eyes focused on the swath of bandages on his left hand.

Even now, when he looked at Susan Steele, he recalled those deeply hidden, silent memories of a summer now long ago. He had only been at St. Joseph's a year or two, when Susan still worked as a nurse at the hospital. She was already going out with Fred Steele, but they hadn't been married yet, or even engaged. And Barbara had taken a trip, with her parents and the children, to Europe for the summer. Jack still didn't know how it had happened, but the delicate scent of her skin and the intensity of her passion were easily remembered. After Barbara had returned, Jack had quickly put an end to it, but for years had lived with the guilt of his adultery and fear that it would be discovered. Susan, however, after it had ended, had never spoken about the affair. After engaging and marrying Fred Steele, distinctly to Jack's relief, she and Barbara had even become fairly good friends.

"How is your hand?"

"It hurts." He gazed at his assistant's wife. "How is Fred doing?"

"He is really concerned about you. And your family. He's working too hard. Doing a lot of surgery..."

"I know." Jack suppressed an ungrateful sense of jealousy, thinking of his own surgical cases that Fred was taking care of.

"I hope that you recover quickly." Susan Steele arose from her chair and looked down at him. Her gaze focused upon his, and then again turned briefly to his injured hand. "Do you need anything?"

"No. I'm alright for now." The woman turned to go. "Susan, thanks for coming to see me."

"Goodbye, Jack." The door opened, and then closed, and she was gone.

In the evening, Jack tried to get some work done. He opened the briefcase and lifted out the final chapter of the AVM book. But he found the room distracting, with the noise of the nurses and patients outside in the hallway, and it was uncomfortable trying to sit on the bed, keep his injured arm elevated, and do anything constructive. And, repeatedly, he found his attention turning to the white mound of bandages on his left hand. Finally, he put the material back in the briefcase and got out of bed in disgust. He walked out into the hallway, where an overweight uniformed police officer was sitting on a chair, just outside the door. The man glanced up at him from the newspaper he was reading.

"I'm going to take a walk, OK?"

The officer looked at him. "Want me to go with you?" His tone made it clear that he hoped the answer would be no.

The neurosurgeon shook his head, and then turned and began to walk down the hall, keeping his bandaged hand elevated protectively against his chest. Without thinking about it, he went to the elevator and pushed the down button, waiting silently until a car came and the door opened. He was alone in the car, and by reflex he pushed the button for the seventh floor, where he would have access to the Neurological

Insitute, and his office. A short while later, Jack used the keys that Barbara had brought in to him in the afternoon, to open the door of his office. He walked into the near darkness and gazed around the waiting room and outer office. Everything was the same, as it had been only yesterday when he had left. Yet somehow it was different. *He was different.* He moved to the door of his own office and, still with the lights off, walked inside. He sat down at his desk, in his own chair, turning on a small banker's light, began to absently leaf through some papers on the desk. He felt better sitting there, away from the nurses, and the police officer at the door, and the distractions of his hospital room. It was his world here. Maybe tomorrow he would bring his things back and really get some work done, with Mrs. Brannan to help him. He noded to himself in the darkness. He would have a little more control over things here in the office.

He looked at his watch, which he had needed the nurses help to strap on his right wrist. It was already eleven o'clock. The office was dark except for the banker's light glowing on the desk in front of him. He looked at the picture in the brass frame that sat next to his telephone. It was a photograph of him and Barbara and the kids, taken on the beach at their vacation home on Cortes Island, in British Columbia. Just last summer. He looked at himself in the picture, tanned, and smiling, as he helped Darian hold up a large striped bass that they had caught together. It seemed so long ago. He had been in control of his life then. By reflex, Jack opened and closed his left hand in the bandages, feeling the sharp pain. He'd had ten fingers then, too, he remembered bitterly. The morphine shot was wearing off....

He turned back to the mail and paperwork that Mrs. Brannan had stacked neatly on the desk. There were three manuscripts to review for the Journal of Neurosurgery. He longed to get back to it. And what was happening to the Institute? Mrs. Brannan had told him that Fred was handling the immediate administrative problems. Thank God for that. Otherwise the place would be going down in flames.

His hand was hurting more noticeably now, but still he sat, looking around the room. His work, his life really, was here, in this place that he had built. Finally, he got up out of the chair, a bit stiffly, and walked out of the office. The door closed with a click, and he padded in his hospital slippers back along the hallway towards the elevator and the main hospital. As he passed by the Neurosurgical Intensive Care Unit, the door opened, and one of the hospital assistants came out. Jack recognized the man from the operating room, and nodded at him.

The man smiled in return. "Hello, Dr. Phillips."

Jack glanced through the open door into the unit. Most of the beds were full; the smooth white gauze head dressings on the postcraniotomy patients stood out in the dimmed nighttime lighting inside the unit. He was impressed. And not just a little jealous, he noticed. Obviously Fred was also handling the cases as they came into the Institute. Most of Jack's referring doctors didn't know yet that he wasn't working, and sent the patients down to St. Joseph's simply expecting that he would be available, as had always been the case. He tried to put it out of his mind as he walked to the elevator and waited for a car.

When he reached his own floor in the main hospital, he got off the elevator and began to walk back towards his room. His nurse, a young recent graduate from nursing school, was sitting behind the counter in the nursing station as he walked past.

"I'd like my pain shot when you get a minute," he said.

The girl gave him a bright smile. "I'll be right in with it."

Jack wasn't in the mood for cheeriness. He nodded sullenly and kept walking towards his room. The room was one of the new VIP suites that the hospital had recently opened, set along the north and east sides of the hospital to take advantage of the views of the bay and the skyline of San Francisco. His room was at the far end of the hall, just around a corner.

At one of the pay telephones near the nurses' station, Jack saw the police officer who was supposedly guarding his room. The man was leaning against the wall, and seeing Jack, he lowered his voice as the neurosurgeon passed by. Jack looked at him but continued walking alone down the darkened hallway towards his room. After ten p.m., most of the lights in the hall were turned out so that the patients could sleep more easily.

The pain in his hand was making him irritable. It was doing a lot of good, he thought, that the officer guarding his room was spending his shift talking to his goddamned girlfriend!

In front of him, a housekeeper moved in the same direction. Jack recognized the pale blue jacket that was their uniform. The man was carrying a bucket in one hand and a mop in the other. Jack hardly glanced at him; his hand was hurting badly now and he wanted his pain shot. He was about ten feet behind as the housekeeper reached the end of the hallway and turned right. Jack's room was also just around the corner.

One of the overhead lights in the hallway illuminated the man's face. As the housekeeper turned, Jack glanced at him more closely, wondering idly if he recognized the man, and the housekeeper's head turned towards him. For the briefest moment, their gazes met, and held. And then the man was gone, around the corner. Jack took another step, but then slowed, and stopped. What was it? He swallowed, and blinked as he ran through his mind what he had just seen. Jack didn't recognize the housekeeper, though he knew most of them by sight. They were mostly women, often older; many were black. But this one was a man, a young Asian man. Jack saw in his mind again the face, the dark emotionless eyes under the dim corner light, as they fixed upon his own face.

By involuntary reflex, Jack's entire body became tense as he recoiled, back, away from the corner. Away from his room. He felt a sudden rush of anxiety overcome him as adrenaline flowed though his body. A film of sweat formed abruptly on his scalp, and he felt his breath catch and he held it, so that the housekeeper would not hear his breathing and turn around. He turned and lurched back towards the nursing station and the police officer.

A part of him argued that the man was probably just a new janitor, cleaning up some late night spill in a patient's rooms. But another, less rational and more primitive part of him screamed out that he must get out of there, away from that man. Should he take the chance? *No! Absolutely not,* he thought, as he moved back towards the officer, who infuriated Jack by continuing to chatter on the pay phone. They had taken Christine, and then proceeded to coldly, deliberately stalk him, nearly killing him. He wasn't going to give them another opportunity.

The young nurse was walking towards him, the morphine shot in her hand. He quickly reached to her and stopped her.

"Did you call for housekeeping up here on the floor?" His voice was an urgent whisper.

The girl looked puzzled. "No. I've got your pain shot...."

"Never mind that!" Jack's mind was racing. He felt strangely paranoid. But the guy could have been watching for the guard to take a break.

"Can patients call for a housekeeper directly, from their rooms?" he demanded. But he knew the answer before she opened her mouth.

"No, usually we call them if there is a problem. Is there a problem?" The nurse looked at him with a worried expression. "What's so important about a housekeeper?"

"Don't go near my room!" Jack turned again to hurry toward the officer standing at the telephone.

"What about your pain shot?" the girl asked.

"Forget it!" He didn't turn around but looked directly at the officer as he walked. The man's thick, black leather belt was wedged under a rounded paunch. Jack felt a combined sense of anger and disgust as he approached the man.

The officer looked up at him, and when he saw the expression on Jack's face, he quickly mumbled "I gotta go," and hung up the telephone.

"Why don't you go do your job and take a look in my room!" Jack's voice was loud and even he was surprised at how infuriated he was.

The officer's face turned bright red. "What's the problem?"

"A guy dressed like a housekeeper just went in there carrying a mop and a bucket." Jack wasn't sure that the man had really gone into his room, but he had to say something to get this officer's attention.

"No one called for him, and he's Chinese. I think that I recognize him." That ought to wake him up, Jack seethed to himself.

The police officer's eyes suddenly became wide, and he reached down and unsnapped the leather safety strap from over his service revolver. The officer then quickly started in the direction of Jack's room.

Jack stood next to the telephone, watching him for a moment. He had to get out of there. Without thinking further, he turned and went back to the elevator. He punched the down button, and waited. Quickly a car came, and he got in. He stared at the row of numbers for a moment, and then pushed the button for the floor that would again take him back to the Neurological Institute, and his office.

As he stood, he looked at his own hazy reflection in the brushed stainless steel on the elevator door, and realized that he was shaking uncontrollably. He held up his good right hand. The fingers trembled in front of him. He fought a rising sense of nausea. Within moments the elevator stopped and the door opened. Quickly he got off and walked back towards his office, looking straight ahead as he went past the Neurosurgical Intensive Care Unit. Once he unlocked the door to his office and stepped inside, he hesitated, and then decided not to turn on the lights. He sat down at his desk in the darkness.

As he stared forward and tried to calm down, once again he saw the housekeeper's face, and a jumbled collage of Asian faces, and the orange flash from the assault rifle. He couldn't get rid of the image, or the feeling of being trapped. He jerked involuntarily as he expected the bullet to hit. Terrified, in his mind he tried to twist and get away, but it was too late. And then he saw again clearly on the flattened elephant grass the lacerated scalp and torn temporalis muscle, the fractured, open skull and the pulped brain, with life's last blood pulsing to the ground. His breath caught in his chest, and his pulse raced. Anxiety overwhelmed him, and forcibly he shook his head. *God, what was happening to him! How could he rid himself of these images!* They were just dreams, nightmares, he forced himself to understand. Yet they seemed so real!

He felt hot and nauseated, and realized that he was soaked with sweat. He got up and opened the window near his desk. The coolness of the night air bathed him, and finally calmed him, as he sat down again at his desk and closed his eyes.

Was he just being paranoid about the housekeeper? No, he sensed that he was in real danger. It was like Viet Nam all over again. You couldn't tell who the enemy really was. He remembered the young Viet Namese that lived in the village near the base hospital. The ones that he came to recognize and even became friends with. Later, an intelligence officer had told him that many of the youths were actually Viet Cong, living among the enemy, fighting them invisibly. It was the same way now. And the police seemed unable to do anything about it! *Christ Almighty, his life was coming apart all around him!*

Again, he stared at himself in the picture on his desk. He looked at Darian and Christine. They were worth fighting for. Consciously, he slowed his breathing down, and forced himself to think rationally, as he gripped the edge of the desk with his good hand. The pain under the bandages was intense. What was he going to do? He couldn't sit here all night! He gazed for a long moment at the telephone, then lifted the receiver off the hook, placed it on the desk, and dialed with his good right hand. He picked up the receiver, and listened to it ring four times.

"Hello?" Her voice sounded so normal. As if nothing had happened.

"Barbara?" Jack tried to control his anxiety and frustration as he spoke in a coarse whisper.

"Jack? What's wrong?" Her voicre rose in concern. "My God, what's happened now?"

He took a deep breath. "They're here, in the hospital."

In his heart, he was sure that the man upstairs was one of them. And even if he wasn't, it really didn't matter now. This situation couldn't go on as it was.

"What? I thought that the police were guarding your room?"

"It's not stopping them." He swallowed. "I've got to get out of here. We need to leave here. Leave San Francisco." As he said the words, he realized that this was the answer. The only way that he could survive.

"But your hand! Jack, you can't!".

"It's OK, Barbara. My hand will heal. But the police and FBI have no control over these people. They don't even know who the hell they are!" His voice became urgent, insistent. "I want you to get the kids together and pack the car. We have to get away before they kill all of us!"

"But where will we go?"

Jack's mind raced. Until that moment, he had felt only a frantic, primal need to escape. His eyes focused on the picture on his desk. The family, on vacation last August. That was it! The house on Cortes Island.

"Up to the island. To the summer house," he replied.

"That's a thousand miles away!" Her voice was loud with shock.

"We've got to do it. They won't find us there." He paused. "Barbara, I've got to. I can't stay here."

"But the kids are in school!" she protested.

"We'll take them out for a while. This is more important than school, don't you see? As it is, they're not safe here! I know that now!" His voice was pleading.

"For how long?"

"At least until the police have had a chance to find these people and get them away from us."

There was a silence. What was she thinking, he wondered. It was a

144

final, complete disruption of their lives. They were running away.

"What about the Institute?"

It was a question that Jack had been silently asking himself.

"Fred has been handling the administrative end of things." And somehow, he reflected, the surgical cases as well. "I'll call him and the Chief Administrator in a few days. They'll understand. I certainly am no good here as it is," he said, with bitter remorse.

When she spoke again, her voice was softer, and surprisingly even. "What do you want me to do?" she asked finally.

"Pack the station wagon with the things that we'll need for a winter trip. Clothes, blankets, whatever you can think of." He looked down at his hospital robe. "And bring me some clothes, would you? Then go to the automatic teller at the bank and get out as much money as you can. How much do we have in the checking account?"

"About six thousand dollars," she replied.

"We can take it out as we go up the coast."

As they talked, Jack could hear the sound of a siren in the distance. It rapidly became louder and then was in front of the hospital. He went to the window and looked out. Below him he could see an SFPD patrol car pulling into the emergency entrance, its lights flashing in the darkness. *So maybe they did find the housekeeper in my room,* he thought. It only gave him more resolve to do what he needed to do.

"Barbara, I'm going to get out of here and take a taxi across the bridge. Can you meet me in Sausalito? At the ferry terminal?" He looked at his watch. Nearly midnight. "How about at one-thirty? Can you do that?"

"Jack, are you absolutely sure that we should do this?" Again her voice was hesitant. "Did you talk to Emory McTaub? I trust him."

Jack froze in the darkness. He had't told her about McTaub when she had been there earlier during the day.

His voice was quiet. "Barbara, Emory McTaub is missing." He paused. "Apparently for a a couple of days now... the FBI are looking for him, too."

"Oh, my God! Could these people?"

"They don't know. But it's possible. And it's one more reason for us to leave."

There was a long silence on the telephone.

"OK, I'll meet you at the ferry terminal at one-thirty. The kids are both asleep. I'd better go and wake them up to tell them."

"I love you, Barbara." Jack said the words, hearing them echo in his ears, and feeling them deeply. For the first time since Christine had been kidnapped, he felt as if he were in at least some kind of control over his life. "It won't be for long Honey, I promise," he assured her again.

As he hung up the telephone, Jack winced. Any movement of his left arm now caused pain to radiate from his hand all the way up to his shoulder. He used his good hand to gently move the left arm with its bandages into a more comfortable position. I've got to get that morphine shot, he decided. But he couldn't go back to his room now. He didn't want anyone to know of his plans, including the police. They would try to keep him from leaving, he was sure of it.

He thought for a moment and decided that he really couldn't do this alone. He could nurse his own hand once he left, but he needed a supply of bandages and dressings, and something for this pain. He picked up the telephone again and dialed the beeper number for the neurosurgical resident on call. After hearing the triple high-pitched tone on the line, he quickly punched in the telephone number for his office and hung up. Within seconds the telephone rang.

"Hello," he answered.

"This is Dr. Chin."

Jack hesitated. Tonight Mark Chin, the resident on his research rotation, was on call in the hospital for the Neurosurgical service. Jack knew the young Asian physician well, but in his paranoid state couldn't help wondering if he could trust the resident. He shook his head, angry with himself for the thought, and replied.

"Mark? This is Dr. Phillips." He paused for a moment. "I need your help. Would you come down to my office when you get a minute?"

"Yes sir. I'll be right there." The resident didn't ask any questions, but quickly hung up the telephone. Jack waited silently in the darkness. In less than three minutes, he heard the door to the outer office being opened with a key. He saw light under his door as the resident turned on the overhead lights in the outer room. There was a knock on his door. Despite his pain, Jack smiled a little. At least the resident remembered the right way to enter his office.

"Come in".

Mark Chin opened the door and stared at Jack, sitting in the darkened room, hunched over, protecting his bandaged hand. The resident looked bewildered.

"Mark, do me a favor and turn out the lights in Mrs. Brannan's office. Then come back in and sit down."

When the resident returned, he asked, "What's going on, Dr. Phillips?" The concern was obvious in his voice, as he looked at the pale and drawn figure of his Chairman sitting in the darkness in obvious pain.

"Mark, what I'm going to say to you has got to remain between the two of us. OK?"

The resident nodded silently, and then spoke in a low voice. "I'm awfully sorry about what's happened to you, Dr. Phillips. All of the residents are."

146

"Thank you, Mark." Jack took a deep breath. "So am I, believe me."

He paused for a moment. "You should know that since that patient Twan died in the operating room, a..." He hesitated again. Mark Chin was a native of San Francisco. His parents still lived in the city. Jack wondered what the resident would think about his problem. "A Chinese gang has been after me and my family."

The resident's eyes widened. " What? That's just crazy, Dr. Phillips!"

"Well, they don't see it that way. Somehow they think that because this man died in the operating room, I'm responsible for his death. They want some kind of revenge. They kidnapped my daughter. When that didn't work..." He weakly held up his left hand. "Now this. But more importantly, tonight another one has tried to get into my hospital room upstairs."

The resident was on his feet, the anger on his face plain in the darkness. "What are the police doing about it?" he demanded.

"As much as they can, I guess, but it's not getting anywhere." Jack looked up at the agitated resident.

"Sit down, Mark." His voice had taken on an edge of impatience; the pain in his hand was becoming intolerable. "I've decided to leave for a while, to get away from this gang, until the police and FBI can find these people. I don't want anyone to know about it, to protect all of us. But I need your help. I need some things to take with me for my hand."

He motioned to it with his good hand. "Dressings and bandages. And I need some kind of pain medicine. This thing is killing me."

The resident was silent for a moment in the darkness. "The dressings are no problem. But the pain meds, let me think about how I can come up with enough to last you for a while. You want oral meds, right, Dr. Phillips?"

Jack nodded. Even though he was still on morphine shots in the hospital, he knew that it would be much harder for the resident to get morphine without being noticed; all of the injectable narcotics were kept under the tight control of the nursing staff in locked drug cabinets within the hospital.

"Yes. Codeine, or something like that. Whatever you can come up with. Get me what you can and then call in a prescription for me to an all-night pharmacy, up in Mill Valley somewhere. My wife can pick them up."

Mark stood up, but hesitated for a moment. "Where are you going?" he asked finally.

Jack looked at him. He had trusted the young man this far. "Up to a vacation house that we have. It's safe, where they won't know to look for us, until the police have a chance to find these people and this thing blows over."

The resident nodded and left, closing the door behind him. Jack continued to sit at his desk, waiting. By now he was sure that the police would be looking for him. *They probably think that I was kidnapped by the gang.* Good, he thought. Maybe that will motivate them to figure this thing out and stop these sons of bitches before they really do get to us. The minutes went slowly, and he sat, trying not to move, because any movement now caused his hand to ache even more. He could clearly feel his heartbeat, identified as individual waves of pain as the blood pulsed through the injured flesh. His thoughts were a jumbled collage of the events of the past days. His injury, the surgery, his terrible nightmare visions afterwards, and his plans for escape. Going to Canada.

Twenty minutes later, he heard the keys in the door again, and Mark walked into his office carrying a small box.

"I've got gauze sponges, cloth bandages and tape here." He pulled out each one as he spoke. "And I found a bottle of oral cephalosporins in case the wound gets infected." Jack nodded.

"What about the pain meds?"

The resident smiled. "No problem. I wrote out a prescription for one of the patients being discharged in the morning and took it to the pharmacy myself. Told them that she wanted to leave real early, and would they fill it tonight. You've got a hundred and twenty codeine tablets here." The young man held up a long brown plastic cylinder.

Jack held out his hand and took the container. He tried to open it, but with his bandaged left hand he couldn't get the child-proof safety lid off. He handed it back to the resident.

"Open it and give me two, would you?" Mark squeezed the lid down and twisted. He shook two tablets out into Jack's open palm. The neurosurgeon swallowed the pills. They were dry and bitter in his mouth.

"Do you want me to let anybody else know that you're gone?" The resident look worried.

"No, Mark. You'll be safer if you forget that we ever saw each other tonight. I'll call Fred Steele myself, probably in two or three days time."

"Dr. Phillips, I just want you to know had badly I feel. This thing is so unfair! You were just trying to help the guy, and look what happens." The young man shook his head, staring at the floor. "It makes you wonder about treating anybody who's been assaulted."

Jack nodded. "Mark, I know how you feel. But you can't treat patients selectively like that. You have to do the best you can, all of the time. If you don't, or if you start to second-guess yourself, then eventually someone that really needs you won't get your help. And they'll die as a result."

Jack got up from his chair. "Thanks for your help, Mark. I really do appreciate it." He shook the young man's hand.

The resident left the office. Jack picked up the telephone again, dialed information, and got the number for Yellow Cab. Then he dialed again.

"Hello. I need a cab, from the side entrance of Saint Joseph's Hospital on Taylor Street, as soon as possible."

After he hung up, Jack looked down at his hospital pajamas and robe. He couldn't leave like this without raising suspicion. He opened his closet and pulled out one of his long white hospital coats. In the bottom were some fresh surgical scrubs. He slowly pulled off his pajamas, trying to move his painful hand as little as possible. The cotton of the scrub suit was cold on his skin. Because of the bandages on his left hand, Jack couldn't tie the drawstring of the scrub pants. Finally, frustrated, he held one end with his teeth and with his right hand tied a clumsy square knot. Then he pulled on the white coat. He looked down at his feet. He was wearing a pair of slippers. He had a pair of tennis shoes for surgery in his locker next to the operating rooms. He could go get those. Jack hid his pajamas and robe in the bottom of his closet, picked up the box of bandages and codeine tablets, and left the room.

Quickly, he walked down the darkened hallway towards the stairs. He passed the Neurosurgical Intensive Care Unit once again, but this time he kept his eyes looking straight ahead. He didn't want anyone to see him leave; there would be less chance that the gang could track him down. He went down the stairs and came out into the hallway one floor below, near the double doors leading into the operating rooms. He moved carefully towards the doorway. Sometimes they had emergency cases going at night. He looked in, but saw no one, and so he continued to walk towards the door for the men's locker room.

As he reached the door, Jack had to put down the cardboard box and use his right hand to punch in the correct number sequence to open the security lock. As he pushed each button, there was a distinctive electronic tone, the metallic beeps loud and echoing in the dark quiet hallway. He looked over his shoulder, hoping that none of the nighttime staff were close enough to hear. As he completed the sequence, the door clicked, and he leaned on it with his shoulder and entered the locker room. He spun the combination of his locker, and then pulled out his tennis shoes. He wrapped his slippers in a dirty scrub shirt and hid them in the back of the locker. His left hand was feeling a little better now that the codeine was taking effect.

Jack left the locker room and, picking up his box of supplies, again went to the stairwell. He continued to go down the stairs until he was at the ground level. Through the small glass panel in the stairway door, he could see that the hall on the ground floor was dark. Just ten yards to the left of the stairs was the side entrance to the hospital. At this time of night the doors were locked to the outside, but one could still get out onto the street. Jack couldn't see the entrance through the window. Slowly, he opened the door and looked towards the entrance. He froze. Outside, on the sidewalk, stood a bulky dark form. The man was facing the street, and Jack couldn't see his features.

As Jack watched, the yellow cab he had called for pulled up to the sidewalk and stopped. The passenger side window of the cab rolled down, and the man standing outside the doorway paused for a moment but then walked to the vehicle and leaned into the window, talking to the driver. Jack's mind raced in panic. Whoever the man was, he was going to find out that someone called for a cab to this entrance. If he were one of "them", the man would stay there, waiting for the assigned prey, *the intended victim,* himself, Jack Phillips.

To Jack's horror, the cab jerked into gear and pulled away from the curb. Then the man outside turned and began to peer through the glass door, into the hallway. Jack didn't know if the man could see him, and he still couldn't see the man's features. He couldn't tell if the outlined form was Asian or not, but it didn't matter. Jack couldn't risk using the exit. As the doctor watched from the darkness, the man abruptly grabbed the push bar on the glass door at the entance and began to shake it, trying to open it against the lock.

The neurosurgeon jerked back into the stairwell, pulling the hall door closed. He must have seen me! Jack shuddered and asked himself: *What the hell am I going to do now?* He was covered with sweat, as terror gripped him.

Without thinking, he climbed the stairs to the next floor and went out into the hallway. On this level was Radiology. He walked through the darkened halls. Jack looked at his watch. Twelve-twenty. He had to get out of the damn building somehow! Maybe he could go through the loading docks, in the back of the hospital. He went down another stairway which he knew reached the basement level. As he neared the lowest level, he stopped. There was a noise above him. A door slamming. Now he could hear footsteps echoing down the stairwell! They were coming towards him! He ran down the last stairs, taking them two at a time. With each step, he felt a jolt of pain down his left arm. He reached the bottom level and dropped the cardboard box, using his good arm to twist the door knob. He pulled the door open and kicked the box through.

It was warmer in the basement, the ceiling lined with insulated water pipes, heating ducts and electrical conduits, and the walls of the hallway covered with pale green tile. Although he hadn't been to the loading docks for years, he remembered that they were near the laundry, and the morgue, and he ran in that direction.

Behind him Jack heard the door at the bottom of the stairs open, and slam closed. He ducked into another hallway and followed it. After forty feet, he saw a small sign above a wide doorway. It was the morgue, which was located directly in front of the loading docks. Maybe he could get out through there. He tried the door handle, and was surprised when it turned easily. He slipped inside, and locked the door behind him.

150

He winced and blinked in the bright fluorescent lights of the outer office. He was alone in the room. He locked the door and walked towards the dissection laboratory, which was through another set of double doors. Behind them he could hear voices in conversation.

When he reached the laboratory door, he turned the handle gently and opened it until he could just see into the room. Two men were loading a body onto a light aluminum stretcher. One of the men had a dark blue nylon jacket on, and he could see "Medical Examiner" printed on the back in block letters. They were from the county coroner's office, making a pickup for an autopsy! Behind him Jack could hear footsteps, and then the outside door handle being tried. He swallowed, and opened the door into the dissection room and walked in.

The two men now had the cadaver onto the stretcher, lying in an open plastic body bag. They were starting to close a heavy plastic zipper that ran the length of the bag. One was holding the two sides together and the other was pulling the zipper closed. As Jack walked in, they both stopped and looked at him curiously. The body was that of a woman, Jack noticed. The face was young, but held the waxen grey color of death.

"Hi". Jack tried to sound normal, and relaxed. He certainly didn't feel it. Neither of the men responded as they stared at him.

"I've got a problem. My car is stuck in the garage with a dead battery."

After a prolonged pause the taller man spoke. "What can we do for you?"

'I was wondering...I live downtown, near the coroner's office. Would you guys mind giving me a lift?"

"Why don't you take a cab?" He was the shorter of the two. The man was looking at the bandages on Jack's left hand, and eyeing his surgical scrubs.

Jack tried to laugh, and motioned to his scrubs. "I don't have enough money with me. I was in surgery all day today, until I cut my hand this afternoon...in surgery," he added after a moment. *Christ, this sounds stupid!* he thought angrily to himself.

"How did you know that we were here?" It was the shorter one again.

"One of the patients on the ward died this evening." He nodded towards the lifeless form between them. "I knew that she was going to be a coroner's case. I figured that you'd be here soon."

"I don't know," the shorter man spoke again. "It's against regulations." The man was looking at Jack's white coat. "Are you Dr. Phillips?" The name was embroidered over the breast pocket of his coat.

"Yes, Jack Phillips."

"Oh come on, Jerry!" The taller one looked at his partner. "Let's give him a break."

"We could be in a lot of trouble for this!"

"Who the hell is going to know? It's the middle of the night, for Christ sakes!"

"Oh, all right." The shorter one shook his head. "But if we get into trouble..." his voice trailed off uneasily.

"Don't worry about it. Just wait a minute, Doc, while we finish loading up and getting the paperwork straight."

Jack watched as they finished getting the zipper shut, fully enclosing the cadaver. He leaned casually against the door that opened into the front offices, praying that whoever was out in the hallway wouldn't start pounding on the outside door.

At last they were ready to go. Jack walked behind the two men as they wheeled the body out of the back of the dissection room past the refrigerated storage units and onto an enclosed loading dock. They opened the rear doors of a dark blue van, which also had "Medical Examiner" printed on its sides in white lettering. After they loaded the body, they slammed the rear doors shut, the noise echoing in the silence.

In his thin surgical scrub suit, Jack shivered in the cold night air, and his breath formed a cloud of moisture against the bright overhead lights. Once the taller man had gotten in on the driver's side and the shorter one had squeezed into the middle, Jack climbed into the passenger side of the cab. The van smelled faintly of disinfectant. Disinfectant and something else...death, Jack decided. He shivered in the cold, as he tried to protect his painful left hand from being bumped by the man next to him.

The driver started the van up. As he began to pull out, an SFPD patrol car drove past in front of them. Jack could see the two officers in the car, looking up at them in the glare of the van's headlights. He prayed they wouldn't stop the van to talk to the drivers. As the patrol car rolled by, a spotlight on one side swept along the van's length. Then the driver pulled the van out and onto the pavement behind the hospital.

"I wonder what they're up to," the taller one muttered, as he lit a cigarette.

"Who knows,?" said the other. Jack remained silent as they drove into the dark night.

12

McAllister awoke with a start at the harsh rattle of the telephone next to his bed. He lay in his underclothes, on top of the covers. The television was still on, casting dull reflections on the ceiling above him. He cleared his throat.

"McAllister here." He couldn't hear over the sound on the television, some mindless talk show. He mumbled, "Wait a second," and got up heavily and shut the TV off, then went back to the telephone.

"Yeah?" He looked at his watch. Nearly one o'clock in the morning.

"This is Officer White. Sorry to wake you up, Lieutenant. I'm at Saint Joseph's Hospital. The sergeant on duty said to give you a call."

McAllister was more awake. "What is it?"

"I was on duty guarding Dr. Phillips, and..." The man hesitated, "...I found a suspect in his room. An Asian male, about twenty-five years of age...." His voice trailed off.

"If you were on duty, how the hell did he get into the room in the first place?" McAllister didn't hesitate to let the irritation show in his voice.

The officer paused. "I was on the telephone for a minute, down the hall. He was dressed like one of the housekeepers here at the hospital, carrying a bucket and a mop. I guess he slipped by."

The man quickly went on. "But I surprised him in the room. He had a handgun, a snub-nosed thirty-eight, hidden in the bucket."

"Where's Phillips?" The detective sat tensely on the edge of his bed, trying not to get overly concerned or excited. But he realized that this was a terrific break in the case.

"That's the weird thing, sir...he's gone!" I saw him in the hallway just before I noticed the suspect, and that was it. I haven't seen him since!" The officer refrained from mentioning the neurosurgeon's comments to him at the telephone.

McAllister stared at the telephone. "You've searched the building?"

"No, we haven't yet, sir." The man's voice quavered uncertainly.

McAllister's words were quick and harsh. "There may be others with the one you apprehended! They could have snatched him right out from under your goddamned nose! Do it, for Christ's sake!" The detective was furious. No wonder this guy was on guard duty!

"How many men have you called in for back up?" he demanded.

"There are two patrol units here."

"Well, call in three more, and have all of the hospital exits covered as soon as possible. We've got to find Phillips. Where is the suspect?"

"We're taking him to Central Station, sir." The man tried to sound at least slightly proficient.

"OK. I'm on my way. Let me know right away if anything else comes up." McAllister went into the bathroom and slapped cold water on his face. Jesus, he thought, looking at himself in the mirror: he looked terrible. There were layers of wrinkled yellow skin hanging beneath his bloodshot eyes. He was elated about finally getting a break in the case, but worried about Phillips. But then he considered. After all this, if I knew some Chinese guy were in my room, I'd get the hell out of there, too. Quickly, he dressed and pulled on his shoulder holster. Then he left the house. Low fog had enveloped the neighborhood. He started the car and pulled out of the driveway, his headlights glaring in the mist. There were no other cars on the street, as he accelerated and drove towards downtown.

*   *   *

"Who are you?" His voice was loud and threatening. It wasn't a question so much as a statement establishing who was in control. But the young man remained silent. They were inside one of the glass- enclosed, soundproof interrogation rooms at the Central Station. It was two-thirty a.m., and McAllister was alone with the suspect.

"I said, who the hell are you?" He snarled again.

The young man was sitting in a metal chair which was bolted solidly to the cement floor. A single bright spotlight focused on his face and upper body. He was still wearing the pale blue janitor's gown from the hospital, now unbuttoned and falling open, nearly casually, exposing a simple white t-shirt beneath.

With a quick motion McAllister was above him, leaning down, his face inches away from the boy's. Still the youth wouldn't speak.

"I'm tired of fucking around with you, punk! I expect some answers." The detective's voice was a menacing growl. But the Chinese boy stared at him, and his lips curled slightly into a faint smile. McAllister looked into his eyes. They were black, rebellious eyes.

Suddenly, the detective couldn't control himself. The chance to unlock this case was here, in front of him. He had to make this suspect talk. A deep fury welled up inside him, focused on the remorseless, smirking face. The sound of the detective's hand was sharp and loud in the enclosed room, as McAllister slapped him. It had happened suddenly, the aging detective knowing as it he did it that he was over the limit. The Miranda Act was supposed to prevent things like this. But strangely, he just didn't care. The young man's expression changed into one of pain as he clutched the side of his face. Tears involuntarily came into his eyes.

"You can't do this to me! I've got rights!" His voice was high and whining.

"In here, right now, you've got no rights. There's no one else here. Who are people going to believe? Me? Or a punk like you?" McAllister could see a faint edge of fear come into the young man's eyes. He kept his own face close to the suspect's, whose sallow cheek was beginning to flush to a bright red. Still the boy remained silent, until again in the darkness another slap rang out.

"Quan, my name is Wilbur Quan."

"Good, Wilbur. Now we're getting somewhere," a note of triumph in the detective's voice. "Tell me what you were doing in Saint Joseph's Hospital tonight?"

The boy became silent again. McAllister didn't hesitate this time before he hit him again with his thick hand. As the sound died out in the darkened room, McAllister reflected with an eerie, strange sadness that never before had he allowed himself to use this kind of physical force, to break the rules that were established, *that he had established for himself,* so many years ago. It confirmed for him that he wasn't the same man he used to be, but only the ineffective, dying shell of that man. Then he remembered the anguished face of Dr. Phillips, the young brain surgeon who now had only eight fingers.

"I want a lawyer," the boy whined.

"Fuck a lawyer. Answer my question."

Wilbur Quan remained silent until he again saw the detective start to bring his hand up. What the hell, he decided. He was going to be out of here and gone, as soon as the lawyer arrived. No reason to let this cop beat him to death.

"All right, man! Don't!" He swallowed, wondering briefly what the consequences within the tong would be if they found out that he talked. "It was a hit. I was supposed to hit the guy in the room."

McAllister slowly brought his hand back down, a vague satisfaction sweeping through him. "Who authorized it?"

"I don't know." The thick hand came up again. "Wait a minute man! I got the word from a guy. His name was San Li!"

"Where do I find San Li?" McAllister kept his face close to the boy's.

"I don't know. Chinatown maybe. He runs a flower shop there."

"Who is Gojin?" The question came abruptly in the stillness of the night. Under the harsh white light, the detective watched as the young man's face tightened, his lips becoming thin and colorless.

The boy was silent for a long time. It had all gone so well for him until now. For some reason, he recalled the night, a few years before, when he had kneeled proudly in front of the red-painted face of Kwan Tai, the God of War, and it had been his time to drink the mixture of cock's blood and wine. He had risen rapidly, from selling heroin in the streets and schools. And soon he was to get into the real money, the real power. He would truly be a *boo how doy*. A hatchetman. Feared, respected. The elders had assured his future. But first he had needed to prove himself worthy. To perform the utmost service for Gojin, alone and unafraid. They had said that, even if he were caught, they would have the best lawyers available for him. That he would be out on bail and taken to Hong Kong under a new identity before the police could do anything about it. That was before this crazy policeman, he thought to himself, as his disdain for the detective crystallized.

"Fuck you, old man."

It was as though McAllister's mind suddenly went numb, disconnected from his body, and his actions. As he heard those words, his entire pent-up frustration and fury rose, and finally overcame him, and overwhelmed any sense of control that he had left.

"Answer... my... question," McAllister's words were punctuated with short, vicious blows as he began to beat the boy mercilessly.
The youth shrieked with pain and fell completely off the metal chair as the detective hit his raw face once more. The boy lay on the floor, breathing hard as blood oozed from his split lip onto the cold cement. Finally, he turned to look up at McAllister with hatred and fear in his eyes.

"It's not who. Gojin is the name of the most powerful tong in San Francisco." He spat the words out as he stared at McAllister. "It is because of Gojin Tong that you will die for your actions tonight."

"Don't try to threaten me." The detective roughly pulled him back up into the chair, consciously ignoring the words. "Who is the leader now that Sam Twan is dead?"

Again the youth remembered the meeting of the elders a few months before, and the face in the shadows of the candlelight around Kwan Tai. "I don't know his name." His voice was flat, resigned.

McAllister looked at the boy, who now sat, shoulders tensed, with his eyes closed, waiting for the next blow. But this time the detective believed him. Abruptly, McAllister wheeled and left the boy sitting in the darkness.

*   *   *

156

The orange lights that illuminated the roadway on the Golden Gate Bridge flashed by like a strobe in the darkness as the taxi drove north, away from the city at last. Jack sat, slumped in the back seat, exhausted, his cardboard box next to him.

The taxi driver eyed him warily in the mirror, as he had when he first stopped to pick Jack up downtown. Over the years, the driver had seen a lot of unusual things. A lot of unusual people. But never one quite like this, dressed up like some kind of doctor, with a bandaged arm, and nowhere near a hospital when he had waved the taxi down, below the hanging Christmas ornaments on the streetlights in the financial district. Weird. The driver nearly hadn't stopped, but tonight his fares had been slow, and the lease payment on the cab was due soon. As long as the guy paid his fare, the taxi driver really didn't care what he looked like. The man wondered about the pain that he could see plainly in Jack's face in the mirror, as he took the second exit north of the bridge, and began to follow the road as it wound down towards the bay, and the town of Sausalito.

As the taxi descended through the rolling hills towards the water, Jack watched the glistening lights of the city with a numb sense of sadness. And relief. *At least they would be safe.* For now. The lighthouse on Alcatraz flashed lazily in the distance, as the taxi made a series of sweeping turns and began to pass the houses on the outskirts of the quaint waterfront town of Sausalito. They slowed, past the many shops along the water which catered to the year-round tourist trade. Most of the windows were decorated for the holidays. Finally, the taxi reached the downtown area, and as they came to the bus depot, Jack began to look for the station wagon. He glanced at his watch. Nearly two in the morning. Barbara should be here by now. He asked the taxi driver to pull over at the waiting area in the bus depot. Then he saw the Ford, clearly apparent under the lights in the depot parking lot.

"My wife is in that car over there. The station wagon. I need to get some money from her. Wait for just a moment, would you?" Jack could see the skepticism in the man's eyes, but finally the driver nodded as he climbed out.

Jack picked up his cardboard box and walked quickly towards the station wagon, shivering in the cold night air. Even though the streets were empty, he felt conspicuous in his white coat and surgical scrubs. As he came up to the car, the driver's door opened and Barbara got out. Jack could see both of the kids in the back seat. Darian was asleep. Christine was looking at him, but didn't acknowledge him as their eyes met.

"Are you all right?" Barbara put her arms around her husband and held him tightly for a long moment. Jack put the box of dressings down on the hood of the car and responded to her with his good arm.

"I'm OK. My hand hurts like hell, though. Would you have some money for the taxi?" He nodded back towards the cab driver, who was waiting with his parking lights on and the engine still idling.

"I'll go pay him. Get inside. It's freezing out here!" She could feel Jack's shoulders beginning to shiver under the thin scrub suit.

He opened the passenger door. The heater was on and a blast of warm air greeted him as he got into the car, putting the box of dressings on the floor in front of him. He turned to look back at Christine.

"Hi, babe." His voice was soft so that he wouldn't awaken Darian.

At first his daughter didn't speak. She looked straight ahead, trying to avoid Jack's gaze, until suddenly her eyes filled with tears, her voice broken. "Why do we have to leave, daddy? Why is this happening to us?"

Jack looked at her for a long moment, agonizing in her sadness. Doubt swiftly filled his mind. Was this the right thing to do? To run away? But again, deep inside himself, he knew that he was right. His voice was soft but firm.

"We've got to go, Christine. These people, the same ones who tried to take you away, and tried to kill me, were in the hospital again tonight. Trying to finish the job."

"But my school! Finals are just coming up, and it was hard enough trying to make up for the time I lost before." Her voice trailed off, and Jack could feel her frustration.

"Christine," he persisted, "If we don't go, they won't stop until either they kill me or we're all dead." His voice rose emphatically. "They will not stop. Don't you understand?" Jack gazed at her for a long moment, willing her to believe him. "Life isn't the same as it was, as much as we wish that it were. It won't be the same until these people are found and placed in jail!"

Barbara came back to the car and got in on the driver's side. Jack turned forward and looked at his wife. "How much money did you bring?" he asked as he connected his seatbelt, twisting to use his good hand.

"I had just over a hundred dollars at home, and I took out another three hundred from the automatic teller."

"Good, that's a start." He turned again, looking past Christine into the back of the station wagon. He could see that it was full with bulky luggage and other supplies.

"I brought mostly clothes, some blankets. Everything that I could think of in a hurry."

"That's great, Barbara." He looked at her in the darkness, and then turned again to look at his daughter. "Thank you both for understanding. We've got to do this for our own safety."

"Where do you want to go?" asked Barbara, as she started the car.

"Let's take Highway 101 through San Rafael and then drive towards

Sacramento. If you get tired we can stop anytime, but I want to get some distance away from here first. They might come looking for us at the house."

Barbara pulled out onto the street and they drove silently along the waterfront, past the houseboats on Richardson's Bay north of Sausalito. When they reached the freeway, their taillights merged with those of other cars streaming north in the remaining darkness.

*   *   *

The angry face of Kwan Tai, its red lacquered finish shining in the light of the ceremonial candles, seemed to look down accusingly at Nim Choy. As he kneeled in front of the God of War, he felt a deep, jagged sense of failure. Killing the assassins that had murdered his friend Samuel Twan had given him but temporary solace. It was true, the boldness of that attack had weakened the spirit of Wan Fung Tong, and since then, under the vigorous leadership of Joseph Lo, Gojin Tong had moved in to take away many of the shopkeepers and restaurant owners in Chinatown that had been paying protection to the other triad. The Gojin had violently taken over their gambling houses and the drug trade that Wan Fung Tong had cultivated in the wealthier neighborhoods of San Francisco.

But still, for Nim Choy, these victories were hollow. The bitter hatred that burned inside of him had not left, and would never leave, while the man that he knew was truly responsible for Sam Twan's death was still alive. Alive, and now probably under police protection, because of their own ineptness and embarrasing mistakes. It should have been so easy, and yet three times they had attempted to destroy Phillips and failed. And this last bungling in the hospital was nearly too much to bear. He had argued for sending an older, more experienced man. He had pleaded the elders to let him go himself. But no, they had decided that he was too important to their other missions, and that he knew too much about their methods and the inner workings of the tong. Coveted knowledge were he ever caught. Nim Choy looked up in the flickering light at the leering grotesque mask above him. In the depths of the image, he saw his duty. His one fulfillment.

13

The old man walked slowly but steadily along the dirt trail. Mac, his German Shepherd, ran ahead and down along the quiet waters of the bay, as he had always done. Mac was getting old, too, but you wouldn't know it, watching him on their daily morning walks. The man breathed deeply and felt the cold air cleanse his lungs. It was just before sunrise, their usual time to be out. Therapy for an old man's insomnia, he thought to himself as he walked. Behind him, the sky was beginning to lighten into a salmon pink above the hills of Berkeley and Oakland. In front, the faint silhouette of the Golden Gate Bridge could just be seen, still black against the leaden grey background of the coastal fog.

The man looked at the bridge in the distance as he walked. Fifty years ago he had helped to build that bridge, pounding rivets far above the safety netting and the viscious currents below. It had been hard, dangerous, back-breaking work. Yet it seemed like yesterday. Whenever he looked at the bridge, he felt that a part of his soul was still up there. He stopped, and turned to look east. The sun was up now, having just crested the hills.

Ahead, Mac was running back towards him. The dog was barking like mad. The animal turned again and ran back down to the water, two hundred yards ahead. The old man continued to walk. It was probably a bird or a dead fish on the shore. Mac would sniff at it for a while. But still the dog was carrying on, and so the man began to go towards the animal, off the trail, into the sand down towards the water. It was harder to walk here, his feet sinking into the softer sand on the beach. The water was still a dark metallic grey color, but beginning to brighten in the morning light.

He looked ahead. Mac was stopped, holding his ground, barking at something on the water's edge. The old man peered forward. He could see a mass, a dark form that was partly in the water and partly pushed onto the beach. Probably a seal carcass, he thought. He moved slowly in the sand, his legs beginning to tire. His wife always complained to him about overdoing it.

Now Mac was back next to him, still looking at the thing in the water, and growling. The dog looked nervous and excited.

"Settle down, boy. Let's go take a look at what you've found." As they got closer, he could begin to make it out. But he couldn't be sure. And then he smelled it and stopped. It must be a seal. Dead for a long time. And yet, there was something strange. Mac was whining and started to growl again. The man went to within fifteen feet of the thing to get a better look. The smell was overpowering. Then he realized what it was. He looked at the ground, feeling unsteady and not knowing what to do.

"Get away, Mac, get back!" He yelled and grabbed the dog's collar, turning to pull the dog away up the beach. He had to get help. The old man stumbled as he dragged the dog through the sand and back up towards the trail.

*   *   *

McAllister put the car into second gear and listened to the transmission whine as he let off the gas and coasted down the steep incline. The elegant high-rise apartments of Nob Hill rapidly gave way to older, smaller tenements as he neared the bottom of the hill and continued towards the Chinatown district. It was foggy, cold and wet. A damp mist formed on his windshield, forcing him to turn on his wipers. In his mind, he continued to go over the plans that they had hammered out in the office over the previous two days. He used his radio to contact his partner, Neal Cochran, and checked in. The Captain had finally given in to McAllister's plea for more manpower now that they had gotten a number of important breaks in the case, and had been able to tie Twan's murder into the others in Chinatown. Apprehending Wilbur Quan in the doctor's room at the hospital with a thirty-eight caliber handgun hidden in his possession had definitely been the biggest break so far.

"Neal, are the men in position?"

Cochran's voice was peppered with static. "We're getting there, but one car hasn't arrived yet, so we're still two men short."

McAllister cursed the weather for the radio static. "OK. Let me know when you are all in position. I want to go in there full force, and without giving them any warning."

The detective continued to slowly make his way towards Grant Avenue, but then decided to park and walk in the rest of the way. Stopping his car on the busy city street would cause a major traffic backup that could potentially hamper their access to the area if they needed to bring in additional support.

McAllister radioed Cochran again to confirm his plans and then began to look for a place to park. He found a corner, in front of a fire hydrant. The red paint on the curb was chipped and cracked. He pulled into the No Stopping Zone and got out of the car, enjoying briefly one of the few remaining benefits that his job had to offer: unlimited parking. He checked his gun in the holster under his left arm and adjusted his worn sports jacket. Then he began to walk towards Grant Avenue, and the center of Chinatown.

Out here, away from the four- or five-block square that the tourists saw, small, narrow and busy shops lined both sides of the street. The signs in the windows and above the doors were for the most part written in native print. In many of the small shops there was only a handwritten note taped to the inside of the window, giving McAllister no idea what services or goods they might have been offering. There was little glitter and neon here, but instead only the frugal methods needed to make ends meet in day to day survival. In one window, down a short flight of stairs below street level, he saw a small white-haired woman, sewing at an ancient manual machine; she didn't bother to use additional energy to look up as he passed by.

McAllister checked his watch. He and his people had decided on a particular time for arresting San Li. The informant had said that the man always worked in his flower shop on Wednesday afternoons. The detective felt a small surge of excitement in his throat and began to walk faster.

As he neared Grant Avenue, the street changed. Even at this time of year, tourists crowded the district, taking photographs, sampling Chinese food, and staring curiously at the candied ducks, ginseng and dried sea skates that hung in the windows of some of the shops. Even on this cold and grey winter day, the sights and smells were highlighted by the brightly colored blinking neon lights, these in oriental style, but written in english, clearly for tourist consumption.

McAllister pulled a piece of paper out of his pocket and rechecked the address scribbled on it. He looked at the numbers on the buildings and moved around a couple of obvious tourists and their son as the family stood staring through the window of a shop selling curios from Hong Kong.

"Can I have it, Daddy?" the boy wailed. "Mommy, I want it!"

"Not now. We're just looking, I told you!" the boy's mother replied harshly.

The detective checked the numbers on the buildings again and finally stopped to glance casually across the street. He had purposely come down the street on the side opposite San Li's Flower Shop, and now he looked across at the shop, spotting the small doorway covered by a dark red awning. A few flowers and plants stood in containers along the sidewalk and around the entrance to the shop. The doorway was empty and he couldn't see through the windows of the shop well enough to tell whether there was anybody inside. Automatically, he checked the inner breast pocket of his sports jacket, and could feel the folded search and arrest warrants.

He looked fifty feet to the right of the doorway and saw his partner Neal Cochran, similarly browsing through some produce stacked in wooden crates along the sidewalk. Their eyes met, and McAllister nodded slowly. Then he glanced up and down the street and began to walk across, towards the red awning.

They met at the doorway. McAllister pulled out his gun as they entered the shop, Cochran following behind. A sweet, damp smell of flowers and plants surrounded the men as they went through the door. The unpainted wooden floor creaked under their shoes as they walked towards the counter.

A small middle-aged Asian woman was sitting behind the counter, trimming stems with a small pair of clippers. She looked up as they came in, and abruptly spoke several words in Chinese, showing them a smile with uneven teeth as she spoke.

McAllister flipped open the leather case that carried his badge, and held it up towards her with his left hand as he came up to the counter. In his right hand he held his gun low, pointed down towards the floor. Cochran also had his gun out, gripped in both hands, aimed downward.

"Where is San Li?" McAllister's voice was loud and firm. The woman began with a stream of guttural Cantonese, as she put down the flowers and clippers on the counter in front of her. Her smile was gone.

He shook his head. "Where is San Li?" he said again. *God damn it!* He fumed. *The man was supposed to be here!* He tensely glanced at his partner beside him. "You've got your men covering the back?" Cochran nodded, as the woman continued her irritating, unintelligible chatter.

McAllister ignored her and put his gun back into its holster under his left arm. He moved to a thin plywood gate that hinged on the counter, separating the front of the shop from the area in back, and pushing the gate open, walked past stacked terracotta flower pots, and a low green forest of potted plants. Cochran followed. A wall with a small doorway separated them from a room in back. He could see light coming through a rear window into the back room.

"San Li? We want to talk with you."

His voice rang out in the confined space, as in the front of the shop the woman remained frozen on her seat, staring at the two of them. The detectives moved slowly through the rear doorway, their guns now up in front of them, into what appeared to be a small office. A low wooden desk stood against one wall. A door at the back of the shop was closed, bolted shut from the inside, McAllister noted. After an initial look around the small room, he went to the rear door and unlocked it. Opening it, he looked outside. On an adjacent roof, a uniformed officer stood with his service revolver drawn, wearing a bullet-proof vest zipped on outside his uniform. McAllister looked up at him and the officer nodded. He pulled his head back in and closed the door.

"Damn it, Norm, our information stinks!"

"I don't know what happened, Joe. We figured this was a reliable source. It has been before." Cochran tucked his own gun back into the holster under his jacket.

McAllister looked at him. "Why don't you go see if that woman has learned any English yet?" The younger man nodded, and moved back into the front of the shop. McAllister heard him talking to the woman, who once again began to reply in a string of indecipherable syllables. He stopped listening and began a careful visual search of the room. The detective tried, as he always did, to miss nothing, but to also keep his eyes open for the obvious. He went to the desk first, a small unpainted wooden structure, and began to leaf through the few papers on top. Mostly bills, order forms and receipts written out by hand. The signature looked like San Li's from the photographic samples he had seen of the man's handwriting. McAllister picked up a few of these for a handwriting analysis by the lab later on.

He turned to walk back towards the doorway into the front of the shop and stopped. What was it? He wasn't sure at first. Something had clicked inside of him as not being right. But what? He couldn't put his finger on it. He turned again and went to the desk, looking it over once more. Nothing there.

He shook his head, puzzled, and then slowly looked down at the simple wooden floor. Most of the floor in the flower shop creaked as he walked, the ancient boards bending slightly beneath his significant weight. But here, just under the desk, it was different. To be sure, he leaned forward on one foot. Nothing. The flooring was solid and firm, and there was no sound. No creaking. Odd, he thought.

McAllister pulled a chair out of the way and got down onto one knee to look more closely. Then he saw it. Below the desk there were two pencil-thin cross-cuts in the wooden planks, coming away from the wall, several feet apart. About two feet away from the wall the cuts ended, connecting with the natural gap between the planks that ran the length of the floor. All together they formed a perfect square, with one edge along the wall under the desk.

McAllister suppressed a smile and reached into his pants pocket. He pulled out his key ring and wedged his house key into the outer edge of the square, and began to lift. The small door came up easily, pivoting on well-oiled hinges on an axis a few inches from the wall. He lifted the door open until it leaned against the wall below the desktop.

"Hey, Norm." He listened as the other detective stopped talking to the woman in the front of the shop.

"Yeah?"

"Come and take a look at this." He kept the excitement out of his voice as he looked down into the darkness.

He heard the other man's footsteps creak on the floor behind him. Cochran came around the partition, and his eyes lit up as he saw the opening.

"What the hell is that?"

"Just happened to notice it. I'll bet you lunch that it connects with those tunnels that the FBI found last month."

"Want to take a look? I can get a flashlight from the car."

McAllister considered. San Li could easily have slipped down this way as they had come in...while they were occupied with the woman in front. He would be long gone by now if it did connect to the other tunnels. But there could be other useful evidence down there, that San Li wouldn't have had time to clean out as he escaped. And since they did have a warrant for the search, he might as well take advantage of it.

"Yeah, why don't we take a quick look. Bring along a couple of the other men from outside. And one or two of the big flashlights from the squad cars, OK? Better radio the Captain, too, and let him know what we've found."

"Sure, I'll be right back." Cochran turned around and went out the door in the back of the building.

In the reflected light down through the small door, McAllister could see only the vague shadows of some kind of room below. A narrow wooden ladder led down from the opening in the floor. He turned around and, shifting his bulk over the opening, put one foot down onto the top rung of the ladder, testing its strength. The ladder held his weight easily. Slowly, he lowered himself down into the darkened space. It was noticeably cooler as he finally dropped onto a dirt floor about eight feet below. He was in some kind of small room, with dirt covered walls. As his eyes adjusted to the dimness, he began to look around. On one wall, towards the back of the flower shop, the black mouth of an opening gaped. He also noticed the outline of two low wooden boxes along one wall of the room. Above he heard the back door open again and footsteps echoing on the wooden floor. Cochran's head appeared above him.

"Joe?" The younger detective sounded worried.

"Down here. Thought that I'd get a little headstart. Drop me down a flashlight." The younger detective passed a long rubber-covered flashlight down through the opening. McAllister grasped the light and turned it on. He shined the wide beam on the wooden ladder as Cochran and two young uniformed officers came down into the small room.

Once they were all standing together within the small space, McAllister shifted his light onto the floor, and focused it on the two boxes, one stacked on top of the other. They were made of simple unfinished wood, but were well constructed and nailed shut.

"Got a pry of some sort?" McAllister looked at the others. One of the officers pulled a Swiss Army knife out of his pocket, and snapped open a blunt screwdriver blade. McAllister took the knife and began to work the lid off the top box. Cochran focused one of the flashlights on the box as he wedged the blade under one edge. Finally, he was able to get the end of the screwdriver blade into the opening as the nails on that side pried free. He grasped the edge of the lid with his large hand, and pulled the remainder of the nails out.

Inside the box were four packages, each wrapped in yellow paper. Cochran pulled one out, and began to open the paper. He came upon clear plastic wrapping, and through it they could see a compact brick of dirty white.

"Let's see that, Norm." McAllister took the package in his left hand and abruptly stabbed into the plastic using the the open blade of the knife. He tasted the powder from the tip of the knife blade.

"Cocaine?" asked one of the officers.

He shook his head. "Heroin." He looked at Cochran and smiled grimly. "Glad we looked." He dropped the package back into the box. Nodding to one of the uniformed officers, he muttered, "Go back upstairs and tell the others to place the woman under custody. Then come on back."

As the officer climbed back up the ladder, McAllister handed the knife back to the other uniformed patrolman and took one of the flashlights. He shined it onto the rear wall of the small room, and into a low passageway framed by thick wooden beams. The tunnel went straight back for at least thirty or forty feet, into blackness. McAllister looked at the younger detective.

"What do you think?"

"I'd say that we should take a look. We might find our friend, Mr. Li."

"Don't count on it, I have a feeling that he's long gone." The older detective paused. "But let's go ahead and look around for a bit. Might find some other interesting things." McAllister nodded towards the heroin on the floor. He pulled his thirty-eight out from under his jacket, and began to lead the four of them, holding one of the large flashlights under his left arm. He carried his gun loosely, pointed at the ground in front of him.

The floor and walls of the passageway were formed of dirt, but every ten feet or so there were thick wooden supporting beams on either side. The ceiling seemed to be made entirely from crossing beams of the same thickness. The men were forced to walk in a tiring crouch as the ceiling was only about five-and-a-half-feet high. "Short goddamned people," McAllister muttered to himself, as he finally stopped for a moment to rest. They had gone about forty feet, he figured, well past the narrow alley behind the flower shop. They were probably beneath the apartment building on the other side. Except for their flashlights, the tunnel was completely dark.

"Want me to lead?" Cochran asked. McAllister nodded as he tried to catch his breath, and moved to the side to let the younger man squirm by. Cochran continued forward, holding only his flashlight in front of him with both hands. He went on for another thirty feet, until finally their lights reflected onto a dark wall in front of them. The tunnel appeared to branch towards the left and right. Cochran stopped for a moment to allow the others to catch up. He then paused, momentarily considering his movements, before taking a quick look around the corner, shining his light in either direction.

"See anything?" McAllister's voice was breathy, rasping from the exertion. He noticed a slight twinge of pain and a heavy band of pressure across his chest, but ignored it.

"Yeah, about ten feet down to the left it looks like it opens up; there seems to be some kind of room. I couldn't see anything else. And just a tunnel going the other way."

McAllister had decided that they should give this up and go back. But before he could say anything, Cochran went around the corner towards the left and disappeared into the darkness. The older detective lifted his flashlight and began to follow him. Instantly, the narrow space erupted with noise and filled with choking dust. Cochran fell back heavily against him, and the tunnel went dark as both of their flashlights dropped to the ground. From the sudden weight of his partner, McAllister fell to his knees on the tunnel floor. The younger man was on top of him, pinning his right arm down as McAllister violently tried to pull his gun up and around the man's body. He couldn't breathe from the dust in the air and the choking smell of cordite. There had only been one shot, fired from somewhere in front of them. At last, he freed his gun and pointed it into the darkness towards the room. He fired, again, and again, emptying the chambers, the reports filling the black airless space, the noise deafening.

One of the young uniformed officers grabbed Cochran by the coat and began to pull him back around the corner. McAllister held onto the younger man and brought himself to his feet. Together they dragged Cochran back along the tunnel several yards and gently laid him down to the floor. In the angular and moving flashlight beams, they could see a dark stain forming and enlarging on the front of his shirt. His chest was moving air, but there was a sucking sound from the wound. Cochran let out a low moan.

McAllister kneeled down and grabbed the front of the young detective's shirt. He ripped it open. On the right side he could see a small black hole which bubbled with blood as the young man exhaled. McAllister pushed the shirt back down onto the chest wound, and looked at one of the uniformed officers.

"Hold on to that, to stop it from leaking air! Get him out of here!" He could barely hear himself talk; a loud ringing filled his ears from the gunfire. He coughed heavily from the dust, and watched as the two officers began to drag Cochran by the arms back in the direction that they had come. He began to feel the deeper aching inside his own chest once more, which again he tried to ignore. He was furious with himself for letting the younger man lead. It should have been him. He wouldn't have cared if he had been shot, but Norm had a wife, and a small son, he remembered. *God damn it!*

There had been no more noise after the sound of his own gunfire had died out. McAllister reached to the floor and picked up one of the flashlights that lay shining obliquely onto a dirt wall. He moved back, with deliberate care, towards the corner where the tunnel divided, and then, staying behind the corner, he abruptly reached around with his arm and shined the light into the passageway towards the underground room. Nothing.

He still had his gun in his right hand, but reminded himself that it was empty. It didn't matter, he decided. He took a deep breath. The pain in his chest was gone, he noted. Slowly, he turned and faced the underground room.

Faintly, at the edge of his light, he could see a figure, slumped, unmoving on the floor. He went forward in a crouch, the light fixed upon the body. It was a man lying facedown, in a dark pool of blood on the dirt floor. McAllister prodded the body with his foot. There was no response. The chest was still, unbreathing. A gun lay in front of the body and McAllister kicked it away, more violently than was necessary in the enclosed space. He reached down and turned the man over to look at his face. It was San Li. McAllister recognized his face from the photographs that he had studied back in his office.

Deliberately, the detective put his flashlight under his arm and lifted the man by the shoulders. The body was surprisingly light, as he began to drag it back the way that they had come in, toward the flower shop. Again, he felt the squeezing deep pain recur inside his chest. He couldn't ignore it this time as the pain built to a crescendo, forcing him to stop and drop the body to the ground as he doubled over and tried to catch his breath. He crouched with his hands on his knees as the pain slowly subsided. Behind him he heard a noise, and turned to see the passageway reflecting moving patterns of light. One of the young uniformed officers appeared, shining his flashlight into McAllister's eyes.

"Are you all right, sir?" The man's voice was anxious. The light shifted to the body on the ground. "Jesus Christ!"

"Can you get this guy out of here?" McAllister's voice was raspy and weak, as he turned and slowly began to make his own way back along the tunnel.

Captain James' face was flushed and plethoric, a sheen of sweat covering his forehead as he and McAllister stood, looking at the remains of San Li. The young police officer had dragged the body up through the trap door and laid it out on the wooden floor in the back of the flower shop. A single small dark hole could be seen just to the right of the trachea in the neck. He must have strangled in his own blood, McAllister reflected grimly as he looked at the deadly wound.

Paramedics had arrived quickly, responding to the emergency call from the police radio, and the orange and white ambulance unit had already taken Norm Cochran away, with full lights and siren, going to the Trauma Center at the San Francisco General Hospital.

"I shouldn't have gone into that tunnel. It was a mistake." McAllister's voice reflected his shock over the shooting and his anger at himself over his decision to go into the tunnels.

"Look, don't second-guess yourself now. You had a warrant, and you did what you had to do." The captain wiped his forehead with a handkerchief. "I would have done the same thing. Besides, you found that stock of heroin. Now, at least, it won't end up on the street. So forget about it, all right?" He took a deep breath. "Norm's going to be OK."

"This whole thing is maddening! Gang hits in broad daylight in the middle of the busiest parts of town. Teenagers being kidnapped. That guy Phillips getting his hand shot up! Not to mention that FBI guy that just up and disappeared!"

The Captain stood quietly for a moment before speaking. "They found him."

"What?" McAllister gazed at his senior officer.

"I got a call this morning from the head of the San Francisco office of the Bureau. That guy McTaub. They found him." The Captain's voice suddenly sounded tired. "Washed up off of Fort Point two days ago. Couldn't get prints. It took a couple of days for them to make the ID using dental records."

McAllister turned to stare at the floor, at the body of San Li, and slowly began to shake his head. He felt physically ill with anger and frustration.

"What is it going to take, Bill? I'm back to square one. When am I going to get more help to track down these leads?"

Captain James continued to perspire. "Look, I'm with you on this! And now it's top priority for the FBI. You'll get the help you need, I promise."

The dark blue van from the Medical Examiners office arrived. McAllister watched as the two men loaded the body of San Li into a yellow plastic bag, and onto a light aluminum stretcher. He lit a cigarette, pausing only briefly as he remembered the chest pain earlier in the tunnels, before letting the acrid smoke fill his lungs. He needed a stiff drink, too, but there was paperwork to do. A lot of it. He turned and walked through the front of the flower shop and onto the street. A wide strip of police barrier tape had been placed across the doorway. He stooped under it, and worked his way through a cluster of tourists standing on the sidewalk, and staring curiously into the flower shop, before he could begin the slow walk back towards his car.

14

The four-lane highway cut like a wide, gaping incision through a dense forest of fir trees as they drove north, through Washington State. The road was flat and straight and slate grey, mirroring the overcast sky above. A dusting of snow covered the coarse stubble of brown grass on either side. For the hundredth time, Jack shifted in his seat, trying to ease the stiffness in his back and shoulders The pain in his left hand had settled down to a dull, constant ache, only marginally controlled by the codeine tablets.

The first night, they had gotten only as far as Sacramento when Barbara had begun to have trouble staying awake behind the wheel. They then had rented a motel room, and while his wife and the kids slept, Jack was again tormented by the vivid images. As he lay in bed, staring at the blackness above him, he had consciously tried to force the ghosts in his mind away, as his pulse raced and sweat soaked his bedclothes. Finally, three more codeine pills had allowed him a few hours of troubled sleep.

By ten the next morning, they had eaten, filled the car with gasoline, and continued to drive. Darian was excited by the trip, happy to have escaped the last weeks of school before Christmas vacation. But Christine remained sullen, and Jack worried that she might be developing a true clinical depression, first over the kidnapping, and now by suddenly being uprooted out of school yet again. Jack had sat in the back seat, with his good arm around his daughter's shoulders, as Barbara drove the car.

"Once we get up there, I'll give the principal a call and talk things over with him. I know him pretty well. I think that he'll understand."

"It's not just that, daddy. It's the whole thing. Even before this happened. I was just starting to catch back up with my school work." The tears began to roll silently down her cheeks. "And after I came back, my friends were avoiding me."

It tore at Jack to see his daughter so distraught. "I'm so sorry, honey. It must be awful. None of us wants this. I know that the police will stop these people so that we can get back to our lives. But until they do, we've got to be safe. Try to understand." Yet his words seemed hollow, even to himself. Barbara had remained silent as her daughter had spoken, staring at the road ahead of them, carrying them northward.

They had driven along the winding highway through Northern California, and first saw snow high on the peaks of Mount Shasta. Further north, through the hilly green forests of Oregon, where the smoke curling from the stacks of countless timber mills cast a blue hue in the cold air. Jack had always loved the ruggedness of this region the many times they had traveled this route in previous years. This time the pain and fatigue dulled his awareness of the beauty. The trip became something that he simply had to endure.

They had stopped in mid-Oregon to eat lunch, and Barbara had changed the outer layers of the dressing on Jack's bandaged left hand. The deepest layers of gauze were crusted with dried blood and adherent to the suture lines over the outer edge of his hand and at what was now the tip of his fourth finger. Jack hadn't wanted to change those. It would hurt badly. But more importantly, he hadn't wanted to face seeing his hand, or the amputated fingers, although a thousand times he had stared at the bandages and imagined what the fingers looked like. Until he saw the amputations, he wanted to try and forget about them, as if they might not really be there. That night, near the border of Washington State, they had found a motel room along the highway. Finally, from the fatigue and medication, Jack had slept a numb, dreamless sleep.

Now they had driven past the massive Boeing factory, and then past the busy skyline of Seattle, still under the heavy overcast skies. Barbara continued north. It was nearly three p.m., and Darian began to squirm in the back seat.

"Mom, I've got to go to the bathroom!" he cried.

"OK. We need gas anyway. We'll take the next stop." A few miles later, they saw a restaurant and gas station in a small valley off the highway. She steered the station wagon down a gentle incline onto the exit and pulled into the gas station.

Jack got out, stiff from sitting, and stretched his muscles. It was bitterly cold and damp outside the car.

"I think I'll give Fred a call," he told Barbara, as he walked over to a telephone booth next to the garage. He dialed his private number at the Institute, collect.

"Hello?" It was Louise Brannan. She accepted the call with a hurried "Of course," after the operator had identified him on the line.

"Dr. Phillips! Are you all right?" Jack could sense the concern in her voice.

"I'm fine, Louise. I decided to take a little vacation, to get away for a while, that's all." He paused. "Is Fred there?"

172

"Goodness, yes! The police were here yesterday. They told us that there was a man in your room the other night, dressed as one of the housekeepers! He had a gun!"

Jack felt his body stiffen as he caught his breath. So he had been right! *Thank God that he had trusted his instincts!*

She continued. "They found your night clothes in your office closet."

"I put them there, Louise." He hesitated. "I guess that I left kind of abruptly." Jack watched his breath vaporize in the cold air as they talked.

"Well, I'm just glad that you're OK. Thank God for that! Let me connect you with Dr. Steele. He's in his office."

The line clicked and then he heard Fred's familiar voice. "Jack! Jesus, you gave us all a scare! Where the hell are you?"

"I'm in Washington State, Fred. I'm going up to our summer house for a while, while things cool off down there." He took a deep breath. "Until the police find that gang and get them out of my life!"

"Well, they apparently got one of them the other night in your hospital room."

"Yeah, Louise told me. That's great. Maybe now they can find the rest of them."

"They also told me that the guy was out of custody by the next morning. Sprung by some sleazeball attorneys."

"What?" Jack's reply became a near shout. He was incensed, his earlier sense of euphoria vanished. "How the hell could they let that happen?"

"Don't ask me. But they seemed more sure that they would break this thing." Fred was silent for a moment. "Jack, how long are you going to stay up there....What's the name of that place again?"

"Cortes Island." Jack rubbed his forehead in frustration. "I don't know, Fred. Until my hand heals up." His anger at the injustice welled up inside him. "Until they stop these bastards! Jesus, I can't believe that they let the guy go!" He paused for a moment to calm down. His hand was starting to throb in the wet cold. "I've got to go now Fred. Listen, don't tell anyone where I am. Not even the police. OK?"

On the other end of the line, Fred Steele was silent for a moment. "I got you, Jack. Take care of yourself, OK?"

He slowly hung up the telephone and stared into the distance. *They let the son of a bitch go free!* Out on bail! It was unbelievable! He turned and walked numbly back to the station wagon. Christine and Darian came out from the restrooms and climbed into the back seat. Jack reached into his leather athletic bag and pulled out the plastic bottle of codeine tablets. He handed it back to Darian, who used both of his hands to twist it open. Jack took two of the bitter white pills and swallowed them down without water.

Barbara started the car and pulled out onto the freeway. A light rain began to fall, and turned into a frozen slush which began to build up on the sides of the windshield.

"They did find someone in my hospital room. With a gun." Jack's voice was quiet. He knew that the kids were listening, but he had to tell Barbara, to get it off his chest. He stared at the grey road through the rain as his wife drove.

Barbara turned to look at his face. "Did they catch him?" she asked hopefully.

He nodded. "But Fred said that by the next morning they let him go on bail! Can you goddamn believe it?" He shook his head angrily.

"Oh no!" She looked at him in disbelief, as his words sank in. "No! How could they do that?"

"He didn't say."

"Did they find anything out from the man, at least?"

"God, I hope so!"

An hour and a half later, they reached the small town of Blaine, and just a bit further north, the Canadian border. There was little traffic crossing into Canada. It was still raining, and the light was already beginning to fade as they drove up to the customs booth. A stern appearing white-haired man stood inside the booth wearing a heavy coat over his uniform.

Barbara held out her and Jack's driver's licenses. The man bent down and peered into the station wagon at the four of them.

"Purpose of the visit?" His voice was curt, as he scrutinized their identification.

"Vacation," she replied.

"How long do you expect to be staying?" He was looking into the back of the station wagon at the luggage. No skis, he noticed. Most people vacationing in Canada this time of year came to ski.

"A week to ten days. We have a place up near Lund."

"Lund, aye?" The customs officer was looking at Jack's bandaged hand. He hesitated for a moment, but it was cold and he wanted to close the window of the booth. "OK, go on then."

They continued on across the border into British Columbia, on to the King George Highway, following it over gentle hills and then down into the wide Fraser River Valley, as the last light of the day faded into a purple and azure darkness towards the west.

"What do you want to do?" asked Barbara. All of them were tired from the long day of driving. Darian was squirming in the back seat, trying to read a book under the small overhead light. Christine sat staring out the window.

"I'll tell you, let's check the ferry schedule for Victoria. If we can get over tonight, we could stay at the Empress Hotel and then drive up Vancouver Island in the morning. Or we could stay in Vancouver tonight. I don't care. It's about the same distance either way to get up to the island."

Barbara glanced at the clock on the dashboard. "Well, it's five-thirty now. We're going to hit rush hour traffic if we go into Vancouver. How about the ferry?"

"That sounds good." Jack pulled the maps out of the glove compartment and looked at them under the overhead light. One was for British Columbia, and he opened it up onto his lap. "It's the exit up here, to Tsawwassen. Another few miles ahead, I think."

It was stuffy inside the car. Jack opened his window a little and let the cold air blow onto his hair. It felt good, and took his mind off his hand, which was again beginning to ache. Barbara watched him as he gently readjusted the bandages on his lap.

"How is it?"

"It hurts, but it's better than yesterday. I don't want to take any more of those codeine tablets." Like most physicians, Jack had an inordinate fear of taking narcotics, even though for post-operative pain he knew that their use rarely, if ever, led to addiction. He had never liked to take any medication; taking pills made him feel dependent, and unsure, as if he were no longer in perfect control of himself.

Barbara took the turn off towards Tsawwassen, and the ferry terminal for Victoria. They drove through several small farming towns near the mouth of the Fraser River, which flowed into the straits that lay between Vancouver Island and the rugged coast of the mainland of British Columbia.

As they arrived at the ferry terminal, they pulled up to the ticket window. The next ferry departed in forty minutes. Barbara bought passage for the car and then drove up to the rear of a short line of vehicles that were already waiting for the ferry. During the summer months, the wait was often several hours because of the busy vacation traffic onto the Island. Now the traffic was very light. She stopped the car and shut off the engine.

"I want to get out, Dad!" said Darian. Jack got out of the car with his son, and went to the back of the station wagon and searched through the bags until he found a thick, goose down-filled ski jacket. He pulled it on. The sleeve was tight around the bandages on his hand and wrist. They walked towards the end of the pier. A cold wind was blowing in from the sea. In the darkness, a half mile or so to the north of them, a large freighter sat at anchorage at the end of a long pier, bathed in lights.

"What are they doing, Dad?" Darian pointed to the ship.

"It's being loaded with coal, brought down from the Canadian Interior by train."

"Where does the coal go?"

"They send it off, in those ships, and sell it to other countries."

The two of them watched in silence for a few minutes.

"Are you going to be OK, Dad?" Darian's voice was high, but steady. Jack put his right arm around his son's shoulders. It saddened him to think about how little time he had ever really spent with his son. That it took something this tragic to force him to be with the boy....

"I'm going to be fine. Don't you worry."

"Can you do your surgeries with your hand like that?"

Jack was silent for a moment. It was a question he had been asking himself. "Yes, after I heal up, there shouldn't be any problem." He listened to his own words, attempting to make his voice sound confident, not only for his son.

A few minutes later, they walked over to an enclosed snack shop lined with vending machines. Jack bought Darian some peanuts, and got himself a cup of cocoa, which was weak and much too sweet. But at least it was warm. They walked back to the car.

The large white ferry eased silently into its berth, and ramps were lowered onto its two auto decks. Twenty or thirty cars arriving from the Island drove off, emptying the ferry, before men with flashlights began to wave the outbound cars onboard. Barbara started the station wagon, and they followed the other cars in line and pulled forward, parking in rows on the lower level of steel decking. They all climbed out of the car and walked up two flights of metal stairs to the enclosed passenger deck. The interior of the boat's cabin was pleasantly heated.

Jack had always liked the smell of the Canadian ferries: a mixture of tar and diesel oil. He had spent many summers of his boyhood in British Columbia with his parents. His father had loved the western coast of Canada. Riding the ferries had been one of Jack's great pleasures. The ferries now were newer and bigger than in those days, but they still had the same smell. It reminded him of those childhood vacations, and to a degree made him forget about the problems of today. For the first time in weeks, he felt hungry.

"It's time to eat," he announced to his family.

They went into the dining cabin and selected their meals as they walked with plastic trays along a long counter. Jack loaded his tray with baked chicken, a vegetable, salad, apple pie for dessert, and coffee. Barbara looked over at his tray and then at him. "You must be feeling better," she said, smiling.

"I am. I really think that this was the right thing to do. I feel so much better up here, away from the hospital, away from San Francisco." The relief was evident in his voice.

They found a table and sat down. The tables had low wooden rails on each edge to keep the trays and plates from sliding off in rolling seas. The ferry shuddered as its big diesel engines strained and the boat began to pull out of the Tsawwassen harbor to begin the trip to Vancouver Island. Usually the passage took about an hour and a half.

"Dad, can we go fishing when we get up to our house?" asked

Darian.

"You bet!" replied Jack. This could be the time that he had been meaning to spend with the kids, he told himself.

"Well, I hope that we aren't up here too long," said Christine. She didn't look very happy as she poked at her food with her fork. "What is there to do in the winter? It's going to be boring."

"Well, you can get a different type of education than what you get at school," Jack replied. "We can visit the paper mill and the fishing fleet, and the Indian reservation near Lund." He tried to sound enthusiastic, but sensed that his words were falling upon deaf ears.

"When we're in Victoria tomorrow, we'll go to some of the bookstores and get a supply of novels, too," said Barbara. "You have been wanting to try some creative writing. Maybe now is the time." She smiled at her daughter. "It shouldn't be that long, anyway," she added. Jack didn't miss the subtle but firm undertone in her voice.

They finished their meal. Barbara looked at Jack's bandaged hand. The outer dressings were frayed and dirty. "Jack, I want to change that dressing. I'll go and get the things from the car, OK?"

He had been looking down at his dessert and for a long moment he didn't lift his head. He was still avoiding doing anything to the hand. The pain had quieted down and was controllable now. "Not just yet, maybe when we get to the hotel, all right?"

She shook her head. "No, let's do it now. It needs to be done. Then, tonight, when we get in, you can sleep."

He sat, brooding silently as she went down to the car to get the supplies. When she came back, they walked to the forward part of the passenger deck, where there weren't many people. They found a small men's room, entered it and locked the door.

Barbara pulled the bottle of codeine tablets out of the cardboard box and opened it for him. She gave him two, and then gently began to unravel the gauze from his hand and wrist. The outer layers came away easily enough, but the deepest layer was crusted with blackened blood and stuck down to the sutured hand and finger. He winced as she tried to pull the cloth off the incision.

"Wait a minute." He turned on the water and ran it until it was lukewarm; then he soaked the dressing under the stream until it softened. He used his right hand and pulled at the gauze. It felt like it was tearing his skin off. Finally, though, as he let out a gasp, it came away.

Jack stared at his hand for a long moment. At the smooth, clean line of blue nylon sutures where his fifth finger used to be, running up from the outer side of his hand. He could see that it was healing well there. But at the stump of his fourth finger, where it had been amputated at the first joint, the skin edges were red and angry-looking, and swollen around each of the sutures.

He looked away, towards the floor, forgetting about the pain.

"Jack, you're going to have to learn to live with this." She put her hand on his shoulder. He barely noticed. "You have to be strong," she continued, her voice firmer. "Dr. Williamson said that you would be able to operate with your hand. That this shouldn't stop you."

"He doesn't have to do it!" His voice was sharp and bitter.

"But you do!" Her voice rose further and became emphatic, and a little angry. "For God's sake, face up to it, will you!" She paused. "None of us ever expected this to happen to you, but it's not the end of the world!"

He nodded silently. Steeling himself, he again held the hand up and looked at it again for a long moment, his attitude changing as his wife's words echoed in his head. "I think that the fourth finger may be getting infected at the end," he said finally. He moved the stump up and down. "But it's not that painful, and doesn't feel warm. I won't start those antibiotics yet. But we should keep an eye on it."

"When we get up to Powell River you can see that friend of yours. Gordy?" Barbara started to wrap fresh gauze on the hand.

"Yeah, Gordy Jefferson." He had met Gordy Jefferson in college at McGill University in Montreal. Gordy was a Canadian. When Jack had gone down to Stanford for medical school, Gordy had gone to the University of British Columbia. He had done his Internship and Residency in General Surgery at the Vancouver General Hospital, then he had moved up the coast to the small mill town of Powell River. Somehow they had stayed in touch through the years. As Jack had pursued the heights of academic neurosurgery, Gordy had lived a quiet life, caring for the needs of the people in the region. It was partly because of him that Jack had kept the summer house on nearby Cortes Island.

Jack smiled slightly. "Yeah, Gordy could look at it, and even culture it if we need to."

Barbara finished dressing the hand and then put the supplies back into the cardboard box. As she turned to leave, Jack reached for her with his good arm.

"Thank you," he whispered, and kissed her firmly on the lips.

Later, he and Darian walked onto the outer deck, moving to the bow of the ferry. They were bundled in their sweaters and down jackets against the biting wind. In the darkness all around them, they could see but few lights as the ship moved through the archipelago of small islands that surrounded the southern tip of Vancouver Island.

"Who lives there, Dad?" asked Darian.

"Fishermen, mostly. Some others. Retired people, vacationers."

"But they're so far away from everything."

"Some people like it that way." He paused, thinking to himself. "I'm beginning to see their point."

Jack enjoyed the coldness of the wind on his face. Somehow it took away the pain in his hand. At the front of the ferry, they could hear but not see the water below, sliced by the bow. Jack felt a sense of safety here, standing with his young son, moving between the islands, protected by the distance and the isolation and the darkness.

Later, they climbed back into the station wagon as the ferry pulled into the harbor at Swartz Bay on Vancouver Island. After the trucks disembarked first, they drove forward and up a metal ramp onto the roadway. In thirty minutes they were in downtown Victoria at the Empress Hotel.

The Empress was originally the final one of a series of grand hotels of the Canadian Pacific Railroad which dotted the country from east to west. They had stayed in the Empress a few times during previous trips in the summertime. Now, during the winter, the hotel's Victorian elegance was quieter, more subdued, although a huge evergreen decorated for Christmas graced the lobby.

All of them were exhausted when they finally arrived in their room. The kids quickly went to bed. Barbara decided to take a bath before going to sleep. Jack took two more codeine tablets, tasting their bitterness as he swallowed them, and then lay down on the bed. He stared at the ceiling, listening to the water running in the bathroom. Tomorrow they would be on Cortes Island, and in safety. No one could get to them there, hidden, isolated, surrounded by the cold grey water of the northern Pacific. Maybe he could even get back to work on his book. Barbara had brought a copy of the manuscript along, hoping that it would give him something to do. Something to focus on. Yet, he reflected, given everything that had happened to him, the importance of the manuscript, so paramount just a few weeks ago, dimmed to insignificance. It was a part of his old life. That life felt like an abstraction, long ago and a million miles away now. He drifted off, wondering vaguely if it would ever be the same again.

15

The computer printout was folded haphazardly on the grey metal desk, and one end of the length of paper spilled down onto the floor. As McAllister leafed through the printout, he drank stale coffee from a styrofoam cup. There were thousands of active accounts with the First Bank of Num Hoy, and so McAllister had just run the ones in which there had been deposits or withdrawals within the months of August and September. It was still a hell of a lot of names. The detective scanned through them looking for large amounts of money. Deposits or withdrawals, he didn't know. It was a shot in the dark. Another possible source of leads that had to be looked into. He shifted his weight to put his feet up on the edge of the desk, and kept scanning the printout.

The telephone rang. He grunted from the effort as he bent forward to reach the receiver. It rang twice more before he managed to get to it.

"Hello?"

"This is Doug Mason, with the FBI office in San Francisco. Wanted to let you know that the Hong Kong police have located your boy, Wilbur Quan."

"No kidding. In Hong Kong, huh? That's great! Can we extradite him?" McAllister could have predicted that the kid would disappear once bail had been posted. He was amazed that the FBI had found him. But once that agent McTaub had been found washed up in the bay, the Bureau had started concentrating on the case with a grim new determination. Obviously, it was paying off.

"He's an American fugitive, it won't be any problem. But it'll take a week or ten days with the paperwork."

"This time maybe the judge will be a little more cautious about setting bail."

"This time there won't be any bail, I can guarantee you."

"Do you know anything about whoever it was that did post bail for him? Or who arranged his passage to Hong Kong? There must be some names somewhere."

"We've talked to the lawyer that arranged his release, a sleazeball from south of Market named Bloomington. Strictly a gun-for-hire type. The guy that paid him was named Chan. That's it." The FBI agent paused. "You know how many Chans there are in San Francisco?" He laughed out loud over the telephone. "But we've got excellent relations with the Hong Kong Police. Especially now that they are coming out from under British conservatorship in a few years. They're real interested in keeping their friendships alive." The FBI agent paused. "The more interesting thing is that Wilbur Quan was holed-up in an apartment building in the trade district of the city. The building is owned by a man named Joseph Lo. This guy Lo happens to be an American citizen, and has a local address."

"Here in San Francisco?" McAllister's interest increased slightly as he squirmed on his chair once more.

"You got it," said the FBI agent.

"Kind of a long shot, isn't it?" McAllister took a swallow from his coffee cup.

"Well, there's something else about Mr. Lo. Seems that he recently took over as the CEO of a bank in Chinatown. Want to guess which one?"

McAllister glanced again at the computer printout on his lap as he felt his pulse quicken. "You've got to be kidding! The First Bank of Num Hoy?"

"In the personal footsteps of one Mr. Samuel Twan," replied Mason.

"What happened to that other guy, what was his name, Robert Chun Ling?" McAllister was irritated that he had not been aware of a change in the leadership at the bank.

"We're not really sure."

"What are your plans for Lo?"

"Well, we may get more information on Mr. Lo once we extradite that kid from Hong Kong and talk to him. That's going to take a week or so," replied Mason.

"Maybe we should sit tight and just put this guy Lo on surveillance, so we don't scare him off until then." McAllister had to suppress the urge to go and lean on the guy now, but he knew that at this point they didn't have direct evidence against him for any crime, never mind kidnapping and attempted murder.

There was a pause. "Yeah, probably the best bet. We question Lo now and he'll end up pulling a dissappearing act himself," said Mason.

McAllister thanked the FBI agent and hung up the telephone. He went back to his computer printout, and traced up to the L's. There were seven named Lo, but only one with a first initial J. McAllister looked at the monthly transactions. Several withdrawals, of mostly small amounts. The detective's eyes focused and narrowed as he peered at the typed numbers, indicating a fifty-thousand dollar deposit,

182

on September eighteenth. The Twan shooting had been on the eighth of September. He stared at the impersonal black numbers on the computer printout for a long moment, and then slowly circled the transaction with his pencil. Then he went back through the folded sheets of paper again. Another series of transactions had earlier caught his eye, and now he looked at it again. A similar fifty-thousand dollar deposit, and then a withdrawal of the same amount, all within a two day timespan. From an account under the name of S. Chien. He looked at the dates of the transactions, and then slowly wrote the name and account number down on a small scrap of paper. He took a last swallow from his coffee cup and left the office.

*   *   *

The Air Canada flight was at thirty-two thousand feet, flying over Portland. To the west, above a solid cloud cover, the textured pinks and fading blues of a winter sunset unfolded, as the airline crew prepared to serve the in-flight meal.

"Chicken or fish?" The blond stewardess smiled mechanically as she repeated the question at each row. Deftly, she unwrapped the aluminum foil from the small ceramic plates and placed them on plastic trays, to be passed to each passenger. With dinner service running late, she had to hurry, as it was only a two-and-a-half hour flight to Vancouver.

In row seventeen, in the non-smoking section, on the port side, aisle seat, a thin, serene young man sat quietly. He nodded when the stewardess said fish, and ate the meal in silence, not glancing at the sunset, which had transformed into a spectacular vista of red and gold below a darkening purple sky. Next to him sat a plump middle-aged woman, who glanced over hungrily at the chocolate cake that remained uneaten on his dinner tray.

"Can I have your cake?" she asked, looking at the young man and smiling sweetly. He nodded without interest, and continued to look straight ahead, ignoring the woman as she lifted the cake over to her empty plate.

"Coffee or tea?" The stewardess was coming down the aisle with the drink cart for one last time before the meal trays would be cleared and stowed. The young man shook his head as she passed.

"Oh, yes. Tea please." The stewardess refilled the woman's cup as she finished the second piece of cake.

The flight arrived on schedule at seven-fifty, and Nim Choy continued to sit in his seat until most of the other passengers had started to move forward, letting the heavy set woman work her way past, pulling a large flowered canvas bag with her down from the overhead luggage rack. He carried only a single small bag with him, and no other luggage.

At Customs he showed them his California driver's license and passport, and opened the bag for inspection. The uniformed Canadian Customs agent seemed very bored.

"Purpose of the trip?"

"Business."

"How long do you plan to be in Canada?"

"Two or three days." His voice was quiet, and polite, his accent gone for many years now, lost during his childhood and adolescent years in the streets of San Francisco.

The customs agent nodded and waved him through after a cursory glance at his luggage. It would not have mattered had the agent searched it carefully. He wasn't so foolish as to attempt to bring a weapon across the border with him. He walked through the front doors of the airport and got into one of the taxis that sat idling at the curb, placing his small bag next to him on the seat.

"Where to?" The driver looked over his shoulder at the new passenger, who pulled a small piece of paper out of his jacket pocket and looked at it in the dim light. "Downtown Vancouver, near the Gastown district."

The driver jammed the car into gear and flipped the flag down on the meter. It was a common enough request from tourists coming into the city from the airport.

Nim Choy got out of the cab at Pender Street near Gastown and paid the driver. He didn't ask what the current exchange rate was for American currency, and the driver didn't offer it. After he paid the man, Choy looked up at the numbers on the buildings and began to walk, following the street signs at each intersection.

It was a clear, cold night, with a wind that cut into the thin cloth of his jacket. He walked quickly away from the renovated section of the waterfront, Gastown as it was called, with its fashionable shops and restaurants and cobblestone streets, towards a more rundown part of the city. As he walked, he looked with slight curiosity at the bars with two sets of doors, one marked "Men only" and the other marked "Women and Escorts". He passed drunks lying on the sidewalk despite the cold. Some were native Indians. Others were men from the logging camps, who came down to the city from the Interior for the winter season, while the camps were closed, spending their season's earnings in one long binge, living in the cheap hotels, drinking until their money ran out.

And as he continued to walk, the texture of the city changed once again, gradually, below the bright harsh glare of neon lights. Now there were open vegetable and fish markets, where ginseng and dried cottle fish hung suspended on dark twine. As he walked past, Nim Choy listened to the Cantonese of two busy stockboys as they strained to move a large white display case full of oranges and Chinese pears off the side-

184

walk and into their shop for the night.

Nim Choy continued through Vancouver's Chinatown until he reached Harrison Strcet. There he turned right, and followed the street numbers to a large and decrepit Army-Navy Department Store. He stopped next to the store, in front of a small wooden door with peeling paint. He looked again at the number on the slip of paper, and then put the paper back into his pocket and turned the doorknob. As he had expected, the door was unlocked. He pushed the door open further and moved quietly inside.

Later, in a small room above the department store, where he would remain until his weapon was delivered to him, Choy sat on a hard narrow cot and laid his things out in front of him, under the light of a single bare bulb. Still over a thousand dollars in cash, some of which would pay for the gun. His false California driver's license and credit card. And the pictures of the house on Cortes Island. He had found those when he had broken into the doctor's home in Mill Valley the day before, in one of the photo albums in the study. They were vacation pictures, apparently taken within the past few years. Nim Choy stared at the pictures of the house, trying to memorize its details. Abstractly, he looked at a photograph of Jack Phillips, laughing, sitting in front of the house with his daughter and son. No longer did Nim Choy rage at the thought of this man. Somehow time had lessened the burning pain in his heart. Phillips was no longer a person to him now, but merely something to be disposed of. He stared at the doctor's laughing face in the picture, his own face remaining impassive in the shadows of the light above.

*   *   *

It was raining. McAllister sat in the back seat of the Plymouth sedan as Frank Mason, the FBI agent, drove along Market Street towards the Financial District. Mason and his partner had decided to pick the detective up at the Central Station, and drive together to see Joseph Lo. They turned left on Columbus Avenue, and followed the street as it changed from the tall marble and steel buildings of the Financial District to the small storefronts and restaurants of Chinatown. Mason began to look for a place to park. Finally, the FBI agent found a slot next to a movie theatre, and pulled the sedan in. He fished a quarter out of his pocket and fed it into the meter.

The three men walked a half block up the hill to the First Bank of Num Hoy. The two FBI agents wore their customary overcoats, ignoring the rain on their heads. Joe McAllister had an umbrella which he opened up and held over himself as they walked.

A different woman than the one McAllister remembered was at the information desk behind the massive golden Buddha in the lobby of the bank. She was on the telephone only briefly before directing them to the elevators. They stood in silence as they rode to the fifth floor. Once again McAllister walked through the elegant display of oriental art.

A middle-aged Asian woman sat at a desk facing them. The spectacular view behind her was dulled by the leaden overcast and the rain, which formed rivulets down the glass walls.

"Mr. Mason?" Her voice was soft and pleasant.

"Yes." The agent nodded toward the others. "This is Mr. Wilson and Detective McAllister, who is with the San Francisco Police Department. We're here to talk with Mr. Lo. I called earlier."

"Yes, you did. Mr. Lo is expecting you. Won't you take a seat for a moment?" She directed them to several chairs placed around a low, black laquered table.

A few minutes later the telephone on the woman's desk rang. She didn't speak, but after a moment hung up the receiver and arose from her desk to direct them towards the inner door. It was the same inner door, and the same office, that McAllister had been in when he had seen Robert Chun Ling a month earlier. But it was different now. The French Provincial furniture that had seemed out of place before was gone, replaced by strikingly angular modern pieces. A large red, blue and black abstract oil by Calder hung on one wall, the simple images suspended and balanced on the white canvas. It looked like an original.

Behind a wide rosewood desk in the middle of the room, a small man, elegantly dressed, stood up. He remained behind the desk, as if protected by it, but extended a thin bony hand to each of his guests in turn. His grip was firm and sure.

"I am Joseph Lo. What can I do for you?"

Mason introduced the three of them. They remained standing until Lo motioned them to several chairs in front of the desk. Mason's partner didn't sit, but instead chose to stand further back, near the door.

Mason began. "Mr. Lo, the reason we're here is that a young man, a fugitive from San Francisco named Wilbur Quan, was found hiding in a building in Hong Kong." Mason glanced at a piece of paper in his hand, "At 22 Queens Place." The agent paused. "Have you ever heard of this man?" McAllister watched Lo's thin shoulders tighten imperceptibly as he listened to the FBI agent.

Lo shook his head firmly, his words clipped. " I've never heard the name that you mentioned. Of course, that is my building, but it is managed locally by my business associates in Hong Kong."

"How about San Li, who owned a flower shop on Grant Avenue in Chinatown?"

Lo stiffened for a brief moment, but then again shook his head, a slight frown creasing his forehead. "No, I don't believe so."

186

"You were a business acquaintance of Mr. Samuel Twan, the previous chairman of this bank?"

"Of course. Until his...demise. Most unfortunate." Lo seemed to relax slightly.

Mason continued. "Could you tell us what type of business you were in together?"

"Well, investments, primarily. I worked with many of his clients here, in international investments mostly. That's what I have done for many years, here and abroad, mostly in Hong Kong."

McAllister spoke up. "Mr Lo, several weeks ago I came to this bank and spoke with the president, then a Mr. Robert Ling. I'm just curious. Where is Mr. Ling now?"

"Mr. Ling was actually acting-president after the death of Mr. Twan, as another chief executive officer was elected by the Board of Trustees. Sadly, his health, too, was also failing...." Lo's voice trailed off.

"Mr. Lo," Mason chose his words carefully, as he leaned further forward on his chair, watching closely the face of the man in front of him. "Each of the people that we have mentioned–Wilbur Quan, San Li, Samuel Twan, and Robert Chun Ling, has been linked to a group, an organization, called Gojin. This group, Gojin, has been connected to a variety of criminal offenses. Did you know that?" All three of them stared at Joseph Lo.

"No." The word was soft, but sharp, and spoken a little too quickly, as Lo sat more upright and forward in his chair. The FBI agent at the door tensed, as by reflex his right hand moved up and under his coat. "No." he paused with a calmer voice, "I have not heard of this...this Gojin." He continued to gaze at the FBI agent.

"I don't believe you, Mr. Lo. I don't believe you because this morning you were identified as the new leader of Gojin. As the man who followed in Samuel Twan's footsteps not only here, in the bank but within Gojin as well." He paused for a moment. "You were connected with all of the organization's activities; heroin and cocaine trafficking on the streets and in the public schools, money laundering, extortion, prostitution. And murder."

"I don't know what you are talking about! I told you, I have never heard of any of these people, or any such thing!" Lo's face was dark, impenetrable. "Gojin Tong you say! Who would put up these false accusations! "

Mason stood up and leaned over Lo's desk, putting his face directly in front of the other man's. His voice was soft but firm. "Tong is your word, not ours, Mr. Lo." He paused. "And it was Wilbur Quan. This morning at nine a.m., here in San Francisco, Wilbur Quan identified you as the man responsible for directing the murders of three members of the Wan Fung Tong in a Chinatown restaurant in the middle of the day, among thousands of tourists back in October!" The FBI agent pulled an envelope out of his coat pocket and slapped it down on the desk. "This is a warrant for your arrest. Read it!"

"This cannot be!" A look of shock and anger took over Lo's face. "He would not." Lo's eyes, wide with controlled rage and dismay, fixed upon the three men. "He took a vow to never tell....." His frail body seemed to collapse into the large chair in which he sat.

"Wilbur Quan is now in the Federal Witness Protection Program. He bought his freedom by breaking his vow to you."

Joseph Lo was silent for a long moment before he spoke again, nearly to himself. "How was I not informed that you had found him in Hong Kong. I had him in the building, specifically to be watched." He stared into the distance, at some unseen image beyond the confines of the room.

"Your informants were, shall we say, temporarily subdued, so that they couldn't reach you."

Lo was pale, and began to tremble slightly. Joe McAllister saw that now was the time. His voice was quiet and emphatic. "Have you heard of a man named Dr. Jack Phillips, a neurosurgeon here in San Francisco, who practices at Saint Joseph's Hospital?"

Joseph Lo looked at him blankly. He had collapsed even further into his chair, as though he might disappear completely into the cushions, and remained silent.

"Do you know the man I'm speaking of?" The detective's voice was sharper.

"Yes." They could barely hear his reply.

"Why in God's name have you been trying to kill him? Why? After he tried to save Samuel Twan's life?" McAllister was on the edge of his chair, staring hard at Lo.

The thin man began to shake his head. "But he was a part of it. He was responsible for Sam Twan's death."

"The man's injuries were fatal! Not even God could have saved him!"

"He failed on purpose."

"So you want to kill him for revenge, like you killed the others?"

Lo sat silently, unmoving, still staring ahead at nothing. McAllister's hands clenched involuntarily as he gazed at Lo. He had to get this man to talk, to bring together the things he didn't understand.

"Mr. Lo, why did you deposit fifty thousand dollars into your personal account in this bank, on September 18th of this year?"

The two FBI agents both looked at McAllister with surprise, and then back at the small man behind the desk.

Finally, Lo spoke with slightly more strength. "Gojin Tong has existed, grown and flourished, and protected its members and their families since the reign of terror by the Guilds in Chinatown more than a hundred years ago! Under Samuel Twan, Gojin had remained all powerful. But the Wan Fung Tong, they were growing too, dangerously, because they have no respect, and they wanted what was ours."

Joseph Lo paused, and then continued, as if he were speaking to himself. "After Twan's death, they had to be controlled, to be shown a lesson. A sudden blow to weaken them. It was necessary. It is the way of the Tongs."

"The fifty thousand dollars?"

Lo remained silent for a long time. "To kill for revenge alone is foolish, Mr. McAllister. We are not a foolish people." He paused again, looking into the detective's eyes. "In business, all things have their price...."

McAllister stared as the remark burned in his mind. He couldn't believe what he was hearing. "Then the money was paid to you for Jack Phillips' death?" he asked, incredulous.

"It was a simple matter to arrange. Once the members of the tong, the young warriors, believed that he had a part in Samuel Twan's death...that he was actually responsible for their leader's death...he became the most guilty one of all." He paused. "But I will say no more. I must speak to my lawyer now." The frail man's black eyes focused on McAllister, and held him, motionless, for a long moment.

"Who is Chien? S. Chien?"

Lo continued to stare at him. "A woman. A woman that I have met only once. After Samuel Twan's death."

"Now you will have it stopped." McAllister's voice was firm. It wasn't a request. "Gojin must leave Phillips alone. He did nothing wrong. He was not influenced by this Wan Fung Tong! He tried to save Twan, not kill him for God's sake! You know that! It must be stopped." He stared at Lo.

It took a long time for Lo to answer. He coughed slightly. "It can't be stopped."

"Why?" The aging detective was on his feet in front of the man.

Lo's voice seemed resigned, as he looked with distant eyes at the detective. "Many years ago, there was a boy, an immigrant boy from Taiwan, without parents, who ran in the streets of San Francisco alone. He had nothing. He was nothing. Samuel Twan took this boy, and raised him, fed him, taught him to fight, to survive and to be proud. He looked upon Samuel Twan as a father." Lo paused. "For him the death of this doctor is much more than a business arrangement, and has little to do with the survival of Gojin." Lo stared up into McAllister's eyes. "It is more than for revenge...."

"Where is he? We must find him."

"You won't find him now. He left San Francisco yesterday."

"Where did he go?" McAllister's voice was abrupt, angry, and frustrated. Lo remained silent. Suddenly the detective reached over the desk and grasped the man's shirt, pulling him up out of his chair.

"Hey!" Mason and the other FBI agent jumped up and tried to pull the big man away. But McAllister held on, bringing Joseph Lo's face close to his own.

"Where? Tell me!" His gaze bored into the man, ignoring the two FBI agents tearing at his arms.

Lo's voice was a choked whisper. "Canada."

16

In the low, late afternoon sun they drove along a wooded peninsula lined with dark rocky beaches. They had spent the day driving up Vancouver Island, theirs one of the few cars on the highway, passing through one small resort town to another. The towns were all but closed up for the winter, save for the few retirees and working people that lived there year round. It was cold, but clear, with high clouds that stretched above them, coming over the island, from the west. They had stopped a few times, to get out of the car for a brief while, and look at the views to the east, of the smaller islands in the straits between Vancouver Island and the mainland. They stopped once to eat in a roadside diner. Afterwards, back in the car, Jack unfolded a ferry schedule on his lap and then pulled his wristwatch out of the glove compartment and glanced at it.

"It looks like we can make the four o'clock ferry at Comox if we hurry." He glanced at Barbara, as she concentrated on driving the narrow road. "What time is it now?" she asked.

"Nearly three-thirty." He folded the schedule back up and stretched his arms, tensing and relaxing his shoulders. The pain in his hand was much better, even with the dressing change that they had done that morning, before leaving the Empress Hotel in Victoria. The infection seemed to be clearing.

"Dad, what's this ferry like? Big like the last one?" Darian stuck his head over the back of the seat and looked at his father.

Jack turned towards him and ruffled his son's hair. "No, a lot smaller, as I remember. More like the ones I used to ride on with my father when I was your age."

"Neat! How far is it across the water to where we're going?"

"I'm not sure, probably eight or ten miles."

Barbara turned onto a smaller road where a sign directed them to the ferry terminal. They drove away from the beach, into a densely forested area, the road cutting through the middle of a high growth of evergreens across a peninsula. After ten minutes more, the forest opened up at a narrow but deep water bay, the road ending at the wooden structure of the terminal. A small ferry, white-painted and open at both ends, was docked in the berth, loading the few cars and trucks that were making the trip. Barbara pulled up to a small booth, and bought passage for the car. Then they drove forward and down the ramp onto the back of the ferry, waved forward by a crewman in greasy overalls. The boat rocked a little on the water, as they got out of the car and went up an enclosed flight of narrow stairs into a small sitting area and galley.

"Do you want anything?" Barbara asked Jack as she went up to the service line and bought a cup of coffee for herself. Darian had a soda, and was eyeing the corn chips behind the glass counter. Jack shook his head. They sat for a while at one of the formica tables. A few minutes later, Jack got up and walked toward the back of the cabin. He opened the door and stepped over the high sill and onto the outer deck. The ferry was beginning to move, the deck shuddering under the force of the diesel engines. He watched the ferry terminal, falling away behind them. Behind the terminal, to the west, the sun was beginning to drop behind the island mountains, the sky above turning a faint salmon pink.

"How is your hand, daddy?" Jack hadn't noticed Christine come out onto the deck behind him. He turned and smiled at her.

"It feels a lot better today, thanks." He paused for a moment "How are you doing?" Jack looked closely at his daughter. All day she had still been quiet, not herself. He was still worried about her.

"I'm better. I don't know. I still feel...so weird. It's so unfair what's happening to us!" She looked down at the grey deck.

"It *is* unfair, Christine!" He took a deep breath. "It is...but it's something that we don't have any control over. Those people have no sense. They can't be reasoned with. The only thing that we could do was to get away from it, for now." Jack spoke softly, emphatically "But we will be back. Our lives are not over, thank God. And we have each other, that's the most important thing."

They stood together, silently, looking at the water which had turned a metallic grey-blue under the darkening sky, reflecting the variegated reds of the high cumulus clouds in the sunset. The ferry moved quickly through a low chop.

"I killed him, daddy," Her words were soft, so soft that he nearly didn't hear them above the rumble of the diesel engines. Christine continued to gaze into the distance.

"What?" Jack reached forward and gently turned her face towards his own. Her eyes were filled with tears. "What did you say?" he whispered.

"I killed him daddy. I know I did!" Her words were anguished. "The man in the tunnels, the one that I hit to get away! I hit him again and again, with the board. I couldn't stop! Until he wasn't breathing! I feel so...so badly about that!" She buried her face in her father's shoulder.

Jack stood in numb silence. Emory McTaub had reported to him that they had found an Asian man's body, and that it had probably been the one from the tunnels. But the FBI agent had said that the man they found had probably died from a drug overdose. That is what they had told Christine, later on, and Jack had believed what the FBI agent had said.

He took a deep breath, holding his daughter tightly to him. "Christine, listen to me! Whatever you did, you had to do to escape from there. It was in self-defense. They weren't going to let you go!"

Jack felt a quiet sadness as he thought about what she had said. His daughter now lived with the burden of knowing that she had taken away the life of another. He looked, unseeing, over the darkening and roughened texture of the ocean for a long moment. Then he continued on, in a quiet voice. "Don't you ever think that you did anything wrong." He pulled her head up again and looked into her eyes. "Do you hear me? Don't ever think that!"

"But I feel it, daddy!"

"Don't!" He held her tightly in his arms. "Please, don't." Jack had witnessed, and in his practice, he had lived through, so much death. Patients that could not be saved, during his training, in Viet Nam, even now. And occasionally it was the death of a patient that could, perhaps, have been saved, but hadn't. It frightened him to realize that in the process he had become numb to it, that he had begun to view death as just another routine part of the profession that he had chosen. But Christine. That she, at such a young age had been forced to witness it, to feel responsible for another person's death. *The burden that she must feel....* Jack closed his eyes as he held her close to him. Deep hatred for the ones that had caused this welled once more inside him.

"Jack?" Barbara had opened the door of the cabin and leaned out into the evening air. "Isn't it cold out here?" She looked at the two of them, seeming slightly puzzled.

"We'll be in in just a minute, OK?" He tried to control his voice, but kept his arms around his daughter, who, to his extreme gratification, held onto him tightly. Barbara closed the door and went back inside the cabin. After a few minutes more of silently holding his daughter, he looked down. "Are you OK?"

She nodded, her head still pushed into his jacket.

"Let's go inside."

Forty minutes later the ferry slowed, as the lights of the harbor terminal at Powell River grew larger. They went back down the stairs and got into the car once again. Slowly, the boat docked, and a steel ramp was lowered, clanging onto the end of the ferry. Barbara pulled forward and up the ramp onto the access road.

"What do you want to do?" She glanced over at her husband.

"Why don't we have dinner, and then try to find some groceries to take out to the island. I can call up to Lund, and let Mr. Svensen know we're coming up."

The Lund hotel was run by an elderly couple, the Svensens. The husband, a longtime friend of Jack's father, occasionally checked on Phillips' house out on Cortes Island during the winter months. They also had a boat that Jack used whenever he and the family came up to the island.

Barbara drove through the small town of Westview, a mile south of the huge pulp and paper mill which sprawled below the dam at the mouth of the Powell River. When she found an open restaurant, she pulled over and parked the car.

An hour later they had eaten, and picked up groceries at a small convenience store. They drove through the town of Powell River, with its one movie theater, and two banks. A few Christmas decorations hung in the store windows, somewhat forlorn in the darkness. It was seven o'clock now, and there were few people on the street. The town was set on a hill above the paper mill, and below, clouds of white steam poured from the massive stacks. A small city of lights illuminated the mill and lent a glow to the steamy haze overhead. The paper mill ran at all hours, day and night, the workers rotating on three overlapping shifts.

They crossed the narrow bridge spanning Powell Lake above the dam and followed the two-lane road eight miles further up the Malaspina Peninsula, through dense forests of fir and alder trees, past the Indian reservation, and finally to Lund, at the northern tip of the peninsula.

Swedish immigrants had named the town after the city of Lund, when they had come from Sweden to British Columbia in the 1800s. Lund had always been as it was now, a village formed by a cluster of houses and a small hotel set on the edge of a small sheltered bay. Lund stood at the northern end of the coastal highway; a road that began in South America and ran the length of the continent went no further than this. The general store and post office next to the hotel served the more isolated people who lived further north. Some of the men in the village fished for a living, but most worked in the logging camps.

Jack's father had been a close friend of the Svensens. When Jack was young, they would come up here to fish, and in the summers, to camp and swim in the clear water.

Barbara pulled the station wagon into the parking lot in front of the hotel. It had recently been expanded, with a large white clapboard structure that had added ten rooms. The older part of the hotel was really just a large house, where they had been renting rooms for more than forty years. The house was also painted white, and the Svensens lived here, with a few long-term boarders.

As they climbed out of the car, the front door of the house opened and out came a short man with a shock of white hair. At seventy, Per Svensen was still strong and active.

"Well, I'll be. Jack, it really is you! And Barbara and the children!" Svensen still had a noticeable accent despite his fifty years of residence in Canada. He shook Jack's hand briskly, with a strong grip. "I couldn't believe it when you called earlier. Come in, come in! Mrs. Svensen is waiting for you!"

They went into the house and into the living room, which was dominated by a large fireplace, over which hung a moose head. Every time they came up to Lund, Darian had to hear again how Mr. Svensen had shot the animal and dragged it out of the woods by himself, many years before. In one corner, a small evergreen had been brought in and decorated for Christmas in the traditional Swedish manner, with delicate homemade wooden and paper ornaments, cookies and other edibles, and real candles. The candles would be lit only for a brief time on Christmas Eve.

A large woman came in, carrying a tray with coffee and cookies. "Welcome to our home! It's such a surprise to see you this time of year!" Mrs. Svensen also ran the store and was the local postmaster. She put the tray down and hugged each of them. Then she poured coffee, and juice for the children.

Per Svensen sat down in a large leather chair. Jack saw him looking at the bandages on Jack's hand. "So you decided to celebrate your Christmas up here in the wilderness?"

"We decided to come up kind of suddenly." He nodded to his bandages. "I got hurt, and can't work for a while."

Jack paused. He had been wondering about what to say to them. "Actually, Per, I was shot." Jack heard Mrs. Svensen let out a short gasp. She stood holding the tray and staring at him.

"It's kind of complicated, but some months ago I operated on a man, apparently the ring leader of some kind of gang, and he died. He had been shot in the head and wouldn't have survived either way. Somehow, though, this gang has held me responsible for his death. Since that time, there have been several attempts on my life. Once they kidnapped Christine. We decided after this," he held up his left hand, "to get away. To leave San Francisco for a while. I don't know how long we will be here, but hopefully not for too long."

Per Svensen had been sitting quietly in his chair, his face becoming grim. "What about the police? Can't they stop these people?"

"They have been trying, and the FBI, too. But so far, nothing."

"Well, you will be safe here. We know who comes and who goes from Lund."

"Very few people know that we are up here. We should be safe," Jack replied.

"You will be safe! Tonight you will stay with us. In the morning we can go out to your house on the island." Mr. Svensen turned to look at Darian. "And you! This time I will finally teach you how to fish properly!"

The next morning, they got up late. Jack was finally sleeping more soundly, no longer haunted by the violent images and nightmares of just a few days ago. He looked out the window. There was a high overcast, but otherwise the weather was clear. Darian was already up, out on the docks looking over the boats with Mr. Svensen. Later, they ate a large breakfast prepared by Mrs. Svensen. Afterwards, they loaded the supplies and luggage onto one of Svensen's boats, a wooden, thirty-two foot cruiser with an enclosed cabin. Jack had used this boat before many times. It was old but in excellent condition.

Jack started the inboard engine and let it warm up. The smell of oil and gasoline filtered up from the bubbling water at the exhaust pipes, behind them. Barbara and the children got into the boat; with a push from Mr. Svensen, Jack pulled away from the dock and started out into the deeper water. It was calm in the bay as Jack opened up the throttle. They picked up speed and the bow came up as the boat began to plane. He headed towards the northern edge of the bay. Cortes Island was a mile or so north of them. Even within the enclosed cabin, the winter air was cold, and quickly Jack's left hand began to throb and hurt. He tucked the hand inside of his down jacket and steered with his right hand.

Jack followed the coast, staying a quarter of a mile off the shoreline, where dense forest reached down to the water and narrow rocky beaches. As they got out of the bay and into more open water, a low rolling chop came up, and Jack pulled back on the throttle, allowing the boat to drop back down, deeper into the water.

Jack enjoyed the feel of the boat underneath him. It was good to be away. *To be here.* He felt isolated and protected. Darian stood beside him looking through the plexiglass windshield of the boat. Barbara and Christine stayed down in the cabin, out of the cold.

After ten minutes, they could see the silhouette of Cortes Island directly ahead. It was about a mile long and a half mile wide, separated by a shallow passage of clear water, four hundred yards off the mainland. Their's was the only house on the island, set on the leeward, protected side. The boat moved steadily through the rolling ocean. To their left, Jack could see the other islands in the archipelago: Savory, Kinghorn, Twin, Redondo and Hernandez. And further west on the horizon he could see the vast outline of Vancouver Island, which protected the entire coastline here from the open Pacific Ocean beyond.

Jack steered in towards the shallow straits to the lee of Cortes Island, staying away from the cluster of underwater rocks that he knew bristled just under the surface along its southern tip. He motored into the passageway for two hundred yards. He could see his house now, set on a rocky embankment above the water, the wooden structure dark under the overcast sky. Their dock extended north of the house, into a small, well-protected bay. Jack's father had first built the home, actually just a cabin really, when Jack was a young boy, from logs hand-cut in the nearby forest. After his father had died, Jack had kept the place, although he hadn't come up for years during medical school and his residency in neurosurgery, because there was just no time. After finishing though, he had started to return again, bringing his family up during the summertime. Later, Jack had done major renovations to the house, enlarging it, providing Barbara with the comforts that she had wanted.

"OK, Darian, can you get ready to secure the bow line? Be careful, the deck may be icy." Jack watched carefully as his son climbed out onto the bow, and as Jack guided the boat up to the dock, Darian threw the bow line over and then jumped onto the wooden structure. The boy looped the rope around a low stanchion, as his father had taught him during their summers here. He began to pull on the line, holding the boat as Jack swung the stern in, and then shut down the engine. Jack went back and threw the coiled stern line onto the dock. Then he got off and secured the line onto another stanchion, as his son tied the bow line down. Finally, Jack reached for the spring line, and snugged the boat up against the rubber padding on the side of the dock.

"Good job!" Jack smiled at his son, as Barbara and Christine came out from the cabin of the boat, each struggling with an armload of supplies.

Barbara looked around them at the inlet, and then at the house, and finally up at the darkening sky. "I like it here better in the summertime," she said simply.

"Think of it as a rustic Christmas this year." Jack still felt slightly euphoric about being on the island, released from the tension of the past several days. They all helped to move their supplies up the wooden walkway to the large deck that surrounded the house. Darian ran back and forth, helpfully carrying bags of groceries and other supplies, as Jack began to unlock the doors.

Inside, it was cold, and the wooden floor creaked as they walked into the unused rooms. Barbara began to open the shutters and pull the dust covers off the furniture, as Jack went to the back of the house with Darian and brought logs from a sheltered woodpile back into the fireplace. After a time, they got both the wood stove in the kitchen and the fireplace in the living room started. Slowly, the house began to warm.

Later, a light rain began to fall, and Jack stood looking through the large picture window which faced towards the south. Across the grey water he could see the tip of the Malaspina Peninsula. To the left, a dense growth of alder trees came abruptly down to the water's edge along the rugged coastline. The trees appeared dark and heavy in the rainfall. The house was warm now, and the kids were lying on blankets and large pillows in front of a blazing fire in the living room. Jack gazed at his children. *It wasn't perfect, but by God they were alive and now they were protected.* He felt secure here, finally in a safe place. Unconsciously, Jack clenched his left hand, and felt the painful tightness, and for a long time he watched the water and the trees.

*   *   *

"I don't know where Dr. Phillips is, I told you." Mrs. Brannan sat at her desk outside of Dr. Phillips' office, and looked up at the big man standing in front of her. Joe McAllister leaned forward and put his hands on the edge of the desk.

"He hasn't called since he left? I told you, we have reason to believe that his life still may be in danger. We need to contact him as soon as possible, to warn him."

McAllister's voice reflected his exasperation as he looked at the woman. "We think that he may have gone to Canada. Someone may be following him there. Do you know where he might have gone?" He watched the middle-aged woman shake her head. "Does he know anybody there? Relatives? This is very important. Please, think!"

McAllister had come to Saint Joseph's Hospital directly from the Central Station, after he and the two FBI agents had taken Joseph Lo into custody and questioned him further. The detective was hoping that he could get some information, a phone number, anything, to warn Phillips.

Joseph Lo hadn't known the details, or if he did know, he wasn't willing to divulge them. All they could get out of him was that a young lieutenant within Gojin, by the name of Nim Choy, had broken into the Phillips house and found something, some information, Lo didn't know what, and had abruptly left for Canada two days before. Nim Choy would continue to hunt Phillips down until he found him. For this young man, said Lo, revenge on Jack Phillips, the man that he held responsible for Sam Twan's death was much more than a simple business arrangement. It was a personal vendetta.

But that led to another part to the puzzle: Joseph Lo. Apparently, for Lo, the doctor's death was motivated by one thing, pure and simple, and that was money. Lo himself had admitted to them that he had concocted the story about Phillips letting Twan die on the operating table, to manipulate the other members of the tong into going after the surgeon. The real question was: *who else wanted Jack Phillips killed?* Enough to pay Lo fifty thousand dollars to arrange it? It just didn't make any sense. They had gone over Phillips with a fine-tooth comb looking for a reason that someone would want him dead. He was squeaky clean. Well, they hadn't completely finished with their questioning of Lo, and already McAllister had someone working on the identity of the woman who had paid him the fifty thousand dollars.

Louise Brannan's voice broke into McAllister's thoughts. "Sometimes he went to Canada for vacations. He had gone there a lot when he was younger. But I really don't know where. And he hasn't called to tell us where he is." Mrs. Brannan was firm. Dr. Phillips had not wanted anyone to know where he was, and she wasn't going to breach that trust. But her doubts and fear began to grow when the detective mentioned Canada. How could the police have found that out?

"Do you mind if I take a look through his office? You don't realize how important this is." McAllister knew that he didn't have a search warrant. She didn't have to let him in if she didn't want to. "Please?" His voice was pleading.

Mrs. Brannan looked at the man more closely. His grey hair was too long, and obviously hadn't been washed in days. And his clothes were rumpled and worn. So far, she reflected, the police had been of absolutely no help to Dr. Phillips. Why should it change now? But the big man remained standing in front of her desk, and continued to look at her, imploring, waiting for an answer.

"All right," she said finally, "in here."

The secretary directed McAllister into Phillips' office. After a preliminary glance around the room, taking in the tasteful and expensive furnishings, he sat down at the desk. Louise Brannan followed him in, and stood at the door watching the detective as he began to look through the drawers. He didn't really know what he was looking for. McAllister flipped through the files: they appeared to all be medical in nature. He glanced up at the secretary.

"Did he have a personal address book?"

"Usually it's right there on the desk, or in the first drawer." Mrs. Brannan walked over to the desk, and looked herself. "It's gone. Sometimes he kept it with him in his briefcase, though."

"We have that. The briefcase was still in his hospital room after he had left. The address book wasn't in it." McAllister continued to rummage through the material in the drawers. Nothing. He closed the last drawer and started to get up from the chair. Frustrated, his eyes scanned the desk top once again.

"What's this?" He picked up the small wooden-framed picture. It was Phillips, and his wife and kids, standing in front of a house of some sort. It looked like it was taken during a vacation. "Where was this taken?" His voice was louder, as he looked more sharply at the woman. "Tell me!" he demanded. The secretary stood unmoving, staring at the picture that she had forgotten was there. She opened her mouth to speak, but no words came out.

"Cortes Island." Louise Brannan froze, and then turned towards the male voice that came from behind her, in the doorway of the office.

"That's Cortes Island, in British Columbia. It's OK, Louise, let me talk to him." She moved to the side a little as Fred Steele came in and slumped onto the couch under the Leroy Neiman painting. He was still wearing his green surgical scrubs, under a wrinkled white coat. He looked exhausted.

"In Canada?" McAllister sat back down at the desk. He noticed Louise Brannan quietly leave the room.

The grey-haired neurosurgeon nodded, as he fished a cigarette out of a packet in his white coat. He lit it and took a deep pull. "That's probably where he went. He called me, a few days ago, and said that he was in Washington State, on his way up to Canada. He was with his family, driving in their car. He has a place up there, on this small island north of Vancouver. They usually go there during the summertime."

"Is there a telephone there, or some way to contact him?"

Steele shook his head. "I don't think so. It's pretty rustic. He likes it that way. I'm not even sure exactly where it is, actually." He leaned forward and stretched his aching shoulders. "What's going on, anyway?"

"Apparently one of the members of this gang that's been after him broke into his house up in Mill Valley. He must have found something there that gave him an idea of where Phillips was going. Now he's left for Canada to finish the job. That's all I know." McAllister shook his head. "I'm just hoping that this guy doesn't know exactly where this Cortes Island is. That might give me a little time to warn Phillips."

"Christ Almighty! Why don't these people leave him alone! Jack never did anything wrong! Don't they know that?" Steele shook his head, as he finished his cigarette and got up.

"Apparently not. Not this one anyway." McAllister also stood up. He looked more closely at the neurosurgeon. The man looked worn and haggard. "You all right, Doc?" he asked.

Steele smiled slightly. "Been pretty busy, with Jack's practice to keep up and all. I just did a big aneurysm case." He paused. "With Jack gone, I'm responsible for the Institute. Look, keep me informed about what's going on, would you? And if there's anything else that I can do to help, let me know."

The younger man nodded at McAllister and then turned and left the detective standing in the office alone with his thoughts. After a moment, he sat back down at the desk and dialed the Central Station number. He glanced at his watch. Nearly four o'clock. He reached the captain and quickly detailed the new information to his superior.

"Well, we can get a hold of the RCMP in Canada, and give them a description of this guy, Choy," the captain replied. "I'll have them pull his file, if he has one, and we can FAX a picture up to them. Maybe we'll get lucky and they will pick him up. They can probably get out to that island by boat or something and warn the doctor."

As he sat listening, McAllister's eyes focused on the picture of Phillips and his family. He felt a subtle, vague, squeezing pain in his chest. He thought about the pain. It had recurred several times in the past week, but he refused to go and see a doctor about it. His own life was nearly finished, he knew. And actually he looked forward to the time when he would be free. Free to be with his wife again, finally. But this man Phillips, he reflected as he stared at the smiling, confident face in the photograph. The man was young, smart, and had everything to live for. The detective made up his mind.

"Listen, Captain, would you leave that picture on my desk when you get it, and have one of the girls try to get some maps for me, of British Columbia, around Vancouver? I just want to take a look at the area that we're dealing with here."

"No problem."

"Thanks." McAllister hung up the telephone for a moment as he considered objectively what his gut was telling him to do. Then he dialed once more.

"Information, may I help you?"

"Yes. Give me some airlines, would you? Air Canada, Western, and TWA." He crimped the receiver into the side of his neck and with his free hand lit a cigarette as he began to scribble down the numbers.

17

Nim Choy walked away from the wooden doorway next to the Army-Navy department store. It had snowed overnight, and the curbs and sidewalks were covered with an icy white layer except where the early morning traffic had left tire tracks on the street. The drunks on the sidewalks were gone now, driven into doorways and shelters by the snow. The collar of Choy's thin jacket was turned up, as he walked north towards the high-rise buildings and elegant hotels of downtown Vancouver.

In his right hand, Choy gripped the handle of his black vinyl satchel. Hidden in it was the thirty-eight caliber handgun that his contact had finally brought to him the night before, with one box of ammunition. Unmarked, untraceable weapons were apparently harder to get in Canada than back in the United States. It had taken an extra day of waiting. A day Nim Choy had spent hidden in the small room, reviewing maps, photographs, and making his plans. He had committed to memory the location of Cortes Island, imagining how he must get there on the water from Powell River, or further north, from the smaller town of Lund. He would avoid Lund, if possible, he reflected as he thumbed through Dr. Phillips' address book. In the book there was an address in Lund, next to the name Svenson. Probably a friend of the doctor's, he guessed. What he didn't know was exactly where the doctors house was located on the island. The photos that he had in his possession gave him no clue. But the island didn't look that big. He was confident that he would find it.

Choy turned and walked into the bitter wind towards the west, up a rising hill several city blocks, to the Hotel Vancouver. He walked into the hotel through the heavy brass front doors, and went directly to the Bell Captain's desk.

"Where are your rental car offices?" His voice was soft, nearly gentle. The man directed him towards several discreetly situated cubicles near the back of the building.

Choy waited in a short line of people, most of them in business suits, and when his turn came rented a compact car. He used the same California driver's license and a credit card he had used to buy his airline ticket. The name on the license was John Chan. He smiled to himself as the girl behind the desk busily filled out the papers. How many John Chans must there be in the world? He had used the same credit card to hire the lawyer that had gotten Wilbur Quan out on bail in San Francisco.

He placed his satchel on the passenger seat and started the car, letting it warm up as he turned the heater onto high and consulted a map of the city. The car was equipped with snow tires, but he was not accustomed to driving in snow. As he pulled out of the driveway of the hotel, he drove carefully, making his way towards the Lyons Gate Bridge. The narrow three-lane bridge was busy with morning commuter traffic coming in from the other direction on two lanes as Choy drove on the single lane moving north, away from the city. He followed the road signs towards Horseshoe Bay, to the northwest of Vancouver, where the first ferry would be leaving to head up the coast, towards Powell River.

Choy was hungry, but ignored the discomfort. Perhaps he would eat on the ferry. As he finally reached the highway, the traffic was heavy and moved slowly because of the snow. He checked his watch. He had thought to give himself extra time to get to the ferry terminal, but he was becoming alarmed. It was ten or twelve miles to Horseshoe Bay. Should the slow traffic continue, he might miss the first departure at nine a.m. It would be a two-hour delay until the next ferry would be leaving. A light snow began to fall and collect on the edge of the windshield wiper. He turned the wipers on. The snow from the previous evening had been transformed into a dirty brown slush as it built up on the sides of the road. The highway switched back and forth, winding uphill along the coastal mountain range north of Vancouver. Ahead, a sedan went into a sweeping turn a bit too fast. The driver, an American, and not used to snowy conditions, quickly jammed on the brakes to slow down, which immediately locked all four wheels, forcing the car into a skid on the icy road. The sedan crashed heavily into the adjacent embankment, which forced the car behind to slow abruptly. This driver, a Canadian, pumped his brakes expertly, avoiding a skid; however, to his disgust, as he watched in the mirror, he was promptly rear-ended by a woman driver, distracted by her child in the back seat. All of the traffic behind them came to a complete halt. Angrily, Nim Choy pulled to a stop as he surveyed the scene ahead of him. There obviously was no way to get around the multi-car accident, and he watched and waited in frustration as the drivers and passengers of the damaged automobiles got out and began to inspect the damage in the dampness and the cold.

*   *   *

"Look Dad, it's snowing!" Darian ran to the large picture window in the living room and stood looking out at the white scene. The wooden deck that surrounded the house was covered with snow, and across the water on the mainland, the trees were becoming frosted with a new layer of white. Darian watched the light flakes fall gently to the ground.

"Looks like it's going to be a real Christmas this year!" Jack sat drinking coffee in the kitchen, which opened out into the living room. He had gotten up at six-thirty, and had already worked to get the fireplace started, and refueled the woodstove which had burned throughout the night, warming the house. Then he had made coffee and puttered around the kitchen. He was beginning to use his left hand more now. He had taken the bandages off the night before and decided to leave them off. The infection on the fourth finger looked better, he thought. As he had gone through his morning chores, his eyes had repeatedly been drawn to the red incision. It was still a shock not to see his fingers where they should be. Finally, he had forced himself to look away. But, he reflected, thank God that it was his left hand. Had the injury occurred to his extremely dominant right hand, he was quite sure that he could not return to practicing neurosurgery, regardless of what the Chief of Orthopedics had to say.

"Can we go outside?" Darian came back and sat down in a chair next to his father.

"Later, we sure can. Why don't we go find ourselves a Christmas tree and cut it down?"

"OK! That sounds great, dad." Darian kept gazing out the window. "Won't it be cold though?" His voice was hesitant.

"Not if we dress for the snow. Do you want something to eat?"

"Yeah, I'm hungry. Can we make eggs?"

Jack nodded, and turned to see Barbara coming out from the bedroom. Still sleepy, she went to the stove and poured herself a cup of coffee.

"Good morning." Jack smiled at his wife. She nodded glumly. Barbara had never been a morning person.

"I'm going back into town later today, to see my friend Gordy Jefferson, and to call down to San Francisco. You want to come?"

She nodded. "I'd like to get some Christmas gifts, and pick up a few things I need for the house."

Jack got up out of his chair and began to prepare breakfast. The kitchen was fully equipped. In the early years here, Jack's father had cooked using only a wood stove. But after Jack had begun to bring his family up here, he had redone the kitchen with all of the modern conveniences. The appliances were powered by a gasoline-driven electrical generator in back of the house. Jack focused himself on making the eggs and bacon, and enjoyed the feeling of being useful once again.

Later they dressed, and he and Darian went outside. Jack could fit his left hand into a mitten, which kept the hand warm and prevented the incisions from hurting too badly. They walked out behind the house towards the center of the island, through which trails veined the pervasive, thick evergreens and scrub plants which covered most of the island. But the trails were overgrown now from disuse, and father and son were forced to move slowly, pushing the overhanging branches to the sides. The snow had stopped, but the air was bitingly cold, and their breath formed dense clouds of vapor in front of them.

"There's a good tree, Dad!" Darian excitedly moved off the trail a few feet and pointed at a small evergreen surrounded by low bushes. It was about six feet tall.

"That does look like a nice one," he agreed. "Do you want to take it?"

"Yeah!"

Jack used a small hatchet that he had brought, and cut away some of the brush from around the base of the tree. Then he gave the hatchet to his son. It looked big in his gloved hands.

"Now be careful. Try to cut it low, near the ground. Jack pushed on the upper trunk of the tree to bend it as Darian kneeled on the ground and chopped at the base. The wood was hard and brittle in the cold and it was slow going, but he kept at it, chopping until Jack felt the trunk finally start to give way. He kept pushing as the tree leaned further over, until finally it fell to the ground. Darian stood back up excitedly, breathing hard.

"Good job!" Jack grinned and patted his son on the back. "You've chopped down your first Christmas tree!"

Together they pulled the tree out of the scrub and began back along the trail towards the house. When they got the little tree onto the deck, Jack used the small axe to trim some of the bottom branches.

"When we go into town, we can get a metal stand for it, and some Christmas decorations." He leaned the tree up against the railing on the deck, and Darian went inside the house to bring his mother and sister out to look at his find. Jack stood with his family and admired the tree in the flat winter light. Even Christine seemed to be getting a bit more into the spirit of things, as she smiled approvingly. This wasn't turning out too badly after all, he reflected, with a subtle, rising sense of inner peace.

*　　　　　*　　　　　*

McAllister stood in the small office and stared at the manager of the air transport service.

"I told you, right now it looks like we will have to cancel the flight. It's still snowing all along the coast to Powell River."

The manager looked at the bulky, aging man in front of him. Even if this guy's story were true and he was a police detective, the manager wasn't about to risk one of his airplanes until the weather had cleared. He looked at the clock on the office wall. Ten minutes to nine. He turned back to McAllister.

"I'll be getting the next weather report at nine-thirty. I'll make a decision then, OK?"

McAllister had arrived in Vancouver at eleven-thirty the night before. He had quickly found that it would be impossible to get up the coast to Cortes Island right away. There were no flights at night, and the ferries didn't run again until the next morning. He had gotten a few hours of troubled sleep in a cheap motel near the airport, and at seven in the morning had been back to the ticket counter at Sunshine Coast Air, the only passenger airline that regularly serviced the coastline north of Vancouver. McAllister soon found that all flights had been canceled for that day due to weather. The ticket agent had told him that the only flights that might go up would be by a small, private air transport service that flew mostly cargo, and at the detective's request, pointed out where the office was located.

McAllister then had called the Royal Canadian Mounted Police, Powell River, but they were of little help. They promised to warn Dr. Phillips about the "possibility that the man had entered Canada", but they were unwilling to offer additional assistance for an unconfirmed threat. Their computer check had shown no one by the name of Nim Choy that had come through Customs. As if he were such a fool that he would use his own name, McAllister had fumed to himself.

The detective was waiting at the door of the air transport service office when the manager had arrived at eight a.m. Now he looked out at the leaden grey sky and then up at the clock, waiting for the nine-thirty weather report.

"You want some coffee?" The manager came back into the front office carrying two styrofoam cups. McAllister nodded and took the cup of steaming liquid.

"If they tell us the front is moving through, we can be in the air by noon." The small airline's usual cargo was packages and private mail, not passengers. But after McAllister had related his story, and backed it up by showing his gold detective's badge and two hundred dollars cash, the office manager was convinced. And willing to bend the rules a bit. The manager went back into the rear of the office to call the weather service once again.

McAllister continued to wait. He thought about Nim Choy, wondering what sort of weapon the man had. It was doubtful that he would have tried to smuggle one across the border. More likely that he had picked something up here. McAllister had left his own weapon behind. There had not been enough time to make the necessary arrangements to bring it with him on the flight. He hadn't even told the captain that he was leaving. To hell with it, he thought. They could take this trip out of his vacation time. Once again he opened up on his lap a detail map of Vancouver Island and the coast of British Columbia and looked at the small oval spot that was Cortes Island. One of a cluster of small islands between the northern end of Vancouver Island and the mainland in a place called Desolation Sound. North of a town called Lund. He folded the map, and rubbed his eyes.

The manager walked back out shaking his head. "Not yet, I'm afraid. Still snowing up north. The airport at Powell River is still closed." He paused. "Might be all day."

"Shit!" McAllister stood up, shaking his head and looking up at the clock once again. "You have any ideas on how I can get up there more quickly?"

"Well, the ferries are running, but by the time you rent a car and drive up the coast, it's going to take a good while. It's about a five-hour drive all together, with the two ferries and the island in between."

McAllister considered. And that's if you knew exactly where you were going. Just getting through the city of Vancouver could be slow going. He decided to wait it out.

"OK. I'm going to go get something to eat and make some calls. I'll be back." The manager nodded as McAllister went through the door. He went to a pay phone and once again dialed the local RCMP station in Powell River.

"Have you reached Dr. Phillips yet?" McAllister was brusque on the telephone.

"No, sir. We haven't sent a car up there yet. We've got a problem here in town that's tying up all of our units." McAllister stared at the telephone receiver with rising anger. Obviously, he was talking to some kind of a green, cub scout type. The officer's voice was high and nasal, with a polite exactness to his voice that the detective at this moment found irritating.

"When are you going to get around to it, for Christ's sake?" McAllister's frustration was obvious.

"We'll do it as soon as we can. Not yet, sir."

"How about a road block then?"

"Do you have any solid information that the suspect is coming into the area today?"

"No, I don't!"

"Then we can't do it."

He didn't bother responding to the guy, but viciously slammed the receiver down on its cradle, ignoring the few people in the terminal that were staring at him.

                    *   *   *

Per Svensen pulled on the bow line that Barbara threw to him and pulled them into the dock. He tied the rope and then quickly went to the other end of the boat and secured the stern line. Jack shut off the engine and stood up from the vinyl-covered captain's chair.

"So! How is your house? Is it still there?" Svensen smiled as he helped Darian and then Christine out of the boat and onto the dock.

"Just the way that we had left it," said Barbara.

"So you are back down already for a visit?"

"We're going into town for a few things." She looked at the kids. "For Christmas."

"I cut down our Christmas tree!" Darian exclaimed.

"Well, such a woodsman! Sometime I will take you to the real woods, where the trees are two hundred feet high!"

"Do you need anything from Powell River?" Jack asked the older man.

He shook his head. "No, we have everything we need. Have you eaten breakfast?"

"Yes we have, thank you, Per," said Barbara.

"Well, come in for a cup of coffee anyway! You must!"

Jack and Barbara looked at each other, and Jack shrugged his shoulders.

"You're sure that Mrs. Svensen won't mind?"

"Mind? Of course not! She would be angry at me for not making you stay, at least for a little while! Come in, come in!"

A half an hour later they began the drive back down the Malaspina Peninsula towards Powell River. As they drove by the Indian Reservation, with its small school house and low wooden buildings, Jack noticed an RCMP car pass them going the other direction, towards Lund. It was pleasant to see the police and not have their presence remind you that you had to watch where you went. That you had to fear for your life, because a group of maniacs were trying to kill you for no good reason.

They drove across the metal suspension bridge over Powell Lake, above the dam. Powell River was covered by the billowing steam from the smoke stacks of the paper mill. As they neared the mill, they could see men walking towards the front gates with their lunch pails. It must be change of shift, Jack thought; the men on graveyard switching with those on the morning shift. The mill ran continuously day and night to supply newspaper for the entire west coast, as far south as Los Angeles. His friend, Gordy Jefferson, once had told him that many of the men worked in the mill their entire adult lives. And usually their sons found jobs there as well, right out of High School. Several generations of men sometimes worked on the same massive piece of equipment. The mill was the economic and industrial core of the entire region.

Jack parked in the middle of town, near the shopping area. Most of the small, modest shops had Christmas decorations in the windows.

"I'm going to give Gordy a call, and find out what he's doing. Maybe

I'll walk up to the hospital and see him for a few minutes," Jack said, as they got out of the car.

"OK. Maybe Christine and I will go and do some shopping. And I need to exchange some American money for Canadian at the bank. Do you want to meet in an hour back here?" Barbara looked at him pointedly, nodding slightly towards Darian.

"That's fine." Jack glanced at his son and grinned. "Darian, do you want to go with me?" Barbara wanted to get their son's Christmas present without his being there.

"Yeah, OK. Can we look at some fishing poles and stuff?"

"Sure." Jack patted his son on the back and they began to walk towards the hospital, set on a hill above the paper mill.

*   *   *

The dark blue RCMP patrol car pulled into the parking area in front of the Lund Hotel. The officer, wearing a heavy coat, got out of the car and went to the front door and stepped inside. Mrs. Svensen was working at the small desk that served as an office in the front hallway of the main house. She was surprised by the visit. The police rarely came up the Lund unless there was a call about some kind of trouble or a road accident. She recognized the police officer from town but didn't remember his name.

"Good morning. Can I help you?"

"Maybe." The man pulled a notebook from the pocket of his coat and looked at a scribbled note. "I need to speak to an American. Doctor Jack Phillip is his name. I was told that he's probably out on Cortes Island. He apparently has a house or cabin out there?"

"Why yes, he does. But they aren't there now. In fact, you just missed them. About twenty minutes ago they from left here to go into town. What is this about?" Shielding the concern from her eyes, Mrs. Svensen looked at the man.

"I'd rather talk with the doctor about it directly, if I could."

"Please, speak to my husband. He's known Dr. Phillips since he was a boy. They are very good friends. We watch over their place when they aren't up here."

The officer hesitated. He wanted to get back into town. It was getting near lunch time. "All right, where is he?"

"I'll get him. Wait just a minute, please!" Mrs. Svensen hurried outside and towards the docks. In a few minutes, Per Svensen returned with her.

"Hello. What is the problem, officer?" The old man's face was flushed from exertion.

"We were contacted by an American detective, from San Francisco, who says that he has been working on a case that involves this Doctor

210

Phillips. Apparently, there have been some kinds of attacks on this doctor and his family."

"Yes there have, officer. Jack has told me so himself. It is a gang from San Francisco who have been doing this."

"Well, this is unsubstantiated, but the detective says that a man has entered Canada, and is coming up here, apparently intending to harm or even kill this doctor. The RCMP as yet has had no confirmation of this."

"What! Jack came up here thinking that this was safe, that no one would know that he was here! Do you know where this man is? Can't you stop him?"

The officer shook his head. "Right now we are awaiting confirmation from the Vancouver office, and from San Francisco. We don't know what the man looks like at this point, no way to prove his identification at all yet. When will Dr. Phillips be back here?"

"I'm not sure, probably in a couple of hours. They just went to do some shopping in town for Christmas."

The officer started towards the door. "Have him call us when he gets back, aye? And call us yourselves if you see anyone that is acting suspect or looks like they aren't from around here."

"I will. Thank you for coming." The officer left as Svensen looked at his wife, his face dark with concern. Then he walked back into his study. On the wall there was a polished wooden and glass cabinet. He unlocked the door and opened it, lifting out one of his hunting rifles.

His wife watched him from the doorway. "Per! What are you doing?" her voice anxious.

"We should be prepared. I am just checking to make sure that the gun is clean and ready, if we need it."

"You should leave this for the police!"

Per Svensen gazed at his wife for a moment, but then turned and walked with the rifle into the kitchen.

*   *   *

Jack sat on the edge of the paper-covered examining table, as Gordy Jefferson finished unwrapping the gauze dressing over his left hand. Jack watched his friend's eyes as the general surgeon held his hand by the wrist. Gordy appeared unperturbed as he inspected the incision over the amputation site. The stump of the fourth finger was still red and swollen around the blue nylon sutures, and Jack flinched as his friend pressed on the incision, trying to express any purulent fluid.

He looked up at Jack. "I'd say that they did a very nice job putting this back together. How does it feel?."

"The pain is a lot less than it was earlier, and so is the redness and swelling."

"Any fever?"

Jack shook his head.

Gordy pulled a roll of gauze out of a drawer and began to wrap the hand up again. "Well, it doesn't look like it's seriously infected. In a way, you were luckier than you might have been. If the bullet had gone through the center of the hand, there could have been damage to the median or ulnar nerve, as you very well know. At least as it is you'll still be able to operate."

"Yeah." Jack's voice was noncommittal.

"Those sutures should come out in a few days. I'll do that here for you if you want."

"I'd appreciate it."

"And how is the rest of you." Jefferson looked at the dark rings that were still under Jack's eyes. "Are you sleeping?"

"I am now. But boy, up until a day or two ago I was having these terrible nightmares. Not nightmares, recurring images really. I couldn't sleep, and would just lie there, bathing in sweat." He paused as he remembered the tortured nights after his injury. "It was bad."

Gordy Jefferson sat down on the edge of his tired wooden desk and regarded his friend curiously. "What kind of images?"

Jack hesitated. He didn't want Gordy to think that he was nuts. And Darian was right there, sitting in the large chair next to the desk.

"Well, it was kind of crazy. It was always the same image, of someone lifting a gun, a rifle, and firing...more like the Viet Namese during the war. It first started after I was shot." Jack glanced down at his son. Darian was looking up at him, listening intently. Jack dropped his gaze towards the floor.

"Well, we can talk more about it later." Gordy turned and looked at Darian. "Your dad's going to be all right. Are you two going to do some hunting with me while you're up here?"

Darian had kept looking up at his father, but then turned to the other man. "Sure, Dr. Jefferson."

Gordy looked at his wristwatch. "I think that I can probably get out of my afternoon appointments. It's pretty light today. What do you say we go down to my place for a visit?"

"I'll have to ask Barbara, but I think that would be fine."

"I'd like to hear a little more about this problem of yours. You remember how to get to my house, down at Grief Point?"

"Sure. What time do you want us there?"

"Come for lunch, and we can spend the afternoon. I'll finish up here and call Jennifer."

Jack put on his jacket and shook his friend's hand. "Thanks for taking a look at it."

"No problem at all. You know that. I'll see you later."

Jack and Darian left the hospital and walked out into the cold winter light of the morning.

18

Nim Choy stood on the upper deck of the ferry, watching the water move past as the large boat worked through the Jervis Inlet towards Saltery Bay, the final ferry stop before Powell River. He stood outside the plexiglass windbreak, at the railing near the front of the boat, feeling the cold air on his face and in his hair. He relaxed his mind, assured that things would go as planned. Kwan Tai was with him, guiding him. He had nearly missed the morning departure at nine o'clock because of the road accident. But the local police had arrived quickly and begun to direct traffic around the mishap. After he had been waved past the wreckage, he had driven as quickly as he dared, and made it just in time for the first ferry out of Horseshoe Bay. The ship's passage had taken nearly an hour. From the next terminal, at Langdale, he had driven north the length of the rugged island. Driving had been slow because of the snow on the roads, and the many logging and freight trucks in front of him, but he had made this ferry in ample time, and had even had time to stop and eat at a small roadside diner along the way near the small town of Gibson's Landing.

Now he walked back inside the ferry's heated cabin and bought another map which detailed the topography of the Inside Passage and, further north, Desolation Sound. The map showed all of the small islands which dotted the straits between the main coastline and Vancouver Island. To those that might notice, he looked like any other passenger, browsing through the map and the ferry schedule that came with it. His eyes scanned the open page until he found what he was looking for. Cortes Island looked like a small comma on the map, between a narrow peninsula that protruded from the mainland towards the north, and the large land mass of Vancouver Island to the west. To the north of Cortes was another, larger island called Quadra Island. Choy then looked at the pencil-thin line on the map that indicated a road. It continued up from where he was about to land at Saltery Bay, to the northern tip of a narrow peninsula. The end of the road was marked by a small dot, labeled Lund. And there it stopped; there was

213

no road going any further than Lund. From the scale of the map, he could guess that Cortes Island was at least a mile or two beyond the road, further north and west. He would have to get a boat somehow, to get out there. He looked down the map. A few miles south was a larger town, Powell River. Maybe a boat from there would be better. This place, Lund, was at a dead end, and he guessed that it was a very small town. He would be conspicuous there. And the doctor might well have someone keeping watch for him.

The ferry slowed, and straight ahead Nim Choy saw the wooden framing of the ferry terminal, still small in the distance. He got up, folding the map, and stretched the muscles of his arms and back. He walked towards the metal staircase that led down to the car deck, and felt the diesel engines slow further as the ferry began to approach the berth. The few other passengers on the ferry were starting towards their cars as well. Nim Choy got into his rental car, and checked the black vinyl satchel. It was still there, under the seat. He felt the hard muzzle of the gun, and it was somehow reassuring. He waited patiently, quietly contemplating what lay ahead. Soon the aching in his soul would be over.

He watched as the heavy steel ramp was lowered onto the bow of the ferry. He continued to wait as they waved the middle row of heavier trucks off first. And then finally the cars were waved through, first one side, and then the other. Choy was at the end of the first line of cars as he drove slowly up a hill and onto a narrow two-lane road. A sign on the side of the road read fifteen miles to Powell River. Fifteen miles. He could have patience for fifteen miles. He concentrated on driving carefully, staying well back from the car in front of him. To the left, below the road and through the trees, he caught glimpses of the dark water of the straits. He tried to remember the features of the road. It might be useful later on, when he was through. Not that it mattered, he reflected. *His destiny was in the hands of Kwan Tai.*

He remembered the first time that he had seen the God of War, on a night that Samuel Twan had taken him, as a nervous young boy, to meet the elders of Gojin Tong for the first time. Samuel Twan had taught him respect, and committment to an ideal. And perseverance. Yes, he reflected silently, he had learned perseverance.

The road ran through a thick growth of evergreens for many miles. Then, finally there were a few houses on either side of the road. He dismissed his thoughts. He must be coming into the larger town of Powell River a few miles south of the island. He glanced at his watch. After three o'clock. It would be dark fairly soon. To the west he could see a heavy build-up of winter clouds around the falling sun.

Choy had already decided that it would be safer to try and get a boat from here than drive to the end of the road at Lund. As he got into a small downtown area, he turned at an intersection and followed the road downhill towards the harbor. The boat landing was protected by a long rocky breakwater. He pulled into a gravel parking area and got out of the car, pulling his black vinyl bag from under the seat. He locked the car and walked out onto the landing carrying the satchel with him.

Anchored out in deeper water, he could see several large fishing boats. He wanted something smaller and faster. Nim Choy continued to walk towards the end of the landing, but he saw no one in any of the boats.

He went back to a small wooden hut next to the gasoline and diesel pumps near the end of a concrete boat ramp. A man in overalls was kneeling, working on a small outboard engine next to the pumps. The man looked up at him as he approached. His hands were covered with black grease.

"I would like to charter a boat. Do you know who I could talk to?" Choy swung his black bag slowly in his right hand.

The man shook his head. "Pretty late in the day to be getting a charter. Maybe in the morning. Besides, a storm is coming in." The man continued to work on the engine.

"It's very important that I go tonight."

"Where do you want to go?"

Choy hesitated for a moment. "Quadra Island." The less the man knew the better. "A friend of mine lives there and I need to see him tonight."

The man stopped working again and shook his head. "That's a good nine or ten miles up the coast. With the storm, it's too dangerous." He paused again. "There aren't many people that live on Quadra Island year around. You sure he's there?"

" Yes. I can pay as much as necessary. Is there anyone that I could ask to take me?"

"Well," The man stopped his work and looked more closely at him. "Fred Collins might, I guess. You can find him up the hill at the Sunset Hotel." He nodded towards a large building up past the parking lot, as he wiped his hands on a red rag. "In the bar." Choy nodded, and then turned and began to walk up the road towards the building. The hotel was wooden, three stories tall and badly in need of paint. As in Vancouver, at the bar entrance there were two doors, one marked "Men only" and another one next to it marked "Ladies and Escorts". Nim Choy gazed with mild curiosity at the two and then entered through the "Men only" door. Inside, it was dark, and it took a few moments for Choy's eyes to adjust to the light. There were five or six men sitting at the bar, looking at a small color television set bolted to the ceiling at one end. Nim Choy felt their eyes turn towards him as he came into the darkened room.

He went up to the bar and nodded to the bartender. The man was in his fifties, and continued drying glasses with a towel as he came over.

"I'm looking for Fred Collins. I was told that he would be here."

"That's right." The man raised his voice over the noise of a hockey game being broadcast on the television. "Fred!"

A thick, plethoric man turned on his seat and stared at them. He slowly got up and made his way along the bar, none too steadily.

"Yeah?" He had a deeply lined, tanned face, but his nose and cheeks showed the reddened capillary blush and coarsened features of an alcoholic.

"I need to get to Quadra Island. I was told that you have a boat, and might be willing to take me there."

The man looked back at his seat, and then at the clock above the bar. "Now? Hockey game's just bloody well started!"

"I need to go tonight. I'll pay whatever you want, in cash. Can you take me?"

"Well, the charter business is a little lean this time of year." The man regarded Choy for a moment, but then wistfully glanced at the TV once more. "How about a hundred and fifty dollars?"

Choy nodded.

"Yeah, all right. I'll need that now, if you don't mind." He waited as Nim Choy pulled out the wallet with the false identification, and counted out the money in American bills. He gave it to the man.

The boat owner turned to the bartender, who was still drying glasses behind the counter, watching the two of them curiously. Collins peeled four twenties out of the money. "Willy, here's my tab for the month." He stuffed the rest of the money into his pants pocket and looked at Nim Choy. "I'm ready whenever you are."

The younger man nodded and, holding his black vinyl bag firmly, followed the man out through the front door of the bar.

*   *   *

"We're on! It looks like it's clearing." The manager walked out from the back of the office, grinning. McAllister smiled thinly, and got up and stretched, looking at his watch. Nearly three in the afternoon. Jesus the wait had been frustrating!

"When can we go?"

"The airplane is fueled and the pre-flight check has already been done. Twenty minutes, maybe."

"Good."

The snow had been blown off the tarmac and formed a thin brown crust on either side of the ramp as the small twin-engine turbo prop taxied out towards the runway. McAllister sat in the co-pilot's seat, and watched the wet surface pass under them. The pilot was ex-Canadian Air Force, pleasant enough, but to the point, and busy with the details of the final pre-flight checklist and take-off sequence. He gave the detective a pair of headphones to wear so that he could hear clearly.

The pilot concentrated on their taxi position between the larger commercial aircraft, taking care to keep the smaller plane out of the jetwash. In the back of the airplane was a flat cargo area. On this flight there were only a few packages going north. The main cargo today was McAllister.

The pilot spoke with the tower in a clipped, business-like manner as he finally pulled the turbo-prop out onto the runway, facing due west, directly into the low winter sun. They waited, and McAllister checked his seatbelt once again and pulled it even tighter across his lap. As they were cleared for takeoff, the pilot smoothly pushed the throttles forward, holding the plane with the brakes until the airframe began to vibrate and rattle with the force of the engines. He released the brakes, and with a jolt they were accelerating. The detective watched the tarmac move beneath them, faster, into a blur, and then the runway receded below them and they were off.

The pilot immediately dropped into a banking turn towards the north. To their right, McAllister could see the city of Vancouver spread out below them. They crossed over a narrow inlet lined with factories and warehouses. Further north, above the city, he saw a suspension bridge, tall and very narrow, and hazy in the winter air. It reminded him of the Golden Gate. Below them, in the wide ocean inlet, ships were lined-up off Vancouver Harbor.

"Going to be a little rough. The weather service said that we're in between storm fronts." The pilot's voice was loud in the headphones. "Keep your seatbelt tight." The detective nodded as they moved up into the clouds and the scene below them vanished in a white veil.

McAllister tried to relax, realizing that the muscles in his shoulders and back were contracted and tense. He looked at his watch. Three-thirty. The flight would take forty-five minutes. They stayed low, mostly under the cloud cover, following the coastline north over Howe Sound, and past Gibson's Landing and Earl's Cove, and finally over Saltery Bay. To the west, over the dark mass of Vancouver Island, McAllister could see a huge build-up of clouds which filled the afternoon sky. He tried to relax as the small plane bounced and jolted in the burbulent air. Later, up ahead another, smaller billowing mass of clouds or steam seemed to rise up from the ground on the coastline.

"What's that?" McAllister pointed at the white, rising mass.

"The paper mill at Powell River. That's just a little south of where you want to be going," the pilot replied. He banked the plane, turning inland towards the airport, and slowly began to bleed off his altitude.

McAllister felt his ears pop, and he swallowed to ease the discomfort. Below him rose a forest of dark trees. To the east, in front of them, was a rising mountainside. The pilot made a sudden, hard turn to the left, and rapidly descended. Through the angled window, the detective could now see the airport, small below them, set on a plateau in the rising hillside and surrounded by tall trees.

"We'll drop down pretty fast here. Got your seatbelt on tight?" The pilot looked at him and grinned benignly. He continued to talk on the radio to the control tower, and then abruptly they descended further and were down low, the trees speeding past them in a blur of dark green. McAllister felt the wheels skid, first the left, for just a moment, and then both were down and the airplane slowed rapidly. Ahead he could see at the end of the runway a sudden wall of the same tall trees. The airplane slowed further, and the pilot turned and began to taxi back towards the terminal, a simple low wooden structure next to a small glassed-in control tower set on wooden piers.

The daylight was nearly gone as McAllister got out of the airplane. He thanked the pilot, and felt a few drops of cold rain on his face as he began to walk towards the terminal. He entered a small waiting area and went to the pay telephones. Next to the telephone was a thin directory. Quickly, he leafed through it and found the number again for the Powell River RCMP office.

"Hello, Officer Kelton." On the other end of the line came a different voice than the one that he had heard that morning. Good, he thought to himself.

"This is Detective McAllister, of the San Francisco Police Department. I called earlier this morning, about a Doctor Jack Phillips. Was someone from your department able to get in touch with him?"

"Phillips, aye? One minute, please," This one was too damned polite to be of any use, McAllister decided. Moments later, the man's voice came back on. "One of our officers went up to Lund this morning. This man Phillips wasn't there. So far, they haven't gotten in touch with him, although they have kept an eye out for his car."

McAllister's anger quickly welled up, fueled by his long, frustrating wait at the airport in Vancouver. "This guy's life is in danger! The killer could be anywhere up here by now!"

The RCMP's voice became muffled once again, as he apparently talked to someone else with him. Then he came back on. "That's still an unconfirmed report we've been told."

"What!" McAllister stared at the telephone in disbelief.

"We are still awaiting word from the Vancouver Office before we can do anything more. As it is, we're short one man, gone down to Victoria for the Christmas holidays."

McAllister tried to control himself. "Listen, for Christ's sake! I've just flown up here from San Francisco, to see Phillips myself, and try to track down this killer!"

"You're here in Powell River?"

"Yeah, just landed."

"Hold on the line, please," McAllister listened silently as the voice became muffled again as the officer talked at length with someone else at the other end of the line.

The man came back on the line, "What's your name?"

"McAllister. Joe McAllister, with the San Francisco Police Department. Detective, Homicide Division."

"You are reminded, Detective McAllister, that here in Canada you have absolutely no jurisdiction over any persons, American or otherwise. Until we have a confirmation on this suspect's entry into Canada, you are advised to do nothing regarding this man. Do you understand?" His voice was firm.

The officer in the small RCMP office in downtown Powell River was staring out the window at the oncoming darkness, as he waited for a response. It was starting to snow again. "Do you hear me?" He paused again, and then looked up at the other man on duty with him. "I think that he's dropped the bloody telephone!"

19

Nim Choy watched the massive complex of lights to the east of them as the boat moved slowly north along the coast. They were about half a mile away from the paper mill, which was blanketed by a thick haze as the steam from the billowing smoke stacks mixed with the clouds overhead. The sound of the boat's engine changed as they worked through increasing seas. Choy could see nothing in front of them but a swirl of snow, which was starting to stick and form an icy layer outside the cabin, on the boat's windows and deck. The windshield wipers swept the snow to the sides of the window, where it collected and then fell in a slurry to the sill. Choy held onto a railing in front of him with both hands, and shivered in his thin jacket. He glanced at the pilot, who seemed unperturbed by either the cold or the movement, as he balanced himself against the pitching of the boat.

"This stretch of the coastline is pretty safe as long as you watch the depth reading. There will be more lights coming up at the Indian reservation here in a bit." The man's drunkenness had seemed to quickly wear off after they had left the harbor.

"How much longer?" Nim Choy raised his voice over the wind, which had begun to make a moaning sound in the rigging overhead.

"To Quadra? About an hour maybe, in these seas. It's past Lund a good ways," replied the captain.

Choy looked down to the floor. Not seeing his vinyl case in the darkness of the cabin, he pushed his foot forward until he felt the heaviness of the weight of the gun.

"You want a cigarette?" The pilot glanced at him in the flare of a match as he let the wheel of the boat go for a moment to quickly light his cigarette. Choy nodded, and took one from the pilot's pack, lighting it with the man's matches. He inhaled deeply, feeling the acrid smoke in his lungs. It was much stronger than the American cigarettes that he was used to.

"Actually, the man that I want to see is on Cortes Island, not Quadra." He waited for a reaction from the pilot, ready to reach for his gun if the man needed convincing.

"Cortes? Then why did you tell me Quadra earlier?" The pilot looked at him again, his voice quizzical, but only slightly irritated. Nim

Choy could detect no suspicion in the words.

"Sorry, my mistake." he replied. "I thought that it was Quadra, but then I looked again at my directions and saw that I was wrong."

As far as the pilot was concerned, exactly where they were going didn't really matter. The man had already paid his money and where he wanted to go was his own business. But he turned again to the Oriental. "This guy on the island a friend of yours?"

Choy hesitated. He didn't want to talk to the man any more than he had to; the pilot probably knew most of the people that lived in these islands.

"Yes, a friend. " He raised his voice further in the increasing wind.

"There's only one house on Cortes. I go by the place from time to time, on fishing charters mostly," The pilot's cigarette glowed in the darkness. "It's usually empty. Nice place though. They've done a lot of work on it. Where are they from?"

"San Francisco," he replied, irritated by the man's curiosity.

"That where you're from?"

Choy hesitated. "Yes," he said finally, as he suppressed a chill going through him. The pilot had just sealed his own fate, he decided.

"I've never been there myself. Lived here in B.C. my entire life. They say it's nice down there, aye?"

Choy nodded in the darkness; as he finished his cigarette, he threw the butt onto the deck and stepped on it. He grabbed the railing and held on as the bow of the boat suddenly fell hard into a trough in the deepening swells. The pitch of the boat's engine rose as the stern rode high and nearly out of the water for a moment. The pilot seemed unconcerned.

"There's the reservation." He pointed with his free hand toward the coastline.

At the pilot's direction, Choy could see a collection of lights along the water. They were dim and hazy through the snow. He couldn't make out any buildings and began to worry about the visibility.

"Will you be able to find the house in this weather once we get to Cortes Island?"

"It shouldn't be a problem if they have their lights on. Like I said, it's the only house on that island. If we can't find it, I'll take you back and drop you off at Lund. You can stay in the hotel until morning and go out then."

Choy stiffened. "I must get there tonight," he replied.

"We'll try." The man lit another cigarette in the darkness and offered the pack again. Choy shook his head as he held onto the railing and gazed into the darkness ahead of them.

A half an hour later they passed across the mouth of a small bay.

"Lund," the pilot said simply, nodding towards a small cluster of lights. The wind and snow had lessened somewhat.

"What's there?" Nim Choy asked. He could just make out a small harbor area lit by lights strung above on tall poles.

"Hotel, post office, store. That's about it," the pilot replied as they continued past the mouth of the bay. "Cortes is about a mile directly north of here, close to the main coastline. We should start to see their lights soon."

Choy said nothing. He pondered the options. He wanted to get onto the island without giving Phillips warning of his arrival. With the weather as it was, he doubted that he could land on another part of the island and then find the house.

"Are there other docks on the island?" He tried to sound as if he were just making conversation.

"Don't know of any."

If they had to land right at the house, it was sure that Phillips would see them come in. All surprise would be lost. Unless he could do what he had to do quickly, right there on the dock, as the doctor came down to the boat.

They continued for another quarter of an hour, the pilot following the compass and beginning to watch the luminous red numbers on the digital readout of his depth gauge. Nim Choy looked at the glowing numerals. Thirty-two fathoms. Close to two hundred feet, he calculated.

"We should be seeing lights any time now. " The pilot peered forward into the darkness. There was no moonlight, and around them the clouds and ocean met as a solid wall of blackness. The snow continued to fall lightly onto the deck and windows of the boat.

"When we start to lose depth on the gauge, I'll turn on the spotlights, so that we can see the shore."

"No!" At his sudden outburst, the pilot looked over at him in alarm. The Asian lowered his voice. "I mean, they might obscure the lights from the house."

"We get close and I'm going to want to see the shoreline, mate. There are submerged rocks. And we can follow the island along until we reach the inner straits, where the house is." The pilot turned back to watch in front of them as the boat worked through the swells.

Why were there no lights, wondered Nim Choy? As his anxiety rose his mind began to race. They must have electricity on the island, don't they? He remained silent as he watched the glowing red digits of the depth finder. Still twenty-eight fathoms. He looked at his watch but couldn't see the dial in the darkness. It couldn't be later than six o'clock. They couldn't be asleep yet. Were they not there? The pitch of the engine abruptly decreased and then steadied as the pilot slowed the boat. It wallowed in the swell. In front of them remained only the snow and blackness. And then, slowly at first, the red numbers on the depth finder began to fall as they neared the shore. The number dropped more rapidly, twenty-two, eighteen, sixteen, ten fathoms. Sixty feet.

"Looks like we're getting close," said the pilot. He pushed a button on the readout that changed the numbers into feet. Fifty-two, forty-eight, they continued to blink downward. "I don't see a thing," the pilot added. He slowed the boat even further. "I'm turning on the spot-lights."

Nim Choy could sense the man reaching for the control panel, and instinctively began to stop him. But he realized that it would be foolish to continue on with nothing to guide them, and silently pulled his hand back.

With an audible click they were suddenly bathed in brightness from the light reflecting off the fog and swirling snow. The water was a mov-ing, flowing blackness below them. Abruptly, the pilot began to vio-lently spin the wheel and the boat heeled over as the bow began to turn to starboard. Then with a sickening realization, Nim Choy himself saw plainly in the lights the shining darkness of rocks, protruding out of the water within twenty or thirty feet of them. He tensed and clenched his hands on the railing as the pilot continued to turn and apply power to the engines. The boat shook as the propellers cut into the water to push them away from the deadly coastline.

"Good God, man! The island is right in front of us!" the pilot's voice was high and tense as he guided the boat out to a safer depth. "I think that we should turn back." The pilot's voice quavered with anxiety. "I'll take you into Lund."

"Keep going." Choy replied firmly.

The pilot stared at him sharply. He wasn't going to risk his boat for any charter. "Look mister, I'm making the decisions here." In the dim-ness of the cabin light, he saw his passenger reach down into the black vinyl bag at his feet. He continued to turn the boat to starboard, head-ing away from the island.

"I said keep going!" Choy barked over the noise of the engine.

"You're crazy! We'll both be killed on those rocks!" Then he fo-cused on the muzzle of the gun in Nim Choy's right hand. His anger turned to incredulous fear as he gazed back at the Oriental man's face. "Good Mother of God!"

"Take me to the house. You said that it was along the straits."

The pilot continued to stare at his passenger, not believing what he was seeing. The boat continued to move forward slowly, wallowing in the swell. The pilot turned back to look out the window. Choy re-mained motionless, his eyes fixed on the pilot. He felt the boat begin a gentle turn back to port, as the other man began to follow the shoreline towards the narrow straits near the mainland. They moved at a crawl as the snow began to fall more heavily and the wind picked up again. Choy looked at the glowing red numbers on the depth gauge. Three fathoms. Eighteen feet. Through the windshield, and the still swirling snow he could just see the low dark mass of the island to their left, close to the boat.

The pilot looked at him again, his eyes drawn down to the gun. "What do you want here?"

"Never mind what I want. It has nothing to do with you."

"OK, I'll get you there," replied the pilot. His thoughts raced ahead, with illogical hope. If he didn't give this man any trouble, maybe he could just drop him off on the island. "But I want to move a little further out from the island. It'll be safer."

The depth gauge increased to twenty-five feet, and then stayed steady as they moved east. The pilot turned on another spotlight on their port side, illuminating the island. They turned slowly to the left as they followed the mass of the island.

"We're coming into the straits now," said the pilot. He continued to peer forward. "Lights!" The relief was clear in his voice.

Choy looked out and a hundred yards in front of them and to the left he could see a few small lights near the water.

"Shut off the spotlights!" he barked.

"We won't be able to see the dock," the pilot replied.

"Do it!"

The pilot flipped off the switch and, again enveloped in darkness, they continued to move slowly forward.

"Where is the dock?" Nim Choy demanded.

"Should be where those lights are, but I can't be sure without the spotlights. It's in a small bay, to the left of us." The pilot slowed the boat even more. As they came closer they could see the lights vaguely illuminating a small dock, below a ramp running up onto the island. Nim Choy could see that there were no boats at the dock, and no lights in the house above. It didn't look like Phillips was there.

"There may be rocks around us! I need the lights!" warned the pilot.

"No! Just get us in there!" Choy angrily waved the gun in the man's face. They made a broad circle to the left, the pilot scrutinizing the depth gauge continuously. Finally, they were fifty yards away from the dock. The pilot directed the boat towards the far side of the dock and finally began to turn to port to swing the stern in. "You'll have to handle the bow line," he said.

"You do it!" Nim Choy didn't want the man to get him on to the dock and then suddenly take off. The pilot looked at him again, and brought the throttle back to an idle.

"OK, whatever you want. You'll have to bring us up to the dock, then. I can't do both." As the pilot went out through the narrow rear door, a blast of frozen air swept into the cabin. The man went around to the starboard side and then along the icy deck towards the bow. He clung to the railing with his hands as he moved onto the snow-covered bow and lifted the coiled line. Nim Choy grasped the steering wheel and continued to guide the boat towards the dock under the lights.

As the boat approached the dock, the pilot jumped over the low railing and onto the wooden surface. The bow rose and fell, the icy water slapping against the hull each time as the pilot tried to steady the boat and push the bow away, to line the boat up next to the dock. Nim Choy pulled the engine out of gear and kept the throttle at idle as the pilot secured the bow line and then quickly moved back to the stern of the boat. He came back on board, collected the stern line and threw it over the side onto the dock. Then he jumped off again and tied the line down to the cold metal stanchion on the wooden dock.

Nim Choy watched the ramp and the dark bulk of the house above from the cabin of the boat. No lights came on, and no one came out of the house. He knew that Phillips did not expect to be followed up to the island, and if he were here would have already come out to investigate them. It was obvious the doctor wasn't here. He turned his gaze to the pilot, and decided that he must deal with this problem first.

As the pilot worked, he was thinking that he wouldn't even keep the money from the passenger. He'd give it back. He had done a good job getting the man here safely, under the circumstances. For God's sake, just let him leave with his boat and he would call it even. *By Christ, he could use a drink!* As he stood, he looked up onto the stern of the boat and his face changed to horror as he saw the Oriental man standing, facing him with the gun trained on his chest. He tried to speak, but no words came. He could feel the absolute coldness in the other man's eyes, colder than the wind and the falling snow around them. He knew then that there would be no talking, no bargaining. No other choice but what lay ahead. Nausea welled up, and he swallowed and tried to control it. He watched, nearly abstractly, the orange flash from the gun, and listened to the sound of his own death, which was quickly swept away by the wind.

Nim Choy quickly climbed over the railing at the stern of the boat. He pushed the pilot's body off the dock, and it fell heavily into the blackness of the water. With a clinical eye, he looked and saw that no blood had spilled onto the deck surface. Then he moved along the dock and untied the bow line, and pushed the bow out, away from the dock. He went back into the cabin of the boat, hurrying because of the extreme cold and his resolve not to be caught off guard by the doctors sudden return. First, he searched the control panel and found the switches for the deck and running lights, and turned all of these off. The engine had been left idling, and now he pushed the throttle forward. He felt the propeller kick in and the boat start to move slowly forward until it began to strain the stern line. He pushed the throttle slightly more, and then quickly picked up his black vinyl satchel and left the cabin, jumping carefully over the stern of the boat back onto the dock.

With the thrust of the propellor, the boat had swung like a pendulum, the bow now pointing out, towards the straits. The stern had dropped down into a boiling white foam from the propwash, the stern line stretched and taut with the strain of the engine. Nim Choy pulled out his gun again and touched the line with the blunt muzzle. He fired, and the rope severed partially, and then suddenly snapped. The boat jumped forward, and moved away from the dock.

Nim Choy stood and watched as the boat disappeared into the darkness. Phillips would have to have his own boat to get here; Nim Choy would use that to get off the island when the time came. Then he picked up his vinyl bag and turned and moved up the ramp towards the house.

*   *   *

Jack watched the whitecaps in the straits between the coastline and Texada Island, two miles to the west. Heavy clouds were moving in, and now the water was a deepening grey, nearly black in the distance. He sat in a comfortable reclining chair, protected from the weather within a fully glassed-in porch off Gordy Jefferson's living room, a space heater near his feet warming the area. His friend's house was situated fifty yards above the water at Grief Point, a small peninsula south of Powell River. Below, there was a private dock where the surgeon had his own boat tied down securely for the winter.

"So now what?" His friend sat next to him, drinking a cup of coffee. They had long finished lunch. and had been out on the deck for nearly two hours. Gordy had listened quietly as Jack talked about the Twan case, and afterwards about being driven off the mountainside in the car, and Christine's kidnapping, and later the two attackers. Being shot in the hand, his surgery, and finally the hospital janitor and the decision in the middle of the night to leave San Francisco. To run away. At times, Jack had rambled nearly aimlessly with his conversation, piecing together fragments of the story, and his feelings, his horror at what this was doing to his family, and the frustration at being completely without control. He had also talked about the terrible images, or whatever they were, that had haunted him in the night.

"I think that I know what's going on there," Gordy asked, after listening to him. "Were you ever wounded in Viet Nam?" Jack had shook his head.

"Even so, it sounds like a post-traumatic stress reaction. You don't have to have been wounded before, but sometimes new trauma, physical injury especially, can trigger off something that brings you back to how you felt during a previous severe psychological stress, like Viet Nam. A fair number of the veterans from that war suffered from it, I believe."

"Some of these dreams are like that. I see it, I feel exactly what it was like to be there again. The same sense of fear. It's like I'm reliving it. And I can't get away from it. God, it's awful."

"They say that it can be so real that some people truly believe that they are back where they were at one time. And they will hide and fight back, as if they're being attacked." Gordy looked out over the water. "I don't really know much about it, but I think that once the new stress—the one that brings it back—is controlled, the symptoms usually go away,"

"I hope so." Jack shook his head. "I really thought that I was losing my mind."

The last light in the clouds to the west was gone now. Through the glass, Jack could see that it had started to rain again, the drops pattering against the greenhouse around them.

"So now what?" Gordy asked a second time.

Jack tried to collect his thoughts. "We're going to stay up here until the police and FBI find these people, this gang, and get them away from us, for good."

"What about your practice?"

"It's just going to have to wait. The Assistant Chief is running things for the time being. It's more important that my family is protected." Darian came into the room. He and Christine had been watching a movie on Gordy Jefferson's video system. Jack looked at his watch. It was nearly six o'clock.

"We should get going, so we can get back to the island before the weather gets too bad."

They walked out into the kitchen, where Barbara sat drinking tea and talking to Jennifer, Gordy's wife. She had been having her own conversation with Jennifer about what had happened in San Francisco. At least, she had reflected, the ordeal had brought them back together again as a family. It had forced Jack to be with the rest of them and at least for a while, to halt his insane, overly-driven life in neurosurgery. She hoped that when he got back to it he could do so with better balance in his life. If so, despite what they had gone through, it would have been worth it. She looked up at Jack as he entered the kitchen.

"Are you two all through?"

He nodded. "We had better think about heading back soon. It's starting to snow, and it's at least a thirty-minute drive back up to Lund."

They got their things together. Gordy and his wife walked with Jack and Barbara and the two kids out to the front of the house. As they went outside, the air felt even colder than before. The rain had turned into a wet snow, which formed an icy film over the windshield of the car.

"Be careful driving back, and getting out to that island of yours," warned Gordy.

"If it's too bad, we'll just stay with the Svensens at his hotel until morning," Jack replied as he shook his friend's hand. They got into the car and pulled away from the house and into the darkness.

20

Per Svensen came out to the front of the hotel at the sound of the desk bell. An older, heavyset man stood there, waiting silently, appearing somewhat disheveled. He had no luggage, Svensen noted, and was immediately on guard.

"What can I do for you?" he asked cautiously.

"My name is Detective Joseph McAllister. I'm with the San Francisco Police Department." McAllister pulled his badge out and showed it to the man. "Do you know Dr. Jack Phillips?"

Svensen hesitated. Jack had said that the police in San Francisco were trying to stop that gang that was after him, but Svensen didn't remember Jack mentioning any names.

"Yes, yes I do," he replied finally. "Come inside and sit down." He directed the man into his den.

The two of them sat down, and Svensen looked at the detective closely. The man didn't look well. His skin was yellow and pale, and he seemed to have some difficulty breathing. "What are you doing here, in Canada?" he asked.

"Doctor Phillips is in serious trouble. Has he told you about his problems in San Francisco?" McAllister watched Mr. Svensen nod in reply. Despite his attempt to ignore them, the chest pains had been coming more frequently, squeezing down on him, like someone standing on his chest, making it difficult to breathe. He tried to slow and steady his respirations so that he could speak. "One member of this gang is up here in Canada, looking for him. Somehow the man knows about his place on Cortes Island. He's a killer, and he's here for only one reason, to finish the job that they were trying to do in San Francisco. He'll keep trying until he's succeeded, or stopped."

"The RCMP were here today, looking for Dr. Phillips, too. Are you the detective that they said had called them?"

McAllister nodded. "They don't believe it, though! Because they haven't verified that this man has entered Canada yet, they won't do anything to help, except warn him."

"And is that why you are here? To stop this man?" asked Svensen.

McAllister nodded. "These people had slipped by us for months, until recently. Because of them, an FBI agent has been killed and another San Francisco police officer wounded. But now we have the leader of the gang in custody. And others as well, except this one. His name is Choy, Nim Choy. McAllister pulled an envelope from his pocket and withdrew a small black and white photograph from police files, taken several years earlier. "This is the man."

Svensen looked at it. "Well, so far he hasn't been around here. I would probably know. This is the end of the road going north. You can't go any further except by boat or seaplane. Since Jack came back and told me about this situation, I've been paying particular attention. Even more so since that officer came by earlier today."

"Where is Dr. Phillips?" the detective asked.

"That's the funny thing," replied Svensen. "They had some breakfast with us here this morning, and then he and his family left to go Christmas shopping down in Powell River. They haven't been back since then."

"Would they necessarily come back through here?"

Svensen nodded. "They always use one of my boats to get to and from the island. Yes, I'm sure that they would come back here first."

McAllister relaxed slightly. They would be much harder for the killer to find if they had been out in their car and shopping all day.

Mrs. Svensen came into the room. Her husband introduced her to the detective. Her demeanor was cool as she studied McAllister for a moment. But then she seemed to warm slightly. "Would you like something to eat or drink?" she asked.

McAllister hesitated, but then nodded. It had been a long day and he was actually quite hungry. She turned to go to the kitchen. McAllister wondered if perhaps the best thing to do would be for him to wait for Phillips here at the hotel.

After a moment, Per Svensen spoke up. "It seems such a tragedy what has happened to him. So unfair, after trying to help that man that was shot in the first place."

McAllister looked at the older man, with his ruddy, healthy appearance, and suddenly envied him, and his quiet life out here in the country. "That's not the whole story," he replied simply.

Mrs. Svensen interrupted them with coffee and a tray of cakes. McAllister murmured his thanks as they drank in silence for a few moments.

"Mr. Svensen, is there any other way out to the island?" McAllister was still worried that somehow Phillips might have gone back out there without them knowing.

"Well, of course you could get there easily from Powell River, or across from Vancouver Island. It's just a longer trip," replied the older man.

"How long from Powell River?" McAllister asked.

"Maybe an hour, an hour and a half."

"Doesn't he have a telephone on the island?"

Per Svensen shook his head. "A telephone is one of the things that Jack feels is a nuisance when he's up here."

McAllister considered. It was quite possible that Choy might not come all the way to Lund before going to Cortes Island, this being such a small place, and with only one road in or out. The only other choices would be to come up from the larger town, Powell River, by boat, or across from Vancouver Island. Then local police road blocks would be useless. He hadn't thought about that possibility before now.

"Funny that you should ask about Powell River, though," Per Svensen said. "Just before you came in, I was out on the dock, finishing my work, and a boat went past, close to shore, heading north." He paused as he realized the possible significance of what he was saying. "In the direction of the island. It was too dark to tell whose boat it was."

McAllister stopped drinking his coffee and looked at the older man. "Is that unusual? To have boats go past here, I mean."

"This time of year it is," replied Svensen. "Not many commercial fishing boats out right now. It's between seasons, and with Christmas and all. Could have been one, but she was running awfully close to shore for a commercial boat. And charters are unusual this time of year too."

"How about other people that live north of here?"

"They mostly dock here in Lund, like Jack," replied Svensen.

McAllister was uncomfortable as he pondered this new piece of information. Could it be Phillips? Finally, he asked, "Does Dr. Phillips have other friends here, in Powell River?"

"Yes, I think so, another doctor I believe, and he knows a few other people as well," replied Svensen.

"So it's possible that he could have come up from Powell River by boat then? I mean, conceivably?"

"Well, I guess that it's possible. But not very likely, given this storm and the added distance. It would be much easier to drive up to here and then go out to the island. A much shorter trip. It is what Jack would usually do."

That answered it for him. If the boat were going to Cortes Island, it could only be one person. He decided on what he must do.

"Mr. Svensen, I want you to take me to the island."

"Do you think..." replied the old man. But the look on McAllister's face told him the answer. Per Svensen could feel more than see his wife tense and begin to say something. He quickly held up his hand, stopping her.

The detective spoke as the thoughts came to him. "It could be Dr.

Phillips, who left from Powell River because he had to. He may have seen the man who is after him." McAllister was silent for a long moment. The more he thought about it, the more he was sure of his instincts. "Or it may be this man Choy, going out to the island. I don't think that he would come all the way up here first. This place is too small, and with only one road in or out, it would be too easy for him to be trapped." He paused again. "And he expects Dr. Phillips to be on that island. You'll have to take me out there, Mr. Svensen."

Mrs. Svensen could contain herself no longer. She burst out. "Per, you can't! Call the RCMP! Leave it for the police to take care of!"

Svensen looked at his wife angrily. "Brigit! This man is trying to help Jack. The police here won't do anything! You heard what he said!" He looked back at the detective. "I'll take you. We will go right away!"

"Thank you," replied McAllister, feeling his body tighten with excitement. *Finally, alone, on even terms, I can end it here tonight.*

"No!" With surprising quickness, the big woman came completely out of her chair. "You are an old man! And a fool!" She took a deep breath. "For once, I won't let you go. It is too dangerous. For the love of God Per, call the police!"

Per Svensen stared at his wife standing above him. For over forty years, she had been the quiet, stoic, good Swedish wife that he had come to expect. Never complaining when he had gone into the woods to hunt by himself, or out to sea in one of his boats. This new outburst was unexpected, and so unlike her. And he knew in his heart that she was right. He was an old man now. He understood her need to protect him, for both of their sakes. But he was torn with his desire to see justice come for Jack, his good friend's son. And somehow he believed in this worn policeman that had come to his door from San Francisco. Slowly, he relaxed back down into his chair for a moment as McAllister gazed at him. He looked over at the detective and shook his head slightly.

"OK, Brigit. You are right." He paused. "I will go and call the police, as you say." He turned to McAllister as he got up. "Come with me."

Together they walked back towards the rear of the house, as his wife stayed seated in the living room still trembling in anger, having surprised herself at her own explosion of feeling. Never before had she so forcefully contradicted her husband. But even so, as she sat and stared at the fire that was now only smoldering embers, something edged into her thoughts. It took a few moments for her to realize what it was. It was her surprise that he had given up so easily.

Next to the back door of the house, Per Svensen silently opened a closet and pulled out two heavy coats and a dark woolen cap. He handed one coat and the cap to McAllister and then, without hesitating, opened the door silently and quickly led the detective out into the darkness.

"Follow me," the old man whispered. McAllister was surprised at how well he could hear the other man, before he noticed the deep silence and the falling snow that surrounded them.

"But we don't have any weapons," he protested. He had hoped that Svensen would have a pistol or a rifle or something to arm themselves with to go to the island.

"I put one of my hunting rifles in my boat today, after the police were here, as a precaution." He laughed grimly. "I'm glad that I did."

"What about your wife." McAllister asked, as they walked quickly down a slight incline towards the dock.

Svensen paused before replying. "After forty years of marriage, she will understand. She is a good woman, Brigit."

As they reached the dock, the snow began to fall more heavily, the wind gusting from the west. McAllister could feel the snow sift under the collar of his coat. He lifted the collar up, and pulled on the dark woolen sailor's cap that Per Svensen had given him.

He followed the old man onto the snow-covered wooden dock, their footprints dark and wet on the white surface. On either side the water glimmered black in the hard light from the overhead lamps. Svensen led him to a cabin cruiser, about thirty feet in length, of wooden construction, and quite old, by the shape of her. Per Svensen briskly climbed aboard and held out his hand to help McAllister onto the boat. The deck was slippery with the layer of new snow, and the detective moved gingerly towards the cabin door. Svensen unlocked the narrow door, opened it, and stepped through into the cabin of the boat. McAllister followed him in and stood shivering in the cold, as Svensen quickly put a key into the ignition and turned it.

"I will go and untie the lines now, before I start the engine. Wait here." He went back outside and untied the bow and stern lines, then he loosened the spring line, and pushed the boat with his foot, making it drift away from the dock. Deftly he jumped back on board and came inside the cabin once again. He went to the steering wheel and pushed a button on the control panel. There was a deep groan as the engine turned over, and then came to life with a muffled roar. Svensen flipped on several switches, and running lights around the boat began to glow, and the windshield wipers began to scrape across the frozen glass, as he let the engine warm up.

Above the dock, McAllister saw the front door of the large house open, and the bulky silhouette of Mrs. Svensen fill the lighted space. "Here comes your wife."

Per Svensen abruptly pulled the throttle into reverse, and the boat jerked as the propeller drive engaged, and they began to back away from the dock. He turned quickly to starboard, bringing the bow around. When they had pivoted nearly completely, he jammed the throttle forward and accelerated towards the mouth of the small bay towards the west.

McAllister watched behind them silently for a full minute as they moved away from the lighted dock, and the lights of the small harbor receded behind them. Then he turned forward and peered out the icy windows in front of them. "I can't see a thing," he muttered.

"We can get out of the bay and begin to go north by compass. I've been around this coastline for many years," replied Svensen. "Don't worry."

McAllister pulled his heavy jacket closer to him. The coat was too small for him, and his arms stuck out from the sleeves several inches. He crossed his arms and huddled in the cold and stared out at the blackness and the swirling snow.

*   *   *

Nim Choy stood near the large picture window in the living room and watched the snow gust and blow before falling to the ground. He had first carefully circled the house, to be sure that no one was there, and then broken a small window in the back door, away from the boat dock and ramp. Inside the house it was quiet and cold, but as he moved around he could see that he was in the kitchen. The family had been there, he was sure. There was fresh food in the refrigerator, and a quick search through the house had turned up clothing and personal belongings in the bedrooms. Not the way it would be if no one had been living in the house recently.

And now he waited. In a corner of the living room he saw a small evergreen, leaning against the fireplace. Obviously placed there for Christmas, but the tree was yet not on a stand and without ornaments. Nim Choy regarded the tree impassively. And that was how it would remain, he knew. Undecorated, untouched further by human hands in celebration of a false God. He pulled his arms tightly to his sides and suppressed another shiver as he rubbed his hands together. He looked forward to getting away from this god-forsaken place, back to San Francisco, and his home.

Abstractly, his mind focused on Joseph Lo. He didn't yet trust the man, and he wondered about the future of Gojin. Life in the tong was all that he knew. He would simply have to adjust to Samuel Twan not being there. They would triumph over the Wan Fung Tong...and anyone else who dared to cross them! But first, he must finish what he had set out to do. It had gone perfectly so far, even better that he was here on the island, waiting for Phillips. One thing that he could not criticize Joseph Lo for was his information. Somehow the elder had known exactly where Dr. Phillips had fled to. Within two days of Phillips leaving San Francisco, Lo had personally instructed him to go through the doctor's home to find pictures of the house on this island. The wind made a low moaning sound through the trees outside the house.

By reflex, Nim Choy crouched down. To the south there were lights, moving on the water. A boat, he was sure. It must be them! He felt excitement and anticipation rise in his throat, and he made no attempt to suppress the emotions, but allowed them to blossom, to nourish and strengthen him for his task ahead. The boat was still far off, the lights moving slowly, irregularly on the water. But steadily they advanced as he waited in the darkness. Nim Choy paid silent tribute to Kwan Tai, for he could see that had the doctor been here earlier, the man surely would have been warned of his own presence by the lights on the pilot's boat.

Soon the boat was below him, rocking hard from side to side in the swell, then moving into the straits between the island and the coastline to the east. He could see the outline of the boat, and he watched silently and prepared, checking the clip in the gun and flipping off the safety.

Slowly the boat began to turn in, toward the dock at the edge of the tiny bay. The spotlights on the boat were bright and reflected the flurries of snow blowing in from the west. The boat moved up to the dock and eased closer, the bow sliding in towards the wooden pier. Nim Choy could see the silhouette of a figure jumping from the side of the boat, and moving to the bow to crouch forward, securing a line. The shadow then moved to the stern, and as Nim Choy watched, another figure came out of the cabin but stayed on the boat. He strained to see, but the faces of the two were in shadows, and the spotlights on the boat still blazed, painting the side of the house and the window on a glaring light. The light forced Nim Choy to move further back, into the center of the living room. Was it Phillips? Who was the other person? It looked like another man! Furious at the possibilities, Nim Choy wondered if this even was the doctor's house. Could the pilot have brought him to the wrong island? If it weren't Phillips, he would have to kill these two and take the boat, he decided, as he waited, clenching the gun in his hand in the darkness.

Crouched forward in the wind and snow, the lone figure on the dock began to move up the ramp towards him. The other one was remaining on the boat. As the silhouette drew nearer, Nim Choy prepared to simply shoot the man through the window as he approached the house. And then the Oriental recoiled in horror, gasping audibly. For it wasn't Phillips at all. Even silouhetted in the glare of the boat lights, he recognized the bulky form of the detective from San Francisco. He remembered standing on the sidewalk in a crowd of curious onlookers, across the street from San Li's flower shop when this man had ducked under the yellow police tape across the front door to leave the building. Nim Choy had been going there to see his trusted friend...who by then was already dead...at the hands of these police!

In unthinking hatred, Nim Choy lifted his gun and fired at the bulky figure through the plate glass window. The glass shattered with a crash and a freezing wind swept into the house. He turned and ran back into the kitchen and out through the broken back door, into the darkness of the snow behind the house. His mind was racing. How many more men might be inside that boat! Quickly, he retreated fifty feet, up a rising ascent into the forest of trees behind the house. Then he turned and watched and waited.

The house was still and dark against a halo of snow brightly reflected in the lights from the boat in the harbor beyond. After a time Nim Choy moved between the trees towards the house. As he came to the edge of the woods the loud report of a rifle echoed in the night. The sound and a brief flash came from the direction of the rear doorway of the house. Nim Choy fired back, towards the door again and again, shooting in fury until his clip was empty. Each report from his gun was quickly muffled by the wind. He waited, breathless, unmoving, forgetting the cold and feeling only the blood pulsing in his face and temples. And then it was quiet, and the house was still.

He pulled another clip from the pocket of his thin jacket and loaded it. Slowly, he began to move back towards the rear of the house. His movements were stiff and clumsy from the cold. He bent forward into a crouch and tried to run to the back wall of the building, away from the doorway, but as he ran he slipped and fell in the snow. He bounded to his feet, slowed and rendered numb by the intense cold. As he got up, he swore at himself as he moved to the wall of the house, and continued to inch forward, towards the kitchen door, alert for any movement or sound. In the doorway he saw a figure, still and face down on the floor, a rifle partly hidden underneath the body. It was an old man, he was surprised to see, with a shock of white hair. Slowly he moved closer and inspected the body. The man was still breathing. Nim Choy lifted his gun again, pointing it at the rising chest, and began to squeeze the trigger. Then he stopped. Not yet. Not until he knew where the policeman was; if he were still alive, a shot would notify the man of his presence.

Deliberately, the assassin stepped over the wounded old man on the floor, into the kitchen. Where was the other one? He must have hit him with his first shot through the window. He hadn't been sure, it had been too fast...*too uncontrolled*, he chided himself! The house was silent except for the howl of the wind through the broken windows, and the rooms were still washed in the light from the boat in the harbor. He stood upright and began to move tensely, slowly forward, towards the spray of shattered glass in the reflected light of the living room....

The hatchet struck Nim Choy in the chest, on the right side, up high near his shoulder. He could feel its sharp pain before he saw the movement of the big man near him, in the darkness. He felt an abrupt tingling, burning discomfort envelop his right arm moving like a wave down to the fingertips, followed by numbness as the hatchet pierced the bone of his clavicle. The nerves of his brachial plexus were crushed and severed against the first rib by the sharp, heavy blade. He heard his gun fall out of his hand to the floor, but felt nothing, with the now useless, hanging extremity. The blow had pushed him back, standing him upright. And then the man hit him again. This time the pain was lower down, a more glancing blow in his abdomen. Nim Choy bent forward, and jerked towards the left as suddenly the detective was upon him. He fought against the weight of the man, ignoring the pain, trying to lift his paralyzed right arm, as the detective pulled him down to the floor. He felt smothered under a heavy coat, as McAllister began to hit him with his fists. Nim Choy felt the bones of his nose break with one of the blows, and began to feel nauseated and faint.

But then the large form on top of him slowed, and stopped his assault all together as the detective lifted both of his thick hands up to grip his own chest. In the dim, light Nim Choy could see, through the hatred in the face above him, a grimace of pain. And suddenly he was aware of the man's breathing. It was labored, gasping, and then it became a cough. A weak breathless cough.

Frantically, Nim Choy began to struggle again as the detective fell down fully on top of him, seemingly unable to move, clutching at the front of his own coat. The detective's eyes were open, staring at him in hard anguish, wanting only to finish what he had begun. But then the eyes lost their sharpness and turned towards the floor as the man struggled simply to breathe.

Nim Choy tried to push the weight of the detective off with his good left arm. The sharp, electrical pain in his chest and shoulder was unbearable as the heavy body lay on his paralyzed right arm. Waves of nausea overcame him as he finally rolled and was able to get the man off him. He felt dizzy, and on the ceiling above him he saw the glaring reflected lights from the boat changing, becoming bright, reinforced and transformed into new, unreal angular patterns and shapes.

Nim Choy lay on the cold floor, fighting for breath, and then slowly he got to his knees, holding himself up with his good left arm, his right arm dangling uselessly at his side. Nim Choy fought the spinning inside his head and forced himself to look around the room. His eyes fixed on his own gun on the floor several feet away. He began to crawl towards it, each movement, each breath, forming a jagged edge of pain. The wind from the winter storm howled through the room, slowing his movements further with the freezing cold. At last he reached the gun. With his good arm, he lifted it up. The metal was heavy and foreign in his left hand.

He turned towards the other man, and saw that the detective had revived slightly, and now was struggling to turn and face him. Nim

Choy forced himself to lift the gun, training it on McAllister. At least he could redeem the honor of San Li, he thought with slight satisfaction, as he squeezed the trigger. He watched the orange flash in the blackness, and listened as the roar overcame the howl of the wind. But there was something very wrong, for the gun had jerked to the side, the orange tracer angling up and away towards the ceiling, as his shoulder was struck from behind. He fell to the floor, but with an inborn reflex of survival rolled onto his back to face his new attacker. Somehow he kept the gun in his good, left hand, and as his eyes focused above him, his expression froze. In realization and final fulfillment, the assassin began to fire at the standing form.

*   *   *

Jack Phillips had been near the point of giving up finding the house in the rising storm, as the boat he had taken from the dock in Lund lurched and crashed in the huge waves. The engine dangerously over-revved as the prop lifted completely out of the water before the boat slid down into another steep trough. Visibility was limited to only a few feet, and Jack had been sure that he would end up crashing on submerged rocks when finally he discerned a faint glow in the distance through the swirling snow. Fixed in his memory was the anguished face of Mrs. Svensen as he and his family had arrived at the hotel. He had steered towards the light, searching for the inlet to the straits along the southeastern side of the island. The light was too low to be coming from his house, he thought.

With palpable relief, he had felt the swell lessen as he motored into the calmer waters of the straits. As he moved towards the lights, he realized that they came from a boat moored at his own dock. He quickly pulled his own boat towards the dock and came up alongside the other craft, recognizing it as one belonging to his friend, Per Svensen. He shut down the engine and quickly moved to the gunwale. His hands were stiff and frozen, and his amputated fingers ached with pain as he lashed his boat to the cleats on the outer side of the one already docked. The two vessels grated roughly against each other in the moving black water.

Phillips ignored the snow and wind as he climbed over into the bigger boat. With a quick look, he found that the boat was empty, and so he continued forward to the dock. There were no lights visible above, at the house, and he could hear only the howling sound of the wind as he negotiated his way up the icy wooden bridge towards the deck. As he reached the house, he felt the shards of broken glass grate under his shoes, and realized in horror that the large picture window to the living room was gone. In the rocking spotlights from the boats below, his shadow formed a grotesque caricature on the outer wall as he moved towards the front door in the semi-darkness. What would he find inside

238

the house? Where were the detective McAllister and Per Svenson? With a deep breath, he reached down and turned the knob and opened the door.

After the glare of the lights outside, it took a moment for his eyes to adjust to the darkness. It was only because of the movement that he focused on the dim silhouette of a figure kneeling before him. The man was facing away from him, slowly raising an arm. Jack peered through the darkness and recognized the struggling form of the other man on the floor. Without further thought, he leaped forward, striking the kneeling figure with his fists and arms. Immediately, the man rolled and turned to face him. In the weak cold light, Jack focused on the figure below him. He stared in fear and fascination, at the man's face, at his eyes. As he stood motionless, mindless of the cold, and stared into those black eyes, he saw...nothing...they were devoid of emotion, lacking that essential spark of humanity. He realized that he had seen many times before what he saw now, in the eyes of the ruined young men in Viet Nam, in the faces of patients who had finally comprehended the hopelessness of their condition. They were the eyes of death.

In that moment, Jack Phillips understood the unrelenting force that pursued him. And in a flood of emotions, he realized that this force would not leave him alone, would not be stopped by anything the police could do. Lying before him, within his grasp, was the embodiment of all that he and his family had suffered. The one responsible for trying to take away all of the things that were most important to him, the essence and meaning of his life. The shocks of pain from his amputated fingers went unnoticed as his fists clenched uncontrollably. It was only with the burning tug of a bullet through his jacket near his shoulder that he realized abstractly that the man was shooting at him. The percussion rang in his ears, and the bitter smell of cordite filled his nostrils as Jack leaped forward onto the Asian, trying to reach the man's throat with his hands. Only one thing would satisfy the need that Jack felt. To cleanse the open wound that was his life, he had to destroy the thing that was before him. Yet battling with his emotions were his basic nature and years of medical training: *to above all preserve life.*

A pain arose in his side as another bullet from the assassin's gun penetrated his clothing. As he fell to the floor on top of the assassin, his right hand came upon the smooth roundness of wood. He gripped the handle of the hatchet and frantically arched back as he saw the dark muzzle of the gun turn towards him once more. With all of his effort, Jack brought the hatchet down, as the explosion from the gun rang yet again.

As he saw the blow coming, Nim Choy tried to fire and at the same time twist away from Phillips. He lurched as he felt a pain at the base of his skull, and a sudden, sharp, tingling numbness spread throughout his body as the blade of the hatchet severed his spinal cord cleanly. He dropped backward to the floor and struggled to take a breath, but somehow couldn't expand his lungs. And for a timeless, locked-in moment he could see but couldn't feel, couldn't move, couldn't respond as he looked at the face above him. And Choy's expression turned to one of quiet surprise. For he never expected it to happen this way. The face seemed to recede further and further away in the darkness. His last mortal sensation was that of a bandaged hand gently helping his head down onto the floor. And then the coldness of the room was gone.

21

The brown sedan turned into the parking lot south of the Golden Gate Bridge. The headlights glared in the fog as the car parked on the edge of the lot overlooking the bay.

They sat quietly for a moment, and Jack looked up at the span, the roadway illuminated by a row of yellow lights. The orange bulk of the south tower rose and disappeared into the fog and darkness above.

"How is Svensen?" asked the detective.

"He's OK," Jack replied. "It turns out that the gunshot wound was pretty superficial. He probably slipped or fell when it happened, and had a concussion. My friend Gordy Thompson is taking care of him at the hospital in Powell River. Per's a tough old guy."

The detective looked at his watch. Six-forty. A few more minutes yet.

Jack gazed out at the moving fog. "It was her maiden name, Chien. Susan Chien." He shook his head. "I've known her for all these years. Even before they were married." He had decided, as soon as he had been told the true circumstances of his ordeal, to say nothing of their affair to anyone, including McAllister. He shuddered at the thought that it might be uncovered at the trial; after all these years of hidden guilt. After what they had all gone through, how could Barbara and his family withstand yet another blow like that. Jack would deny it, of course, and suggest that it was a cruel ploy to raise sympathy for the two of them.

The detective remained silent for a long moment. "It might have been her, you know, pushing him into it." He looked again at the fog. "The money you make. The power you have at the Institute....I can imagine her wanting all of that." His voice trailed off.

"Who knows," Jack replied softly, as he reached for the handle of the passenger door.

"Do you want me to come with you?"

Jack paused. "No, I want to go alone," he said finally, and opened the door and got out of the car. The detective watched him as he made his way up a long embankment, and began to walk onto the bridge. He went slowly, past the heavy concrete pillar that formed the base of the massive suspension cables. As he walked on the span, he looked straight ahead, concentrating on the walkway in the distance. The fog and seaward wind joined to bathe Jack's face with moisture. But even now, in January, it felt warm after Canada.

A young couple walked by, going the opposite way, their arms around each other. Then there was no one else. Jack thought about what he would say. What was there to say? Anger had faded into a lingering sense of disbelief, and betrayal. He flexed his left hand and felt the aching pain where his fingers should have been. He glanced towards the city as he walked, but could see only a hazy glow of lights in the distance through the fog.

He reached the south tower, and went around the base to the other side. He could see the thick orange suspension cable dropping down out of the fog, at mid-span, and then rising up, to disappear once again, further in the distance. As he walked, he felt a twinge of pain from the healing flesh wounds in his side from the bullets. The pain was not severe, and reminded him of his fortune. Had the bullet's trajectory been by chance just a few degrees different....

Under the yellow lights he saw a single figure, coming toward him, small and vague at first, in the fog and the distance. He slowed, but kept walking towards the center of the bridge, as the figure became larger, and Jack recognized the steady unvarying stride of the runner. He had seen it before. Steadily, the runner came closer, and Jack could see the arms and legs working mechanically, synchronously, in a seamless rhythm. The man's head was down, fixed on the cement sidewalk in front of him, the grey hair clinging to his head, wet in the fog. They were nearly together now. Jack stopped and stood silently, waiting. He was actually surprised at how little anger he felt. The runner was thirty feet away, and still hadn't seen him. Twenty feet.

"Fred!" Jack's voice was loud. Louder than he had meant it to be. The runner, startled, stopped abruptly in his tracks. Fred Steele's glasses were covered with moisture, and he quickly pulled them off, squinting myopically at the figure in front of him. But he had recognized the voice, and stood motionless, except for the heaving of his chest.

"Jack?" His voice was charged with incredulity.

Jack stood silent as he gazed at the younger neurosurgeon. "It was you Fred. You all along." In the background, Jack Phillips could hear the sound of the tires from the passing cars reverberating on the wet roadway of the bridge. "You were the one that told those people that Twan could have lived!" And the anger rose once again inside as he had before him the last man responsible for his pain, for his family's agony. "And it was Susan who paid them fifty thousand dollars. So that they would force me away from San Francisco. Clean, simple, no bloodshed! Just a little terror for my family to drive me away!"

Fred Steele wiped his glasses with the edge of his shirt and put them back on. He focused his gaze on Jack's face, not knowing what to do.

Jack's voice was softer now. "But that didn't work, did it, Fred?" He lifted his left hand, holding the amputated fingers of his left hand up in the yellow light. "So you decided that you would ruin my hands, too? Is that it? That would fix it!"

Steele stared at the irregular scars, the amputated stumps on Jack's hand, white in the cold.

"That's not true, Jack," he pleaded.

"Don't bother, Fred. Please, don't disgrace yourself. Joseph Lo has told us everything." Jack's voice rose in outrage. "And when I did leave, finally driven away to protect my family, you even told them where to come and find me in Canada!"

Steele's shoulders slumped, as he gazed down at the concrete. "I never meant for them to hurt you. You have got to believe me. They forced me to tell them where you had gone...." He looked back at Phillips, tears coming to his eyes as he formed the thoughts that tumbled through his mind.

Fred shivered in the wind and fog swirling across the Golden Gate. "I tried. Oh God, how I tried. But don't you see? I could never succeed with you there! You dominated everything. All of the surgery. The research." He shook his head. "My research! It became yours! My years of work! But the Institute was you! Always, and only you!"

Jack Phillips felt the wind across his face. *Of course he dominated the Neurological Institute.* He was the reason for its success in the first place. The idea, the first spark of creation had come from him. He had nurtured and developed the idea into a reality, and through his own efforts, into national prominence. Jack was the driving, guiding light. Without him, it would never have happened. He had always rationalized that his drive, his integrity and his dominance were necessary for the good of all of them working there. The others, under him, understood that, didn't they? It had never occurred to him that his vision, his passion, could become so destructive.

Fred Steele held his hands out in front of him in a gesture of supplication. "And the residents. The only one they really looked up to was you. Not me! Don't you see, Jack? I was a failure until you were gone. And you were never going to leave. But now I'm the one directing the Institute. Doing the real cases. I'm needed and necessary for the first time in my life!" Steele began to shiver in the wind. "But I never, ever wanted to hurt you. It got out of control."

"Did you think that I would stay away forever?" Jack clenched his throbbing hand and held it up to the other man's face. "Do you think that this will keep me away now?" He felt the anger well-up again inside him.

"It won't Fred. This won't stop me, and you won't stop me!" Jack felt sickened and saddened for the man standing in front of him.

Slowly Fred Steele began to shake his head, the wetness dripping off his face.

"It all started with Susan. She had always wanted me to be what you were. She wanted us to have what you had. The power, the money..." Fred's words were bitter and broken. "She wasn't satisfied to be married to the just the Assistant Director of the Institute. When I told her about the surgery on Samuel Twan, she already knew all about him. And his gang connections.

Jack was silenced for a moment, the memories of his illicit affair with Susan surfacing again to quiet his anger. Was she the cause, moreso than Fred? As the question formed in Jack's mind, Fred Steele answered it for him.

"I knew about the two of you, you know...she told me, to make me hate you. And I did hate you for it! She married me only because she couldn't marry you. She couldn't pull you away from Barbara and your family." Fred Steele shivered in the cold and the fog. "In time she and Barbara became very close."

Fred Steele slowly turned and began to move toward the railing on the side of the bridge. In the yellow light the swirling, moving fog enveloped the two of them. Jack took a step toward him as Steele stopped and turned back to face him "And what about Barbara?"

"Barbara is at home now, with the children. What about her?" Phillips demanded.

Steel gazed at him. "Barbara was the one who gave Susan the fifty thousand dollars."

"What!" Jack stood frozen in horror as the words crashed through his head. "You're lying!"

"I'm not lying, Jack. Susan went to Barbara soon after you had operated on Twan. They came up with this idea together, to drive you away from the Institute. To have this gang threaten you, to stop your work, and bring you back to your wife and your children. But it got out of control, all of it, from the kidnapping of Christine," He paused. "and your hand...none of us ever asked them to do that."

Jack still couldn't believe was Fred was saying. He had known, in his heart, that Barbara had in reality always hated his devotion to his work. For the Institute, as a goal and ideal he had spent nearly all of his waking hours for the past decade, literally the best moments of his life. His wife had rarely had him at home, and his children had been growing up without him. But he had always felt that she understood, that this was the way he was, and the only way that he could be. For her to want to destroy it all was inconceivable. And the fifty thousand dollars...that undoubtably came out of Barbara's own trust account, given to her by her parents. They were worth millions, and money was of little issue for his wife. Another though crystallized in Jack's mind. "Fred, did Barbara know about my affair with Susan?"

Fred paused before answering. "Yes she did, Jack. As I said, they were very close." Fred Steele now stood with his back to the railing, a vast canopy of black space open behind him, and began to shiver with the chill of the swirling fog. "Where is Susan now?" he asked.

Jack gazed at him, but in the confused shock of the true reality of his life, could feel no more remorse for Fred or his wife. "They have her in custody," he replied simply.

Fred Steele's shoulders began to shake as tears formed in his eyes and flowed down his face. "I really love her, you know. And now they will take away everything else that means anything to me." He looked at Phillips and slowly became more calm. "Goodbye, Jack."

"No!" The echo of Phillips' voice surrounded him as he lunged forward, but Steele was up onto the orange railing, and then going over, dropping toward the black void below. Jack grabbed at him and caught hold of his wet shirt. A jolt of pain ran through his left hand and he gasped, but held on, pulling the man back up, away from the darkness below. As he strained, his face came closer to the other man's, and he could see into Fred Steele's eyes. They seemed to plead with him to let him go, to end it here. And Jack realized that it would be so easy. So simple to just let go. This man had tried to destroy him! Tried to take away all that he lived for! Inside of Phillips the hatred kindled once more and began to burn, and he tried to fight it, his basic instinct for the preservation of life battling with his anger and his instinct for his own survival. Fred reached up and struggled to loosen Jack's grip. Jack felt the tortured incisions on his left hand give way first, and then his right hand gave way and then Fred Steele was gone, disappearing into the darkness below.

Jack stood at the railing and stared down for a long time, as he listened to the gentle sound of the wind. Then he turned and slowly walked back towards the south end of the bridge. As he walked he reflected upon his wife. It could only be the case that Barbara's involvement would be uncovered as they investigated the source of the fifty thousand dollars that Susan used to pay Joseph Lo. He would probably be asked if he were going to press charges against her. Jack pondered that thought as he walked, and slowly opened and closed the fingers of his left hand in the cold. Yes, he could operate with that hand, he decided. It would not slow him down. Not at all. His gaze fixed upon the wet concrete of the sidewalk in front of him as he came to the south end of the bridge. *Nothing would slow him down at all.* McAllister was waiting for Jack at the concrete pillar. The detective looked at him quizzically.

"He jumped," said Phillips. "He admitted it all, and then he jumped off the bridge."

McAllister gazed at Jack's face, weighing the words in his mind. The neurosurgeon's grey eyes were calm, placid now. A wide damp stain across the front of Phillips' jacket engaged the detective's attention. The material was wrinkled, as if there might have been a struggle. Had Fred Steele jumped, or not? The detective listened to his heart, beating softly inside his chest. And then he smiled slightly and nodded, and the two men turned and walked back towards the car in the fog.

THE END